FRANKIE'S LETTER

The Jack Haldean Mysteries
by Dolores Gordon-Smith

A FETE WORSE THAN DEATH
MAD ABOUT THE BOY?
AS IF BY MAGIC
A HUNDRED THOUSAND DRAGONS *
OFF THE RECORD *
TROUBLE BREWING *

* *available from Severn House*

FRANKIE'S LETTER

Dolores Gordon-Smith

This first world edition published 2012
in Great Britain and 2013 in the USA by
SEVERN HOUSE PUBLISHERS LTD of
19 Cedar Road, Sutton, Surrey, England, SM2 5DA.

British Library Cataloguing in Publication Data

Gordon-Smith, Dolores.
  Frankie's letter.
  1. World War, 1914-1918–Secret service–Fiction.
  2. Country life–England–Fiction. 3. Spy stories.
  I. Title
  823.9'2-dc23

ISBN-13: 978-0-7278-8217-2 (cased)

All Severn House titles are printed on acid-free paper.

Severn House Publishers support The Forest Stewardship Council [FSC], the
leading international forest certification organisation. All our titles that are printed
on Greenpeace-approved FSC-certified paper carry the FSC logo.

MIX
Paper from
responsible sources
FSC
www.fsc.org   FSC® C018575

Typeset by Palimpsest Book Production Ltd.,
Falkirk, Stirlingshire, Scotland.
Printed and bound in Great Britain by
MPG Books Ltd., Bodmin, Cornwall.

Dedicated to Jessica
With love

HISTORICAL NOTE

*F*rankie's Letter is, of course, fiction, but one of its chief characters, Sir Charles Talbot, is based upon a real person.

William Melville, the man who would become the Secret Service's 'M', was an Irishman, born in poverty in County Kerry in 1850. He ran away from home and in 1872 joined the London police. He made a name for himself as a quick-witted and capable officer, who, among other things, arrested Fenians and anarchists, was involved in the search for Jack the Ripper and was appointed as the royal bodyguard. He retired, at the peak of his career, in 1903, with the rank of superintendent.

The retirement was fictional; what Melville actually did was to set up a small office near Scotland Yard under the name and title of *W. Morgan, General Agent.* As W. Morgan, he looked after both espionage and counter-espionage. His job was entirely hands-on. That not only suited Melville's character, it was necessary. As he had agents but no staff, he had little choice.

In 1909, the service expanded, taking on Captain Vernon Kell, of the South Staffordshire Regiment, and the flamboyant, swordstick-wielding ex-Naval officer, Mansfield Smith-Cunningham ('C') to run various sections of the infant service. All three men, in their separate offices strung out along the Thames, were unofficially supported and officially unacknowledged by the government – a state of affairs which suited the modest William Melville very well indeed.

If anyone is interested in finding out more about this fascinating man, I can recommend Andrew Cook's *M: MI5's First Spymaster* as a reliable and thoroughly absorbing account.

ONE

Terence Cavanaugh steadied himself against the rain-sheened wall. The pain in his chest, where the bullet had struck home, flared into agony as he tried to move. He had to get to Anthony Brooke. He just *had* to get to Anthony Brooke.

He scrunched his fist against the wound, steeling himself to walk. For virtually the first time in his life, he felt helpless. He had always been tough, a fifty-year-old fighter of a man. Now his eyes blurred and he felt his way along the wall, sensing the rough, uneven bricks under his fingers. A few steps more . . .

Jagged fingers of pain clutched his heart in an intense, serrated grip and he whimpered out loud, forcing himself to stay upright by willpower alone. He *had* to get to Brooke. The rain slashed down, a vicious icy squall from the Baltic. The violence of the rain cleared his head and he saw the steps of the house. He grasped the railing and climbed. One, two, three – my God, that third step was a long way – and through the front door.

He leant against the door in the hall, gathering himself for a final effort. Brooke had lodgings here, on the first floor, and he had to climb the stairs. The hall, with its shiny oilcloth and its solid dark furniture, was deathly quiet but, from a room close by, he could hear voices. He looked at the staircase with its polished wooden banister and, calling up the last remnants of his strength, with his fist clenched against the white fire in his chest, staggered across the hall.

Dr Conrad Etriech hurried up the steps, opened the door and stepped into the hall with relief. It was a miserable day. It was April, but the rain, driving in from the sea in ill-tempered gusts, was very far from springlike. It was a relief to be home. Not, he thought, as he put his wet umbrella in the stand, peeled off his gloves, unbuttoned his coat and took off his hat, that this was exactly home.

He was one of four tenants who lived in this tall, thin and quietly respectable house in the Wilhelminenstrasse, together with their tall, thin and quietly respectable landlady, Frau Kappelhoff.

It suited his purposes. The house was in the centre of Kiel, close enough to the docks for the mournful sound of the ships' sirens to be heard but near enough to be in walking distance of the university where he worked. And he was comfortable, as comfortable as Frau Kappelhoff could make him.

Frau Kappelhoff thought the world of him. She was a widow with two sons in the merchant fleet. She was proud of her sons but the person she loved best in the world was her eleven-year-old daughter, Lottie. Dr Etriech hadn't been in the house a month when Lottie was taken gravely ill with pneumonia.

It was a tough struggle, but the little girl pulled through. Dr Etriech's speciality wasn't respiratory diseases but he saved her. Any doctor, he said, to the tearful Frau Kappelhoff, would have done the same, but from then on, Frau Kappelhoff treated him with awestruck devotion.

Dr Etriech looked up with a smile as the kitchen door opened and Frau Kappelhoff peered out hesitantly. His smile became a puzzled frown. One of the ways Frau Kappelhoff showed her gratitude was to look for his homecoming, help him off with his coat and fuss over his gloves and hat. However, just for once she didn't rush into exclamations as to how wet it was or offer to dry his things in the kitchen. Instead she greeted him with downright relief.

'*Herr Doktor*! I'm so glad you've come home.' She looked scared.

'What is it?' he asked, shaking off his wet coat. 'It's not Lottie, is it?'

'No.' Her face softened. 'Lottie's in the kitchen. *Herr Doktor*, I heard someone go upstairs.'

In a house with four lodgers, this didn't strike Dr Etriech as odd. 'It's probably one of your guests,' he said, remembering, with instinctive courtesy, that she didn't like the word *lodgers*.

She shook her head vigorously. 'No, it isn't. Herr Lehmann and Frau Hirsch are in and Herr Klein won't be back till eight o'clock.' She twisted her hands together. '*Herr Doktor*, there's someone in the house, I know there is.' She twisted her hands together. 'Their footsteps were heavy and there was a noise as if they were dragging something. It could have been a sack, a heavy sack.' She glanced anxiously up the stairs. 'We could be being robbed.'

Dr Etriech smiled reassuringly. 'That's unlikely. A burglar wouldn't be carrying something in, would they?'

'Someone's up there,' she insisted with another glance at the staircase. 'It could be a spy. We're told to look out for English spies. This dreadful war . . .'

He laughed. 'You needn't worry about spies, *mein liebe Frau*,' he said in what he thought of as a 'there, there' voice. 'There's nothing to spy on in your house.'

He hung up his coat and put his things on the hallstand. 'I'll go upstairs and have a good look round. If I see any spies, I'll send them back to England, yes?' She smiled at what Etriech privately thought of as rather heavy-handed humour, clearly relieved that the good doctor was taking care of her.

She looked at him curiously. '*Doktor? Herr Doktor?*' Dr Etriech had paused, looking intently at the stairs. 'What is it?'

Dr Etriech turned. 'Nothing, *mein liebe Frau*,' he said carelessly, but there was something. The light in the hall was dim but it gleamed on the polished wood of the banister. Where it struck the rail as it bent round to the first floor, the wood was dull and stained.

He took out his handkerchief and pretended to cough, wetting the corner of it with his tongue. He ran the damp handkerchief over the stain as he walked up the stairs. With Frau Kappelhoff watching him, he couldn't examine it closely, but the cloth came away a deep rusty red. She was right. There was someone upstairs. His stomach knotted as he rounded the corner.

It sounded as if they were dragging something . . . A man drag-ging himself upstairs? English spies. Yes, Frau Kappelhoff would think of that. Kiel was full of posters warning all good Germans to be on their guard. Frau Kappelhoff was frightened of spies, knowing they were alien, vicious creatures. That's why she'd asked Dr Conrad Etriech to go and hunt for them. She trusted Dr Etriech, who lived in her house, asked after her family and ate her stew and dumplings. It would never occur to her that, while the title was real enough, the name was borrowed.

The doctor couldn't be a spy. He was someone she knew. But his name wasn't Conrad Etriech, it was Anthony Brooke and, with that bloodstained handkerchief in his pocket, he was a worried man.

The door to his room was open. With a sick feeling he noticed that the brass handle was stained. He had to get Frau Kappelhoff out of the hall. He stamped his foot, gave as good an impression of a cat's meow as he could, and laughed. 'It's all right, *mein liebe Frau*,' he called down. 'It's a stray cat, that's all. It's gone into my room. I'll chase it out.'

There was a cluck of annoyance. 'Shall I help you, *Herr Doktor*?'

'No, it's nothing to trouble about.'

He heard the rustle of her dress and the sound of the door from the hall to the kitchen closing. Anthony took a deep breath and walked into his room.

He bolted the door behind him. His sitting room looked, at first sight, undisturbed, but the rug was crumpled and there were two rusty splashes on the oilcloth.

'*Hallo?*' he called softly in German. From somewhere he heard a faint gurgling sound, the sound of a desperately fought-for breath. He went into the bedroom and his heart sank.

Terence Cavanaugh lay sprawled on the floor, the bedspread tumbled round him. His strength had failed as he tried to reach the bed. Anthony knelt down beside him and turned his face to the light. Cavanaugh's eyes flickered open. With a huge effort, he focused his eyes on Anthony's face. When he spoke his voice was a breaking whisper.

'Brooke? I'm for it.' He started to cough, a harsh, racking sound. Anthony cushioned his head on his knee, holding Cavanaugh's cold hand. His fair hair was wet with either rain or sweat and a streak of blood creased his forehead. From the way he was breathing, Anthony guessed he had a chest injury.

'Let me see,' said Anthony quietly. The blood didn't show on Cavanaugh's dark coat or jacket, but they were sticky to the touch. He unbuttoned his coat and drew his breath in sharply.

Cavanaugh's shirt was soaked an ugly reddish-brown and the bullet hole was rimmed in black. He'd been shot through the lungs. With compressed lips, Anthony twisted up his handkerchief and pressed it against the wound. There was nothing else he could do. Cavanaugh's eyes had the vacant look of a man on the verge of death. It was a miracle he was still alive.

The cold hand moved feebly in Anthony's. 'I've led them to you. Sorry.'

'Don't worry. I'll—'

'Listen!' Cavanaugh gasped for breath once more. 'There's a spy in England. Gentleman. He must be a gentleman. Seems to know everything. Got to stop him, Brooke.' The words were slow and hard to catch. 'Knew about me. Frankie's letter. Read Frankie's letter.' His eyes flickered shut and he coughed, bringing up blood. 'I loved her . . .'

The end was very near.

'Have you got the letter?' Anthony asked, trying to keep the urgency out of his voice.

Cavanaugh moved with feeble impatience. 'Not that sort of letter,' he answered, then mumbled something Anthony couldn't catch. It sounded like 'star' but there was more. *Anger? Star's Anger?* Cavanaugh gave a convulsive shudder. 'Big ship. Passengers. Americans. Stop them, Brooke. Going to kill the passengers . . .' His voice trailed off.

There was a knocking at the front door downstairs. In the silence it sounded like a clap of thunder.

Anthony laid Cavanaugh's head gently on the crumpled bedspread. In the hall below he heard Frau Kappelhoff, shrill with indignation, arguing with the deep, official voices of men. He crossed to the window, drawing back as he looked down on four soldiers in field grey. There was no escape that way. Anthony glanced at the door, then dropped down beside Cavanaugh once more. He couldn't desert him. The poor devil didn't have long, but that time was going to be spent with a friend.

There was the hurried sound of feet on the stairs and a knock at the door. '*Doktor? Herr Doktor?*' It was Frau Kappelhoff.

Various schemes ran though Anthony's mind. He could hide Cavanaugh under the bed and bluff it out. Cavanaugh coughed once more. Anthony reached out and in the fraction of a second it took his hand to get to Cavanaugh's, Anthony knew that he was dead. From outside the room, Frau Kappelhoff was still calling his name.

Anthony stood up, straightened his tie, adjusted his waistcoat and squared his shoulders. There was nothing for it, he'd have to face the woman.

A freakish memory of years ago came to mind. He had gone through the same ritual of facing up to things as a frightened schoolboy standing outside the headmaster's study. Even with soldiers around the house and Cavanaugh's body on the floor, the ridiculous comparison made him smile. He realized how relaxed he must have looked when he opened the door.

Frau Kappelhoff let out her breath in a rush of relief. '*Herr Doktor*, there are men downstairs. Stupid men, soldiers, who should know better than troubling decent people. They say there's an English spy in your room. I said this is a respectable house and the good doctor, who is so clever, he is quietly upstairs, and then they said . . .' She broke off, her bosom heaving with indignation.

'What did they say?' asked Anthony with as much supposedly casual interest as he could summon.

Her breast swelled and she spat the words out. 'They said *you* were a spy.'

'Ah.' Anthony took her arm and quietly drew her into the room, closing the door behind them. There was, he thought, nothing else for it.

'Frau Kappelhoff, *mein liebe Frau*, I'm awfully sorry but it's true.' She gazed at him in blank incomprehension. He was going to have to spell this out. 'I am a spy. An English spy.'

'You're German.'

'No, I'm not.'

'Oh yes, you are.' She shook her head, bewildered. 'I know you are. Don't pretend, *Doktor*.'

In all the possible scenarios Anthony had ever conjured up for what were probably his last moments of freedom, arguing the toss with a German landlady as to his nationality hadn't occurred to him. 'Frau Kappelhoff, I am an Englishman,' he said sternly. That did get through.

She shrank back against the door in terror. She tried to scream but, thankfully, no sound came.

Anthony had to get her on his side and quickly. 'Frau Kappelhoff! Listen to me!' She tried to scream again and managed a little gulping hiccup. 'I am still the man you know.' The panic-stricken gaze didn't alter. 'Remember when Lottie was ill?' The terror faded with the mention of her daughter. 'She had pneumonia, yes?'

Frau Kappelhoff licked her lips nervously. 'Lottie. Little Lottie. You saved her, *Herr Doktor*.'

'That's right.' Anthony could hear the men below. He was desperate to get her to act but he forced himself to radiate calm.

'Remember how happy we were when we knew Lottie was going to get better?'

'Yes, yes. I remember. You saved her, my precious Lottie.' She covered her face with her hands. 'What shall I do? Tell me, what shall I do?'

'Listen to me,' said Anthony, his voice deliberately gentle. 'I have to leave, *mein liebe Frau*.' He could hear the tread of feet on the stairs. 'I need to escape, yes?'

'Yes.'

'And I need you to help me, yes?' Perhaps the best way was to take her cooperation for granted. 'I'm grateful to you. Just as you were grateful for Lottie's sake.'

'For Lottie's sake. Yes.'

He put his finger to his lips. 'Stay there.'

He swiftly went into the bedroom and opened the window as quietly as he could. With any luck the soldiers would think he'd escaped that way. Then, taking a wad of money from the desk and breathing a silent farewell to Cavanaugh, he returned to Frau Kappelhoff. She was still rigid, her back pressed against the door. The steps on the stairs were, as far as he could judge, at the far end of the corridor. The soldiers knocked at Herr Lehmann's door. Anthony waited, ears straining, for the noises that would tell him they'd gone into Herr Lehmann's room. There!

'Frau Kappelhoff, my friend is in my bedroom. He's dead.'

Anthony immediately realized that was too harsh. She looked as if she might cry out and with every moment precious, forced himself to speak softly. He took five hundred marks and put them on the table. 'This is to give my friend a decent burial. Please, as the good Christian woman you are, do this for me.'

The word 'Christian' reassured her as he'd hoped, countering the idea that the English were all godless monsters. He gently moved her to one side and opened the door a crack. The corridor was clear. He could hear an argument in Herr Lehmann's room. Lehmann was elderly and deaf. It wouldn't take them long to work out he had nothing to hide. This was his only chance.

'You haven't seen me. Remember you haven't seen me and no harm will come to you or Lottie. I wasn't in my room.' She nodded, her eyes fixed on his face. 'Give me a few minutes, then scream as loudly as you can. They won't harm you if you haven't seen me.'

She swallowed. 'But . . .'

'For Lottie's sake you mustn't come to harm. You haven't seen me.'

Leaving Frau Kappelhoff in his room, Anthony slipped out into the corridor and along to the attic. Of all the ways he'd worked out to escape from the house – and that was one of the first things he'd done – this was far and away his least favourite, but it couldn't be helped. He made the safety of the attic staircase and closed the door behind him as the noise of the soldiers' voices increased. They'd finished with Herr Lehmann.

Up the attic stairs, avoiding the creaking boards in the middle, over the dusty floorboards to the window, fumble with the catch . . .

An ear-splitting scream rang out. Frau Kappelhoff had found Cavanaugh's body. There wasn't any suggestion she was acting. A tirade of sobs followed the scream. No, he thought, the poor woman certainly wasn't putting that on.

He took off his socks and shoes, stuffed his socks into his pocket and, hanging the shoes round his neck by their laces, scrambled through the tiny window onto the tiles. He could hear Frau Kappelhoff's sobs and the men's exclamations as they discovered Cavanaugh. He was past all harm, poor devil and, with luck, they should be occupied for the next few minutes.

The rain smacked down in a dreary drizzle. Putting his fears under stiff, if brittle, control, Anthony held onto the window frame, closed the window behind him, and set out to climb the roof.

The window stuck out onto the roof in the shape of a little house. He edged himself round by holding onto the gutter, his bare feet finding a tenuous grip on the wet tiles.

Frau Kappelhoff's house was the last in a row of terraces. The roofs faced the street in a line of inverted V's, like a series of miniature forty-five degree hills. He needed to get over the crest of Frau Kappelhoff's roof to the other side. He sat astride the top of the window, judging the distance. It wasn't very far, but the street yawned below and Anthony hated heights.

At that moment it would have been as easy for him to go back as it was to climb that roof. Easiest of all was to stay put, but that wasn't an option.

He wiped his clammy palms on his trousers, stood up and started to walk. He'd seen builders walk up roofs, shouting to their mates, stopping to light a cigarette, laughing. Laughing, for God's sake!

If they could do it, so could he. But the roof was wet and a tile moved under his foot. In near panic he slipped, regained his balance, and flung himself up the last couple of feet to the ridge pole. Weathered by years of sun and rain, the cement crumbled under his hand. In sheer desperation he shifted his grip and lunged over the apex of the roof, facing the man-made. red-tiled valley of the roof of the house next door.

His breath came in huge, unsteady gulps. Beneath him lay, like the promised land, the slope downwards to the flat parapet which joined Frau Kappelhoff's to the Kolhmeyers next door. He half-climbed, half-slid down and sat on the parapet, shifting only to make sure he was out of sight of the Kolhmeyers' attic window.

The rain drifted down, he was filthy from the climb and his fingers were numbing with cold, but as he lit a cigarette and relaxed, leaning against the slope of the roof, sheer relief made him as happy as he'd ever been in his life.

The April evening in that northern latitude was long and cold. Anthony put on his socks and shoes, bitterly regretting the warm coat, hat and gloves which he'd left in Frau Kappelhoff's hall. He tried to make sense of the noises from the street below. A hubbub of shouted orders came up to him. They were taking Cavanaugh's body away.

Anthony didn't know why Terence Cavanaugh was in Kiel. There were certain questions which simply weren't asked by people in their situation, but he'd liked the man. He'd had a reckless, to-hell-with-it attitude which Anthony, surrounded by careful Germans, found immensely refreshing. God only knew why Cavanaugh was in the war. He wasn't, as Anthony was, fighting for his country. He was an American, a neutral.

Cavanaugh didn't hate Germany and had mixed feelings about England but he had, as he'd told Anthony, a real nose for trouble. The war was shaping up to be just about the biggest load of trouble anywhere on earth and he wanted to be part of it. Well, thought Anthony, smoking his cigarette down to the butt, he certainly got his wish, poor devil.

Feet crunched in step below. There were a lot of troops about, an abnormal number, in fact. Kiel, the home of the High Seas Fleet, was always well patrolled, but this was excessive and Anthony wondered why. It was with an odd stab of surprise he realized they were looking for him.

At long last, when he was thoroughly chilled, the evening turned to dusk. Very, very stiffly he climbed up to the Kolhmeyers' window. It was closed, of course. Anthony's first thought was to slip the catch with his pocketknife but his fingers were too clumsy to open the blade. He wrapped his fist in a handkerchief, smashed the glass and, seconds later, was standing in what was obviously, from the sparse furniture, a servant's bedroom.

From far below came the sound of a piano. He remembered that Mrs Kolhmeyer was musical. He crept down the attic stairs and gently edged back the door. The music, one of the more rumbustious bits of Wagner, increased. There was no one about, as he had hoped at this time in the evening. With only a bit of luck all the Kolhmeyers would stay in the drawing room. He stole along the corridor to the head of the stairs.

The sound of the piano swelled and he shrank into a bedroom. Someone had come out of the drawing room. Were they coming up the stairs? A woman said something about coffee. Anthony breathed a sigh of heartfelt relief.

He couldn't go out of the front door and the back door was in the kitchen. At least one of the Kolhmeyers' two servants would be there. He listened intently for a moment, then slipped down the stairs into the hall.

The door to the drawing room was ajar but the door to the dining room was closed. The piano still played but there was a sound as if a fairly bulky someone had got up from their chair and walked towards the door. Mr Kolhmeyer.

Mr Kolhmeyer wasn't built for speed but even if he'd moved like greased lightning it was doubtful if he would have seen Anthony, the rate he got across the hall and into the dining room.

He stood with his back to the closed door, looking at the dining room. The room was, thank God, empty. It was dominated by a solid table with a green plush tasselled cloth and smelled of cooked cabbage. In the alcove stood an equally solid bureau. His first thought was to get out of the window but the sight of the bureau made him pause. He opened the oak lid and there, as he had hoped, were the Kohlmeyers' identity papers.

Anthony had a twinge of conscience as he pocketed Mr Kolhmeyer's papers, but the chance to get a genuine pass was too good to be missed. Now for it.

He pulled back the heavy velvet curtain covering the sash window and waited. He had his hands on the sash when he heard the tramp of feet. Three soldiers marched by. He waited until the sound of their boots had faded, took a deep breath, mentally crossed his fingers that the window wouldn't stick, and heaved.

Miraculously, the window shot up with only the smallest of squeaks. He bundled himself outside and walked away.

TWO

I t wasn't simple chance which had lead Anthony to pick Frau Kappelhoff's house. Not only was it near enough to the university to fit in with his role as a visiting tutor, but it was less than three quarters of a mile from the Handelshafen where the merchant ships docked. It seemed, as he walked away quickly from the Kolhmeyers, that even that short distance might cause him some problems. Anthony knew they were looking for him but there were, he thought, a couple of things in his favour. Kiel was poorly-lit because of the wartime restrictions on fuel and he had a good knowledge of the less frequented routes through town.

The further he got, the more his spirits rose. The rain and the cold had cleared all idlers from the streets and he took care to slip into the shadows when he heard anyone approach. There were still large numbers of troops about, but, as he saw with relief, even the Kaiser's soldiers were ordinary men and preferred, on this dismal evening, to keep their coat collars up and stay, when not under the eye of a superior officer, under what shelter they could find. He knew the places he had to be on his guard and managed to slip by four danger spots unnoticed.

He was making for The Mermaid on Jensenstrasse off the Katserasse, which ran the whole length of the merchant dock. It was at the corner of the Thaulow Museum, with Jensenstrasse only yards away, that he met his first real obstacle. Two sailors, armed with rifles, were standing forlornly in the rain. After a few minutes of watching them from the shadows, Anthony decided to retrace his

steps and approach Jensenstrasse by another route. It was just bad
luck that one of the sailors glanced up as he moved.

'*Halt!*' the sailor called.

Anthony reluctantly came into the open. He had no hat, no overcoat and was filthy from his climb over the roofs. His wet clothes
clung to him and he looked, he thought, like an absolute scarecrow.
His only choice was to brazen it out.

He swayed gently on the spot as they approached, fixing them
with a delighted, glassy beam. 'Hullo.'

'Your papers, sir,' said the sailor who had shouted for him to stop.

'Papers. Papers, papers, papers,' repeated Anthony in an alcoholic
way. 'I had 'em when I came out.' He saw the sailors swap knowing
looks. 'Never go out without m'papers.'

He started a painfully deliberate search through his pockets and
pulled out an old letter. 'Here we are. No it's not.' He stared glassily
at the sailors. 'M'wife's a harsh woman. Out, she said. Am I drunk?
No. All I had was a tiny little drop, just a tiny schnapps, but out!
No coat, no hat, just out! Her and her mother.'

The sailors grinned, but persisted. 'Your papers, sir.'

He laboriously searched his pockets again and this time produced
Mr Kolhmeyer's card. If the theft had been reported he was for it.
He stuck his thumbs into the lapels of his jacket in an expansive
way, staggered and fell back against the wall. The sailors' grins
increased and Anthony breathed a silent prayer of thanks.

He'd fallen against a propaganda poster, pasted to the wall, one
he'd seen many times before. It showed a caricature of a moustached,
jodhpured figure complete with bulldog, a supposedly typical
Englishman. 'He's the cause!' the poster screamed. 'Why is our life
controlled by rationing?' There was a whole lot more, ending with:
'England is our deadly enemy' and 'Victory for Germany!'.

The sailors, as he had hoped, looked from him to the poster and
laughed. Anthony could follow their thoughts as if they'd spoken
them aloud. He couldn't be an Englishman because an Englishman
looked like the man on the poster.

'He's all right,' muttered the sailor who held his papers.

'I am,' Anthony agreed with intoxicated earnestness. 'Only, dash
it, I keep falling over. Problems with m' legs.' He took back his
papers and put them carefully away. 'Must be off. Bishiness aqua
. . . aqua . . . friend. Want to come?'

'I only wish we could,' said one of the sailors with a laugh. 'Good night.'

Anthony wobbled away, swayed across the square, turned the corner, saw the street was deserted and leaned against the wall in utter relief. For a few moments at least, he looked as inebriated as the traduced Mr Kolhmeyer.

He was on Jensenstrasse. The outer door to The Mermaid stood open, sending a yellow wedge of light onto the wet pavement. Anthony walked into the pub, feeling he had gained some sort of sanctuary.

He was well known in The Mermaid. Lassen, the landlord, was a Dane, one of the many in this north-eastern corner of Germany. When war was declared, the Germans, who had always treated the Danes with suspicion, ordered all men between twenty and forty-five to enlist. That, in Anthony's opinion, was a mistake. He knew Lassen, who had two sons in the army, bore a burning sense of injustice. It was too much to say he was pro-British but he was resentfully anti-German and there were plenty of informers who felt the same.

Lassen was careful not to be curious about Dr Etriech who frequented The Mermaid. Perhaps, for men had learned to avoid awkward questions which could lead them to still more awkward truths, he simply accepted that the doctor liked conversations with all classes and types of customers. If he noticed that those customers were frequently better off as a result, he never mentioned it. Anthony didn't pay much but any extra, in this time of great hardship when even the bread on the table – the miserable gritty K-bread, part flour, part potatoes – was rationed, was welcome.

Anthony made his way to a table close to the stove. The heat made him wince as the circulation returned to his frozen fingers. For a few moments he could think of nothing but warmth and would have given anything for a hot bath and a change. His clothes had begun to steam in the heat before he could bring himself to turn away from the stove.

Lassen stood behind the bar, quietly polishing a glass. 'What can I get you, *Herr Doktor*? You look as if you need something to keep out the cold.'

'I'd like some coffee and an aquavit,' Anthony replied. 'And . . . er . . . would you take a drink with me, Herr Lassen?' He nodded at the chair on the other side of the table.

'I'll bring the drinks round,' said Lassen.

Anthony dropped into the chair. He recognized most of the men in the room. The Mermaid was a comfortable, homely place, smelling of fish, engine oil and wet wool, with its pine boards turned the colour of oak by years of placid clouds of tobacco. It was quiet, with the murmur of conversation broken by the occasional click from a game of draughts and the scrape of chairs on the wooden floor.

Lassen put the tray on the table and pulled out a chair. 'Trouble?' he asked softly.

'Yes.' Anthony picked up the aquavit – an acquired taste – and drank it at a gulp, feeling it sting his throat. No one was paying them the slightest attention. 'I have a passenger for Captain Johannson.'

Lassen stroked the stubble on his chin. 'Yourself?'

Anthony nodded.

'A private passage?'

'Very private.'

'I see . . .' Lassen took his pipe from his apron pocket. He didn't seem remotely surprised. He studied his pipe for a long moment. 'You can pay?'

'Yes.'

'Captain Johannson will not be here for two or three days. Is that a problem?'

Anthony bit his lip. He'd been afraid of this. 'It could be a great problem.'

'I see,' said Lassen again. He picked up his beer, drank some, then filled his pipe thoughtfully. Anthony was anxious for him to speak, but knew better than to hurry him. 'I can pay for accommodation,' he added, watching Lassen closely. 'Pay well.'

Lassen lit his pipe. 'That would be helpful,' he said after a time. 'Drink your coffee, Herr Doctor. Take your time. Then say goodnight as you leave, as you always do, but go down the alley to the left, to the back of the house. Be careful you are not seen. When it is safe, come to the white door. It will not be locked. We'll arrange what happens next when you are safely inside.'

Lassen stood up and went back behind the bar. Anthony felt the reaction from the strain of the escape to The Mermaid set in and he shook himself awake. This was dangerous. The quiet murmur of voices and the chink from the draughts pieces combined to an almost hypnotic drowsiness. He picked up his coffee, but it was nearly scalding. He could feel himself drifting once more. His head grew incredibly heavy and he rubbed his face with his hands.

Then he was completely awake, every sense on edge. The door slammed back, there was a shout of command and four soldiers marched in. They grounded arms and stood to rigid attention as a senior officer, an *Oberstleutnant* entered the Mermaid.

Just as the Germans caricatured the English as John Bull, the English depicted the typical German officer as a Prussian with a monocle, a duelling scar, a bald head and rolls of fat round his neck. This man was no caricature, thought Anthony warily. He was wiry and fair-haired with a long, intelligent face and more threatening than any propaganda bully.

There was a rustle of unease, followed by silence. Anthony guessed he wasn't the only one with good reason to be wary but, still wearing his battered formal clothes and dark tie, he stood out like a sore thumb in that roomful of men dressed in seamen's jerseys and pea-jackets. He decided to play the drunk once more, knowing the generous latitude given to drunks, and only wished he had something more convincing than black coffee as a prop.

He expected the Oberstleutnant to shout, but he didn't. Instead he leaned across the bar and addressed Lassen in a low voice. Lassen, sullen and unhappy, avoided the Oberstleutnant's eyes. He had a towel and glass in his hand and continued wiping the glass automatically, while grunting out answers.

Straining to hear, Anthony caught the words 'spy' and 'sons'. His stomach turned over. Lassen didn't speak but continued to wipe the glass. Then, with a droop of his shoulders, he nodded, as Anthony knew he would, and pointed towards him.

It was no use playing the drunk. The Oberstleutnant's victorious smile told him the game was up. Lassen had been given the choice between the lives of his sons and the life of a stranger and Anthony couldn't blame him for his choice.

Anthony stood up as the Oberstleutnant approached. He couldn't see the point of prolonging the inevitable but he was damned if he was going to let the German know how the sick taste of fear filled his mouth. That was nothing but bravado, but it was something.

As casually as he could, Anthony picked up the coffee and took a sip. 'Do you want me?'

The Oberstleutnant stopped. He was enjoying the moment and his air of triumphant arrogance was so apparent Anthony half-expected him to revert to caricature and say, 'So!'

He didn't. He smiled with a cat-who's-got-the-mouse expression. 'You are – or you have been masquerading as – Doctor Conrad Etriech. Don't deny it.'

'I wasn't going to,' said Anthony with as much urbanity as he could manage.

'You are a British spy.'

'I can't imagine there'd be much point in denying that, either.'

The Oberstleutnant's smile broadened. 'You are sensible not to resist.'

Anthony shrugged. He hoped it looked like unconcern. 'Again, I can't see the point. Those gentry by the door seem to block any means of escape.'

'There is no means of escape.'

'No. I rather thought not.' He took another sip of coffee and the germ of an idea started to grow. 'As we're going to be civilized about this, may I have the pleasure of knowing your name?'

The German drew himself up. 'I am Oberstleutnant von Hagen. I have more men posted outside. You are surrounded.'

'Which, although clichéd, sounds unpleasantly like the truth.' Anthony yawned. 'All right, you win. Let me drink my coffee and I'll come quietly. It's a beastly cold night, I'm tired and hungry and I don't suppose German prisons have many creature comforts.'

He raised the cup once more and hurled the steaming black coffee into the Oberstleutnant's face.

Taken utterly by surprise, the Oberstleutnant staggered back, blinded by the hot liquid. With a quick jerk Anthony upset the table, sending it crashing into him, then, thrusting Lassen out of the way, jumped over the bar and into the rooms at the back, a torrent of shouts following him. A white-aproned woman came into the narrow passageway, her face contorted with surprise. He ignored her screams, ducked past her, raced into the kitchen, flung open the back door and slammed it behind him.

He ran out of the yard and into the alley at the back. Shouts came from the front of the house, but it wouldn't take them long to follow him round here. He ran the length of a few houses, stopped, and tried the latch of a door into a back yard. It was locked. As quickly as he could, he put his hands on top of the door and hauled himself over, his feet scraping on the wood.

The yard was very dark. Anthony crouched by the side of the gate, trying to steady his breathing. In the alley outside were running footsteps and shouts of command. Despite himself, he couldn't help grinning as the Oberstleutnant's dilemma became clear. He had evidently worked out that his quarry could be hiding in any of the yards which lined the alleyway but, on the other hand, he could be getting clean away.

Feet crunched past him on the other side of the gate. Two . . . no, three men. The feet stopped about twenty yards away. That would be the corner of the alley.

'Stay here,' snapped the Oberstleutnant. There was the snap of boots as the soldiers came to attention, then all was quiet.

How many men had the Oberstleutnant left on guard? Anthony felt for the bolt on the back of the gate and tried to draw it back, but it was stiff in its socket. He put his hands on the top of the wall and eased himself to the top, lying along the length of the wall.

In the dim light he saw two soldiers, standing at either end of the alley. Diagonally across from him was another alley, leading, he remembered, into the yard of a small brewery. If he could get through the yard, then all he had to do was climb over the brewery gates and he would be on a main road. He blessed the instinct which had urged him to explore every back street in Kiel.

There was a bunch of keys in his pocket. He wouldn't need those again. Drawing them out carefully, he weighed them in his hand and sent them skimming over the head of the soldier standing at the end of the alley. They clattered on the cobbles. The soldier whirled, bringing his rifle to the ready.

'What is it, Kupper?' called the soldier at the top of the alley.

'I heard something,' answered Kupper. He stooped to pick up the bunch of keys. 'He's here! He's dropped these!'

'Hold on!' The second soldier ran down the alley. As soon as he had gone past, Anthony dropped to the ground and raced for the dark opening of the brewery yard, flattening himself into a doorway against the brick wall.

So far, so good. He could hear the voices of the two soldiers and the crunch of feet as one started to return. He willed himself to look away as the soldier went past, knowing his face would catch the light. Then he was gone and Anthony breathed a sigh of relief.

The back gates of the brewery stood in front of him. They were an easy climb, but he made more noise than he wanted to. He paused for a moment on top of the gate, fearing the bark of a dog or the tread of feet, but there was nothing.

He dropped down into the yard. Hugging the deep shadows beside the wall, he crept through the yard, past the stables of the brewery horses, finding the stable smells and the sound of a soft whinny an inexpressibly comforting sensation.

He edged his way to the front of the building, where two great wooden gates, big enough to take the brewery wagons, barred the way to the road. A wicket gate was set into them, bolted on the inside. Presumably that meant there was a night watchman somewhere. This was the danger point. To get through the gates he had to come out of the shadows. He listened intently. Silence.

It took far less than a minute to open the wicket gate and step through onto the main road, but it was one of the longest minutes Anthony had ever known.

As he stepped through onto the road, he saw a black Mercedes with an Imperial Eagle on the bonnet parked a little way down the street, its hood pulled up against the rain. He couldn't be sure but he thought there was a driver in the car. He swallowed hard. He had to make this look natural. He turned back to the gate, pulling it shut behind him.

'Goodnight!' he called to an imaginary companion. *They're looking for one man, not two . . .*

He'd walked a few steps away from the Mercedes when he heard a shout from the car. It was the driver. The man was leaning out, pointing towards the gate. 'Hang on, mate,' he called. 'The gate's swung open.'

With a sinking feeling, Anthony half-turned. He couldn't ignore the driver but he dreaded him seeing him properly.

'You want to be careful,' said the driver chattily, getting out of the car. 'You never know who . . .' He stopped, and Anthony could see him looking at his filthy, once respectable clothes, so unlike anything a watchman would wear. 'Who are you?' he said in a different voice. 'Let me see your papers.'

Anthony didn't have any choice. His fist shot out, catching the driver underneath his left ear, a wicked knockout punch to the carotid artery. The driver groaned and fell, his knees crumpling beneath him.

Anthony's first instinct was to run but the sight of the driver's cap made him pause. His wretched clothes were a signal to every searcher. Why not take the driver's coat and cap? Come to that, he thought with a grin, he could make a proper job of it and take the Mercedes as well.

The street was deserted, but he could hear the sound of marching feet in the distance. He pulled the driver back to the car, rapidly stripped off his coat and put it on. The tramp of regimented boots was no more than a street away, echoing loud in the quiet night. He hurriedly opened the back door and bundled the driver into the gap between the front and back seats. He was about to get back into the car when the footsteps rounded the corner.

As he had thought, it was a group of soldiers with an officer at their head. His heart sank as a gleam from a street light caught the officer's face. It was, predictably, von Hagen.

There was absolutely nowhere to go. His only hope was that von Hagen would carry on his patrol on foot, but that hope was dashed. 'Report to me at the merchant docks,' rapped out von Hagen to his sergeant. 'Carry on.'

The sergeant saluted, the soldiers marched off, and von Hagen walked towards the car.

Now at this point, a real driver would have stood to attention before opening the back door for Oberstleutnant von Hagen, saluted smartly – Anthony couldn't credit that any inferior would salute von Hagen anything but smartly – walk round the front of the car, climb into the driver's cab and await orders.

As von Hagen approached, Anthony fantasized for a fraction of a second about doing just that. *'Unconscious man at your feet, sir? I wonder how he got there? He wasn't there when we set off . . .'* But, granted that von Hagen was not only armed himself but had a platoon of armed men within hearing distance, that wasn't really on the cards.

The only thing in his favour was that his face was shadowed by the peak of the driver's cap. He compromised by saluting. That, at least, he could do without suspicion. 'There's a problem with the car, sir,' he said in as good an imitation as he could manage of the driver's North German accent.

Von Hagen paused, his mouth tightening in irritation. 'How soon can you get it going again?'

'I'm not sure, sir. It's the clutch. I'll have to take it up and that will be at least twenty minutes or so.'

'Then you'd better get on with it.'

Anthony could hardly believe his luck. He'd fallen for it! He went to the front of the car, stooping down to lift up the bonnet.

Von Hagen walked away, then called back over his shoulder, 'Report to me at the Merchant Docks as soon as you've finished.'

Anthony looked up. It was pure instinct but he cursed himself for a stupid mistake. He knew immediately he'd been caught. He glanced down almost instantly but for a moment his face was clear in the light. Von Hagen stopped and turned back slowly. He opened his overcoat and unholstered a pistol. 'Come here.'

Anthony walked towards him. There was nothing else to do.

'Take off your cap.'

The gun was pointed at his stomach. Anthony took off his cap with a flourish. If he was going to go, he might as well go in style. 'How d'you do, old man?'

Von Hagen gave a hiss of satisfaction. 'You!'

He opened his mouth to shout to the departing troops and Anthony hurled himself forward. The gun flew out of von Hagen's hand as Anthony's fist crunched on the point of his jaw. They rolled over in the road in a desperate struggle.

Von Hagen was wiry and tough but Anthony had the advantage of surprise. Whatever happened, he mustn't call out. Anthony clamped his hand over von Hagen's mouth, trying to bring his other hand round to deliver a knockout blow. His fingers grasped the barrel of the gun. He picked it up and smashed the butt end into von Hagen's temple. The Oberstleutnant's eyes widened and his body went limp.

Anthony got up and wearily lent against the car. In the distance he could still hear the sound of marching feet. What now? He'd better get rid of these bodies. He glanced towards the brewery gates. He could leave them in the brewery. That would do it. More marching feet sounded close by and he groaned inwardly. There simply wasn't enough time.

He bent down to von Hagen, untied the scarf from round his neck and gagged him with it. Then, opening the back of the car, he heaved the unconscious Oberstleutnant in beside the driver, shut the door, climbed into the driver's cab and started the engine.

As he drove off, Anthony totted up his chances. The situation was interesting, to say the least. To drive round the home town of the Imperial Fleet as a known and wanted spy in a stolen army staff car with two Germans in the back, one of whom hates your guts – and, to be fair, von Hagen had been scalded with coffee, beaten up and made to look a fool in front of his men – was not an experience Anthony wanted to prolong longer than necessary.

His only chance of escape lay at the docks. With Terence Cavanaugh dead there was no other agent to turn to and his experience with Lassen showed how dangerous it was to rely on any Dane or German, no matter how friendly they may have been. Both Frau Kappelhoff and the University could give a good description of him and the theft of Herr Kohlmeyer's identity papers would be reported in the morning.

He could try and make a break for it in the Mercedes, but the car would be a dead giveaway in a few hours and he didn't know how much petrol was in the tank. And there was Cavanaugh's message. He had to get that back to England. He couldn't send it, even if he could contact a messenger. *There's a spy in England . . . Seems to know everything . . .* There was no one he could trust.

A groan from behind the seat added an extra spur of urgency to his thoughts. Whatever happened next, he had to deal with those two in the back. With the cranes of the docks visible a few streets away, he turned the car sharply into a side street and drew to a halt.

Holding von Hagen's gun, Anthony opened the back door of the car. The driver, who had started to groan, fell silent as the gun was pressed to his head.

'Listen to me,' said Anthony as fiercely and as urgently as he could. 'I'm an English spy.' The man's eyes rounded in fright. 'One murmur and I'll put a bullet in you. Nod if you understand.' The driver, sprawled across the floor with von Hagen on top of him, nodded. Anthony felt the need of reinforcements, if only imaginary ones. 'There are other men with me. Understand?' The driver nodded again. 'Any sound and you're for it.'

There was a handkerchief in the pocket of the driver's coat. Anthony put down the gun and gagged the driver with the handkerchief. Von Hagen's eyes flickered open. He gave Anthony a look of concentrated hatred, but the scarf stopped him from shouting out.

'Get out of the car,' said Anthony. 'Remember, I've got the gun.'
The two men slowly climbed out.

'Von Hagen, take off your clothes.'

The German's eyes gleamed defiance. Anthony's finger tightened on the trigger. 'I want your clothes,' he said levelly. 'If I have to get them with a bullet hole in them, I will.'

Anthony was bluffing. He couldn't risk the sound of a shot and he knew he couldn't murder a man in cold blood. However, he hoped that von Hagen wouldn't guess that. 'Take them off!'

Von Hagen unbuttoned his overcoat and shrugged it off. His eyes measured the distance between them but the gun made him hesitate.

'And the rest,' said Anthony. 'Jacket, trousers, boots . . . That's the ticket. Sorry if it's a bit chilly, but that's life.'

Quite what he would have done if von Hagen had shouted, he didn't know. Clubbed him, perhaps, and run for it. Anthony could see von Hagen itching to disobey, but he couldn't risk the gun. Fortunately for Anthony, the German hadn't worked out that he couldn't either. After a few tense minutes von Hagen stood in his underwear with a pile of clothes beside him.

'Now, gentlemen, step over to the wall. And, von Hagen, old thing, I'd like some privacy. Turn your faces to the wall and don't look round. I will shoot.'

Anthony wanted to tie them up but he didn't have anything to tie them with, apart from the belt of the driver's overcoat, and it wouldn't do for two of them. Besides that, he had a healthy respect for von Hagen's courage. At a distance he could control matters. If he came too close, he was sure the German would attack. No; dangerous as it was, he had to leave the two men as they were.

As quickly as he could, he took off his clothes and scrambled into von Hagen's discarded uniform. He had to put the gun down to get dressed, and that was dangerous. On three separate occasions von Hagen made as if to turn round, and each time Anthony stopped him. 'Just stay there . . . I've got the gun . . . Watch it! The next time you move, I'll shoot. That's your last warning. Keep your faces to the wall!' The snarl in his voice convinced him; he hoped it convinced von Hagen.

Anthony wasn't proud of what he did next. All he knew was that it was necessary. Holding the gun by the muzzle, he stole up behind the two men and cracked the butt down hard on von Hagen's head.

He slumped to the ground. The driver, still gagged, turned wide, frightened eyes to him. 'Sorry,' said Anthony apologetically, and walloped him, too.

Once on the main road, with the entrance of the merchant docks in sight, Anthony did his best to copy von Hagen's arrogant swagger and strode up to the entrance to the docks, trying to look as if he owned the place.

There were two soldiers on duty at the gates. They saluted as he walked through. So far so good . . . 'Who is the senior officer present?' Anthony barked at them.

'Major Stabbert, sir.'

He nodded curtly and strode on. He might have to talk to the major, or perhaps, with a bit of luck, he could pull this off alone.

The tide was in, the dark water slopping against the quayside. That meant there should be at least one ship getting ready to sail. He walked along the wet cobbles, feeling a stab of joy as he saw the black bulk of a steamer, its funnel pumping out heavy gusts of smoke. A dockhand stood by a bollard, ready to cast off the hawser.

'*Halt*!' Anthony commanded in his best Imperial Army voice.

The dockhand stopped, coming respectfully to attention as he saw an Oberstleutnant approach. 'Yes, sir?'

'This ship. Where is it going?'

'She's for Korsor, sir. Zealand,' he added helpfully.

Korsor! Perfect! If he could get to Korsor, he'd be safe in Denmark and as good as home. All he had to do was get on board.

'Lower the gangplank.'

The dockhand stared at him. 'Lower the gangplank, sir? But . . .'

'I want to go to Korsor,' Anthony snapped. 'Lower the gangplank.' He was an Oberstleutnant in the German Army, albeit on a very temporary commission, and no one was going to stop *him.*

The dockhand looked bewildered. Further up the quay, Anthony could see a group of soldiers and decided to take the bull by the horns. 'You there!' he shouted to the sergeant in charge of the soldiers. 'Bring Major Stabbert to me immediately. Leave that rope alone,' he snarled at the dockhand.

A sailor looked over the side of the ship, some fifteen feet above. 'What's the delay?' he called. The dockhand shrugged.

Major Stabbert hurried up, slowing as he saw Anthony beside the ship. 'You wanted me, sir?'

Anthony looked at him imperiously. 'I am Oberstleutnant von Falkenhayn.'

'Von Falkenhayn!' gasped the major.

Anthony smiled in a wintry sort of way. 'I bear the same name as my uncle.'

He could see the major gulping. The nephew of the Chief of Staff was not someone to be treated lightly. If he was going to bluff, he might as well make it a good one. 'I have urgent state business to Korsor. Secret business, you understand? It is important I leave at once. Command the captain to lower the gangplank.'

'But sir . . .' stuttered the major.

Anthony glared at him. 'Are you questioning my orders, Major?'

'No, sir!' The major looked up to the ship. 'You there! Lower the gangplank at once.'

There was a bustle and shouted orders on board.

'There seems to be a lot of activity tonight,' Anthony said with gracious condescension as the gangplank came over the side of the ship.

'Yes, sir. We are looking for an English spy.'

'Two English spies,' Anthony corrected. He might as well cover his retreat while he had the chance. 'I heard something of the matter. He has a companion with him. I trust you will manage to capture him.'

'We will, sir.'

'He's a clever man, Major. You need to be on your guard.' The gangplank was nearly secured. 'You know he evaded us once before? The road was blocked and guards posted. He waited until a patrol had gone through, then approached the guards. "After that patrol," he said. "The spy is with them." Naturally, the officer in charge sent a detail after the patrol and the spy offered to lead them. I regret to say the spy made good his escape and the officer is an officer no longer. Be careful, Major, if you capture him. He is very plausible.'

'I will, sir.'

Anthony walked up the gangplank and the major snapped to attention.

'Cast off,' Anthony commanded as soon as his feet touched the deck. 'I will talk to the captain later.'

The steamer pulled slowly away from the quay.

Anthony had to fight a huge desire to laugh. Already they were over a hundred yards away from the quay and the bluff – the outrageous bluff – had worked. He leaned over the ship's rail and grinned.

Two men, one wearing nothing but a coat and with his bare feet clearly visible, had come on to the quay surrounded by soldiers.

It was partly ordinary common sense, he knew, but there was a streak of sheer mischief which made him cup his hands round his mouth. 'Major Stabbert! That's the English spy! Don't let him get away!'

Von Hagen gave a howl of protest, jabbing his finger at the departing ship.

To Anthony's intense joy, he saw the soldiers around von Hagen bring their rifles to the ready. Denmark, neutral Denmark, was eight hours away, he was safely on board and von Hagen had been arrested by his own men. There was only one more thing he had to think of. It was unlikely on a ship this size, but . . .

He turned and walked along the deck, stopping the first sailor he saw. 'You there! Take me to the wireless room.'

'We don't have wireless, sir,' said the sailor.

Anthony hid his delight behind a frown. 'In that case, I will speak to the captain now.'

'Yes, sir!'

Really, thought Anthony, the way everyone jumped to his orders was wonderful. The German army might have its faults, but in many ways it was an excellent institution.

THREE

Anthony walked across Trafalgar Square and turned into Cockspur Street. If he hadn't been so tired he would have enjoyed his walk. For some reason Cockspur Street was the home to most of the steamship companies in London and the destinations on the travel posters in the windows – Melbourne, Valparaiso, Cape Town, Lisbon, Karachi and Bombay – transformed this tall, smoke-blackened row of sandstone buildings into a magical doorway to travel and adventure. Not that, he reflected with a wry smile, his life had been exactly lacking in travel or adventure. In fact, just recently, he'd had quite enough to be going on with.

He was looking for the General and Commercial Steam Navigation Company Ltd., or, to be exact, the office above it. He plunged down Angel Alley, a narrow cobbled passage that ran between the shipping office and the Westminster Coke Company, and came to an unobtrusive green painted door marked by a brass plate.

W. Gabriel Monks. Export Agent.

He smiled in recognition. W. Gabriel Monks, strictly speaking, didn't exist. When Sir Charles Talbot, Assistant Commissioner of Scotland Yard, had retired from his post five years ago, the newspapers had reported his farewell dinner and the gift of a handsomely inscribed gold watch, and noted that Sir Charles would be taking up a position in what was vaguely described as either Whitehall or the Home Office to administer police pensions. The dinner and the watch were correct, but Sir Charles's subsequent career had nothing to do with pensions.

He pulled the bell. There was the clatter of feet on the stairs and the door was opened, not, as Anthony had expected, by Sir Charles, but an extraordinarily elegant middle-aged man with silver-grey hair, high cheekbones, piercing blue eyes and perfectly tailored clothes, who looked as if he might be an archbishop or a cabinet minister.

Anthony blinked at this vision. His first impression was immediately overlaid by a second. Although the man looked all right, there was something artificial about him. He was so perfect he was like an archbishop on the stage, rather than a clergyman in real life.

The archbishop, taking in Anthony's dirty, ill-fitting clothes, greasy cap and grimy, unshaven face, regarded him coldly. 'Can I help you?'

'I want to see Mr Monks,' said Anthony, then, before the man could protest, added, 'I've got a cargo for him.'

The man's eyebrows rose. 'I see.' He smoothed back his hair and added in beautifully modulated but reluctant tones, 'I suppose you'd better come upstairs.'

He stepped aside to let Anthony enter the tiny hall. Anthony was prepared to bet the words, 'Wipe your feet!' were trembling on his lips. With a disdainful glance, the archbishop led the way up the narrow staircase into a lobby on the landing and through a door.

Granted the modesty of the entrance, the office was large and very well appointed. The window, protected by bars, looked out onto Cockspur Street, letting in the fitful spring sunshine and the rumble of noise from the traffic below. Two men, evidently clerks, were working at a big oak desk which filled the middle of the room. The bookcases that covered three walls were lined with files and leather-bound volumes. A large safe stood beside the fireplace and on the desk were piles of papers, blotting pads, pens, inkwells and – surprisingly – no less than three telephones.

'I'll tell Mr Monks you're here,' said the archbishop, crossing the room to another door. 'What name shall I give?'

'Brooke. Dr Anthony Brooke.'

He didn't have to knock at the door. Sir Charles Talbot – or, as he was known here, Mr Monks – could evidently hear what was being said in the outer office, flung the door open and hurried into the room.

'Brooke!' he said, his hand outstretched. 'My dear fellow, what on earth are you doing here? We knew something had gone badly wrong, but we've been starved of news.'

Anthony took his hand, moved by the other man's obvious pleasure. Out of the corner of his eye he could see the archbishop's discomfiture at the warmth of Sir Charles's greeting. 'I thought it best not to say too much before I actually got here.'

'I see.' Sir Charles turned to the elegant clerk. 'Farlow, Dr Brooke and I have a lot to discuss. I don't want any interruptions unless it's really urgent. Use your judgement. Unless . . .' He paused, taking in Anthony's battered clothes. 'Have you eaten? You look a bit worse for wear.'

It was typical, Anthony thought, of him to be concerned first about the man rather than the mission. 'I feel a bit second-hand,' he said with a rueful smile, 'but I had some breakfast on the boat. I arrived at Tilbury this morning. I could do with a bath and a shave, but that can wait.'

'Are you certain about breakfast? Well, well, I'll let you be the judge of that.' Sir Charles led the way into his office and closed the door behind them. 'Now,' he said, pulling out a chair for Anthony. 'Sit down and tell me what you've been up to.'

Anthony relaxed gratefully into the armchair. The atmosphere of this inner office was that of a gentleman's club, quiet, unhurried and rich with green leather and dark wood. One of the few touches of modernity was a telephone and even that looked as if it would never do anything as strident as actually ring. From the half-open window the traffic was muted to a background hum. 'Thanks,' he said. He jerked his thumb behind him. 'All those clerks and what-have-you are new, aren't they? When I was here last there was just you and the office cat.'

'The cat's still here,' said Sir Charles, 'but yes, we've expanded.' He grinned. 'They know me as Monks, by the way. Don't disillusion them.' He pushed the cigarette box towards Anthony. 'Help yourself.'

Anthony took a cigarette. In one way it seemed impossible, in this incredibly civilized room, to convey the stomach-churning tension of Kiel, but although Sir Charles didn't look as if he'd understand, Anthony knew he would.

Anthony had first met Sir Charles a couple of years ago when they were fellow guests at the Benhams' house party. Anthony had taken to the plump, balding, good-natured man who always had a bounce in his step. He could imagine him as a well-to-do farmer, a cavalry general who loved his food, his horses and his troops, or a popular businessman, the sort who built ideal homes for his workers, or even, at a pinch, 'mine host' in an old-fashioned coaching inn. Sir Charles was, as he said with a smile, actually a retired policeman who was now 'something in Whitehall', and that was all Anthony knew.

They'd met at infrequent intervals afterwards and, although Anthony never thought about it, he later realized how much Sir Charles had learnt about him. He knew Anthony had been a student at Cambridge when, unexpectedly stony-broke after his father's death, he was forced to take a position as a ship's surgeon.

Anthony had been fascinated by the new world shipboard life opened up and tropical medicine captivated him. He worked hard, saved some money, and invested his precious capital on further studies in Berlin. He found his niche at London University, enthralled by the opportunities for research offered by the School of Tropical Medicine. Anthony couldn't really credit Sir Charles Talbot was as spellbound as he appeared to be by the life cycle of the trypanosomes parasite, but he was a gifted listener.

Sir Charles never mentioned what the 'something in Whitehall' actually was. Then, on the fifth of August, 1914, with the whole country galvanized by war, Anthony was on the point of volunteering for the Royal Army Medical Corps when he received a note asking him to call on a Mr Monks of Angel Alley. To his surprise, Mr Monks turned out to be his old friend, and the nature of the 'something in Whitehall' was spelt out.

And now Anthony was back, sitting by the same desk he had sat at that day in August. It was, he thought, a few months and a whole lifetime away.

Anthony mentally shrugged. There wasn't an easy way to start so he plunged right in. 'The first thing I've got to tell you is that Cavanaugh's dead.'

Sir Charles paused, then sat down slowly. 'Terence Cavanaugh?' he repeated. He rested his forehead on his hand for a brief moment, then looked up. 'Are you sure?'

'I was with him when he died.'

Sir Charles swallowed. 'Poor devil,' he breathed. 'How did it happen?'

'He was shot. I don't know where he was attacked, but he managed to get away. He made it to my rooms in a pretty poor state and what seemed to be half the German army arrived shortly afterwards.'

Sir Charles's eyebrows crawled upwards. 'That must have been awkward. When was this?'

'On the 28th April.' Anthony's mouth twitched in a smile. 'As you can imagine, I had to leave Kiel in fairly short order.'

Sir Charles looked puzzled. 'The 28th? That's over a fortnight ago. Why didn't you let us know? We could have had you home in half the time.'

Anthony tapped his cigarette on the brass ashtray. 'I'll tell you what Cavanaugh said before he died. Then you'll understand why I didn't warn you I was on my way.'

Sir Charles heard him out, writing down the odd note, prompting Anthony with occasional questions. When he heard of the fate of von Hagen, he looked up with a broad grin. 'Do you know, it really is remarkable how the Prussians venerate an army uniform. How did you go on after you got on the boat at Kiel?'

Anthony returned the grin and lit another cigarette. 'I had a talk to the captain, who was a patriotic German, thank goodness.

He appreciated how it could be necessary for a German officer to get in and out of Denmark without being seen. He provided a change of clothes and kindly offered to keep my uniform for me until I could reclaim it. He understood how Korsor might be watched and how careful I had to be, as there were spies everywhere. I mean, look at that business on the quayside as we left.'

He laughed. 'My word, I was lucky to get away with it. It really was funny, you know. I suppose poor old von Hagen managed to explain things eventually, but I'd prepared the major to believe that everything he said was a pack of lies. The only thing I was worried about was that they might send a fast boat after us but, if they did, it was too late. I left the ship near Skjelskor in the south of Zealand, got across to Copenhagen without too much trouble, and headed for home.'

Sir Charles frowned. 'We had no word from anyone in Copenhagen.'

Anthony leaned forward. 'That was deliberate. In light of what Cavanaugh said, I was wary of approaching anyone. I picked up some false papers in Copenhagen and came back as a passenger on a Dutch cargo boat shipping margarine and candles. It was long-winded but I was safe enough. However, it does mean I've been out of touch for a while.'

Sir Charles's eyes widened. 'You've heard the news, though? About the *Lusitania*, I mean?'

Anthony shook his head, puzzled. 'No. What about the *Lusitania*?'

'It was torpedoed and sunk by a U-boat off the coast of Ireland,' said Sir Charles quietly. 'There's thought to be well over a thousand passengers and crew dead.'

Anthony stared at him. 'They attacked a *passenger* ship?' Sir Charles nodded. 'But they can't do that.'

He felt sick. He'd sailed on the *Lusitania*. She was far more than just a name to him. She was a wonderful ship, a vast, elegant Cunarder who had won the Blue Ribbon for the fastest Atlantic crossing, a ship it was a delight to sail on and whose crew felt proud to be on board. He'd been in attendance on Molly Benham's father at the time and had sat beside the old man in the lounge with its ornate plasterwork under the stained-glass skylight, while families, mothers, nursemaids and well-drilled children came and went.

A little girl had jogged his arm and Anthony spilled his whisky, marking the table top. The steward had wiped it up and next morning the table had been lovingly polished so no stain remained. And now sea water covered the polish and the green curtains were a sodden mass of slimy velvet.

In a sudden, vivid moment, Anthony could virtually see the mass of pent-up water, swamping the decks, pouring down the darkened hatchways and forcing its way through the cabin doors, through to the terrified children held by their mothers. A thousand people dead.

Sir Charles looked at Anthony's shocked face. 'Yes, they got the *Lusitania,*' he repeated quietly. He looked down at the notes he'd taken. 'And Cavanaugh said, "There's a ship in danger. A big ship. Passengers." He obviously knew what he was talking about.'

'But why?' demanded Anthony in horrified disbelief. 'It's barbaric. Those people were civilians. Why on earth did they do it? Apart from anything else, the Americans will be up in arms about it.'

'Only if we're very lucky,' said Sir Charles, grimly. 'There were Americans killed all right but, as I see it, President Wilson will send the Germans a stiff note and everything will be as before.'

'But it doesn't make sense,' protested Anthony in bewilderment. 'The *Lusitania* wasn't a threat to anyone. This sort of thing's unprecedented.'

Sir Charles raised his eyebrow. 'Is it?' He rubbed a hand across his forehead. 'I wish it were. You've been out of touch, Brooke, so you won't know, but the *Lusitania* is only their largest victim so far. The gloves are off, right enough. The Germans have declared unrestricted submarine warfare and no ship is safe. A hospital ship, brilliantly lit and showing the red cross, was attacked outside Le Havre in February. In March, three steamers were destroyed off the Scillies in one day. The ships were sunk but the passengers and crew were safe. They were allowed into lifeboats and then the submarine turned her guns on them.'

'They did *what*?'

Sir Charles nodded. 'They fired on the lifeboats. It's nothing less than murder. The list goes on. The *Falaba* was forced to stop by a German submarine. It surrendered, the ship was stationary, the crew and passengers were getting into lifeboats, when the submarine torpedoed the *Falaba*. Over a hundred people were drowned.'

Anthony felt stunned. To attack the ships, yes. That was war, but to fire on the defenceless crew and passengers was against every rule of war, the sea and humanity.

Sir Charles saw his expression. 'Grim, isn't it? Germany's fighting a blockade and she's using fear as a weapon.' He tapped his notes. 'Cavanaugh's warning indicates that the attack on the *Lusitania* was planned. Do you know that doesn't surprise me? The German Embassy in Washington issued a notice to the New York press that any vessel – any vessel at all – was liable to destruction. We're fighting a ruthless enemy who doesn't recognize rules.'

He pushed his chair away from the desk and walked to the window. 'I remember you were shocked at the idea of going into Germany to gather information. I had to persuade you to break the rules, as you saw it. You didn't –' he turned and looked at Anthony '– think it was a pukka thing to do. How do you feel now?'

Anthony shrugged helplessly. 'How on earth can I recall how it felt before the war? It seems a lifetime away. I still don't like it.' He avoided Sir Charles's eyes. 'I'd far rather follow my original notion and join the Medical Corps. I don't know how much use I was in Germany but I know I'd be worth my salt in an army hospital. Besides that, it'd be a relief to be known by my own name and not be on my guard all the time. I made mistakes, Talbot, plenty of them. I covered them up, but you can only get away with it for so long.'

Sir Charles hitched himself onto the window sill and leaned against the frame. He looked at Anthony appraisingly. 'How old are you, Brooke?'

Anthony was puzzled. 'How old? I'm thirty-two. Why?'

Sir Charles nodded. 'You seem older. You've been through it, haven't you? There's more grey in your hair than I remember and you look tired. But we need you, Brooke. You don't just speak the language. You can pass for a native without question.'

'So what?' countered Anthony. 'Yes, I'm a good mimic. You know that.' He looked at Sir Charles, willing him to understand. 'But this is more than a game. It's horribly real. I want . . .' With a stab of shame he heard his voice crack and he forced himself to continue. 'God knows what I want, Talbot, but there are men dying in France, men I can help. Surely that's more important than picking up crumbs of information.' Mortified, he heard his voice nearly break once more. 'It's not worth it.'

Sir Charles walked to the sideboard, took out a bottle and two glasses and poured a small measure of whisky into both. 'Here, drink that,' he said and waited until Anthony, wincing slightly, drank the neat spirit.

Sir Charles splashed some soda water into his whisky and sat down at the desk, looking at Anthony thoughtfully. 'Now the immediate danger's over you're suffering from reaction, and no wonder,' he said quietly. 'You asked if it was worth it.'

He caught Anthony's expression of dissent and held his hand up. 'It's just beginning to dawn on everyone, politicians and people alike, exactly what we're up against. Lord Kitchener never believed the war would be over by Christmas and made no bones about saying so. We're in for a long haul and there are no short cuts to victory.' His voice grew urgent. 'But as that sinks in, as the casualties grow and the restrictions begin to bite, there'll be cries for peace at any price. A quick fight with soldiers to cheer off onto the troopships is what the public loves. For a time it's more fun than football and cricket and people enjoy reading about distant acts of bravery in places with funny foreign names. But this?'

He walked to the desk and stood with his hands braced on the table. 'This is different. You'll hear a lot of talk in the coming months to the effect that the government are senseless warmongers, that all we need to do is to sit down and talk nicely to the Germans with a little sweet reason and everything will be fine.'

Anthony met Sir Charles's serious eyes. 'Wouldn't it? Look, when I think of the *Lusitania*, I want revenge too, but can't we find some common ground? There are plenty of decent Germans.'

'I know there are, Brooke!' said Sir Charles sharply. 'Unfortunately those aren't the ones we have to deal with. Do you remember sending us papers from a contact called Geiss?'

Anthony nodded. He hadn't been able to read the papers but he remembered Geiss, a political insider from Berlin, well enough.

'Geiss wasn't our only source for the information but what was said was so vital that any confirmation was like gold dust. I don't have to look it up, because I'll never forget it. It was notes of what the German Chancellor, Bethmann-Hollweg proposes in the event of a German victory. We're calling it the September Programme, because the notes we've got are dated the ninth of September, at the height of the battle of the Marne. We managed to stop them but only just. Since the Marne we've been holding on with our fingernails. Bethmann-Hollweg wants control of the whole of Europe. The French, the Poles, the Italians, the Swedes will all be under German domination.'

Anthony couldn't quite believe him. 'That's fairly comprehensive,' he said with an ironic twist in his voice. 'What about the neutral countries? Holland and Denmark and so on? Are they going to be part of Greater Germany?'

'Brooke, there won't *be* any neutrals if the Germans have their way. The September Programme talks about economic control for the neutrals. All of Europe will be nothing more than a puppet state.'

Sir Charles was completely serious. Anthony felt his disbelief shifting but damnit, surely all this fight-to-the-death stuff was crazy? Surely this talk of European domination couldn't be anything more than sabre-rattling. He asked the obvious question. 'Where does that leave us? Britain, I mean?'

'Your imagination can supply the obvious answer, but Bethmann-Hollweg dots the I's and crosses the T's. He talks about forcing France to her knees – that's his actual phrase – so that she will accept any peace Germany sees fit to offer, which means they can impose their will on England. That, too, is a direct quote. I tell you, there won't be a Britain if we don't win this war.'

Anthony shifted in irritation. 'That's impossible.'

'You can't see it, can you?' said Sir Charles. 'Very few of us can imagine what it would be like to live in an occupied country.' He leaned forward, his voice urgent once more. 'Can't you see the arrogance, the unconscious, self-assured, dangerous arrogance of that? The Germans can occupy Belgium. Why not? It's only Belgium. France? It's foreign. You expect odd things to happen in foreign countries, but occupy us? Never. This is England. That sort of thing doesn't happen here. It's been a hundred years since this country was truly affected by war and all the fighting was overseas. It's been a thousand years since we faced a real invasion and Britain, so the thinking goes, wasn't really Britain then. The Norman Conquest is tucked away in history books and is just a date for schoolboys to learn. Well, if we don't win the war, there'll be another date for schoolboys to learn.'

Anthony had to admit that Sir Charles was right. He couldn't imagine a successful invasion. 'What about the Empire?'

'Which Empire?' asked Sir Charles with a lift of his eyebrows. 'The British Empire or the empire the Germans propose to carve out of Africa? *Mittleafrikanisches Kolonialreich*, they call it. If we lose the war, that's the end of Pax Britannica. We can lose, Brooke. Believe me, we can lose. The Germans are well-armed, well-disciplined, tenacious and courageous and are horribly inventive about the weapons they're prepared to use. For years they've said that a modern war would call upon every device science could provide. That was horribly proved last month. They used chlorine gas. It's a disgusting weapon. And, just to make things worse in my opinion, the thirst for revenge is so great it'll only be a matter of time before we use it too.'

'Do you really think so?'

'I can't see us not doing. I'd stop it if I could, but I can't. Gas is a loathsome thing, but they started it. We can't let them have the advantage. We've managed to hold them and we've managed to shake them but we haven't managed to beat them. Considering they've had conscription for years and all we've got is our regulars, we haven't done badly. For years we've managed with a small army, a contemptible little army, as the Kaiser put it. Well, that army's swelled considerably over the last few months and we need to train it, equip it and supply it. Supplying it is probably one of the hardest things of all.' He pulled out his chair and sat down at the desk once more. He looked, thought Anthony, very tired.

'I've never thought about that side of it,' said Anthony. He was oddly unsure of himself. Sir Charles was right; it was impossible to imagine life in Britain under the victorious Germans. Arrogance? Yes, he supposed it was.

Sir Charles put a hand to his chin. 'Supplies are the devil. We've had to ration shellfire down to two rounds a gun in some cases – two rounds! – and there's nothing left in the depots. We're supplying ammunition straight from the ships to the field and even that supply has, on occasion, dried up altogether.' He picked up his whisky, swirled it round in his glass and finished it with a gesture of finality. 'Revise your ideas, Brooke. We're fighting because we have to fight and it's a grim struggle for survival.'

Anthony raised his hands in protest. 'All right. So we have to fight. But Talbot, wouldn't I be more use in France than in Germany?'

Sir Charles shook his head decisively. 'We need information. Information that only people like you and that poor devil, Cavanaugh, can provide. Without it we're fighting blind.' He walked to the desk and picked up the notes he had made. '"Spy in England. Gentleman.

He must be a gentleman. Seems to know everything. Knew about me. Frankie's letter. Read Frankie's letter." And then there's this phrase you couldn't catch. *Star's anger*?'

'I don't know what *star's anger* means,' said Anthony. 'I thought it was the name of the ship, but it obviously isn't.'

'*Star's anger* doesn't mean anything to me. What about Frankie's letter? Who's Frankie?'

Anthony shrugged. 'There again, I don't know. I've never heard him mention anyone called Frankie, man or woman. I thought at first Frankie was a girl, a girl he cared about, but now I'm not so sure. He said "Read Frankie's letter", and added, "I loved her". I asked him if he had the letter, but he said – he died seconds later – "It's not that sort of letter." I've had plenty of time to think about it, and I think that the Frankie who wrote the letter and this girl are two separate people. What he meant by "not that sort of letter", I don't know.'

Sir Charles clicked his tongue. 'Frankie's letter . . .' He drummed his fingers on the desk. 'Let's put that to one side for the moment and concentrate on what we do know. "Spy in England." Well, we know there are spies. We even know who some of them are.'

'Do we?' asked Anthony, startled.

'Absolutely we do,' said Sir Charles with a smile. 'If we want snippets of misleading information to be breakfast reading in Berlin, they're invaluable. We have to flavour it with a salting of truth, just to keep the pot bubbling, so to speak, but I watch over the welfare of these innocents like an old mother hen. They aren't all German, of course. Traitors are rare, thank God, but they do exist, and the Germans pay well. They go up to a thousand pounds or so for something really juicy.'

'Good grief,' said Anthony with a lift of his eyebrows. 'That's a sight more than I seem to be worth,' he added.

'Don't underestimate yourself.' Sir Charles leaned forward and tapped the paper. 'This sounds like someone we don't know. "Spy in England. Knew about me. He must be a gentleman."' Sir Charles sat back, frowning. 'It sounds like unfinished business.' He cocked an inquisitive eyebrow at Anthony. 'What do you know about Cavanaugh?'

'I know he was an Irish-American and a journalist. As a neutral and especially an American neutral, he was welcomed by the

Germans. He was about fifty, but as tough as old boots. He'd been a ranch-hand and a prizefighter and a raft of other things in between. He had a pose of being anti-British.'

'That wasn't entirely assumed,' said Sir Charles thoughtfully. 'Cavanaugh wasn't his real name, by the way. He found it necessary to change it. I took a risk with him, but it was justified. As you know, if it hadn't been for the war, the bill granting Irish Independence would have gone through Parliament. Cavanaugh, in common with many others, was certain that independence would lead to trouble as the Nationalists and the Loyalists battled it out. As a journalist he wanted to see for himself what was going on. He joined a New York Irish group called The Hibernian Relief Fund and what he found shocked him.'

Anthony looked a question.

'The Hibernian Relief Fund was supposed to help poor Irishmen and their families, both in New York and Ireland. What it actually did was raise money for arms. Not only was a civil war anticipated but it was being eagerly provided for.' Sir Charles put his hands behind his head and leaned back in his chair. 'Now, before the war, the money raised came from the New York Irish. Guess who else has taken an interest.'

Anthony looked at him sharply. 'Germany?'

Sir Charles nodded. 'Germany. As I said, the Germans aren't stupid. If there's a rebellion in Ireland, we, the British, would have to do something about it. That means troops and supplies tied up in Ireland which would otherwise be used on the Western Front. Cavanaugh was all for a Free Ireland but he didn't want a civil war and he certainly didn't want the Germans involved. He published his story and all hell broke loose. From then on he was a marked man.'

'You mean his life was threatened?'

Sir Charles nodded. 'Several times. Cavanaugh changed his name, came to London and made it his business to get in touch with me. He'd learned enough in New York to realize there was an active Irish-German link in London and was stubborn enough to want to get to the bottom of it. He joined a London group called Sons of Hibernia, which, like its American counterpart, was supposed to be a Friendly Society, aiding poor Irishmen and women. It wasn't, of course. Having learned from bitter experience, he was rather more cautious this time round and he uncovered some very valuable information. However, it was only part of the story. By his own request, he went to Germany to try and get the other end. There are Irishmen in Germany, honoured guests of the German government, and he wanted to find out exactly what they were doing.' His mouth twisted. 'It seems as if they got to him first.'

Once again he looked at the notes he had made. '"Spy in England. Gentleman. He must be a gentleman. Seems to know everything. Knew about me. Frankie's letter. Read Frankie's letter."'

'That sounds as if Frankie betrayed him.' Anthony clicked his tongue. 'And yet, it's odd, isn't it? Frankie and the Gentleman sound like two different people.'

Sir Charles nodded. 'Yes. So we've got a gentleman spy and his assistant, Frankie, who's in touch with the Germans or the Irish in Germany, which is much the same thing. So who the devil are they? A gentleman in England . . . It's not much to go on, is it?' he added in disgust. 'England's full of gentlemen, particularly if you use the term loosely.'

Anthony reached for another cigarette and lit it, smoking thoughtfully. 'D'you know, that's exactly what he didn't do,' he said after a pause. Sir Charles looked at him enquiringly. 'Use the term loosely, I mean,' he explained. 'Perhaps it's because he was American, but I'd noticed that about him before. To Cavanaugh, to call him that, an English gentleman was a fairly technical term. He never used it politely or ironically but meant the sort of bloke who mixes in fashionable society and gets invited to house parties or who is asked to come for a few days' fishing or play a bit of country-house cricket.'

Sir Charles sat very still for a few moments. 'A real gentleman, you mean?' He swallowed. 'My God, I hope not. The information a gentleman spy could pick up is frightening.'

'What are you so worried about?' asked Anthony, his forehead creasing in a frown. 'Unless the gentleman's a military type or got special information of some kind, I can't see they'll know anything out of the ordinary. I don't want to be flippant, but I can't see the Germans would be much wiser for knowing anyone's batting average or how the trout are rising on the Cam.'

Sir Charles shook his head impatiently. 'Of course they wouldn't. But don't you see, Brooke, someone who does know that sort of thing, someone who's really in the heart of English society, could pick up all sorts of gossip. You wouldn't believe what gets chattered about. They could have found out about Cavanaugh quite by chance.'

'By chance? Come on. Cavanaugh's not likely to have told anyone and anyone who did know wouldn't go blabbing it about.'

Sir Charles bit his lip. 'I wish I could be so sure. Anyone who was on the lookout for information could pick up a dickens of a lot, simply by listening to the conversations round him. You know how people talk.'

Anthony remained sceptical. 'There's bound to be a lot of chit-chat, I grant you, but something really serious, like Cavanaugh's mission, would be kept under wraps.'

'Would it?' Sir Charles steepled his fingers and leaned forward. 'Tell me, Brooke, would you say what I told you about the shortage of munitions was serious? Something the Germans would like to know?'

'Of course I would,' said Anthony with a short laugh. 'They probably have an idea that things are tight but if they knew exactly how tight, they'd keep on fighting, even if it seemed hopeless.'

'And yet I'm certain the Germans know as much as I do about our shell shortage. You won't have seen *The Times* this morning but there's a telegram from the Front spelling it out.'

Anthony gaped at him. 'It's printed in *The Times?*'

'Not only that,' continued Sir Charles, 'but I'm prepared to bet the information came from none other than Field Marshall, Sir John French. He's extremely friendly with Repington, their chief correspondent.'

'*What?*' Anthony was utterly bewildered. Not only did it seem to fly in the face of common sense but coming, as he was, fresh from Germany, it seemed akin to treachery. He couldn't imagine what they'd do to a German general who broke ranks in that spectacular way. Nothing very friendly, he thought, and you definitely wouldn't read about it afterwards in the newspapers. 'Doesn't the fool realize that this will be meat and drink to the enemy?'

'That's the price of having a free press.' Sir Charles shrugged. 'The trouble is, that as far as the shell shortage goes, Sir John French isn't fighting the enemy, he's fighting Lord Kitchener. We've got a whole new front opened up in the Dardanelles, and to have any chance of success, ammunition has to be diverted from France. The generals are at each other's throats about it. The fact that the Germans will be a fascinated third in the quarrel doesn't seem to have impinged on anyone. For all the British reputation for having a stiff upper lip, we must be the most garrulous society on earth.' He leaned his elbows on the desk and shook his head wearily. 'Good God, Brooke, when I think of what I've heard casually chatted about over dinner, my blood runs cold. As an American in England, Cavanaugh would stand out. He could easily have been one of the subjects for discussion.'

'I suppose he could,' said Anthony soberly. 'Yes, in light of what you've told me, I suppose he could.'

'I'll tell you something else, too,' said Sir Charles earnestly. 'If there really is a gentleman spy on the loose, then we're in trouble. Big trouble. I understated it when I said things were chatted about over dinner. I've heard whole plans of campaigns discussed, for heaven's sake. There aren't, thank God, rules about who can be in and out of society. It's all more subtle and elusive than that, but once you're in, you're in. If there really was someone who was accepted, then they could hear virtually the whole of our war plans without much effort. All they'd have to do is talk to the right people and keep their ears open.' Sir Charles got up and strode to the window. 'My God . . . The more I think about it, the more horrifying it is. We're so sure of ourselves, so willing to take people on trust.' He clasped his hands together, looking at the palms. 'Will you do it, Brooke?' he asked suddenly.

'Do what?' asked Anthony, startled. He wasn't aware of having been asked to do anything.

Sir Charles rounded on him impatiently. 'Investigate. Find the spy, if there is a spy. Find Cavanaugh's gentleman. This could be nothing more than a nightmare, but we need to know if it's true.'

Anthony drew his breath in. 'You want me to be a spy in England?' he said slowly. He knew he was being squeamish, but the idea repelled him. It seemed so underhand.

'That's right.' Sir Charles saw his expression and became urgent. 'Don't you see, man, we have to get to the bottom of this. If there really is a spy – a gentleman – we have to know. Otherwise many more lives besides Cavanaugh's will be endangered.'

'That's true.' It was true, but Anthony still winced from the idea of poking into people's private lives. He thought, not to put too fine a point on it, it was rotten.

And that was arrogance, he said ruefully to himself. He was suffering from what Sir Charles had called arrogance. Although Cavanaugh's use of the word *gentleman* had to mean someone inside society, he didn't know if he really believed it. True enough, there were all sorts at the average dinner and many a hostess would sponsor a guest who was deliberately provocative, to throw some sparks into a dull gathering. But that wasn't the kind of man he'd be looking for. Once he'd discounted the brilliant gentlemen of foreign extraction, the tamed anarchist and the ruck of wastrel sons and ne'er do wells – types which surely even the dimmest port-encrusted general would feel shy of confiding in – that left the Sound Chaps, Salt Of The Earth, Trust 'Em Anywhere, Good Man In A Tight Spot and all other clichés which added up to the sort of person who really was trustworthy. Or, at least, appeared to be.

He smoked his cigarette down to the butt and crushed it out. When he'd agreed to work for W. Gabriel Monks, he'd agreed to obey orders, whatever his private feelings may be.

'Very well. I don't see I've got much choice. Where do I start? If it comes to that, *how* can I start? I can hardly wander round Britain hoping to get on the chap's trail on the off-chance.'

'Start with Cavanaugh's friends,' said Sir Charles promptly. 'If any of them have links to Ireland, that gives us another clue. I'll do what I can with Sons of Hibernia, but the ringleaders are all accounted for and none of them could have been called gentlemen, to use the word in Cavanaugh's sense. The journalism angle might throw up a useful lead or two, as well. I'll do what I can. Cavanaugh was a beggar for keeping his cards close to his chest, so I can't suggest any names, but you ought to be able to find something out if you ask around. There's this girl he was keen on, as well. I don't know anything about her.'

'She could be anywhere in the world,' Anthony said wearily.

Sir Charles nodded. 'I know how you feel about this, Brooke. It goes against the grain but it's got to be done.' He looked at Anthony appraisingly. 'You're going to have to ask questions, Brooke. The trouble is, people are going to ask questions back and it might be awkward for you to answer them.'

He picked up his pen and tapped it idly on the blotting pad. 'I think it might be best if I arranged for you to have a temporary commission. The Intelligence Service would be best, as everyone will expect you to be cautious about what you say. Colonel Brooke? That's got quite a nice ring to it. When it's convenient, call round to Gieves and Hawkes and get yourself measured for a uniform. Don't worry about that side of things. I'll arrange it. The other thing I want to mention is this.'

He opened the desk drawer and, drawing out a thin silver card case, opened it and gave Anthony one of the cards it contained. It wasn't a visiting card but a picture of St Michael the archangel, fiery sword in hand. 'Put that somewhere safe.'

After a moment's thought, Anthony slipped the card into his cigarette case.

'The idea was suggested by the name of this street, Angel Alley,' continued Sir Charles. 'I'm Gabriel Monks, but I'm not the only angel in London. There's three of us altogether, myself, Michael and Raphael. Should you ever get stuck – this is for dire emergencies only, mind – you can go to the War Office and either show them that card or mention angels.' He smiled. 'With any luck that'll bring a heavenly host out on your side. Now, about your search for Cavanaugh's associates. Let's think out some details . . .'

FOUR

Anthony made his way to his club through the crowds of Regent Street. Before the war he'd had rooms in Sadlers, a club which, for no apparent reason, attracted a large number of medical men, and his things were still stored in a trunk in the basement. He certainly needed a shave, he thought, ruefully rubbing his hand over his chin, and the idea of a warm bath and a change of clothes filled him with eager anticipation. With any luck he could get his old rooms back.

It was strange to be back in London again, to hear English spoken so casually by the crowds, to see all the old shops and landmarks, grubby with soot and so unexpectedly, so heart-tuggingly familiar, they were oddly beautiful in the spring sunshine. He would never have described Swan and Edgars, for instance, with its display of linen, haberdashery, corsets and socks, as beautiful, yet the sight of the shop with its curved glass windows, there as it had always been there, gave him a lump in his throat.

He expected London to have changed and in some ways it had; there were far more soldiers on the streets, for a start, and some buildings were swathed in steel netting. He couldn't think why, at first, then realized, with a shock, it was to ward off damage from bombs dropped by Zeppelins.

It seemed incredible that war could touch London. He thought of Sir Charles's idea of arrogance with rueful agreement. Paris, he knew, showed its wounds openly, gashed by air raids, its public spaces from the racecourse at Longchamps to the Palace of Versailles, neglected and overgrown. Paris was like a deserted city, with virtually every other shop closed and bearing the notice that the owner was fighting the Boche. What happened to Paris could surely happen to London and yet . . . Sir Charles was right. It was French, it was foreign, it was safely overseas. He couldn't make himself believe it could happen here.

Anthony stood on the corner of Regent Street and Piccadilly, amidst the growl of motor cars, the hubbub of passers-by, the clatter of hooves, the creak of wheels and the shouts of street vendors, trying, amongst all this noisy, careless unconcern, to imagine London scarred by war. It was no use; the city was simply too big and too vibrant.

Not that the war was entirely absent, of course. There were war posters plastered on the hoardings. They lacked the angry bite of the posters in Berlin and Kiel, consisting mainly of injunctions to the able-bodied to join up. Of course! The Germans didn't need to urge men to enlist. Conscription took care of that. Remembering the crowds of volunteers that had besieged recruiting sergeants in Trafalgar Square last August, Anthony was surprised that any more men were needed. About a hundred thousand men had joined in the first few heady days of the war, but, going off the message on the posters, that wasn't enough.

Women of Britain say – 'GO!' That was rather moving, with a picture of a little boy clutching onto his mother's skirts, as she sadly watched a line of departing Tommies march past the window. There was a real sacrifice implied there. She might be saying, 'Go!' but she didn't look very happy about it.

At The Front. Every fit Briton should join our brave men at the

Front. Enlist Now. Although the image was dramatic, it was hardly enticing. A team of horses pulling a wagon had suffered a near miss from a huge shell. The horses reared in panic and the driver was hanging to the reins for grim death. At least it gave the prospective recruit some idea of what he might be in for.

Halt! Who goes there? If you are *a friend join the British ranks and help the brave lads at the Front.* That was illustrated by the lonely silhouette of a solider against the skyline, with rifle at the ready. And, thought Anthony cynically, if the idiot stood out in the open like that, bellowing challenges to all and sundry, his military career was likely to be very short indeed.

A painful jab in the ribs made him spin round angrily. Two women with ferocious expressions were standing behind him. One, hefting an umbrella, looked as if she was about to assault him again. 'Did you just hit me with your umbrella?' demanded Anthony incredulously, rubbing his side.

The women exchanged meaningful glances. 'I most certainly did, young man,' said the umbrella-wielding woman, her double chin wobbling with indignation. 'How you can look at those pictures of our brave boys and their selfless sacrifice without feeling utterly ashamed, I do not know.'

She surveyed his clothes and his stubbly chin with a sort of loathing horror. 'Why are you not at the Front? You speak like an educated man. Whether you have come down in the world through drink or wanton fecklessness, I do not know, but surely you can see that the war is your chance to redeem yourself, to put good some of the ravages your path – your manifestly unsatisfactory path – in life has led you down.' She took a white feather from her bag and brandished it like a weapon. 'It is my duty to give you this!'

Anthony, his side throbbing from the ferrule of her umbrella, didn't know whether to laugh or tell her to mind her own business. The White Feather movement had started before he'd left London and hundreds, if not thousands, of women had enthusiastically taken upon themselves the task of handing out white feathers to those whom they considered to be shirkers.

She leaned forward, seized the lapel of his jacket, and made to insert it in his buttonhole. 'Enlist today! There is still a chance to make good! Be a man amongst men!'

Anthony's sense of humour won. To be taken for a tramp and an inebriate tramp at that, to be upbraided for cowardice, urged to enlist and to be able to produce a white feather was, properly considered, very funny indeed. Sir Charles would love the joke.

His hand closed over hers. 'Thank you,' he said brokenly. 'You have pointed out the right path to me.' The women looked at him dubiously, wondering if he was serious. 'It was gin that brought me to this,' he said earnestly, trying to keep the laughter out of his voice. 'I shall reform and—'

'*Star anger.*' It was a clear, high voice, the speaker close at hand. The words cut through the welter of noise surrounding them.

Anthony, the ferocious woman still clinging on to his lapel, whirled. Standing by a taxicab, outside Swan and Edgars, with a commissionaire in attendance, was a well-dressed, middle-aged man in a top hat and a coat with an astrakhan collar. He stood back to allow his companion, a woman in a blue velvet coat and a wisp of a hat, get into the cab. The sight of the man struck a vague chord of memory. The woman looked up at him, smiling as he bent over her. Anthony could have sworn she'd said 'Star anger'. Then, for a fleeting second, he saw her face.

It was as if he had been drenched with icy water. She was, quite simply, the most beautiful woman he had ever seen and the shock brought him up dead. For a moment – it was like a moment outside time – London seemed to freeze.

The White Feather women, the crowds, the noise, all stopped. Then, with a shock like thunder, the implication of what she'd said crashed in upon him. *Star anger.* She knew what *star anger* meant!

Anthony tried to run towards her but the ferocious woman held him back. He ignored her, intent on getting to the woman in blue. 'Hoy!' he shouted as loudly as he could. 'Stop!'

The woman in the blue coat didn't hear him. She gathered her skirts together and disappeared into the taxi. The man climbed in the cab, the commissionaire closed the door and the taxi pulled away from the kerb.

Anthony unclasped the ferocious woman's hand from his lapel, took the white feather and, shaking off her clutching hand – she clearly thought he'd gone mad – strode rapidly to the commission-aire. 'Excuse me,' he said crisply. 'Who were those people? The man and woman who just got in the cab?'

The commissionaire blinked. Anthony could see him contrasting his voice and his clothes. 'What's it to you?'

Anthony pulled out a sovereign – the only English money he had was a roll of sovereigns – from his pocket and pressed it into the man's hand.

The commissionaire's bewilderment increased. 'I'm sorry, guv, I can't help you. They were going to Waterloo, if that's any use.'

The White Feather women joined them. 'Did you give this man money?' demanded the ferocious woman.

'Yes,' said Anthony desperately. 'I'm an eccentric millionaire. Now hop it, will you, my good woman.' He turned to the commissionaire. 'Call a taxi for me, please.'

'*My good woman!*' repeated the ferocious woman, shrill with indignation. 'How dare you!'

The commissionaire put his whistle to his lips and blew.

Amidst a stream of recriminations from the women, a taxi drew up. The driver looked doubtfully at the embattled and down-at-heel Anthony.

'He's all right,' said the commissionaire with a grin. He had thoroughly enjoyed listening to the women on the subject of Anthony's shortcomings. 'He's an eccentric millionaire.'

'Aren't we all,' said the taxi driver looking at Anthony and his unwanted companions disparagingly. 'I'm not taking that lot on board. This is a cab, not a circus turn. Millionaire! Pull the other one, mate.'

He put in the clutch and drove off, leaving Anthony on the pavement. Anthony sighed in exasperation and, leaving the women arguing on the pavement, made for the underground. It was hopeless, of course. He couldn't buy a tuppenny ticket with a sovereign, so had to stop at the news kiosk for change, which meant further delays.

There were lots of trains leaving from Waterloo, he thought despondently, as he stood on the station concourse. Lots of trains from which, if you made the right connections, you could get to any destination in Britain. His hand curled over the white feather in his pocket. If it wasn't for those blasted women he'd have caught the man in the top hat and the woman in the blue coat.

Maybe – just maybe – it was as well he hadn't. After all, what would he have said? If he had caught them, he might have given the game away. Cavanaugh said they were looking for a gentleman and the man in the top hat was a gentleman, sure enough. What's more, he was certain he'd seen him somewhere before. And the woman? His stomach turned over as he recalled that fraction of a second when she'd looked in his direction.

'Would you recognize either of them again?' asked Sir Charles, when Anthony telephoned his private line from Waterloo station.

Oh yes, he would certainly recognize them again. He couldn't, although he didn't say as much to Sir Charles, get the woman in blue's face out of his mind.

There was something else too, he added to himself as he plunged back into the underground. Whatever *star anger* meant, it meant something to the woman in blue. Somehow or other, he would see her again.

Fortunately, MacIntyre, the porter at Sadlers, remembered him well, otherwise Anthony might have had trouble being admitted to his old club.

'I've been abroad,' he said, as carelessly as he could, trying not to laugh as MacIntyre's raging curiosity visibly diminished. That respectable doctors should turn into tramps, inebriate or not, the minute they set foot abroad was clearly nothing more than MacIntyre expected and part of the dangers inherent in foreign travel. 'I don't suppose my rooms are still free?'

They weren't, much to MacIntyre's sorrow. 'Another gentleman's got them now,' he said, apologetically. 'He's a very nice gentleman,' he added, as if that made up for it somehow. There were, however, two fine quiet rooms at the back, next to the fire escape. He was sure that Mr Walbreck, the secretary, would be glad to arrange everything for him.

Richard Walbreck, the secretary, did indeed arrange everything. That had all been simple enough, thought Anthony. He could only wish the task of finding Frankie would prove as simple. It sounded impossible to hunt through the biggest city on earth for someone called Frankie, but he had hopes that someone would remember Cavanaugh.

Following Sir Charles's suggestion, he didn't start his hunt until his new uniform arrived. He unpacked the box, put on his clothes and, knotting his tie, looked at the military figure reflected in the mirror. It struck Anthony as sheer make-believe. To be a colonel with no regiment and no men had a comic opera, Gilbert and Sullivan quality about it that was as unlikely as his mission.

He wasn't sure if he liked what he saw in the mirror. He'd spent months trying to be unremarkable and the uniform, with its green cap-ribbon and tabs, singled him out as a member of the Intelligence Service. But that, according to Sir Charles, was a very good reason for wearing it. Sir Charles reassured him that he couldn't have a better camouflage than khaki. It would also, he had added with a grin, save him from being presented with any more white feathers.

During the next couple of days, Anthony tried to hunt up his old friends, but most of them had joined up and Cavanaugh's acquaintances proved even more elusive. There were men who remembered the passing American visitor but, despite Sir Charles Talbot following up every lead, there was no result. They seemed, thought Anthony with frustration, on the afternoon of the fourth day, to be getting nowhere. Even an investigation into Cavanaugh's journalism proved fruitless. He had written pieces for the American press, but had published nothing in England. And the quest, as Anthony quickly realized, was urgent.

Cavanaugh had died because a gentleman in England had betrayed him. What else that gentleman could pick up was deeply worrying. Anthony was stunned by the facts which were freely floated round London drawing rooms and not so much whispered, as openly discussed after the port.

Some of the talk was harmless chit-chat, such as Tom receiving his commission in the Blues and Royals, Dick getting the MC and Harry being sent to Gallipoli. That went with the discussions about which rifle it was best for an officer to carry, now rifles had replaced the traditional swords, and if a soldier who threw a hand grenade should be called a grenadier or a bomber, but he could, with very little effort, have written a fairly detailed report on the situation in the Dardanelles, given the inside story of Aubers Ridge and Festubert and found out about the new bombsight being developed by the Central Flying School. He learnt Italy was about to declare war, who was likely to be who in the forthcoming coalition government, how the army had first won, then lost, then drawn the battle of Neuve Chapelle and the vicious infighting between Field Marshall Sir John French and virtually everyone else.

It mainly came, as most information does, in bits and, naturally enough, Anthony couldn't know if it was accurate but anyone with their eyes open would know where to go and who to ask to check their facts.

Sir Charles wasn't remotely surprised. 'You can't stop people talking,' was his comment when Anthony called to see him. 'We're convinced that anyone we meet over dinner, who speaks as we do and knows the same crowd is fundamentally safe. For instance, who told you about the new bombsight?'

'That was Kenneth Bourne after dinner two nights ago but a fair few people knew about it. Shelia Matherson mentioned it too. I've known them both for years.'

'So it wouldn't cross their minds it was something they shouldn't talk about. The more I think about it, the more worried I am. To be totally accepted in English society must be one of the most casual and yet one of the most difficult tricks in the world. We don't ask for a man's credentials or ask to see his papers. We know that sort of thing by instinct.'

'Well, so we do,' Anthony replied. 'Either you know someone or you know someone who knows someone or you know what school they went to or where they come from. It'd be difficult for a foreigner or an outsider, however plausible, to break in to that circle, unless you're suggesting a disguise or a false identity.'

'I can't see it working like that. I'm convinced Cavanaugh was on the right lines. Our man's working on the inside. He's doesn't need a disguise or a false name. This is much more subtle.' He shook his head with an anxious frown. 'He's one of us. Damn it, Brooke, Cavanaugh must have talked to *someone*. We have to find who.'

Anthony had been in London for over a week when he got a break. He'd bumped into an old friend, Jerry Ross, in the Savoy. Over the second whisky-and-splash he pitched in with his standard gambit. He'd run through the usual list of friends and their doings before casually asking, 'Do you remember that American chap who was here before the war? Terence Cavanaugh. Quite a character.'

To his delight, Jerry frowned. 'Was he the bloke who'd been a cowboy or something?'

'That's the one,' said Anthony, keeping the raging urgency out of his voice.

'I don't know how many of his tales I believed, but yes, I knew him. A friend of my sister's introduced him. He was a real tough egg, I'd have said, but pleasant enough.'

With painful carelessness and another one for the tonsils, Anthony elicited the information that Ross's sister's friend was a Miss Tara O'Bryan. And that, the sum total of Jerry Ross's knowledge, was to prove priceless.

Next morning Anthony had a visit from Sir Charles's assistant, the elegant Farlow. 'Colonel Brooke?' he murmured in inaudibly cultured tones. Anthony had to smother a grin. He was sure MacIntyre, the porter, who was watching them from his desk in the hall, thought he was entertaining a duke or an earl, at least. Farlow leaned forward confidentially. 'I've come from Mr Monks.'

'What is it?' asked Anthony quietly.

Farlow cleared his throat. 'Mr Monks wants you to meet him in the bar in the Melbourne at quarter past twelve. Lunch,' he added languidly. 'Oh, and Mr Monks said to come in uniform. Create the right impression, don't you know?'

'Who on earth,' demanded Anthony when he joined Sir Charles in the bar of the Melbourne, 'is that chap Farlow?'

Sir Charles grinned broadly and picked up his sherry. 'Bertram Farlow? He's one of the stars of the department. I use him to fetch and carry and do odd jobs. He's not very bright, but he looks impressive, doesn't he?'

'Very.'

'I hide behind him on occasion, so to speak. One look at Farlow and no one takes any notice of me. He used to be an actor and, despite looking as if he's too aristocratic for words, he's actually the son of a Lancashire millworker.'

'Good grief. Anyway,' said Anthony, mentally dismissing Farlow, 'why did you want to see me? Have you got a lead?'

Sir Charles drew his chair closer. 'We have. Incidentally,' he said with a look at Anthony's clothes, 'the uniform suits you.'

'Never mind my uniform. What about this lead?'

'Ah, but your uniform is part of my scheme. It was your pal Ross with his sister's friend, Miss Tara O'Bryan, who led us in the right direction. Have you ever heard of a man called Sherston? Patrick Sherston?

Anthony frowned. 'Somewhere or other. The name rings a bell.'

He clicked his fingers. 'Hang on! I've got it. He was the man getting into the taxi! I couldn't place him but I knew I'd come across him. He's Irish, isn't he, Talbot?' He lowered his voice. 'Could he be one of the Sons of Hibernia?'

'If we suspected every Irishman of being involved with the Sons of Hibernia and their ilk, we'd have to keep an eye on half the army and most of the police,' said Sir Charles. 'However, he does have a link to Cavanaugh. Tell me what else you know about Sherston.'

Anthony shrugged. 'As I recall, he's a newspaper man and a pretty big cheese. He owns the newspaper, I mean. I met him at the university once. He was at a dinner hosted by my crowd at the School of Tropical Medicine, the neuropathology and parasitic diseases people. There was a fairly big donation in the offing. He made a speech about the Congo, Uganda and German East, setting the scene for everyone. It was a pretty good speech as these things go. I swapped notes with him afterwards. He sounded as if he knew Africa like the back of his hand, but he admitted his experience amounted to a holiday on the Cape and ten minutes with an encyclopaedia. I think I'd always treat him with care but I rather took to him.'

'That's the man. Well, I didn't know you'd met him, but he's joining us for lunch at one.'

Anthony sat up. 'Is he, by George? What's his association with Cavanaugh?'

'All in good time,' said Sir Charles with a grin. 'To go back to Mr Sherston for a moment, it's because we're meeting him for lunch that I particularly wanted you to wear uniform. It commands respect, you know.'

'And why do you want me to command Mr Sherston's respect? Particularly, I mean.'

Sir Charles sat back in his chair. 'Because, as you said, Patrick Sherston is a newspaper man. You said he was a big cheese. That, if anything, is an understatement. He owns the Sherston Press and is, in consequence, a very important person indeed. He owns the *Examiner,* the *Mercury,* the *Sentinel* and a host of others. As well as the big papers he's got lots of little magazines with names like *Modern Poultry Breeding* and so on.'

'Crikey. The *Sentinel?* We're moving in elevated circles. Does he know who you are?'

Sir Charles shook his head. 'No. He knows I work in Whitehall, but he thinks I've got something to do with police pensions. I've known him in a vague sort of way for years and would never have thought he'd had any connection with Cavanaugh if it hadn't been for your friend Ross mentioning Miss Tara O'Bryan. Sherston is Miss O'Bryan's uncle.'

'Is he, by jingo?' murmured Anthony. 'Are they close?'

Sir Charles nodded. 'Very. Miss O'Bryan's father is dead and both she and her mother, Veronica O'Bryan, Sherston's sister, live with him. You might have heard of Miss O'Bryan's father, Bernard O'Bryan. He was a well-known poet and literary figure in Dublin twenty-odd years ago.'

'I'm sorry,' said Anthony. 'I don't know much about poets.'

'He made quite a name for himself. He was an expert on Irish folklore and mythology and fiercely pro-Independence. He was a fiery sort of beggar, calling for young men to sacrifice themselves on the altar of freedom and so on. I don't know how much was poetic licence and how much was meant, but it's violent stuff. Sherston's pro-Independence but so are many people, on both sides of the Irish Sea. He's never made any secret of it and it might or might not be important. I hope it isn't. What *is* important for our purposes is the name of his house. Guess what it is.'

Anthony shrugged. 'It could be anything, I suppose.'

'It's Starhanger.'

'*What?*'

Sir Charles smiled triumphantly. 'Starhanger. And if that's not Cavanaugh's *Star anger* I'll eat my hat.'

'That's incredible!' Anthony couldn't keep the excitement out of his voice. 'And the woman I saw – the woman in blue – could she be Miss O'Bryan?'

'How old was she, would you say?'

Anthony had thought about this. He had thought about the woman in blue intently ever since that life-shattering glimpse. 'She'd be in her twenties at a guess.' He wanted it to be her. He very much wanted the woman in blue to be her.

'That sounds about right,' said Sir Charles. 'There is a Mrs Sherston, Mrs Josette Sherston, but we don't know anything about her. What does worry me is that Sherston is undoubtedly a gentleman.'

Anthony gave a low whistle. 'I see where you're going. Surely you don't think Mr Sherston might be our gentleman?'

Sir Charles looked at him with a twisted smile. 'It seems incredible, doesn't it? And yet in many ways he fits the bill. He's had a few swipes at the powers that be in his time, which is probably why he isn't Lord something or other. He might resent that, you know. He was very pro-Boer and, as I say, he's all for Irish Home Rule. He's run many an article about John Bull's other island, as he usually calls it. He might see his role as Cavanaugh's gentleman as a way of paying off a few old scores. Granted what Cavanaugh said, I can't deny he fits.' He paused. 'There's another thing, too. I looked him up in *Who's Who*. His second name is Francis.'

Anthony stared at him. 'Francis? And we're looking for a Frankie? That's a coincidence.'

Sir Charles held up a steadying hand. 'And that could be the top and bottom of it. I hope to God it's not him. There'll be hell to pay if it is. Since the war started, Sherston has become the patriot of patriots and has some very influential friends. He's also put his money where his mouth is as regards the war. Any member of his staff who joined up has been guaranteed full pay for the duration of hostilities and he's raised no end of money for various good causes associated with the services. If it's a front, it's a very good one. He regularly dines with Asquith and other members of the cabinet.'

'He's in a perfect position to have valuable information.'

'I agree. However, you see what I mean when I said he's someone we have to treat with caution. We've got a free press and Sherston knows how to use it. If this goes wrong, Sherston can make such a stink it'll wreck the department. It's hard enough to justify our work to some of the bigwigs in the War Office as it is, without giving them that sort of ammunition. We can't afford to let him have the faintest suspicion we're looking into him and his affairs, but it's important that we do. I want you to be invited to Starhanger. You can find out an awful lot very quickly about a man in his own home. I'd like to be there as well.'

Anthony raised his eyebrows. Considering he'd only met the man once, the assumption Sherston was going to immediately offer him bed and board seemed a bit cool. 'How on earth am I going to manage that? And how are you, for that matter?'

Sir Charles smiled once more. 'I'll see if I can swing it. As for you, Sherston's a newspaperman, yes? I made a point of running into him at the Garrick last night and you came up in conversation. I didn't know you'd met him, of course, but he was interested, and I offered to introduce you. After all, you've been in Germany. That's a pretty good inducement for any newspaperman. He'd love to get your story. You'll be surprised when he suggests it, of course, but a series of articles about your exploits as Herr Doktor Conrad Etriech should make good reading. Don't give them to him for anything less than an invitation to Starhanger.'

'I can't blab to the newspapers!' said Anthony, horrified.

Sir Charles spread his hands out in enquiry. 'Why not? You can't go back to Germany as Doktor Etriech so you might as well tell Sherston about the good doctor's doings. He'll invite you to Starhanger right enough.'

Anthony winced. The habit of secrecy was so ingrained that to talk to the popular press went against all his instincts. Sir Charles saw his expression. 'Come on, Brooke. There'll be no pictures, of course. You'll be totally anonymous but we have to offer Sherston something to get you into Starhanger.'

Anthony didn't like it. Despite his respect for Sir Charles, he thought he was mistaken. That he was later shown to be right gave him no pleasure at all. He tried to pin down why he was so uneasy about the idea. After all, Sir Charles was his chief and should know what he was doing. Maybe, he thought, it came down to experience. Sir Charles was lacking the edge, the raw instinct for survival, that had developed during those months in Germany.

Anthony said as much but Sir Charles wasn't convinced. Reluctantly, Anthony allowed himself to be persuaded. 'Well, if you're sure,' he said grudgingly. 'You say Sherston knows about me?'

'He's very keen to meet you,' said Sir Charles. 'He's got a certain impression of me, which I don't want to disturb. Follow my lead, won't you?' He laughed. 'Relax, man. No one will know it's you behind the stories in the papers unless you tell them so.'

'Perhaps,' Anthony said dryly. He'd seen too much of the gossipy nature of London society to believe there was any such thing as a secret any more. Still, if Sir Charles believed it would work, it probably would, he reassured himself glumly, no matter how his feelings were lacerated in the process.

'Now, once we're at Starhanger, there's another scheme I want to try.'

'What's that?'

Sir Charles sat forward in his chair. 'Cavanaugh was betrayed. He thought his betrayer was associated with Starhanger, but he could've been mistaken. With someone like Sherston involved we have to be completely certain. I want you to give out some false information once you're in Starhanger, something that's so delectable it's bound to be picked up and acted upon. If it's picked up, then we'll know that Starhanger is definitely where our gentleman operates from. Once we know that, we can start identifying exactly who he is.'

Anthony lit a thoughtful cigarette. This was more his sort of thing than Sir Charles's newspaper scheme. 'You haven't worked out the details yet?'

'No, not yet.'

Anthony knew what Sir Charles was after. They needed to sell Fritz a pup, but it had to be the right sort of pup. 'What about troop movements?'

Sir Charles frowned. 'Perhaps. I suppose we could invent a lot of troops massing for an attack and see if the Germans fall for it by bringing artillery to bear, but by the time we've warned any real troops to keep clear and posted observers to see what actually happens, we've involved a dickens of a lot of outsiders.'

'What about a ship? If I put it about that a ship carrying a highly desirable cargo was to be in a certain place at a certain time, that'd do it.' Anthony could tell Sir Charles wasn't convinced.

'We can't risk an actual ship,' objected Sir Charles. 'We don't want another *Lusitania*. On the other hand, we need a real ship to observe the action. Maybe if we could have a dummy of some sort . . .' He shook his head impatiently. 'We'd still need some crew on board, even if it's only two or three men, to make it look alive. If it was just a hulk, a U-boat wouldn't attack and if there is something there, any U-boat attack might be nothing more than coincidence. Besides that, it means involving the Admiralty. They might not cooperate and, as I said, the fewer people who know about our idea the better.'

He stroked his chin, thinking out the flaws. 'I could do with something on a much smaller scale,' he said eventually. 'Something we can control from beginning to end. And something, as well, where it's not obvious afterwards that the Germans have failed. If it's clearly a fake then they'll know we're on to them and I don't want to give our gentleman and his friends any more warning than I can help.'

This was going to be more difficult than Anthony had anticipated. 'Let me think it over,' he said. 'I might be able to come up with something.'

Sir Charles nodded. 'Good man.' He glanced at his watch as the waiter approached. 'It's after one. I imagine Sherston's here. Don't worry about the invitation. Follow my lead and with any luck it'll all come quite naturally. You're a club acquaintance of mine, by the way and I've been impressed by your adventures. Pitch it strong.'

'All right,' said Anthony, with a feeling of distinctly modified rapture.

'Mr Sherston's in the lobby, sir,' said the waiter.

Sir Charles put his glass on the table. 'In that case, let's go and meet him, Colonel Brooke.'

FIVE

Patrick Sherston was standing by the fireplace in the lobby. He looked up as they entered, smiling as he saw Sir Charles. 'Hello, Talbot. I'm sorry I'm late. I was held up by a minor crisis at the *Sentinel*. I hope it hasn't put you out.'

'Don't apologize' said Sir Charles heartily. 'This is the man I wanted you to meet, Sherston. Colonel Brooke, allow me to introduce Mr Patrick Sherston.'

Anthony remembered Sherston immediately. As they shook hands, he wondered how such a vigorous personality could have ever slipped his mind, even if, when he had seen him outside Swan and Edgars, his attention had been entirely taken up by the woman in blue. (Tara O'Bryan? Tara was a lovely name.)

Vigorous was a very good word to describe Sherston. He must have been, thought Anthony, in his early fifties, a strong, broad-shouldered man with a healthy, outdoor complexion, grizzled dark hair and piercing brown eyes with a commanding, let-me-mould-your-future expression in them. He spoke in a soft Irish brogue but the softness was deceptive.

Sherston was a man who was always going to amount to something. Anthony had seen the same look of authority in various ships' captains, a headmistress of a girls' school and assorted Prussian officers. Mr Sherston, thought Anthony warily, was a man who was accustomed to have people jump when he said so. Patrick Francis Sherston. Patrick *Frankie* Sherston?

'Brooke told me he'd met you before, Sherston,' added Sir Charles, chattily.

Sherston drew back. 'You'll excuse me, Colonel, if I say I can't quite recall it.'

'Don't apologize,' said Anthony easily. 'It was some time ago now. I was one of the hosts at a dinner given by the School of Tropical Medicine. You gave a speech about life in the Congo and so on, and we swapped notes about Africa afterwards.'

Sherston's face cleared. 'Of course.' He looked at Anthony's uniform, his gaze resting on the green tabs of the Intelligence Corps. 'Excuse me, Colonel, weren't you a doctor? I seem to remember you were engaged in research.'

Anthony appreciated the cleverness of the remark. Virtually everyone at that dinner had been a doctor engaged in research, but it made it seem as if Sherston really did remember him. 'That was before the war,' he agreed. 'I'd been to Lake Victoria, tracking down tsetse flies and their distribution.'

'Ah yes. You were one of the experts I was wary of. I remember feeling quite intimidated by the audience I was facing.' He gave a short laugh. 'I'm hardly an expert on Africa or tropical diseases. I was glad to get through it without being heckled.'

That, thought Anthony, was pure flannel. If a man was going to give a large amount of money to an impoverished university – all universities were impoverished in Anthony's experience – it would be sheer folly to find fault with even the most lacklustre speaker. 'I thought you carried it off in great style.'

Sherston smiled complacently. Anthony had obviously given the expected response. 'It's very kind of you to say so.' He glanced at Sir Charles. 'Shall we go into lunch, Talbot?'

'By all means,' agreed Sir Charles, leading the way across the lobby into the dining room. 'I'm looking forward to this,' he added with a hint of civilized excitement. He put a hand on Sherston's arm. 'Wait till you hear Brooke's exploits, my dear fellow.'

Anthony had to hand it to Sir Charles. He seemed subtly changed, not a leader anymore but a follower and of very much less account. 'Much more exciting indeed,' Sir Charles added, consciously basking in reflected glory. It seemed perfectly natural that he would say it in that way.

'Sir Charles said you'd been in Germany, Colonel,' said Sherston.

Anthony winced. He couldn't help it. He knew he was there to play a part but it still seemed wrong to blurt out the facts so openly. He saw Sherston register his discomfort. 'People ought to be more careful,' he said, playing the stiff-upper-lipped hero. It was a useful pretence. He couldn't think what the devil to say. Sherston looked at him inquisitively. 'Stories get about,' continued Anthony. 'You never know who's listening.'

'Oh, you're amongst friends,' said Sir Charles breezily. 'There's too much of this secrecy nonsense if you ask me. Damnit, there's no Germans here. We ought to be proud of what we've achieved.' The waiter showed them to a table. 'It's a great shame,' he continued, picking up the menu, 'that the really thrilling stories of the war can't be told. When I think what Brooke's been up to . . .' He broke off, shaking his head. 'Shall we have a bottle of the '98 claret? My doctor wouldn't approve, but a little indulgence never did a man any harm.'

Once again, Anthony mentally congratulated him. Without over-doing it, Sir Charles managed to convey the exact impression of a man who had had slightly too much to drink. He saw Sherston's smile of understanding.

'An excellent choice, Talbot. Colonel, were you really in Germany?'

Anthony nodded reluctantly.

Sherston pursed his lips in a silent whistle. 'How long for?'

'Since last September.'

The expression on Sherston's face was, Anthony had to admit, flattering.

'But that's wonderful!'

His admiration was so sincere Anthony had to get a grip on himself. Even if it was only a stunt for the press, he could see the role as a raconteur of My Thrilling Life being a damn sight easier than he'd anticipated.

Sherston picked up his napkin and sat with it held loosely in his hand. 'Where did you get to?'

There was an almost imperceptible nod from Sir Charles. Anthony took a deep breath and plunged in. 'I really shouldn't be telling you this, but I know it won't go any further. I started off in Berlin and ended up in Kiel.'

Sherston froze, his gaze drilling into Anthony. 'The headquarters of the Imperial Fleet? My word, Colonel, you're a hero.'

'I'm no hero,' said Anthony deprecatingly, deploying the stiff upper lip once more.

'How on earth did you land up in Germany?'

'I'd studied there before the war. That helped.' Talking of help, Anthony felt in need of some from Sir Charles, but he seemed to be concentrating solely on the menu.

'I'm going to have soup and lamb cutlets,' said Sir Charles fussily. 'I recommend the thick soup. They do it rather well. Look here, Brooke, it's all very well saying you're not a hero but we stay-at-home types have got to have someone to look up to, you know. From what I've heard if you aren't a hero, you're next door to it.'

'But I'm not,' protested Anthony. So Sir Charles had come to his aid after all. He tried hard. 'I had the occasional close shave, but that's all part of the job. I'll have the soup and steak and kidney pie.'

'What sort of close shave?' asked Sherston. He waved a dismissive hand at the menu. 'I'll have anything you recommend.'

'You got on a U-boat, didn't you?' said Sir Charles, seeing Anthony's hesitation. 'And didn't you dress up as a guard and join the hunt for yourself at one point?' He gave the order to the waiter. 'This is the real stuff, Sherston. Brooke had to escape over the rooftops to shake off the Germans. Wasn't that after that newspaper chap you were telling me about died, Brooke?'

'Terence Cavanaugh?' Anthony asked, picking up the fairly obvious cue. This was the story they had agreed earlier. They could hardly tell the truth about Cavanaugh. It would spark off far too many questions to say Cavanaugh, a neutral, had been shot, so, as far as the outside world was concerned, Cavanaugh was a journalist who'd died in an accident.

Anthony saw Sherston twitch at the name.

'I know a Terence Cavanaugh,' said Sherston. 'You say he's dead?'

'I don't suppose it's the same chap,' said Anthony with a

light-hearted laugh. 'My Cavanaugh was an American. He must have been about fifty-odd or so. He was quite a character. He'd been everything from a ranch-hand to a prizefighter and threw in a bit of journalism to go with it.'

Sherston looked at Anthony, then dropped his gaze. There was an odd pause. He pulled his napkin straight, fiddling with the corners. 'The Cavanaugh I knew was American,' he said. 'I imagine he called himself a journalist.' There was a hard edge in his voice. Anthony saw Sir Charles flick a quick glance of surprise towards Sherston. 'He was distantly related to my brother-in-law, Bernard, and made the acquaintance of my sister, Veronica. My brother-in-law has been dead for many years and my sister's devoted to his memory. Veronica welcomed Cavanaugh into the house. Cavanaugh presumed on the relationship.'

Presumed, thought Anthony, was a fairly loaded word. The soup arrived and there was silence for a few moments. 'So he's dead?' repeated Sherston. He picked up a piece of bread and crumbled it in his fingers. There was a restrained violence in the gesture. 'Dead, eh?' He sounded satisfied.

Anthony, intrigued by Sherston's reaction, answered without emotion. 'He died in Germany.'

'How very sad.'

He didn't sound very sad, thought Anthony. Gratified if anything.

Sir Charles finished his soup and pushed the bowl to one side. 'Tell us how you got into Berlin, Brooke,' he said with cheerful eagerness. 'I bet that's a story worth hearing.'

The look Sherston gave Anthony made him feel like a pig being prodded by a cautious farmer at a livestock market. With Sir Charles's careful guidance he embarked upon the more lurid of his adventures. He appreciated just how good a newspaperman Sherston was. His questions were designed to draw Anthony out, and, as he spoke, Anthony could feel Sherston warming to him. He was a knowledgeable interviewer, too. Anthony guessed some of his early questions were tests, designed to show if he really knew what he was talking about.

After about quarter of an hour of thorough grilling on Sherston's part and some solid hard work on Anthony's, Sherston laid down his knife and fork. Anthony was sure he hadn't noticed what he'd been eating. 'This is truly remarkable, Colonel. I wish I could bring your story to the public. Why, what a series of articles you could write!'

'I've got no hand for writing,' said Anthony modestly. He wasn't going to leap at the first opportunity. 'I haven't got the popular touch.'

'That's no problem,' said Sherston encouragingly. 'If you'd give an interview to one of my men, he can write it up.'

Anthony tried for an expression of sincere regret. 'It's one thing talking to you, Mr Sherston. I know you'll treat it all in confidence. It's quite another publishing it in the press.'

'I think you should,' said Sir Charles, a shade more definitely than a completely sober man would have done. 'We all need a boost. There's too much bad news knocking about. Why don't you get permission, Brooke?' he said, with an almost imperceptible wink.

Anthony pretended to chew the matter over.

'I urge you to consider it, Colonel,' said Sherston persuasively. 'The public will be inspired by your exploits. No names, of course, but simple facts.'

Now this was all very well, thought Anthony, but he hadn't been invited to Starhanger. Maybe that would follow, but he wanted to be a bit more secure, so . . .

'I'm not sure,' he said, after what he hoped seemed like a reasonable amount of cogitation. 'I can't see why, given the proper safeguards, there should be any real objection, but I was hoping to have a few days in the country. I want to have some fresh air, get some fishing in, that sort of thing and I don't want a pack of reporters clamouring at my door.' He nodded at Sir Charles. 'Talbot here has offered to show me one of his favourite haunts.'

'Absolutely, my dear chap,' agreed Sir Charles heartily. 'I'm looking forward to our little holiday.' He looked at Sherston. 'I was thinking of Melton on the Bewl, Sherston, down in Kent. Do you know it? It's a delightful spot.'

'Indeed it is,' agreed Sherston mechanically, his eyes abstracted. 'It's not far from my place. In fact . . .' He leaned forward. 'Perhaps, Colonel, you would agree to kill two birds with one stone, so to speak,' he said persuasively. 'I would be delighted if you could manage to put in a few days at my house, Starhanger. You too, Talbot. You'd both be very welcome. As far as fishing is concerned, we have a first-rate trout river on the estate and my wife is an excellent hostess. As far as the articles are concerned, all it would entail is having roughly the same conversation we've just enjoyed and I can guarantee you will not be troubled by pressmen.'

'That's a very generous offer,' said Anthony. 'Talbot, what do you say?'

'I think it's a splendid idea,' said Talbot enthusiastically. 'Absolutely first-rate. I'm much obliged to you, Sherston.'

'What do you say, Colonel?' asked Sherston.

'It's very kind of you,' said Anthony, privately congratulating Sir Charles. His scheme had worked, sure enough. If Sherston had been given a doormat he would have written *Welcome* on it. 'I'll have to get permission to go ahead, but I accept with pleasure.'

Sherston folded up his napkin. 'Good. We'll consider it settled.' He drew out his card case, took out a card and jotted a number on the back. 'That's my private number. Let me know as soon as you have permission and we'll arrange for you to come down.' He turned to Sir Charles. 'You can get away from the office, can you, Talbot?'

'Absolutely,' said Sir Charles cheerfully. 'Not that I'll be missed. To be honest I don't know why I stick at it, but someone's got to see that form CH 123 is filled in triplicate. Now most of my young clerks have joined up, I'm left with the halt and the lame and the old. How anyone expects me to run a government department with the staff I'm left with, I don't know. I suppose you've got much the same problem with your newspapers, Sherston.'

'It's a burden, certainly. However, talking of newspapers, Colonel, I appreciate you'll have to consult with the powers that be, but I'd like to run an article as soon as possible. Now, what I'd like to suggest is sending one of my men round . . .'

'What did you think of Sherston?' asked Sir Charles as he and Anthony crossed St James' Park after lunch. 'D'you think he could be Cavanaugh's Gentleman?'

Anthony scratched his ear. 'To be honest, I don't know if Sherston would fit Cavanaugh's ideas. He's rich and powerful and wears the right clothes, but his accent's against him. I'm not sure if an Irish-American would think another Irishman could be an English gentleman, if you see what I mean. I tell you something that I did think was odd though, and that was the way he talked about Cavanaugh.'

'You're right,' agreed Sir Charles. 'I don't know why. It could be nothing more than some trifling love affair with his sister – you remember Sherston said Cavanaugh presumed on the relationship? – or Sherston could be our man and realized Cavanaugh was on to him. We'll find out more at Starhanger.'

'Let's hope so,' Anthony agreed. 'By the way, you know we want a scheme to sell the Jerries? I've got a glimmer of an idea. It was all the talk about Africa which set me off, but I need to think through the details.'

The next morning Anthony telephoned Sherston to say the necessary permissions had been granted.

He was rewarded by an invitation to Starhanger for the following Friday and a visit from a senior reporter from the *Sentinel*. The day after that, he had the dubious pleasure of reading about his own anonymous exploits under the title 'Germany! The Truth! One Intrepid Briton's Account Of Life Under The Kaiser'.

He couldn't complain about the lack of enthusiasm shown by the writer but he wasn't prepared for the amount of interest it stirred up.

He got his first inkling when Diana Willis sprang to her feet as he was announced. She was his cousin's wife and he'd been invited for tea. The room seemed to be a sea of great-aunts, a sprinkling of youths in uniform and a few men too old to be in the army.

She drew him to one side, her eyes sparkling. 'Anthony, it's you, isn't it? The man in the paper, the One Intrepid Briton? I knew you'd done something *frightfully* brave but I had no idea what. Listen everyone!' she said, addressing the room. 'You've all got to be most fearfully respectful. This is Anthony Brooke, the man in the paper, the one who's just got back from Germany.'

'Cut it out, Diana,' he said, laughing. 'I don't know what you're talking about.'

But nobody believed him.

That the article was to have another and unwelcome consequence was brought home the next morning.

Bertram Farlow called with a note from Sir Charles asking him to call at five o'clock. Anthony, who was just off to lunch, invited Farlow for a bite to eat in Simpsons. As they walked down the

Strand, Anthony felt an indefinable prickle at the back of his neck. He knew someone was watching him.

He walked on a few steps before stopping by a newspaper vendor. He bought a paper, then turned casually, looking at the crowds on the pavement. Nobody. He stepped into the shelter of a shop doorway and, beside a curved glass window, stopped and glancing in idle interest at the packets of tea and granulated sugar displayed in the window.

There he was! Reflected in the curved glass was a man in a dark overcoat and bowler hat. He had a split-second glimpse of startled eyes, distorted in the glass, then the man disappeared into the crowd. Damn! Anthony waited a few more minutes, apparently intent on the headlines, but, although at least five bowler-hatted, dark-coated men walked past, Anthony knew his watcher wasn't amongst them. He folded up the paper, tucked it under his arm, and mounted the steps into Simpsons.

'I'm being followed,' he said to Farlow in a low voice, once they were inside and had been shown to a table.

'Indeed, Colonel?' asked Farlow in a voice that sounded as if he was about to announce the next hymn. 'Can you describe him?'

'Apart from the fact he's average height with a dark overcoat and bowler hat, no. I saw him reflected in the tea shop window. He knows his stuff. He knew exactly what I was up to and scarpered before I could get a proper look.'

'Perhaps he'll be there when we leave,' suggested Farlow. 'Let me go first. I'll cross over to the other side of the road, to March and Weeks, the umbrella shop. I'll see if I can spot anyone taking an interest in you.'

However, when Anthony joined Farlow outside March and Weeks, Farlow, peering into the window, shook his head as if gravely dissatisfied with the sticks and umbrellas on display. 'Not a trace of him, Colonel.'

Anthony nodded. The prickle at the back of his neck had disappeared. He kept a careful lookout as he walked back to his club, but could see nothing out of the way. Then, as always, doubts crept in. Had he been mistaken? Perhaps he was simply being overly sensitive.

A succession of late nights had made him tired and, although it was only quarter to three in the afternoon, he curled up in an armchair with a book. It was a long-winded Victorian thing he'd picked up in the library downstairs and could induce sleep after a couple of pages. He wouldn't mind a rest before he went to see Sir Charles.

He was halfway down the page before he realized he'd read the account of tiger hunting in Garhwal before. That was odd. His bookmark was in the wrong place. He couldn't be bothered to find the right page and let the book drop to the floor. Although tired, he was unable to settle. His suspicions were pretty nebulous but even a nebulous impression was probably worth reporting. He got up and went to the desk, intending to jot down exactly what he had seen.

His pen had been moved. It was at that point his senses flared. The few papers in his desk had been searched, he was sure of it. He sat rigidly still. Very faintly from the next room, his bedroom, came a tiny succession of noises.

He got up and crept to the door, resting his hand on the handle. There it was again. Tensing himself, he flung back the door and erupted into the room.

Anthony felt a complete fool. Standing by the bed, duster in hand, brush and pan beside him, was a club servant, dressed in the standard uniform of black trousers and striped waistcoat, covered by a khaki apron. He looked up with justified astonishment.

'What the devil are you doing in here?' Anthony snapped.

The man fingered his wisp of a moustache, nervously avoiding Anthony's gaze. 'I'm sorry, sir,' he said in deferential Cockney. 'I was just finishing your room. I didn't hear you come in. I'm sorry if I disturbed you. We got behindhand this morning and Mr Baxter told me to catch up while you were out.' He was the picture of aggrieved innocence.

Baxter was the chief caretaker and his name was reassuring. Anthony relaxed and stood away from the door. 'I'm sorry if I startled you. I heard someone creeping about and wondered who on earth it was.'

'Not at all, sir,' he said, obsequiously, picking up the brush and pan. 'It's all done now. Terribly sorry, sir.'

He left and Anthony flung himself back into a chair. Damnit, *had* his papers been moved? He looked at them again. Yes, they had. Anything else? He went back into the bedroom.

The window was open at the bottom as well as the top. He hadn't left it like that. The fire escape ran underneath and someone could enter that way. He pulled out the top drawer of his bedside cabinet. He knew there was something missing. He looked at the drawer for a few moments, trying to place what it was, but the memory stayed frustratingly elusive.

He pulled down the window, locked the door, and went to hunt up the secretary, Richard Walbreck. Walbreck left Anthony in his office and was back in twenty minutes.

'No one's been in your room this afternoon, Brooke. I've had a word with Baxter and it was cleaned this morning. What did you say the chap looked like?'

Anthony scratched the side of his chin. 'A bit nondescript, really, a weedy sort of bloke in his late twenties, I'd say. He was about average height, I suppose, with sandy hair, a small moustache and a little chip of a scar on the left hand side of his chin.'

'That isn't one of the servants,' said Walbreck with a puzzled frown. 'Dash it all, Brooke, I don't like the sound of this. I certainly don't like the fact he was wearing the club uniform and knew enough to use Baxter's name. Was anything taken?'

Anthony clicked his tongue in dissatisfaction. 'Nothing valuable, that's for sure. I've got my money and various bits and pieces on me and there's damn all else to take.'

'I'll warn the porters there's a petty thief about,' said Walbreck. 'It sounds as if he could be a former servant, looking for easy pickings.' He shrugged. 'All I can do is apologize.'

Anthony went back upstairs but he didn't go to his room. Instead he turned into the bathroom on the corridor. The window was open and, stacked neatly in a corner, were the duster, pan, brush and apron. He nodded in understanding. Those were the man's props. He looked out of the window. It was an easy climb to the fire escape beneath. It wouldn't have taken much for the man to have climbed in and out that way, find the caretaker's cupboard and rig himself out as a servant.

Sir Charles Talbot, when Anthony told him about it an hour later, was worried. 'What did you say he looked like?'

Anthony shrugged. 'He wasn't a man you'd look at twice. He was a weaselly, insignificant little chap.'

'Weaselly,' repeated Sir Charles, drumming a tattoo on the desk. He pushed a notepad towards Anthony. 'Write down as good a description as you can and I'll get it checked.' He chewed his lip anxiously. 'It's that blasted article that's done it. I'm sorry, Brooke. I had to get you into Starhanger and this seemed the most obvious way. Damn it! He's bright enough to have found out the caretaker's name.'

'That's what made me think he was genuine,' admitted Anthony. 'I'm at fault. I should have hauled him down to Walbreck there and then. That would have settled his hash.'

'Yes, it's a pity you didn't.' Sir Charles sighed uneasily. 'I had no idea this would happen. I should have realized the risk.'

'No one can really know the article's about me,' said Anthony. 'They might guess but they can't be certain.'

'They might be able to guess enough to want to be certain. Did you have anything in your room relating to your time in Germany?'

'No, I . . .' Anthony stopped. He suddenly realized what was missing. When he'd gone to the club after arriving in London, he had emptied his pockets into his bedside drawer before going for a bath. There wasn't much, but there were a few Danish kroner in notes and some öre coins, amounting to a few shillings in English money.

He hadn't considered the Danish money of any importance. After all, Denmark wasn't an enemy country. There weren't any kroner or öre in the drawer now.

He felt chilled. The fact that the worthless kroner had been taken spoke for itself. That, together with that wretched article, spelt out he'd been in Germany and escaped through Denmark. So much for anonymity.

Sir Charles listened gravely. 'I can only apologize, Brooke,' he said, digging bits out of his blotting pad with the nib of his pen. 'I hope to God I haven't put you in danger.'

Anthony hoped so too, but the fact was that the enemy knew exactly who he was and where he was. He didn't like it.

SIX

Sir Charles stood up and, with his hands clasped behind his
back, walked to the window, gazing unseeingly at the traffic
on Cockspur Street. He turned, looking at Anthony wryly.
'I've put you in danger. If you want to join the Medical Corps, I
won't stand in your way.'

Anthony jerked his head up sharply. 'What about Frankie?'

'Damn Frankie,' muttered Sir Charles. 'The Germans know who
you are.'

Looking at Sir Charles's crestfallen face, Anthony felt torn. He
wanted to join the Medical Corps but he had a huge reluctance to
leave a job undone. He seemed to hear once again the desperation
in Terry Cavanaugh's voice as he died. *Gentleman. He must be a
gentleman.*

There was a gentleman in England and Cavanaugh thought he
was at Starhanger. Tara O'Bryan was at Starhanger . . .

'No, Talbot,' he said firmly.

Sir Charles's eyes widened. 'No?'

'No, damnit. I said I'd find Frankie and I will. The Germans must
think I'm a complete dud. I wouldn't think much of an enemy agent
who boasted in the newspapers and was fooled by that cringing
little weasel who searched my room. Good. I won't be caught
napping a second time, by the Weasel or anyone else. They think
they've got away with it. Let them. Don't forget, I can recognize
at least one German agent. That might prove very valuable.'

'It might,' conceded Sir Charles. He cocked his head to one side,
raising his eyebrows. 'Are you sure?'

'Certain,' said Anthony firmly. 'After all, what have we lost? We
think our gentleman might be Sherston and we're fairly sure he's
associated with Starhanger. Sherston is the one person in the one
house in England where I can't pretend to be anyone but myself.'

'That's true,' agreed Sir Charles. 'Well, I'm not going to argue.
You're a sight too valuable for that.'

'Besides, I want to go to Starhanger.' Anthony leaned forward. 'You were looking for a plan, weren't you? Some information so choice the Germans simply won't be able to resist it. I've got an idea.'

Sir Charles listened as Anthony ran through his scheme. 'That's exactly the sort of thing I wanted,' he said enthusiastically when Anthony had finished. 'Would you mind if I worked on the details?'

'Feel free.'

Sir Charles clicked his tongue. 'Thanks to that article, you can't take the principal part. If they use the Weasel again, he'll know you're a fake. Never mind. I'll get somebody else. Leave it with me, Brooke.'

The following morning the ineffable Farlow called on Anthony with a note signed 'Yr affectionate Aunt, Emily'.

Anthony's Uncle Albert, it appeared, was as well as could be expected. Aunt Emily enquired after his health, but Aunt Emily's heart wasn't with her nephew but in her garden. She mentioned her three plum trees were in blossom but her budding roses were afflicted with greenfly. She'd sprayed them four times with soap solution and was going to try two applications of a nicotine spray before seeking advice from Mr Thornbury – Anthony remembered Mr Thornbury who'd been such a help to Mrs Rycroft – who had done so well with his roses at the Chelsea flower show.

Anthony had an Aunt Constance and an Aunt Cicely but no Aunt Emily, or, come to that, no Uncle Albert either. These relatives were convenient fictions. Anthony thought they appealed to Sir Charles's sense of humour.

The innocent-sounding message, when read properly, told him to ask for a Mr Rycroft at 42, Thornbury Road, Chelsea at three o'clock that afternoon. That Sir Charles had written in code, even when the note was delivered by his own messenger, told him how much the Weasel had rattled him.

'Tell Mr Monks I'll meet him in Aunt Emily's garden,' Anthony said to the waiting Farlow.

42, Thornbury Road was a neat Georgian house, a few streets away from the Embankment. As the chimes of the clock from the Old Church sounded the hour, Anthony was shown into the sitting room where Sir Charles was waiting, accompanied by two men.

Sir Charles introduced the first man as John Rycroft, the owner of the house, and the second as Michael Greenwood. Greenwood, an open-faced, bright-looking lad with a shock of ginger hair, wore the uniform of the Intelligence Corps. 'Greenwood's our stalking horse, Colonel, if I can put it like that.'

'It sounds like a very easy assignment,' said Greenwood cheerfully.

'I hope so,' said Anthony, accepting the chair Rycroft offered. 'Incidentally,' he added, 'I've been followed. It wasn't the Weasel but there was a man on the tube. I managed to lose him.'

'Was he carrying a bag of workman's tools?' queried Sir Charles, then continued in response to Anthony's nod. 'He's one of ours. He was watching for anyone interested in you. Incidentally, I want you to make sure you're seen with Greenwood this evening. Dinner at the Savoy should do it.'

'That's fine with me,' said Greenwood so enthusiastically Anthony had to hide a smile. Dinners at the Savoy were obviously not an everyday occurrence to this particular young officer.

'Now,' said Sir Charles, 'to business.'

He unlocked an attaché case and drew out a small wash-leather bag. He opened the bag and spilled lumps of soapy-coloured pebbles of various sizes onto the table. 'These, gentlemen,' he said, 'are uncut diamonds.'

Anthony's eyebrows shot up. Michael Greenwood gave a low whistle of surprise.

Sir Charles smiled. 'I'm glad you like them. There's half for you, Brooke, and half for Mr Greenwood.'

Anthony picked up a handful of stones, rubbing them between his fingers. 'This is very generous of you,' he said with a smile. 'I didn't expect you to take my grumbles about pay to heart quite so radically.'

'Unfortunately they're just on loan. I'd be obliged if you didn't lose them. His Majesty's Government has promised to make good any loss but, between ourselves, His Majesty's Government would rather not. Our plan is to catch an enemy agent by giving them some irresistible information. Colonel Brooke will pass on this information to a select few and if it's acted on, we'll know that our agent is one of the people he's told.'

He looked at Greenwood. 'Mr Greenwood, your part is to play the role of a prospector, a miner, who's just arrived in London.'

'I see,' said Greenwood doubtfully. 'Do I have to dress up? I don't fancy going round London with a pickaxe or what-have-you.'

Rycroft laughed. He was a stocky man with the faintly yellow complexion of someone who'd spent a lot of time in strong sun. 'I'm a prospector, young man, and I don't have to carry a spade to let people know I'm good at digging. All you have to do is stay in a hotel and act the part.'

Greenwood looked moderately reassured. 'I see,' he said once more.

'Don't worry,' said Rycroft. 'You'll be fine. If, by any chance you do run into anyone who knows their onions, say that you're onto something but you don't want to talk about it. I'll teach you some of the jargon and there's a couple of books you can read to get into the spirit of the thing. Now then, to details.'

Rycroft took a folded map from a case on the bookshelf and opened it out on the table. It was a large-scale map of the African Central Highlands, showing the border between British East Africa, Kenya and German East. 'Your story, Mr Greenwood,' he said, lighting a thin black cigar, 'is that you've found a diamantiferous area.'

'I've found a what?'

Anthony was glad Greenwood asked. He wanted to know as well.

'A diamantiferous area,' said Rycroft patiently, 'is an area which produces diamonds.'

'That's a diamond pipe, isn't it?' put in Greenwood intelligently. 'Blue clay and all that.'

Rycroft shook his head. 'You're thinking about Kimberly.'

'Am I?'

Anthony felt himself warming to the young man. Greenwood's knowledge of diamonds was obviously about as profound as his own and he didn't mind asking obvious questions.

Rycroft smiled. 'I think you found your diamonds in a river, Mr Greenwood. River gravels and sandstones can be very productive. That's where the majority of diamond finds are made in India and Brazil and in some parts of Africa, too. As I said, I'll give you the technical knowledge you need. Now the region I suggest for your find is here –' he tapped the map with a stubby forefinger – 'in the waters coming down from Mount Erok. That's in Ukambaland, just over the border from German East.'

Anthony nodded in satisfaction. When he'd sketched out his ideas to Sir Charles, what he had in mind was something hugely valuable, like a gold mine, but diamonds, which a lone prospector could apparently find tumbling about in a river seemed to fit the bill better.

Sir Charles nodded. 'Mount Erok it is.' He looked at Greenwood. 'The idea is that if the Germans hear you're in an unguarded hotel bedroom with maps of a valuable diamond find, especially one so close to the borders of German East, they're more or less bound to try and steal them. Your cache of diamonds will add a bit of substance to the maps. I can't see them failing to take the bait. Like the rest of us, they're desperate for diamonds.'

Anthony was surprised by the word *desperate*. He wouldn't say no to a few diamonds himself but he'd never been desperate for them. Greenwood was about to speak but thought better of it, so Anthony was forced to display his ignorance. 'Why? Does the Kaiser want a new necklace or something?'

Sir Charles swapped a long-suffering look with Rycroft. 'It's industry, man. The Germans don't want diamonds for jewellery, they need them for industry.'

Now Anthony was really puzzled. 'Industry?' Admittedly, what he knew about diamonds could have been comfortably written on a stamp, but he associated them with expensively dressed women, not smoky factories.

'Industry. Drilling, engraving, making scales and meters, turning metal and so on, to say nothing of wire making.'

'We're using a fair bit of wire in France,' put in Greenwood.

'As you say.' Sir Charles interlocked his fingers and braced his hands in a satisfied way. 'Yes, that all hangs together. Mr Greenwood, I've arranged a false identity for you. Mr Rycroft has kindly offered to take you on as his nephew, so I want you to rid yourself of your uniform and reappear as Martin Rycroft. Once that's taken care of, you need to book into a hotel. The St George's in Cheshire Place will suit our purposes very well.'

'Right-ho, sir.'

'As well as the maps, you'll have various documents to support your story of a find, but the principal prop is your cache of diamonds.' He rose to his feet. 'I think that's all I need to say at this stage. Thank you very much for your help, Mr Rycroft. Brooke and I will leave you in peace to give a few pointers to Mr Greenwood.'

That evening Anthony dined with Michael Greenwood who, enthusiastically throwing himself into the part of Martin Rycroft, seemed to have picked up an extraordinary amount of miner's slang in his session with 'Uncle John'.

The following afternoon he departed with Sir Charles and his valet, Sedgley, for Starhanger.

The train, as was commonplace in the war, was delayed, re-routed and shunted into sidings on what seemed to Anthony to be nothing more than a whim. They had the compartment to themselves, Sir Charles's valet travelling in another part of the train.

Sir Charles hoped to get the ball rolling that evening. Bertram Farlow and another assistant, Peter Warren, were in a room in the St George's, across the corridor from Greenwood, with instructions that one of them should be on watch all the time. Greenwood, for his part, was to leave his room locked but empty for reasonable periods of time.

Farlow and Warren had instructions not to interfere. What Sir Charles wanted wasn't some wretched agent of the Weasel variety but confirmation that the gentleman was at Starhanger. Naturally enough, Farlow and Warren were ignorant of what lay behind their assignment; all they had to do was watch.

As they dawdled through Kent, the conversation lapsed. Sir Charles buried himself in the *Morning Post* and Anthony, an unread newspaper on his knee, sat in the corner of the carriage, sightlessly looking at the rain-sheened patchwork of fleeting woods and fields, savouring his thoughts. Every rumble, every bump, brought him closer to Tara O'Bryan, the woman in blue.

It was crazy, he thought. He was a doctor. He knew that hearts didn't really stop – not without grave consequences, at any rate – but in those seconds outside Swan and Edgars, with those wretched white feather women clutching at his coat, he could have sworn his had.

Why on earth the sight of her face should have had such an affect, he'd didn't know. She wasn't the first pretty girl he'd ever seen or the first he'd ever been attracted to. Pretty? That was the wrong word. She was beautiful, the sort of beauty that took your breath away, like dawn behind the mountains or a silver path of moonlight over a shifting sea. In those few seconds his life had changed beyond all calculation. What the future held he didn't know. For the moment he was content it held her.

They were met at the tiny station of Swayling Halt by Sherston's head groom, Kindred, driving a pony and trap. Their luggage was loaded onto the back. The rain had stopped, the clouds cleared away and they clip-clopped through the lengthening evening shadows through the village towards Starhanger.

As the trap turned into the drive, the bulk of Starhanger appeared in the distance. It was an ancient black-and-white timber framed house with what Anthony guessed was the original great hall, flanked by two sympathetically constructed wings, complete with tall Tudor chimneys and leaded windows, sparkling gold in the western sun.

'I hope the plumbing's up to scratch,' muttered Sir Charles softly. 'I've suffered before in these historic gems.'

The door was opened to them by a butler whose name, Anthony later learned, was Vyse. There was, it seemed, a dinner party that evening, and the guests should be arriving soon. Mr Sherston and the rest of the household were, said Vyse, with an air of deep regret, dressing for dinner. Their late arrival was unavoidable, with the trains in their current parlous state, but if the gentlemen would care to be shown to their rooms . . .?

Anthony washed, shaved and scrambled into his dress uniform at breakneck speed, crammed the diamonds into his pocket and made it, together with Sir Charles, down to the hall before the dinner gong rang.

He squared his shoulders as he walked into the crowded room, eagerly scanning the faces. With a twist of disappointment, he saw the woman in blue wasn't among them.

Sherston looked up with a welcoming smile as they walked in. 'There you are!' He laid a friendly arm on Anthony's elbow. 'Let me introduce you to everyone. It's quite a crowd,' he added in an undertone, 'but only you and Sir Charles are staying for the weekend.'

Anthony, with Sir Charles by his side, was introduced to at least five or six local worthies and their better halves.

Anthony was struck how well Sherston fitted into this milieu. Admittedly, the man was among his own guests in his own house, but county society was notoriously stiff-necked and reluctant to accept incomers. Yet Sherston, with his shrewd eyes and Irish brogue, was obviously accepted and liked by people as diverse as the fiercely moustached retired General Harker, Sir Gilbert Ward and the benignly smiling Mrs Morpeth, the doctor's wife. 'And this,' said Sherston, completing the introductions, 'is my sister, Mrs O'Bryan.'

Anthony looked at her with sharpened interest. So this was Tara O'Bryan's mother. There wasn't much family resemblance. She was a striking-looking woman with piercing green eyes and dark hair streaked with iron grey. For some reason she radiated disapproval.

She eyed him up warily before extending her hand. 'So you're the Colonel Brooke Patrick's been so excited about.' She, it was perfectly obvious, didn't share her brother's enthusiasm.

There wasn't really any answer to that, so Anthony compromised with a conventional mutter of, 'How d'you do.'

Sherston coughed awkwardly, aware of his sister's antagonism. His face lightened as a young lady came down the stairs. 'Ah,' he said, with scarcely concealed relief. 'This is my niece, Tara. Tara, my dear, come and meet Colonel Brooke.'

Anthony had eagerly anticipated this moment for days. The woman in blue! . . . Only she *wasn't* the woman in blue but a complete stranger.

She held out her hand and Anthony took it mechanically.

'Uncle Patrick's told me such a lot about you,' she said with a friendly smile.

Tara O'Bryan? This *couldn't* be Tara O'Bryan. She was good looking enough, he supposed, with dark hair and green eyes, but she wasn't Tara. She *couldn't* be Tara. Only she was.

His dismay must have shown. Anthony, his world turned upside down, managed to say something – he wasn't sure what – and Tara, puzzled by his response, put her hand on her uncle's arm. 'I'm not the last to arrive, am I, Uncle Patrick?'

'No, my dear,' he said affectionately. 'Josette hasn't come down yet.'

'Josette?' asked Anthony, numbly.

'My wife, Colonel,' replied Sherston briskly. There was the rustle of a dress on the stairs. 'Here she is now.'

And there, her hand lightly poised on the banister, as she looked across the hall, was the fair-haired woman in blue. She still wore blue, a velvet gown, with sapphires and diamonds at her neck and a clasp of sapphires and diamonds in her hair. Anthony felt as if his stomach had gone down in a lift.

'This is my wife, Josette,' said Sherston, as if to hammer the last nail into his hopes.

My wife! What the devil was Sherston, the middle-aged Sherston, doing with such a wife? Sherston was old and she was adorably young. Far too young to be married to *him*.

She held her hand out to him, smiling in welcome, a smile that dimpled her cheeks. 'You must be Colonel Brooke. We expected you and Sir Charles earlier but these trains are dreadful, aren't they?'

Anthony took her hand, feeling as if every eye in the room was fixed on him. His whole arm was tingling at her touch. He'd been so anxious to hear her speak that the sense of what she said took him a moment to grasp. He managed a reply and inwardly cursed himself, knowing how awkward he must seem.

He looked away and saw Tara O'Bryan's watchful, intelligent eyes fixed on him. She was someone to be reckoned with. As surely as if he'd shouted it out loud, he knew she'd guessed his secret. He felt a spot of colour flame his cheeks and then, thank God, the gong in the hall sounded and they went into dinner.

Talk about saved by the bell, thought Anthony ruefully as he took his place, and tried very hard to interest himself in his companions.

He was sitting between a Mrs Moulton and a Mrs Farraday. The meal dragged on interminably. Anthony wanted to be alone, to try and sort his thoughts into some sort of order, and all the time Josette was there, real, so real, and yet as utterly unobtainable as a saint in a stained-glass window.

She was married.

So what? demanded a voice at the back of his mind. The answer to that was that he didn't want an affair. He didn't have affairs. They were messy and awkward and upset his ideas of right and wrong.

A wild hope bit at the edges of his mind. If *Sherston* was the spy, Sherston was guilty of High Treason. That meant the death penalty. He writhed away from the thought. That was far too like murder for comfort. Echoes of the Biblical story of David and Bathsheba occurred to him. David wanted Bathsheba. She was married to Uriah, so David had Uriah killed. David wasn't the hero of that story.

But if Sherston was their man? Anthony tried to choke down the hope, but hope, even a forlorn hope, was like bindweed, hard to root up and nearly impossible to kill. *He's possible. Well, so he is.* But granted all that – and it was a lot to grant – Josette was rich and he wasn't. At a guess, a single stone from Josette's necklace amounted to a year of his income.

Mrs Moulton, a stout, salt-of-the-earth type, who must have enjoyed a challenge, grilled him on the topic of diet and health in the army, amongst other conversational gambits. Although he found Mrs Moulton trying, he was grateful not to be sitting next to Tara. Those perceptive eyes had found out far too much about him than he was comfortable with. And all the time, Mrs Moulton talked to him about bully beef and plum jam for the army because he was a doctor and a decent man and ought to take a decent interest in ordinary, decent conversations.

The main course, which he ate mechanically, was mutton and artichokes. As he watched, Josette laughed, sat forward in her chair and ate a forkful of mutton. It seemed incredible that she should move, breath and eat, especially something as mundane as mutton and artichokes.

All he really wanted to do was look at Josette. At the same time he had enough wit to see that he couldn't simply gaze at her like an urchin looking into a baker's shop window and, predictably, overdid things the other way.

He felt ridiculously self-conscious and found it a thankless struggle to take any sensible part in the conversation. Even the redoubtable Mrs Moulton tired at last and addressed her remarks on the importance of pigswill to her other neighbour, Elstead, Sherston's secretary, a middle-aged man of comfortable proportions, who made all the right remarks in the right places.

The ladies departed at last, the port was brought out and the room filled up with the fug of cigar smoke.

'What the devil's the matter?' asked Sir Charles in an undertone when they were at the sideboard together.

So much for his powers of concealment, thought Anthony ruefully. 'Nothing,' he said shortly. 'Mutton doesn't agree with me.' He didn't know why strong emotion should look like indigestion but it seemed to satisfy Sir Charles.

How on earth he got through the next half-hour or so he didn't know. He seemed to be existing on four levels. On the surface he chatted politely. He could hear himself doing it. Next, he wondered what he was going to say to Tara O'Bryan. At the same time he passionately wanted to get out into the fresh air and think but, most of all, he had the aching desire to see Josette again. Eventually, thank goodness, Sherston decided it was time to go into the drawing room. Anthony got to his feet with relief but Sir Charles called him back with an almost imperceptible flick of his eyes.

'Have you got the diamonds?' he asked softly.

Anthony nodded.

'Good,' said Sir Charles. 'Watch for your cue and follow my lead. See what you can get out of Miss O'Bryan about Cavanaugh.'

They followed Sherston across the hall and into the drawing room.

Josette was there. He watched hungrily as she flicked a wisp of fair hair over her perfect ear-lobe. The sight of her didn't make him happy; she seemed so utterly out of reach.

Vyse, the butler, brought in coffee and Josette busied herself with pouring it out. Standing in front of the hearth, Sherston, Sir Charles, General Harker, Dr Morpeth and the other men were discussing Gallipoli. Mrs Moulton was holding forth on the problems besetting the village sewing circle, a discussion in which Josette showed a surprising degree of technical knowledge about which fabric was suitable for what purpose and Veronica O'Bryan was buried behind a magazine.

Tara handed Anthony a cup of coffee. Mindful of his instructions, Anthony followed her to the sofa and sat down beside her. He was casting around for a way to bring up Cavanaugh's name when she solved the problem for him.

'Colonel,' she said tentatively, 'Uncle Patrick said you knew Terry Cavanaugh.' He nodded. She ran her finger round the top of her coffee cup, obviously bracing herself. 'How did he die?'

Anthony was prepared for this. Out of the corner of his eye he could see that although Veronica O'Bryan was still apparently deep in her magazine, her body had stiffened in attention. Although Tara was unaware of it, Veronica O'Bryan was listening keenly. 'It was in Germany,' he said, seeing how Mrs O'Bryan's fingers tightened on the magazine.

Tara gave a little cry of surprise. 'Germany? What was he doing there?'

'He was reporting for an American paper, I think,' said Anthony casually. This was the story he and Sir Charles had worked out. 'He injured his foot in an accident, I believe, and died of blood poisoning. At least, that's what I heard.' The fingers on the magazine relaxed.

Tara's face twisted in compassion. 'Poor Terry,' she murmured. 'I liked him, although . . .' She broke off.

Anthony's mind worked quickly. Sherston had told them that Cavanaugh was related to his sister's family, that it was his sister who had made his acquaintance, but it wasn't Veronica O'Bryan who wanted to know about Cavanaugh, it was Tara.

Cavanaugh had, according to Sherston *presumed on the relationship*. Did that mean an affair with Tara? Sherston obviously cared about Tara deeply and a fifty-odd-year-old ex-ranch-hand with no fixed income or position wouldn't be anyone's ideal choice for a young girl from a wealthy family.

'How did you meet him?' asked Anthony gently.

'He came to stay here for a few days. My mother met him at a charity function in London and it turned out he was a relation of my father's, so naturally he was invited to stay. My father's been dead for years, and it was nice to meet someone from his side of the family.'

Anthony eye's widened. A charity? This sounded promising. 'Which one?' he asked with what he hoped sounded like nothing but polite interest. Tara O'Bryan looked surprised. 'I did quite a bit of work with charities, one way and another, as a doctor before the war,' he explained. 'I wondered if it was one I'd been involved with.'

'I'm not sure. It was an Irish Friendly Society in Camden Town.' She glanced at her mother who was seemingly intent on her magazine. 'My mother does a lot of charity work with poor Irish families. My father was devoted to Irish causes and she's picked up the torch,' continued Tara. 'What on earth was the name? Something Hibernia, I think, but I can't be sure. It doesn't matter, anyway.'

Anthony made a little noise in his throat. Something Hibernia! Bloody *hell!* An Irish charity? *The* Irish charity, more like, a front for German-Irish links.

Veronica O'Bryan was suddenly very still. Tara, her attention fixed on Anthony, was unaware of her mother's tension but Veronica O'Bryan was as taut as a stretched bowstring.

Anthony deliberately relaxed his shoulders and sat back in an attitude of interested calm. 'No, it doesn't matter. I thought I might know it, that's all.' Out of the corner of his eye he could see the strain ebbing out of Veronica O'Bryan. 'Are you particularly interested in Irish affairs, Miss O'Bryan?'

'I think any intelligent person has to be concerned about Ireland, wouldn't you say? All the news is about the war, but the Irish problem hasn't gone away. There will be Home Rule for Ireland, but on what terms, I don't know. My mother's got very strong views on the subject.'

She glanced at Veronica O'Bryan, still, to all appearances, deaf to what they were saying. 'If my father had lived, he would've been in any Irish government. He died when I was very small, and I can't remember him, but my mother says he would have been a great man if he'd lived.'

Anthony, who had read a fair sample of the late Bernard O'Bryan's works the previous evening, couldn't agree. The man had been eaten up with hatred of the English and obsessed with honour, blood, sacrifice and death. Anthony had disliked it very much.

'He wrote poetry,' said Tara O'Bryan in a wary way. 'I don't know if you've ever read any?'

Anthony, torn between truth and tact, chose tact. 'I'm sorry, I don't read a lot of poetry.' It might have been his imagination, but Tara O'Bryan seemed relieved.

'Terry Cavanaugh was a great supporter of Home Rule, too,' said Anthony, steering the conversation back on track. 'I was surprised how well informed he was, considering he was American.'

Tara O'Bryan laughed. 'He might have been born in New York but he was Irish and proud of it. As I said, he was one of my father's relations.'

That wasn't a bad idea on Cavanaugh's part, thought Anthony. If Cavanaugh really was on to something, it would make an investigation a lot easier if he posed as a relation rather than a chance-met acquaintance.

'Anyway,' she added with a shrug, 'I liked Terry. He was different from anyone else I'd ever met. My mother thought the world of him at first.' She shrugged once more. 'Then it all went wrong.'

Anthony wanted to ask how but that sort of question wasn't permitted. However, if Veronica realized that Terry Cavanaugh was using her to gain an entrée to Starhanger, then it could have all gone wrong very quickly, even without an affair with Tara.

For the first time he felt a twist of distaste for Cavanaugh. Whatever he'd done and whatever the motives, Tara O'Bryan had been upset. It seemed wrong to use this girl with her bright, intelligent eyes and sensitive mouth as a mere counter in a game.

'I'm sorry he's dead,' said Tara. 'I hate to think of dying so far from home. I suppose his newspaper would have informed his family – if he had one, that is,' she added.

Anthony seized the opportunity. 'He never talked about any family to me. He mentioned friends occasionally. There was someone called Frankie, I believe.'

Mrs O'Bryan's fingers whitened on the magazine again. 'Colonel Brooke,' she said in a carrying voice. 'If you are going to talk about my husband's relatives, you might have the courtesy to include me. What's all this about Cavanaugh's friends?'

'I wondered if they'd heard he'd died,' replied Anthony politely.

Privately he was wondering if Frankie was a member of either the New York or London Hibernian charities. That would add up. Maybe Frankie had been a bit too free with his confidences to Cavanaugh and Veronica O'Bryan knew that. He was sure it was Frankie's name which had prompted Veronica O'Bryan to stick her oar in. 'I heard him mention a chap called Frankie. I wondered if Miss O'Bryan knew him.'

There was a glint of amused triumph in Mrs O'Bryan's eyes. 'I'm afraid we can't help you, Colonel. Terry didn't have many friends and I never heard of a man of that name. That's right, isn't it Tara?'

'If you say so, mother,' said Tara with a frown. 'I don't think he ever mentioned a Frankie.'

Anthony's voice was casual. 'I don't suppose it matters,' he said lightly as he could. Veronica O'Bryan knew something, and he was prepared to bet that one of the things she knew about was Frankie.

He got up and walked over to the coffee tray on the sideboard. He put his cup down and turned, knowing Sir Charles was watching, and gave him the very slightest of nods.

Sir Charles didn't respond but Anthony knew he'd understood. General Harker rumbled something about forcing the Narrows – they were still talking about Gallipoli – and Sir Charles, as if struck by a sudden thought, beckoned to Anthony to join them by the hearth.

'Here's a man who can bear me out, General. My point is that the war won't be won by mere military expertise, important though that is. It's a question of industry and supplies.'

This time it was Sir Charles who gave an almost imperceptible nod. It was Anthony's cue. 'Now, Colonel, who would you say had the greater amount of natural resources at their beck and call? Us or the Central Powers?'

'On the face of it, Germany,' said Anthony. 'However, as long as we can keep the shipping lanes open, we've got the resources of the whole Empire to call on, but we need to sharpen up. I'd like to see a great deal more sense of urgency in the government and powers-that-be. There are too many complacent types running the show.'

Sir Charles looked suitably shocked. 'Complacent, Colonel? Have you got anyone in particular in mind?'

'Not so much a particular someone but a particular something,' Anthony answered. He took the wash-leather bag from his pocket and, reaching for a saucer from the sideboard, poured the diamonds onto the saucer in his hand.

Tara O'Bryan walked forward and looked at the soapy-coloured stones with interest. 'What are they?'

'Diamonds.'

Tara gave a little cry of astonishment. 'Diamonds?'

'Diamonds?' echoed Josette Sherston. She and the other women in the room crowded round. 'Are you sure, Colonel?' she asked. She fingered her necklace absently. 'They don't look anything like my diamonds.'

'Yours have been cut and polished, my dear,' said Sherston. 'How much are they worth, Colonel? Have you any idea?'

'I'm not absolutely certain—' began Anthony when General Harker cleared his throat.

'I know a little about jewellery, Colonel. I knew a diamond-wallah in India.' He reached out his hand. 'May I?'

'Please do.'

The General picked the biggest stone and held it between his thumb and forefinger. Anthony saw his eyes narrow. 'They're diamonds all right. Good ones, too, I'd say. My word, Colonel, you could be holding an absolute fortune in your hand.'

'How did you get hold of them, Colonel?' It was Tara O'Bryan.

'I ran into a friend in London. I first came across him out in

Africa. He's a nice youngster by the name of Rycroft. His uncle's a big noise in the mining world, I understand, and this boy, Martin Rycroft, had a bit of luck.'

Anthony picked up the diamonds and ran them through his fingers. 'This is what I mean about resources. Rycroft's found a rich field, or whatever you call it, that's quite unknown. He found these in a river. It's a bit off the beaten track, apparently, up in the mountains on the borders of German East. According to him it could do with being properly explored. It'd be different in peacetime but he got the wind-up a bit, being so close to enemy territory. There was a Dutchman, a Boer, in his party who he suspected of being pro-German. Rycroft reckoned that if he stayed, he'd have an expedition from German East around his ears in fairly short order, so he played it down and came back to London. He hopes he's put the Boer off the scent but he's not sure.'

Sir Charles looked at Anthony with puzzled, innocent eyes. 'This is all very interesting, Colonel, but you complained about complacency. You'll excuse me if I say I can't see the connection between that and your diamonds.'

Anthony laughed dismissively. 'It's because of complacency that Rycroft lent me some of his haul. When he got back to London he went straight to the Foreign Office to report his find. He's been shunted from pillar to post. That's why he roped me in. He's got it into his head that I know all sorts of people and might be able to galvanize someone into taking action.'

Tara looked at the saucer with her head on one side. 'Why should the Foreign Office be interested in diamonds?'

'Don't be a fool, Tara,' snapped her mother. 'You might think of them as pretty stones but to the government they mean guns. That's right, isn't it, Colonel?' she added defiantly.

'Well, not absolutely, no,' said Anthony. 'I mean, I'm sure you're right, Mrs O'Bryan, but there's more to it than that. You see, industry needs diamonds, even diamonds which would be no good as jewels.'

Mrs O'Bryan's eyes narrowed. 'How?'

'They're used extensively in manufacturing,' said Sherston. 'They're the hardest mineral we know.'

Mrs O'Bryan looked at the soapy-coloured heap in the saucer with more respect. 'That's interesting,' she said quietly. 'Very interesting.'

'Anyway,' said Anthony, 'you see what I mean about complacency. As my friend Rycroft sees it, there's thousands of pounds worth of diamonds lying around, and the Germans could invade across the border at any time. We probably wouldn't even know they were there. As I said, it's pretty wild country. Poor Rycroft's driving himself nuts trying to get some proper action out of the stuffed shirts that run these things. As far as I can make out, he's kicking his heels while a lot of mandarins decide which department he should apply to.'

Sir Charles, in his role as mandarin, tutted and shook his head gravely. 'I'm afraid that story rings only too true, Colonel. Still, even African diamond kings have to follow the proper procedures.'

Anthony gave what he hoped was an ironic laugh. 'Diamond king! He *will* be, if there's any justice in the world. After all, he found the blessed things. It's ridiculous to think he's stuck in a third-rate hotel in Cheshire Place while he knows where enough diamonds are to buy the Ritz *and* take an option on the Savoy while he's about it.'

Sir Charles looked affronted. He did it very well. 'I appreciate your feelings on the matter, Colonel, but Whitehall has its own way of doing things and the proper procedures need to be followed. You can hardly expect His Majesty's Government to rush an expedition into the wilds of Africa on some boy's say-so.'

'He might be young but he's knocked about a bit and his family name should command some respect. Besides that, he's got some impressive paperwork. I've seen it. Maps, geology, the lot, to say nothing of a couple of handfuls of diamonds.'

'I could run a piece on him in the *Examiner*,' said Sherston. 'Rycroft, you say he's called? *How Fortune Favoured The Brave.* That would make a nice headline. There's a few angles I could use with a story like this. That would shake things up.'

'I'm afraid that would never do,' said Sir Charles quickly. Sherston looked rebellious. 'I'm sorry, Sherston, but if the facts are as the colonel has related, then absolute secrecy and discretion must be our watchwords.'

He glanced round the group surrounding the table. 'I must ask you all to keep this to yourselves. I imagine that the enemy would love to get hold of the location of an untapped diamond field. Now you've brought the matter to my attention, Colonel, I will try to expedite this young man's cause in the proper quarters. After all, even as we speak, the Germans may be advancing and the opportunity could be lost.'

Josette came forward and reached out her hand for the saucer. 'May I?'

Anthony gave it to her and she tipped the diamonds into the palm of her hand. 'They look so dull at the moment. *A rough diamond.* I've said that lots of times but I've never thought about what it meant.'

She picked up the largest with a wondering smile and held it up to the light. 'I wonder what this will be like when it's cut and polished?'

Her smile became wistful. 'I love jewels,' she said thoughtfully. 'They're beautiful. There aren't enough things which exist simply because they're beautiful.' She looked at Anthony, a tiny smile curving the corner of her mouth. 'To see them like this is exciting.'

She put the stones back into the saucer and handed it back. With a jolt, Anthony felt her hand touch his.

Perhaps it was his imagination, but her fingers seem to linger on his outstretched palm for a moment longer than was strictly necessary.

'They're like people, you know? Some have all the glitter on the outside and some need drawing out and polishing to show what's hidden.'

Anthony glanced away. It could be nothing more than imagination, but he thought she was referring to him. That little weed of hope started to grow.

SEVEN

Anthony put down his whisky and soda and walked quietly to the door. He had called into Sir Charles's room for a nightcap and, by mutual consent, the two men had talked trivialities until they judged the rest of the household was safely in bed.

He opened the door a couple of inches, listening intently. In the distance he could hear the sonorous tick-tock of the grandfather clock below them in the hall, but it was the only sound in the quiet house.

'All clear,' he said in a low voice, settling back in his chair. 'By the way, there's a very useful creaking floorboard outside your room.'

'I noticed that, too,' said Sir Charles. 'I think the diamond scheme went well. You dangled all the right clues very nicely. If Sherston really is our man, he surely can't fail to follow up your lead to the third-rate hotel in Cheshire Place, as you very happily put it. If that comes off we're really out of the slips and no mistake.'

'Yes, it went well,' said Anthony. 'There's something else I found out tonight. It's about the Sons of Hibernia.'

Sir Charles sat up in his chair. 'What is it?'

Anthony related the conversation in the drawing-room as concisely as he could. 'There's no doubt in my mind,' he finished, 'that Veronica O'Bryan knows a sight more than she should do. I think Tara O'Bryan's in the clear, but if Mrs O'Bryan is involved with the Sons of Hibernia, then we're really on to something.'

'It sounds like it,' agreed Sir Charles. 'Veronica O'Bryan, eh? She's someone we've never contemplated. Where does this leave Sherston? Do you think they're in it together?'

Anthony rested his elbow on the arm of his chair, seeing how the light danced and reflected on the glass in his hand. He was trying very hard to be fair.

'Sherston didn't show any interest in my conversation with Tara O'Bryan,' he said eventually. 'He doesn't seem to fit. I know Cavanaugh thought we were looking for a man. He said we've got to stop *him*. However, I wonder if our man isn't a man but a woman.'

'Veronica O'Bryan?' asked Sir Charles.

'Veronica O'Bryan,' repeated Anthony. 'Thanks to Sherston's social connections, she's in a position to pick up some very valuable gossip. Mrs O'Bryan might disapprove of Terry Cavanaugh for some family reason, such as Cavanaugh falling for Tara – Tara certainly liked Cavanaugh and might have had her head turned, despite him being so much older – or it could be more sinister. I'm sure Veronica O'Bryan knows who Frankie is. What's more, when I said I was looking for a man called Frankie, she seemed very self-satisfied, as if she was congratulating herself I was on the wrong lines. It might be that Frankie's a woman.'

'A woman?' Sir Charles sucked his cheeks in. 'There's no reason why Frankie shouldn't be a woman, of course. Anything else?'

'Only that Frankie may be associated with either the New York or London Hibernian charities. That's a guess, but it might be right.'

Sir Charles sat back and drummed his fingers on the smooth leather of the chair-arm. 'Take it that what you've said is correct. How did it all work?'

Anthony lit a cigarette and smoked it reflectively. 'What I think happened is something like this. Terry Cavanaugh got involved with the Sons of Hibernia, the London equivalent of the New York Hibernian Relief Fund. He starts to uncover the Sons' links between Ireland and Germany. At a meeting of the Sons he came across Veronica O'Bryan and her daughter, and gets invited here. Tara O'Bryan said Cavanaugh was a distant relation of her father's. I'm assuming that's a ruse on Cavanaugh's part, as otherwise it's too convenient for words. What that means, of course, is that he suspected Veronica O'Bryan and wanted to get closer to her.'

'Or to Sherston,' put in Sir Charles. 'He could have suspected Sherston.'

'So he could,' agreed Anthony. 'In any event, we know Cavanaugh fell from grace. He left Starhanger under a cloud and went to Germany. Mrs O'Bryan has his activities in New York investigated and, via Frankie, writes a letter to their friendly German pals, with disastrous results for Cavanaugh. For all I know, she is Frankie. She was certainly smug enough when I mentioned Frankie's name.' Anthony looked at Sir Charles. 'Can you pick any holes in that?'

'Why was there such a long delay?' asked Sir Charles. 'It was a good few months after Cavanaugh left Starhanger before he was killed in Germany.'

'Maybe it took that long for them to be sure. You said Cavanaugh used another name in New York. Veronica O'Bryan might have suspected Cavanaugh but didn't want to act until she was certain. If the Germans arrested an American who really was an innocent neutral, it'd be very awkward for them and their Irish partners.'

'Fair enough,' acknowledged Sir Charles. 'What about Sherston, though? He had a down on Cavanaugh, too.'

'Maybe he's in on it. He could be, you know. After all, his middle name is Francis and if he's Frankie, Veronica O'Bryan might well look smug at my description of him as a friend of Cavanaugh's.'

Sir Charles raised his eyebrows. 'If they're in it together, that might explain something. Sherston's surprisingly well-liked locally, when you consider the crowd here tonight are solid county types and he's an Irish newspaper proprietor of humble origins. Everyone likes Tara O'Bryan, but no one can stand her mother. Mrs O'Bryan's an expert card player, which should make her popular, what with bridge parties and whist drives and so on, but none of the ladies like playing with her. She's got a sarcastic tongue, dislikes her neighbours and, in addition, has a real down on Mrs Sherston. Mr Moulton, quoting his better half, reckoned that Mrs O'Bryan thoroughly enjoyed running the roost and had her nose put out of joint good and proper when Sherston turned up with his glamorous new wife. General Harker agreed.'

This, felt Anthony, was getting onto dangerous ground. 'Glamorous?' he queried.

'Good Lord, man, didn't you notice? She's outstanding. However, apparently Mrs Sherston is content to give Mrs O'Bryan her own way. The General said – quoting his wife – that Mrs Sherston is known for her generosity and kindness. Mrs Harker's opinion is that Mrs Sherston is verging on sainthood for putting up with Veronica O'Bryan. The general opinion is that Sherston should make Veronica O'Bryan an allowance and, for his wife's sake if not his own, issue his sister her marching orders. If they're in it together though, he'd want her close at hand.'

He frowned. 'I just don't know about Sherston. In light of what you've told me, Veronica O'Bryan has to be our chief suspect, but I'm not dismissing Sherston yet. I hope it's not him, though. I can't help liking the man.'

Anthony crushed out his cigarette. 'He seems agreeable enough, I grant you.' And that, he thought, with a dull ache twisting his stomach, was about as much enthusiasm as he could honestly manage.

After breakfast the next morning, Anthony was gathered in politely but firmly by Sherston to be interviewed in his study.

The study was a pleasant, book-lined room, with French windows leading onto the sun-filled garden with the waters of the lake sparkling through the trees. There was a collection of box files on the shelves, each marked with a name of a newspaper or magazine, a solid oak table with the cigarette box agreeably close at hand, some comfortable chairs and a desk which held a neat and crisply new stack of magazines and a serviceable-looking typewriter. Elstead, the secretary, sat waiting, ready to make a shorthand record of the interview.

Sherston, Anthony was surprised to find, was conducting affairs himself. 'There's very few things associated with the newspaper business I can't do, Colonel,' he said with assertive pride. 'Although I say it myself, I'm the best man for the job. You see, I know the entire range of the Sherston Press and I'll think of questions it wouldn't occur to anyone else to ask.'

Or which, thought Anthony, it might be useful for their gentleman to know, but, as the interview progressed, he became more and more convinced that Sherston wasn't their man.

If Anthony refused to answer a question, Sherston moved on, remarking that he didn't want to publish anything that would endanger British interests. He might have one eye on the censor and another on the Defence of the Realm Acts, but he didn't, as Anthony half expected, press him or try and get the information 'just between the two of us'.

However, there was his attitude to Cavanaugh to account for. So far, the idea that Cavanaugh had been smitten with Tara O'Bryan was nothing more than a theory. To try and draw him out, Anthony brought up the treatment of neutrals in Germany, using Cavanaugh as an illustration. That led onto an entirely fictitious story of Cavanaugh's death. To Anthony's disappointment, Sherston listened, frosty-faced but without comment.

It was odd, sitting in that quiet room, with sounds of early summer drifting through the open window, to cast his mind back to those desperate months in Germany. The events he was recalling seemed so far away it was as if he was describing another man's life.

After a thorough grilling, during which Anthony thought he had given Sherston enough material to write a three-volume treatise on Germany, laced with some of his more memorable exploits, his host was in an expansive mood. 'I'm very grateful to you, Colonel,' he said, rubbing his hands together. He turned to his secretary. 'Get those notes typed up, Elstead. The Colonel will want to read them through, I'm sure.'

Anthony wasn't sure he wanted to do anything of the sort. The whole point of a secret agent, he thought ruefully, was to remain secret. The preliminary article had been bad enough but the interview he had just given constituted a spectacular burning of his boats. Still, this was what Sir Charles wanted. 'What happens to the notes now, Sherston?' he asked. 'Are you going to publish them as they are?'

Sherston smiled at this innocent abroad. 'Oh no, my dear fellow. After you've looked the notes over, I'll give them to Lissett, the editor of the *Sentinel*. He's a very sound man. I propose to run a series of articles. We'll drum up some really good publicity and I'll be very much surprised if the *Sentinel* doesn't knock every other newspaper into a cocked hat.'

His air of eager anticipation increased. 'D'you remember the series of invasion stories we ran before the war, Elstead?' he asked, turning to his secretary. 'That was only fiction, of course,' he added to Anthony, 'but my word, it was a stunt and a half.'

'It certainly was, sir,' agreed Elstead with a reminiscent grin. 'We had all our street vendors dressed as German soldiers,' he explained, turning to Anthony, 'with the banner, "This Could Be True", emblazoned on every stand. We had to put out extra editions, it was so successful.'

'We'll go one better with this,' said Sherston happily. 'We'll run the story over a couple of weeks, then put all the articles together and print it as a separate magazine. We're thinking of transforming a few streets into a replica of a German town, based on the information you've given us. We won't have any problems with the authorities, as long as we make the entrance fee payable to a good charity. What d'you reckon, Colonel? The Red Cross should fit the bill, unless you've got a pet charity of your own.'

For a wild moment Anthony thought of saying the Sons of Hibernia, just to see how Sherston would react, but he quelled the notion. 'The Red Cross seems very suitable,' he agreed.

'Excellent!' said Sherston enthusiastically. 'We can dress it up, have soldiers lording over civilians and so on, show them what it's really like to live crushed under the Kaiser's heel. We can even stage a rooftop escape,' he added with a laugh. 'That'll make London sit up.'

Anthony winced. The chances of remaining anonymous after that were virtually nil. 'That'll take some time to arrange, won't it?' he asked hopefully.

'No time at all,' said Sherston, crushing Anthony's hopes as effectively as any heel of the Kaiser's. 'You'll be amazed at how quickly we can put it together. You, of course, will be our consultant on the project, Colonel.'

'I'll have to get permission,' said Anthony, clutching at this fragile straw.

'With any luck there won't be any trouble about that,' said Sherston heartily. 'As well as the *Sentinel* I intend to run pieces in some of our other papers and magazines. For instance, *Hearth and Home* will get a lot a mileage out of the comparison between what a typical German can expect for dinner, say, and an ordinary British working man.'

'What about the *Citizen*?' put in Elstead. 'Banks of the *Citizen* loves the scare stuff and a Hidden Hand Of Germany story. The Colonel's insights will give them a lot of material on how to spot a spy.'

'Well done, Elstead,' said Sherston. 'Note that down.' His enthusiasm increased. 'Why, even *Market Garden and Allotment Times* can run an article on German versus British food production.' Anthony winced once more and Sherston turned on him sharply. 'You mustn't despise any journal, Colonel, no matter how trivial the subject matter may seem.'

That hadn't been the reason why Anthony had recoiled but he didn't feel able to explain himself. At this rate, he thought ruefully, Sherston might as well start a paper called *Intelligence Agent News by Anthony Brooke, Esq.,* and have done with it. He didn't make the suggestion; Sherston might just do it.

'Let me show you the range of the Sherston Press, Colonel,' said Sherston, walking to the desk to where the newspapers and magazines were. 'I have all our papers delivered here, of course.'

He picked up the pile and handed it to Anthony. 'These are today's, together with the current issues of our weekly and monthly magazines. Why don't you look through them? You might be able to see an angle for your story that I've overlooked.'

This seemed monumentally unlikely, but Anthony was anxious to get away. 'Can I take them outside?' he asked, scenting a way of escape.

Sherston opened the French windows onto the terrace. 'By all means, my dear fellow. Be my guest. And may I say how very grateful

I am for your cooperation.' He beamed at Anthony happily. 'My word, this'll cause a sensation.'

Anthony, complete with his pile of unwanted reading matter, went into the garden. He made for the circular seat that encompassed the cedar tree. Here, in the middle of the lawn, under the rustling branches and sun-dappled shade, he was in full view of the house. He was hoping, he realized, to see Josette. His heart leapt as a girl came onto the terrace, but it was Tara O'Bryan. He hid his disappointment as she waved a friendly hand and came across the lawn to join him.

'It's nice to see someone,' she said cheerfully, sitting down beside him. 'The house is like a morgue. I don't know where everyone's got to.' She looked at the pile of magazines and grinned. 'You've seen Uncle Patrick, I take it.'

She picked up *Woodwork And Practical Carpentry*. It was illustrated with a picture of a brightly-smiling man in a khaki apron sawing a piece of wood big enough to be the keel of Nelson's *Victory*. 'I don't know what he looks so happy about,' she commented. 'He looks like he's got his work cut out, to me.'

She laughed. 'Uncle Patrick better not hear me ragging about his magazines. He's terribly proud of them. To be honest, I am too.' She looked at him with a mixture of pride and awkward modesty. She suddenly seemed touchingly young. 'I write, you know. I've always written. That's what I'd like to do, but properly, I mean. I really want to get involved with the war but my mother nearly had a fit when I suggested it.'

'Doesn't she approve of young ladies working?' asked Anthony guilelessly. 'There's plenty of ladies who do work, especially nowadays.'

Tara's face fell. 'It's not so much working, as working for the English that she objects to. She feels Ireland's wrongs very strongly, and, naturally, blames the English for them all. She . . .'

Tara hesitated. 'I know she's my mother, and you probably don't think I should criticize her, but she's a very black-and-white person, if you know what I mean. She takes everything personally. She thought the world of my father and he thought of Ireland and Ireland's past in very romantic, poetic terms, but it's not like that, is it? Real life's a lot more complicated than she ever allows. She was bitterly disappointed when Uncle Patrick nailed his colours to the mast and came out in favour of the war. I'll get involved somehow or other, but the war won't last forever, will it? And in the meantime, I can write.'

'Have you got an article in one of these?' asked Anthony, laying his hand on the stack of magazines. Tara nodded.

Her earnestness was so beguiling Anthony couldn't help teasing. 'It must help having an uncle who owns a string of papers.'

'It doesn't!' she said indignantly. 'Well, I suppose it might, a bit, but Uncle Patrick won't publish anything that isn't up to scratch.'

'Come on,' he said, enjoying her sparky defence. 'I bet your uncle ropes you all in to help out.'

'It's not like that, Colonel Brooke. Journalism is a proper business, you know. Josette used to be a writer but she hasn't written anything since she got married. She said it was far too much like hard work and she's right.'

'Does your mother write?'

Tara laughed scornfully. 'No. Not proper writing, anyway.' Her eyes became abstracted. 'It really isn't as simple as you think, to make something interesting. My mother enjoys cards, you know, and tried to write about it, but it was very wooden. She sets bridge problems, but she can't make the game itself sound enjoyable. I can do it, but I like people, you see.'

Anthony noticed the implied criticism of Veronica O'Bryan. Tara, it seemed, had few illusions about her mother's social expertise. Ordinarily, he'd attribute Tara's attitude to youthful cynicism, but, on this occasion, he thought it was a clear-eyed assessment of things as they really were. It was probably nothing more than sentimentality, but he felt distaste at discussing Mrs O'Bryan's character with her daughter.

'Let's see this famous article then,' he said, steering the conversation into easier waters.

Tara clasped her hands round her knees. 'I'm going to make you guess. At the very least, you can guess which magazine it's in.'

'Do I have to?' asked Anthony with a groan. 'I'm feeling very lazy. I've been hard at work this morning.'

'That's not the spirit,' she said. 'Being interviewed by Uncle Patrick isn't work. Writing the article's the hard bit. What are you doing with all these papers, anyway? Just general interest or have you got a purpose?'

'Mr Sherston asked me to look through them to see if I could find an angle, as he called it, for my interview,' said Anthony with a rueful smile. 'You know, how inferior German carpentry is to British carpentry and so on.'

She laughed and returned the magazine to the pile. Her face grew thoughtful. 'Why on earth are you doing this, Colonel? You don't seem like the sort of person who courts publicity.'

Her eyes were, as Anthony had noticed last night, uncomfortably intelligent. He chose his words carefully. 'It came about by chance. I ran into your uncle in town. He realized what I'd been up to and asked if he could put a piece in the paper about it. He was so insistent, I asked my senior officers if it was all right and they told me to go ahead. Apparently there's a lot of wild stories circulating about how efficient the German spy network is and they thought some genuine information about what we're doing might provide a useful balance. Your uncle's an interesting man,' he added, hoping she'd take the bait. 'I wouldn't mind getting to know him better.'

'Uncle Patrick's an absolute dear,' she said affectionately. She waved an expansive hand at the house and grounds. 'He built all this, you know. The house was a ruin when he bought it. He was a penniless boy, you know. He didn't have any advantages, and neither did my mother. He's never forgotten his origins,' she added, growing serious, 'or tried to pretend to be anything he's not. My mother does. She resents their early life in a way that Uncle Patrick never does. She'll never talk about it. Mind you, my father was well off, or so she thought. After he died, she found all the money was gone, and she was left very hard up. It was just as well Uncle Patrick came to the rescue, or I don't know what would have happened.'

She sat back and looked at Anthony appraisingly. 'Uncle Patrick,' she said with odd deliberation, 'is a generous man, but it doesn't do to cross him. He doesn't like it.'

Anthony dropped his gaze. That was a warning, if he'd ever heard one. 'Did Terence Cavanaugh cross him?' he asked after a pause. 'He obviously dropped a brick somehow.'

She drew her breath in. 'You could say that. Yes, that's one way to put it. Let's just say that my mother discovered he wasn't everything he appeared to be and Uncle Patrick agreed.'

Anthony tensed. *He wasn't everything he appeared to be?* That didn't sound like an attempted love affair with Tara. That sounded as if Veronica O'Bryan had discovered Cavanaugh was a spy. Surely Tara – Tara who appeared so honest and straightforward – didn't know the truth? Veronica O'Bryan, yes. He could imagine her being a ruthless enemy. Sherston? Perhaps. He was a tough man, despite his geniality, and Anthony could well imagine he didn't relish being crossed. But Tara? 'Do you know what Cavanaugh did?' he demanded.

She flinched away from him. 'Not the details, no. I don't want to know.' Again, that didn't sound as if a love affair was the root of the problem. She stood up abruptly. 'Terry's dead. That's all that really matters.' Her voice wavered. 'Look, can we talk about something else?' She shook herself and when she spoke, her voice was consciously cheerful. 'After all, you haven't even tried to guess which magazine I write for.'

He could have insisted; he knew that. He could have demanded that she tell him the truth about Terence Cavanaugh. But where would that get him? For one thing she'd probably walk away and, for another, he couldn't ask the right questions without giving away the answer. *She didn't know the details . . .*

So what the dickens did she know? Nothing, probably, he thought in disgust. No; force was useless, whereas if she simply chatted to him, he might find something useful.

'All right,' he said, tapping the space on the bench beside him where she'd happily been sitting before he started asking awkward questions. 'Come and sit down again and I'll play Guess the Magazine.' He picked up *Woodwork And Practical Carpentry.* 'Somehow I don't think it's this.'

'Correct,' she said with a returning smile.

'And then there's the *Sentinel.*'

'Uncle Patrick's pride and joy? The *Sentinel*'s a bit above my reach at the moment.'

Anthony looked at the heap of magazines. 'I can see this is going to be more difficult than I thought. *The Grocers' and Licensed Victuallers' Intelligencer?*'

'I haven't any intelligence a licensed victualler would be remotely interested in.'

'*Pig-Breeders' Monthly?*'

'I've never bred a pig.'

'*Stamp Collecting For Boys,* then.'

'I was never a boy, either. And, before you ask, it's not *Market Garden and Allotment Times.*'

'*Schoolgirl Chums*?' suggested Anthony.

'That's not a bad guess,' said Tara. 'I've written stories for them in the past but, no, that's not the one.'

Her smile grew as he flicked through a pile of women's magazines. She disclaimed *Pip's Paper*, *Our Lives*, *Hearth and Home* and *Elsie's Own.* 'I've got it,' he said, holding up the next magazine to hand. '*Motoring and Practical Car Mechanic.*' He opened the cover and looked down the contents. 'There's a piece on fettling something I haven't got a clue about. That's surely yours.'

'No,' she said with a giggle, 'but that's the magazine, all right.'

'Is it?' asked Anthony in astonishment.

'Yes, I do the maintenance section.' She pointed to the article entitled, "Everyday care. This month; cleaning your contact breaker." She laughed at his expression. 'I like mechanical things and I get all the real information from Carey, the chauffeur.'

'That's cheating,' said Anthony with a broad grin.

'No, it isn't. It's research.'

'I still think it's cheating,' he said. He picked up the next magazine on the diminishing pile, a superior and shiny publication, entitled the *Beau Monde.* 'I would have thought this was much more your style,' he added, flicking though the pages. 'Fashion and dresses and . . . and . . .'

Anthony froze in his seat. There it was.

Frankie's Letter.

Wedged between an article on hats and a poem about flowers, was 'Frankie's Letter'. He couldn't miss it. The letterhead was in brilliant red type an inch high.

Frankie's Letter: A Look At London and beyond.
This month Frankie sees Lady Cy . . . ia M . . . s in the Park, tries to find a simple blouse and encounters a family of Sealyhams at the dog show everyone's talking about.

He scarcely took it in. This is what Cavanaugh had meant. He remembered the look on his face, the look just before he'd died.

'*Frankie's letter. Read Frankie's letter.*'

'*Have you got the letter?*'

'It's not that sort of letter . . .'

The scene faded. *That's* what he meant. Not an ordinary letter but this, a piece in a magazine.

'Colonel Brooke?' asked Tara. 'What is it?'

'Nothing,' he said as lightly as he possibly could. He had to keep her from guessing anything was wrong. It was damned hard. After all, concealed in the seemingly trivial gossip of 'Frankie's Letter', was a coded message to the enemy. It couldn't be anything else. He'd come to Starhanger hoping to find a spy and here, from the Sherston Press – *Sherston's* press – was the very document Cavanaugh had told him to read.

EIGHT

Tara twisted her head to look at the page open on his knee. 'Oh, "Frankie's Letter". That's one of Uncle Patrick's best stunts. Frankie goes everywhere and sees everyone. It's a real coup to be mentioned in the "Letter". It's such a simple idea and yet it's pushed the circulation past *Vogue* a few times.'

'Who writes it?' asked Anthony. 'You don't, I suppose?' It looked innocent, so innocent. There was no reason why she should deny it . . .

She laughed. 'I wish I did.' Anthony let his breath out quietly. She looked at him enquiringly. 'Haven't you ever heard of it? It's very well-known. Mind you, I suppose men wouldn't be interested but most women are. I thought everyone knew about "Frankie's Letter".'

Anthony laughed. He couldn't help it. The irony of the situation struck him as almost unbelievable. Here was Sir Charles and himself, the Big Cheese of Intelligence plus one of his agents, tearing their hair out chasing the mysterious Frankie, and so far from trying to evade them, Frankie published a monthly column in a magazine with the name in red letters an inch high. So much for the secret service, Whitehall, and all the King's horses and all the King's men. A King's woman, he thought, would have been much more to the point. An empty-headed, gossipy, fashionable woman at that.

'What's so funny?' asked Tara, curiously.

'Oh, nothing,' said Anthony. 'Nothing important, that is. Something just struck me, that's all. So come on then. If you don't write "Frankie's Letter", who does?' His tone held nothing but light-hearted bantering and her cheeks dimpled.

'I can't tell you.'

'Come on,' said Anthony coaxingly. 'I won't split.'

She shook her head. 'No, I really can't. All London's been on fire to know who Frankie is for the last couple of years. No one knows who Frankie is, you see, not even Uncle Patrick.'

Anthony gazed at her in frank disbelief. That struck him as overwhelmingly unlikely. 'You must be joking. Surely Mr Sherston knows who his authors are?'

'Of course he does,' she said. 'All except Frankie. It's part of the mystique. You see, Frankie – whoever Frankie is – obviously knows everyone who's anyone and she's awfully funny about them. It's a real cachet to be mentioned in "Frankie's Letter", you know. She doesn't use anyone's full name, of course, it's all initials, but we know who she means. She's awfully daring sometimes. I've been in it more than once. All nice comments, I'm glad to say. I'd love to know who she is. "Who's Frankie?" is a regular topic of conversation.'

Anthony tried again. 'Mr Sherston must know who Frankie is. He could tell you, I'm sure.'

'He really can't, you know. Even if he could, he wouldn't say. It'd spoil the fun. Everyone wants to know who she is. Ever so many people have asked me. Even Terry talked about it.'

Anthony swallowed. Of course Cavanaugh talked about it. He should have seen that one coming.

'He took a real interest in Uncle Patrick's papers,' continued Tara. 'Mind you, he was a journalist, so he was bound to be interested in a stunt like "Frankie's Letter".'

'Yes, yes, he would,' said Anthony absently. He forced himself to stretch and conceal a pretended yawn, radiating idle good humour. He picked up the pile of papers. 'I think I'll take these back into the house. I really had better look through them properly.' He grinned. 'I got the impression I was going to be quizzed later on.'

He strolled across the lawn, up onto the terrace and into the house. He could still hear voices from the study but the rest of the house was, as Tara had said, deserted. He only hoped Sir Charles hadn't joined the general exodus.

He was in luck.

Sir Charles was in his room, deep in discussion with his valet, Sedgley, about a dress waistcoat. He looked up as Anthony entered. 'Come in, my dear fellow. Close the door, won't you? I've had quite an interesting morning in some ways . . .' He broke off as he saw Anthony's expression. 'But you really must tell me what you've been up to,' he continued, in the same tone. He turned to Sedgley. 'That's all for now, Sedgley. I quite agree with you about the waist-coat. Thank you for bringing it to my attention.'

As Sedgley left the room, Sir Charles turned to Anthony with a smile. 'Valuable feller, that. First-rate at his job. The buckle on my waistcoat is working loose, which is a damn scandal when you think what the tailor charges.'

As he spoke, Sir Charles followed the valet to the door, waited a few moments, then pressed against the door, making sure it was shut tight.

'D'you know,' he added, 'I think I'll close the window. Draughts and so on. I have to be careful of my chest.' He pulled down the sash window then looked at Anthony, his face alive with expectation. 'What is it?'

Anthony put the pile of magazines on the bed and pulled out the *Beau Monde*. 'Look at this.' He opened the magazine at 'Frankie's Letter'.

Sir Charles took it from him with a soundless whistle. 'Good grief!' He shook his head in disbelief. 'Right under our ruddy noses. "Frankie's Letter".'

He sat down on the bed and quickly read it through. 'Genius,' he muttered. 'Absolute genius.'

He quickly skimmed through the rest of the magazine. 'This is extraordinary. If it wasn't for Cavanaugh, I could have read this from cover to cover and never suspected a thing. By jingo, I'll have to get this decoded and as quickly as possible.'

He shook his head in reluctant admiration. 'Women's clothes, weddings, card problems, dog shows – there's nothing here to make the censor stop this leaving the country.'

'My thoughts exactly,' said Anthony. 'It could be freely shipped to Holland and be in Berlin a couple of days after publication.'

'And none of us any the wiser,' agreed Sir Charles. He put the magazine down beside him. 'The question is, who is Frankie? And does Sherston know his magazine is being used?'

'Exactly. I've been talking to Miss O'Bryan. Sherston gave me an armful of magazines to look at. I took them into the garden and she joined me, rather surprised by my choice of reading matter.'

'How surprised?' asked Sir Charles quickly.

'I told her Sherston had given me them to read and she thought it hilarious. Anyway, I was able to ask her about "Frankie's Letter" without it seeming odd. Frankie is a newspaper stunt. According to Miss O'Bryan it sells the magazine. No one knows who Frankie is, but she – or he – goes everywhere and knows everyone in the fashionable world. Who Frankie is, is a much talked-about mystery. According to Miss O'Bryan not even Patrick Sherston himself knows Frankie's identity.'

'That's ridiculous,' said Sir Charles promptly. 'Presumably Frankie doesn't work for free. Someone must get paid to write this stuff.' He picked up the magazine once more. 'Sherston himself could write it.'

'I suppose so,' said Anthony doubtfully. 'D'you think that's really on the cards? I mean, look at it. It's all about shopping and so on. Would Sherston know enough to write it convincingly?'

'Damn it, Brooke, it's chit-chat, not *War and Peace*.' Sir Charles stood up and walked across the room to the fireplace.

Leaning on the mantelpiece, he took a cigarette and pushed the box towards Anthony. 'Why shouldn't Sherston write it? After all, he's worked in newspapers all his life. If he's Frankie, it's no wonder it's such a well-kept secret. Mrs Sherston was a journalist, too,' he added significantly.

Anthony felt his mouth dry up. 'So Tara O'Bryan told me.'

Sir Charles jerked his thumb at the door. 'Sedgley was bringing me up to date before you came in. He's a perfect marvel for finding out who's who. Mrs Sherston,' he repeated. '"Frankie's Letter" is probably more her style.'

'We don't know Frankie is a member of the household at all,' objected Anthony.

'True,' Sir Charles acknowledged. 'But if they are, it accounts for the secrecy, doesn't it? Mrs Sherston was Sherston's Paris corre-spondent. She could very easily write a "Frankie's Letter". She lived in Paris for about four years.' He gave a faint smile. 'Apparently she started off as a dressmaker, but found writing about it rather more rewarding. Sherston went off to Paris about three years ago and returned with a wife.'

'What about Veronica O'Bryan? She could be Frankie just as easily as Mrs Sherston. She certainly knew something about it. I found that out last night.' Anthony walked to the bed and opened the magazine at 'Frankie's Letter' once more. 'She could pick up all this gossip about weddings and fashion and what-have-you without any effort. I imagine any reasonably well-educated person could churn this out. Why, Miss O'Bryan writes for one of Sherston's motoring magazines. I don't suppose she's—'

He broke off. From outside the door came the creak of a floor-board. Anthony and Sir Charles swapped looks with each other.

'. . . an expert in motoring,' continued Anthony, making his voice just that little bit louder. He crept towards the door.

'You can never tell, my dear chap,' said Sir Charles from beside the fireplace.

Anthony stood with his ear against the hinged side of the door. He could hear very faint sounds from the other side of the wood-work. He motioned to Sir Charles to carry on.

'I must say, I'd rather take the train. At least if a train breaks down, I'm not expected to crawl about underneath it and get covered in oil into the bargain. Tyres, now, they're a problem. The wretched things always seem to be going pop for one reason or another.'

The sound of the lunch gong boomed up the stairs. There was a startled hiss from outside. The board creaked once more and there was the rustle of a dress followed by the sound of footsteps as if someone was walking away very quietly.

'Lunch,' said Sir Charles chattily from across the room. 'I must say I'm ready for it. That was a remarkably good dinner we had last night. Mind you, it's easier to eat well in the country, I always feel, with all the fresh eggs and home-grown vegetables and prob-ably home-reared beef and pork as well.'

Anthony put his hand on the handle and very slowly, pulled the door open and quickly glanced out. Almost in the same movement, he drew his head back in. Then, with infinite care, he closed the door and came back into the room.

'It was Veronica O'Bryan,' he said quietly. 'I can't say I'm surprised.' No, he wasn't surprised. Most of all he was relieved.

Sir Charles nodded. 'That's one coincidence too many. Damn! I wonder what she heard?' He bit his lip. 'What now, Brooke? Even now we don't know enough to take definite action.'

Anthony chewed the problem over. 'We need some evidence. D'you know which is her room? If there's anything to be found, that's the obvious place to look.'

'I can ask Sedgley which room she has. I think a search is a good idea but getting her out of the way may be a problem.'

'Let's see what turns up,' said Anthony. 'She's bound to go out sometime.'

'All right,' Sir Charles agreed. 'Come on. We'd better go down to lunch.'

Anthony half-expected Veronica O'Bryan to be absent from lunch but she was there, all right. What's more, the look she gave him and Sir Charles as they came down the stairs convinced him that she'd managed to overhear enough of their conversation to get the wind up. It wouldn't take much, he reflected. All she'd have to hear was the word *Frankie* and she'd know exactly which way the wind was blowing.

That being the case, he was surprised, then pleased, then deeply suspicious when, over the apple pie and cream, she announced her intention of going riding that afternoon. 'I think I'll take Moondancer over to Carson's Water,' she said. 'She needs a gallop.'

Josette Sherston looked up. 'You're going out?'

'You have no objection, I presume?' said Veronica O'Bryan icily.

'Carson's Water's a fair old way,' said Sherston.

'I need some fresh air, Patrick. I probably won't be back for tea.'

'No, you probably won't, if you go as far as Carson's Water,' said Sherston mildly. 'Incidentally, Colonel,' he added, turning to Anthony, 'if you fancy taking one of the horses out, please say so. You too, Talbot. You're very welcome.'

'I think I'd rather have a stroll round the grounds,' said Anthony. 'I'm feeling very lazy. I'd like to take a look round the stables though. I like horses.'

'I'll come with you,' said Tara. 'We'll go after lunch.'

*   *   *

'Did Mrs O'Bryan really go riding?' asked Sir Charles.

They were in Anthony's room. Anthony had been shown the stables by Tara, then retreated to his room, pleading an overpowering desire for an afternoon nap.

Anthony nodded. 'Yes, I saw her leave. Mrs Sherston went out too. It's odd, you know. I could have sworn Mrs O'Bryan heard something this morning. I'd have thought she'd be very cautious about leaving her room unguarded.'

Sir Charles shrugged. 'She might think it's all right. After all, you mentioned Frankie to her last night. You obviously didn't know much about Frankie then. She might not realize you've tumbled to it.'

'That's the optimistic view,' said Anthony dryly.

'Yes . . . She could be meeting someone to tell them about you. I thought of following her, but it's next door to impossible to follow someone on horseback and stay unobserved.'

'It could be a trap of some sort.'

'It's possible,' admitted Sir Charles. He opened the door and looked along the corridor. 'Come on, Brooke,' he said. 'We might as well try our luck. Thanks to Sedgley, I know exactly where her room is.'

The upstairs of the house was very quiet, the sun-filled corridor wrapped in early summer silence. The only sounds were far-off snatches of conversation drifting up the stairs and the rustle of the wind in the trees through the open window at the front of the house. Most of the doors in the corridor stood ajar. Veronica O'Bryan's was locked.

Sir Charles took a bunch of picklocks from his pocket.

'Wait a moment,' said Anthony and went down on one knee beside the keyhole. He drew out a piece of paper that had been stuck in the door. 'She left that as a telltale,' he said. 'I'll put it back when we leave.' He examined the door carefully. 'There's nothing else.'

Sir Charles grinned in satisfaction. 'So she was expecting a visit. That sounds promising.'

Anthony stood to one side while Sir Charles opened the door. 'Stay outside,' he said quietly as the door swung open. 'I'll feel happier knowing you're on guard.'

He took the picklocks and went in. His real fear, that Veronica

O'Bryan had somehow doubled back and was waiting for him, had been quieted by the telltale of the piece of paper. That would be impossible to arrange from the inside. He stood by the door and considered the room.

He hoped that Veronica O'Bryan would have some letters, some papers, even some drafts of 'Frankie's Letter'. They were very private and the presumption was she would hide them in her room. So where would she put them?

There was the bed, of course, its covers laid back to air. It couldn't be anywhere a servant would look, so under the mattress or bed was out. The wardrobe? There was nothing on top and the inside contained only clothes and shoes. Anthony had hopes of the hat boxes, but they held nothing but hats. He pressed his hands against the back and the base of the wardrobe, looking for a hidden compartment, but it seemed solid enough.

Working very quickly, he examined the bedside table, the chairs and the small bookcase. He picked up the rug and ran his hands over the floorboards, but they were all true and well-fitting. He pulled out the drawers in the chest of drawers, rifled through their contents and reassured himself there wasn't the space for a secret drawer. Satisfying himself the drawers looked untouched, he stood in the centre of the room.

The hiding place couldn't be anywhere too difficult or dirty. Mrs O'Bryan needed to get at these papers – if she had any – so a loose brick up the chimney was out. Her jewellery box was on top of the chest of drawers. It was locked, of course, but the folded wire tool in his pocket made short work of that. Nothing.

He replaced the necklaces and brooches in the order he'd taken them out, aware that time was slipping away. Her writing desk was next, a mahogany affair with a sloping top and drawers. The drawers weren't locked and an innocent array of writing paper and pens met his eyes. Again, there was no false back to the desk.

Consciously forcing down his frustration, Anthony sat back on his haunches on the rug. Was there anything to find? His eyes lit once more on the jewellery box. It was a big affair of ebony. Very big for the jewels he'd taken out and yet they'd reached the top of the box.

Impatiently he opened it up once more and took out the glittering contents, slipped his fingers into the box at diagonally opposite corners and pressed down. There was a click as the velvet-covered bottom came away.

He swore under his breath. The space contained a fine ruby brooch, obviously Veronica O'Bryan's most valuable piece, and nothing else. And yet the box was still too big for its contents. Anthony picked it up and examined it thoroughly, then, holding the bottom securely, pushed the side of the box. It slid open, revealing a drawer a few inches deep. It was full of papers. Bingo!

'Talbot,' he called softly. 'We're in business.'

Back in the safety of Sir Charles's room, they opened up the jewellery box.

The contents were damning. There was a series of letters from an address in The Bronx, New York, from a Sean Kennedy. They mainly concerned raising enough funds in America to buy arms in Germany to ship to Ireland, but one letter made the hairs on the back on Anthony's neck stand up.

'Your Terence Cavanaugh sounds like our Patrick Quinn,' wrote Kennedy. There followed a detailed description of Cavanaugh. 'Quinn is a British agent. He escaped from New York but needs to be taken care of as soon as possible. I'll leave the details to you.'

And she had taken care of him, thought Anthony, remembering once more the clutch of the dying man's hand. There were other letters, referring to the 'London end' and – this made Sir Charles sigh with relief – the Sons of Hibernia.

'She's in it up to her neck,' said Sir Charles with deep satisfaction.

'There's no reference to "Frankie's Letter",' though, said Anthony, skimming through the letters.

'Why should there be?' asked Sir Charles with a shrug. 'After all, how Veronica O'Bryan gets information to Germany is her concern, not this Sean Kennedy's.'

'True enough. What's this?' There was a cardboard-backed envelope in the box which, unlike the other letters, had a British stamp on it. 'The postmark's London EC1.'

Anthony opened the envelope and frowned in surprise. There was a photograph, a studio picture, of a little girl about five years old, sitting on a stool holding a toy cat with a curtain draped artistically behind her. She was a pretty little thing with very solemn eyes and someone – an adult – had written across the bottom of the picture 'To Mummy'.

'Who the dickens is she, I wonder?' said Sir Charles.

Anthony scratched his chin. The child in the picture reminded him of someone. Veronica O'Bryan? Maybe. He stared hard at the photograph and the fleeting impression of familiarity vanished. 'Could it be Mrs O'Bryan's child?' he suggested tentatively.

Sir Charles whistled. 'I suppose it could,' he agreed. 'It seems unlikely but it wouldn't be impossible. No,' he added reflectively. 'It wouldn't be impossible at all. After all, how old is she? Early forties at the most, I'd say.'

He carefully replaced the photograph in the envelope. 'If she is Mrs O'Bryan's child, she's kept it very quiet. She'd have to, of course. The scandal if it got out would be terrific. She couldn't live here if it became known.'

He looked at Anthony and read his expression. 'If it is Mrs O'Bryan's child, she'll be protected. I'm not having an innocent child dragged into this, don't worry.' Besides,' he added, looking at the letters, 'we've got more than enough evidence to act on.'

He pursed his lips. 'I think we'll put these back where we found them. I don't want to give the game away too soon. I'll get Sedgley to wire London from the village. That'll mean a telegram here, calling me away on urgent family business. I want "Frankie's Letter" decoded as quickly as possible.'

'What about Veronica O'Bryan?' asked Anthony. 'Do we arrest her?'

'I don't think so,' said Sir Charles. 'I'd like to keep up my pretence as a harmless government official for as long as possible. Besides that, I want to know more. The *Beau Monde* is Sherston's paper. I want to find out how deeply he's involved and if anyone else is in on it. Granted who Sherston is, that's going to be tricky but it shouldn't be impossible. We've made massive progress, but this is just the start. No, sit tight, Brooke, and be as nice as pie to Veronica O'Bryan. I don't want her to realize anything's wrong.'

The telegram for Sir Charles turned up during afternoon tea which was served under the cedar tree. As Vyse, the butler, came across the grass with a salver containing a yellow envelope, they all fell silent. Even in a household like Sherston's, thought Anthony, where telegrams were commonplace, wartime meant telegrams were greeted with apprehension. It was significant that the first thing Sherston said, as Sir Charles ripped open the envelope was, 'Is everything all right, Talbot? Not bad news, I trust?'

Josette Sherston went pale. She'd been tired and nervy during tea, and had obviously found it an effort to keep up with the conversation. 'Is it bad news?' she asked, echoing Sherston's question.

Sir Charles read the telegram quickly. 'It's Uncle Albert,' he said with a deep sigh. 'He's been ailing for some time but he's taken a turn for the worse.' He tossed the telegram onto the table and looked round apologetically. 'I'm very sorry, Mrs Sherston, but I'm afraid I'll have to return to town immediately.'

'What a pity,' said Josette Sherston sympathetically. She turned to Vyse. 'Instruct Sir Charles's valet to pack his things, Vyse, and have the car brought round. I'm not sure of the times of the trains,' she added to Sir Charles, 'but there's a timetable in the library, of course.'

'That went very smoothly,' said Anthony quietly to Sir Charles as he accompanied him back into the house.

'That's the easy bit,' said Sir Charles. 'I just hope Veronica O'Bryan doesn't get the wind-up when she finds I've gone. If she shows signs of making a run for it, you might have to stop her. We can't risk her getting away. You'll have to use your judgement.'

Anthony raised an eyebrow. He was a guest, after all, and apprehending the host's sister-in-law wasn't the sort of situation he'd ever encountered in a book of etiquette. 'Let's hope Mrs O'Bryan doesn't tumble to it,' he murmured. 'It doesn't sound much fun,'

In the event, Anthony needn't have worried. At half-past seven, Tara remarked that her mother was very late. At twenty past eight Sherston wondered if she'd decided to stay with a friend somewhere. At ten to nine, Kindred, the groom, came in from the stables and reported that Moondancer, Mrs O'Bryan's horse, had been found wandering, riderless, over the slough, a marshy stretch of rough ground between Ticker's Wood and the village.

The slough, as Tara said, white-faced, was a treacherous area, full of tussocks, ditches and bogs. By ten to ten, Sherston, Anthony, Tara and four local policemen, armed with torches, were gingerly negotiating the paths through the swampy ground, before abandoning the search, two hours later, as useless.

The search started again at first light. After a fruitless few hours,

Anthony looked wearily over the desolate marsh. In the distance, chopped into flurries by the wind, came the sound of church bells pealing for early service in the village.

He couldn't help feeling a grudging professional respect for Veronica O'Bryan. Because of the paper telltale in her door, he had discounted the possibility she'd made a run for it. That little piece of paper had quieted his fears, persuaded him, hours after she should have returned, that she was coming back.

Perhaps it wasn't so subtle; perhaps she had intended to return but reflected on what she'd overheard, saw her chance and took it. In any event, she had, as he said to Sir Charles, when he finally managed to slip away and telephone privately, completely disappeared.

First round, commented Sir Charles grimly, to Veronica O'Bryan.

NINE

Later that same day, Lieutenant Michael Greenwood stepped out of the lunchtime May sunshine into the gloomy oak panelled lobby of the St George's Hotel. In his role as the newly arrived colonial, Martin Rycroft, he had supplied himself with a Baedeker's guide. That it was also useful to Michael Greenwood, the junior officer, was something he was young enough to conceal from himself.

Baedeker described the St George's accurately, if succinctly. 'Hotels in Westminster and Belgravia', ran the heading. 'Convenient for the Houses of Parliament, Westminster Abbey, the government offices, Hyde Park, etc.'

Westminster and Belgravia did not feature 'Hotels Of The Highest Class'; they were to be found on the adjoining pages: 'In Or Near Piccadilly' and 'In Or Near Charing Cross And The Strand' and their names, to an impecunious second lieutenant, were like spells; Claridges; The Ritz; ('sumptuous') The Savoy; The Cecil; The Waldorf. With 'restaurant, ballrooms, palm courts etc.' (and what 'etcs.' there could be was anyone's guess) their prices matched their status. 'Room 21s, with bathroom from 35s.'

Thirty-five shillings for a room with a tub! By jingo, reflected Michael, that was a dickens of a lot, far more than he could ever afford.

The St George's rates were more modest. 'Room 9s., with bathroom 15s.' His Majesty's Government did not run to private bathrooms, but the 'charge for a hot bath was noted as '1s. Gratuities ('tips'),' Michael had read, thankful for the information, 'should amount to 10-15% of the bill and be divided between the head waiter, the waiter who has specially attended to the traveller, the chambermaid, the "boots" etc.' A prudent note was sounded; 'to produce the best results they should be distributed weekly.' This, Michael, happily aware that it wasn't his own money he was distributing, proposed to do.

One other piece of worldly wisdom he owed to Baedeker. 'Money and valuables should be securely locked up in the visitor's own trunk, as the drawers and cupboards of hotels are not always inviolable receptacles.'

True, 'objects of great value had better be entrusted to the keeping of the manager in exchange for a receipt', but as the sole object of his stay in the St George's was to be robbed, he wanted to make it credibly difficult for any prospective thief, not downright impossible.

The wash-leather bag of diamonds was securely in his pocket, but the maps of the waters of Mount Erok, all beautifully coloured by John Rycroft to show the location of the supposed diamond find, were kept, as Baedeker had suggested, in his trunk. An ordinary thief wouldn't touch them, but if the plan worked, they should draw a German agent like a magnet.

As he crossed the lobby the clerk looked up from the reception desk. 'Mr Rycroft?' He coughed apologetically. 'I'm afraid we've had a small problem.'

'Oh yes? What is it?'

'One of our porters found a man trying to force the lock on your door. Don't worry,' he added hastily, 'the porter saw the man off before any damage was done. Unfortunately O'Dwyer, the porter, suffers from a stiff knee, so although he gave chase, the man escaped.'

'Did he get a look at the chap?' asked Michael.

The clerk shrugged. 'Not really, I'm afraid, sir. O'Dwyer says he was a little nothing of a man with a moustache, but that's all. Naturally, if anything had been taken, we would insist O'Dwyer make a full statement to the police, but in the circumstances . . .' the clerk broke off.

'In the circumstances it doesn't seem worth making a fuss,' Michael said.

The clerk looked relieved. 'Thank you, sir. No hotel likes having the police called in. It doesn't do us any good, sir. The guests don't like it.'

Michael shook his head. 'There seems precious little you could tell them anyway. Thanks for letting me know and –' he reached in his wallet for a ten shilling note '– if you could let the porter have this. Tell him I appreciate what he did.'

The clerk took the note. 'Thank you, sir. Thank you very much indeed.'

Michael walked up the stairs with a frown. It looked as if things were starting to happen. He could wish that O'Dwyer hadn't been so assiduous in his protection of the hotel property, but he could hardly explain that to the clerk.

Maybe Bertram Farlow and Peter Warren could add to the porter's description. They should have seen what happened from their vantage point across the corridor. He just hoped that the man hadn't been scared off completely. Unless the thief went for the maps in his trunk, any burglary could be nothing more than coincidence.

Still deep in thought, Michael turned the key in the door to his room. From the corner of his eye he saw a figure detach itself from the shadow of a pillar next to the door. He half-turned, then there was a sudden thump in the small of his back and a voice whispered close to his ear.

'I have a gun. It is only a small gun and will not make much noise. It might not kill you, but it will certainly cripple you. Open the door.'

Michael froze. He knew that Farlow and Warren were watching from across the corridor and, at the far end of the corridor, a porter was unloading bags. His instinct was to lash out, calling for help. As if the man read his thoughts, the gun jabbed painfully into his back.

'Don't be stupid.'

Michael swallowed and decided not to be stupid. The voice chilled him. He'd expected a thief, not an assassin. There was something horribly compelling about the man's even, articulate, unexcited tone. Michael had no doubt that the man would leave him sprawled in helpless agony, while he walked away. Besides that, he was *supposed* to be burgled. Farlow and Warren must think it was all going according to plan, but it shouldn't have happened like this. He had no idea how scared he would be.

He heard the man's hiss of satisfaction as the key turned in the lock and the door swung open. Then they were inside the room, the door shut behind them. Michael wanted to turn, to see his assailant, but the gun remained in the small of his back. 'What now?' Michael asked. There was a crack in his voice. He wished there wasn't. 'What's all this about?' he tried, and this time his voice stayed steady.

There was a sigh close to his ear. 'Diamonds, Mr Rycroft. Somewhere in this room are your maps charting where you discovered diamonds. Find them for me.'

'Diamonds?'

'Do not waste my time,' the man said in a snarl. 'Your government does not believe you. I do. Get the maps. And don't turn round!' The last words were punctuated by jabs of the gun.

Michael's lips were very dry. He didn't have to act scared, he *was* scared, but more than that, he was angry. 'They're in the trunk under the bed,' he said sullenly.

'Take out the trunk.'

Michael walked across the room, the gun still pressed against his spine, and stooping under the bed, drew out the brass-bound trunk.

Kneeling on the floor, he could see the man's feet and trouser legs. The shoes were long and slim, with thin soles. Expensive shoes, he thought, desperately trying to find something he could describe to Colonel Brooke later. But the shoes were just shoes. There was nothing unusual about them. He unlocked the catch on the trunk and took out his briefcase with the maps in it.

'Stand up,' said the man. 'Slowly.'

Michael stood up and felt the briefcase taken from his hand. There was a click as the briefcase was opened, followed by a rustle of papers and a little breath of satisfaction.

'Good. Now the diamonds, Mr Rycroft.'

More than anything in the world, Michael wanted to lash out. He restrained himself with a physical effort. This is *supposed* to happen, he repeated to himself. This is what we *hoped* would happen.

The gun was anchored in his back. 'The diamonds are in my pocket,' he said.

There was a soft, humourless chuckle. 'Very wise. Take them out.'

If only this wasn't supposed to happen he could have used the bag of diamonds as a weapon to give weight to his fist, struck out with it, kicked backwards, risked the blasted gun. Anything rather than be robbed by this swine with his expensive shoes and clipped voice.

Michael took the wash-leather bag from his pocket and held it to one side. A man's hand, with fair hair on the back and neatly manicured nails, came forward and took it from his palm.

'Very good.' The triumph in the voice was almost unendurable but what he said next startled Michael.

'Stand against the wall.'

'What?'

'Stand against the wall.'

Michael stood with his face to the wall, senses tingling. The muscles in his arms tensed and his fingers bent, ready to spring. The man gave a little, quick breath. For the first time the gun left his spine. Almost immediately it was jammed against the side of his head.

Using his fingers as a lever, Michael hurled himself backwards, smashing his fist behind him wildly as the gun exploded next to his ear.

The man's chin jerked back as the blow connected. Michael threw himself on him. A powerful arm swept across his windpipe, knocking him back. He cracked his head against the edge of the chest of drawers and for an instant the room went black. The man scrambled for the door.

Michael, scarcely able to breathe, heard, through the roaring in his ears, someone knocking. The door opened and Peter Warren stood in the doorway.

'Hold it,' he shouted, then the man raised the gun and fired at point-blank range.

Warren looked down at his ripped, bloodied, shirt front. He seemed about to speak, then he was thrust out of the way as the man leapt past him. Warren, thrown to the floor, clawed at his chest, juddered and lay still.

Michael staggered across to Warren and shook him helplessly. The sightless eyes stared back. He got to the door, in time to see the black-coated back of the man race down the corridor. The porter who had been unloading luggage stepped forward as if to stop him. 'No!' yelled Michael.

The man jerked to one side, evaded the porter's grasping hands and raced down the stairs.

The porter, utterly bewildered, gazed at Michael clutching at the door frame. 'Here,' he called, coming towards him. 'What's been going on?'

He stopped short as he saw Warren's body. 'Oh my God,' he said. 'He's dead.'

Sir Charles lit a cigarette and looked sightlessly at Anthony, his eyes clouded with worry. It was Sunday evening and they were in Anthony's rooms.

He'd been summoned back to London by a telephone call, supposedly from the War Office. He knew something must have gone badly wrong. He'd just found out what.

'That poor devil, Warren,' said Sir Charles. 'He didn't have a chance. When I think we set this up, Brooke . . .'

'We couldn't know the thief was a killer,' said Anthony uneasily. 'He could have walked in, demanded the goods and Greenwood would have handed them over. I think Greenwood's had a very lucky escape. Warren's killer sounds a real swine.'

'He's a cold-blooded murderer,' said Sir Charles with feeling. 'It's a pity Greenwood didn't get a good look at him. I'd like to know who we were dealing with. He's not a professional crook. No professional would rob a hotel room in that way. He obviously didn't know how to pick a lock, so simply waited for Greenwood to come and open the door.'

'Can't Greenwood tell us anything?' Anthony demanded.

Sir Charles shook his head. 'Not much. The killer had a clipped, well-spoken voice, expensive shoes, fair hair and manicured nails and both Farlow and the hotel porter thought he was tall, well-built and wore a soft hat and a dark coat. Greenwood says he didn't have any accent to speak of, certainly not an Irish one. It's not much to go on, is it? He was certainly going to murder Greenwood, even though he'd got both the diamonds and the maps. Warren simply got in the way.'

'Where's Greenwood now?' Anthony asked.

'He's still in the St George's, but in a different room, of course.' Sir Charles got up and stretched his shoulders. He looked very tired. 'I've tipped the wink to Scotland Yard that it isn't an ordinary murder, if there is such a thing.' He sat quietly for a few moments, then stirred. 'One thing Farlow could tell me about was the failed burglary.'

'Failed burglary?'

'Yes. The successful theft was the second attempt. The first one was at half eleven this morning. Eleven thirty-two, to be exact. The interesting thing is that the first attempt was obviously by a different man. Now he did sound like a pro. He was armed with either a long-bladed screwdriver or a chisel and he was just about to get to grips with Greenwood's door, when a porter came round the corner and chased him off. See if this rings any bells. Farlow describes him as a thin, nondescript man of medium height with a small moustache and a scar on the side of his chin. Farlow got a good sideways view of him.'

Anthony sat up. 'He sounds like my thief, Talbot. The one who pretended to be a club servant.'

Sir Charles nodded. 'That's what I thought. So we've got one attempted robbery by someone who sounds like a real crook, followed by the successful one by someone who isn't so much a crook as a killer.'

'The employee and the employer in fact,' said Anthony. 'That's how I see it, anyway. The Weasel bungled the job, so the fair-haired chap took a hand.' He paused. 'The second chap – the well-spoken one – sounds like a gentleman, doesn't he?'

Sir Charles gave an irritated sigh. 'But we'd placed the gentleman at Starhanger, or thought we had. Talking of Starhanger, do you think there's any chance Veronica O'Bryan did have a riding accident? I only ask because it seems odd, if she was planning an escape, that she left the letters.'

'I wondered about that, said Anthony, reaching for the cigarette box. 'I think she must have acted on impulse. Once she'd decided to run for it, she couldn't risk coming back to the house. In any case, she probably thought the letters were safe in the jewellery box. It was a pretty good hiding place, Talbot. It took me some time to find it, and I've done that sort of thing before. She must have had some money on her because, somehow or other, she got up to London and told whoever about the diamonds.'

'Couldn't she have telephoned?'

'I wouldn't like to give a message like that over the phone, I must say. She could have phoned and arranged to be picked up in a car, I suppose. That's something we could probably check. The trouble is, she vanished a long time before the alarm was raised. With a good horse she could've got a long way from Starhanger.' Anthony tapped his cigarette on the ashtray. 'Did you manage to get "Frankie's Letter" read?'

'I did. It was difficult to crack but simplicity itself once the code people had tumbled to it. The code changed with every "Letter". D'you know what the key was? The bridge problems in a completely different part of the magazine. Once that was spotted, it was easy. The numbers on the bridge scores gave the relevant words in the "Letter".'

Anthony nodded. 'Bridge problems ties it to Veronica O'Bryan, all right. Tara O'Bryan told me that setting bridge problems was one of her mother's skills. What was in the "Letters"?'

'Dynamite.' Sir Charles drew a deep breath. 'My people went back over the whole run of the magazine. It started before the war. The first few issues are innocent enough, and then the information starts. There's reports of armaments at Woolwich Arsenal and proposed troop movements by train. There's notes of which ships are in the Chatham Dockyard and how the mouth of the Thames is guarded. It details which regiments are bound for active service and an unbelievable amount about who's who in the government – and whose mistress is whose, as well. The private lives of the senior ranks of the army and navy are recorded in some detail, too.'

Anthony's eyebrows shot up. 'My God! Is the information accurate, Talbot?'

'As far as we can tell, yes. Some of it even we don't know. When we said that someone at the heart of society was the worse sort of spy, I must admit even I had little idea of how much they could pick up. Perhaps the "Letter" which is of most interest to you is the one concerning Cavanaugh. It says he's in Kiel and asks for him to be taken care of.'

'And so they took care of him,' muttered Anthony.

'If that wasn't bad enough, it seems as if there's something big planned. It's hard to make a guess what it is, but it could be a bomb attack or even a full-scale shelling of the coast, as happened on the east coast in December.'

Anthony winced. The bombardment of the east coast had been an act of sheer brutality. There had been no military target. Eight German battleships turned up out of the mist of the North Sea and opened fire on Scarborough, Whitby and Hartlepool, wounding and killing nearly six hundred civilians from a six-month-old baby to an eighty-six-year-old lady. The attack had been celebrated in Germany with the singing of the *Hymn of Hate*. 'We will never forgo our hate; hate by water and hate by land . . .' That was occasionally played by British military bands as a joke. Some joke.

Sir Charles looked, thought Anthony, more than tired. He suddenly seemed grey with worry. 'All we do know is that some particular person or persons are the target, concealed in the general outrage. It says the party in question will be in place on the fourteenth of June.'

'The fourteenth?' repeated Anthony. 'That's less than a fortnight away. Isn't there any other clue?'

Sir Charles shook his head. 'No.' He got to his feet and stretched his shoulders. 'So you see, Brooke, we simply have to find Veronica O'Bryan.'

'Why the devil can't we arrest Sherston? After all, it was his paper the wretched "Letter" appeared in.'

'Where will that get us?' Sir Charles's voice was thin with impatience. 'I've been warned off Sherston. I saw the Home Secretary earlier and was left in no doubt as to what I can and can't do. We *have* to get this right.'

So that was why Sir Charles looked so tired. Anthony was prepared to bet he'd had damn all sleep last night and to top things off, he'd been hauled over the coals by a politician.

'Unless there's real rock-solid evidence,' continued Sir Charles, '*real* evidence, proving Sherston's the gentleman and knows about "Frankie's Letter", then he's in a position to make the biggest stink there's ever been. Sherston is friends with half the cabinet, for heaven's sake. If we get this wrong – if *I* get this wrong – not only will my head be on a platter but the whole service would be torn apart. We'd never recover and in the meantime the Germans, who'd know all about it, would have a field day.'

He leaned his arms on the mantelpiece, choosing his words carefully. 'There's another reason, too. You know how hysterical the spy mania is. Ironically enough, Sherston's helped to create it. If he's innocent, he'd never live it down.'

He turned and looked at Anthony. 'That's wrong, you know. I still care about that. He'd be ruined and perhaps worse, as some half-baked patriot would be bound to take a crack at him. Besides that, if we arrest Sherston, it tells the enemy we're onto them.'

'But Veronica O'Bryan will tell them that anyway,' protested Anthony. 'She knows Frankie is a busted flush.'

Sir Charles shook his head. 'We can't be certain. It looks that way, I grant you, but she only knows what she overheard. We don't know what she *did* hear. What if we apparently do nothing? They must expect us to raid the offices of the *Beau Monde*. Say we don't. Won't that look as if Veronica O'Bryan went off at half-cock and panicked unnecessarily? Publicly speaking, Veronica O'Bryan went horse riding and never came back. It was an accident. Let's play along with that for the time being. They might even think we believe it. We're supposed to, when all's said and done. After all, we don't know how far the ramifications of this thing spreads, especially with the Irish angle. I'm not sure who's involved, but there's a good few politicians and public men who are sympathetic to an Irish National State. The Home Secretary was worried about that. Frankie might just be the tip of the iceberg.' He glanced at the clock and rubbed his face with his hands. 'It's getting late. Let's see what turns up tomorrow.'

Anthony leaned forward and stubbed out his cigarette, sitting thoughtfully for a few moments. 'All right. I agree. In the circumstances doing nothing will confuse the enemy and I'm all for that. I'll tell you something, though. I'm going to make a prediction. Warren's murderer, our fair-haired friend, sounds like the man at the top to me. He's ruthless and efficient. We're going to hear from him again.'

TEN

Sir Charles Talbot leaned forward attentively to the woman across the table. It was lunchtime on Monday and they were in the Criterion on Piccadilly. Under the influence of a bottle of hock, faultless service and excellent food, served amongst marble pillars under the ornate gold mosaic ceiling, the editor of the *Beau Monde*, Miss Rowena Holt was becoming confidential.

'So you're thinking of starting a new magazine,' she said, finishing the last of her chicken pie. 'It's not the right time, you know, what with the price of pulp paper and the war soaking up all the really decent staff. We keep going, but we're a well-known name.'

'A household name,' murmured Sir Charles.

She smiled at the compliment. 'You could say that, I suppose. What you've got to be certain of is your intended audience. Who are your readers?'

Sir Charles was ready with the answer. 'Ladies of some wealth and standing, ladies who, despite wanting to do the very best, both for their homes and their country, still have enough means, leisure and inclination to want to dress and live smartly in accordance with the prevailing modes.'

Miss Holt digested this, together with the chicken pie, as the waiter deftly cleared the plates. 'Hmm. The same readership as the *Beau Monde*, in fact.'

'Exactly,' said Sir Charles smoothly. 'Which is why, of course, I've come to you.'

Miss Rowena Holt, he thought, didn't look as he imagined the editor of an expensive journal for the upper classes would. She certainly didn't emulate the languid beauties who adorned the pages of the *Beau Monde*. She was short – dumpy in fact – and businesslike, with a sensible, well-worn grey alpaca coat and what were referred to as walking shoes.

'Well, you could do worse than talk to me,' she granted. 'At least I'll tell you the real facts and not some flannery. You say this American wants to extend his press to England?'

This was the story Sir Charles had worked out. He had presented himself at the offices of the *Beau Monde* in the guise of a scout for a New York newspaper magnate, and managed to charm Miss Holt out to lunch. He nodded in response to her question.

'I wouldn't mind knowing who it is,' she said thoughtfully. 'Mr Sherston would be interested. I don't suppose . . .?' She saw his expression.

'He would like to remain anonymous for the present,' said Sir Charles regretfully.

'Well, he's probably well-advised at this stage,' she agreed. 'To be honest, I'd tell him to find another readership. What about factory girls? They've got quite a bit of money to throw around nowadays, what with munitions and so on. The top end is very crowded, you know. *Vogue* is the one to beat, but there's plenty of competition. We hold our own, I'm glad to say. Pudding? Oh, thank you. Perhaps one of those strawberry tarts. They looked delicious and marvellously early as well. The thing is, Mr Hargreaves –' Sir Charles had dropped his name and title for the purposes of the interview – 'every magazine needs its own personality, something that will draw the readers back time after time.'

'You've got "Frankie's Letter", haven't you?'

She laughed and reached for the cream jug. 'You've put your finger on it. Frankie is the talk of London. She goes everywhere and knows everyone and there's always that little *frisson* when you think you might have talked to her. There's been lots of guesses who she is, but no one's managed to pin her down.'

'It must be very difficult to keep a secret like that,' said Sir Charles with a smile. 'You must have been tempted to let the cat out of the bag more than once. It must be nearly unendurable to see Frankie at work and be the only one in the room to know who she is.'

'But I don't know,' said Miss Holt, meeting his eyes. Sir Charles looked startled. 'No, honestly,' she said, sprinkling sugar on her tart. 'I grumbled at first, as you can imagine, when Mr Sherston first proposed the idea, but he said it was a condition of Frankie, whoever she is, doing the "Letter" at all. I was very dubious, as it's one thing to make a newspaper stunt out of secrecy and quite another to really mean it. I nearly refused to run the first "Letter", because of the conditions. I'm not allowed to edit them, you know.' Sir Charles's eyes widened. 'I've got to print them as they are. Still,' she added with a shrug, 'it's the first page everyone turns to and the copy's always good, so if that's what Mr Sherston wants, that's what Mr Sherston gets.'

'So it was Mr Sherston's own idea?'

Miss Holt nodded vigorously. 'Yes. He takes a great interest in the content of his magazines.'

'But how does Frankie get paid? Surely she doesn't work for nothing?'

Miss Holt laughed. 'I wouldn't have thought so, but I don't know who pays her. Mr Sherston himself, at a guess. There was some talk that it might be a lady-friend he wanted to oblige, but I scotched that right away. Mr Sherston isn't that sort, and I've seen enough to know. No, I've got a fairly good idea about Frankie, but if Mr Sherston wants to keep it to himself, that's his business.'

'A member of his household?' asked Sir Charles quietly.

'You didn't hear me say any such thing,' said Miss Holt stiffly, then laughed once more. 'It's a good guess, but why spoil the fun? After all, it's not a state secret, is it? Yes, coffee would be very nice, thank you.'

Agnes Prenderville, senior assistant at Hampson and Quinns, the gentlemen's outfitters, walked through the entrance to Southampton Row tram station and down the steep stairs to the gloomy underground platform. The platform was crowded, as it always was at six o'clock, but she jostled her way through until she found a foot-square space relatively free from bags, umbrellas and elbows.

Mondays always seemed longer than other days, for some reason, and she'd been run off her feet today. The place had been crowded out, full of people who'd come to gawp at the German Town being built for some newspaper stunt. They'd had some awkward customers today, too. Honestly, that woman who complained about her husband's socks! On and on, as if it was Agnes' fault they'd shrunk in the wash. Well, they were the right size when we sold them to you, madam. No, that hadn't gone down well. It was dark, under the gloomy subterranean archways of the tram station and, despite the crowd, Agnes felt her eyes closing. She pulled herself together with a start and glanced at her watch.

Ten past six. She had a few minutes yet before the number 31 was due. The watch had been a present from Steve, a pretty thing with numbers picked out in gold. He was on good money now, what with the war and everything. Yes, she'd made the right choice with Steve. Even if the army said he wasn't fit for them, he'd do for her. Steve was a steady worker who could keep a job. Mum said that was important and she was right. Even if there were better-looking men, looks weren't everything. Take the bloke in front of her, now . . .

Partly to keep her eyes from closing again and partly from natural curiosity, Agnes studied the man standing to one side and slightly in front of her, summing up his clothes with a practised eye. The stick he carried was a gentleman's cane of blackthorn topped with a silver handle. The overcoat slung over his arm was a fine wool that must have cost anywhere between seven and eight guineas, and his suit was another cool five or six guineas worth, topped off by a very smart soft hat.

She wished Steve would make more of an effort. Not at those prices, of course, but he could look like a real gent if he wanted to. This bloke was a real gent, of course. Agnes recognized the upright, arrogant stance, the air of one who gave commands, not took them. Good looking though, with fair hair and sharp cheekbones.

A tram – a number 35, not hers – clanked into the station and he turned his face to look at it. She didn't like his mouth. No, she didn't like his mouth, she thought with a sudden chill. It was sharp with a cruel twist to it, not kindly like Steve's. Agnes had a faint sense of something wrong. Although the man was looking at the tram keenly, he didn't seem to want to board it. He didn't straighten his shoulders, readjust the coat over his arm and shuffle forward in the crowd. No; instead he stepped back, watching. That was it. Watching.

The crowd heaved round her, shuffling slowly forward towards the waiting tram. The man walked forward, not towards the tram, but diagonally across the platform. It was as if he was trying to catch up with a friend, but his face wasn't friendly. He shouldered his way through to stand behind a bloke in a bowler hat and paused. Agnes half-expected him to tap the bloke on the shoulder, but he didn't.

She saw his eyes narrow and focus, his lips flatten out to a thin line, then the arm carrying the coat raised up and, so quickly she couldn't work out what was happening, there was a sharp crack.

The gent dropped his arm, turned away, back through the crowd and towards the steps leading up to the street. The bloke in the bowler seemed to stagger and jump forward, clutching at the woman in front of him, his arms round the shoulders of her navy blue coat. She screamed in fright, trying to free herself, to shake off the clutching arms. The crowd heaved and eddied and there was a swell of excited noise as a space appeared around her and the man in the bowler fell to the floor.

The conductor on the tram leaned forward on the lighted landing stage, his voice carrying over the din. 'What's going on?' he demanded. 'Here, stand clear of the car, will you,' he added, getting down from the tram and pushing his way through the passengers. 'What's that lady screaming about?'

'A geezer attacked her,' said an eager-looking man in a cloth cap, over a rolling torrent of explanations. The woman continued to scream. 'Disgraceful, I call it. Grabbed hold of her, he did. I seen it. Bold as brass.'

'He's been took ill,' said a headscarfed woman. ''E collapsed. 'E must've had a stroke. Takes 'em like that, it does.'

The woman who had screamed was standing at the centre of a small circle, a man sprawled out on the platform in front of her. His hat, a bowler, was still jammed tight on his head, but Agnes caught a glimpse of an odd dark stain on the back of his neck.

The conductor broke through into the little circle and knelt on the ground. 'Be hushed, mum,' he said with rough sympathy to the woman who screamed. She was standing with her hand crammed to her mouth. 'No harm done.' He reached out, tentatively shook the fallen man, gasped and drew his hand away.

His voice broke. '*Bloody hell!* That's blood. There's blood all over his collar.' He took his cap off and wiped his forehead with a trembling hand. 'He's been shot.'

Sir Charles was standing at the entrance to the Fennel Street mortuary when Anthony arrived. Anthony knew the Fennel Street mortuary from his time at the School of Tropical Medicine, an unobtrusive building tucked behind the imposing frontages of Gower Street. It was nearly three hours after the murder at Kingsway tram station.

'I got your message,' he said quickly. 'What's happened?'

'You know you said we'd hear from Warren's killer again? I think we have.' Sir Charles quickly recounted what had happened on the tram platform. 'I'm waiting for Superintendent Rothley. The description of the murderer matched Warren's killer, so Scotland Yard got in touch with me right away.'

He looked up as a solid, well-scrubbed man holding a black briefcase, who looked, thought Anthony, every inch a plain-clothes policeman, approached. 'Here he is now.'

The mortuary attendant led them into the clean, cold, depressing reception room. 'This is the most peculiar murder I've ever come across, Mr Monks,' said Superintendent Rothley lugubriously, putting the briefcase down on the table. 'Can you really credit one man would shoot another in that way? It wasn't a chance affair, either. We've got a very sharp-eyed young woman who swears our gunman was looking out for his victim. She was sure the killer was a gent. The real thing, I mean. She described him as a toff by the way he was dressed.'

Sir Charles and Anthony swapped glances. 'A toff, eh?' repeated Anthony. 'A gentleman, you mean?'

Rothley nodded. 'We can take her word for it. Gent's clothes is something she knows about because she works in Hampson and Quinns, the gentlemen's outfitters. I couldn't shake her. She'll be a good witness, which is just as well, because otherwise it beggars belief.'

'How come no one tried to stop the killer getting away?' asked Anthony.

Rothley gave a depressed shrug. 'No one realized what had happened. I mean, I ask you! People were jammed on that platform like sardines in a tin. You don't expect them to start shooting each other. Our witness, Miss Prenderville, saw what she saw, but she didn't believe it. I don't blame her, either. We've identified the dead man. His name was Cedric Chapman. I don't suppose that means anything to you, gentlemen?'

Both Sir Charles and Anthony shook their heads.

'Ah well. It was just a thought. Anyway, Chapman seemed to fling himself forward and make a grab at a woman, a Mrs Ollerenshaw, who screamed fit to bust. She thought she was being assaulted and so did a good few others. When he collapsed, everyone thought he'd been taken ill, Mrs Ollerenshaw wouldn't stop screaming, the conductor was bellowing at everyone to clear the car and the platform and so on and, what with one thing and another, our man calmly turned on his heel and walked away without anyone lifting a finger to stop him. I've never come across anything like it. If he really is the same bloke who killed your Lieutenant Warren, the sooner we get our hands on him the better, but it's going to be hard.'

'Why?' asked Anthony. 'Why should it be especially hard, I mean?'

Superintendent Rothley looked at him morosely. 'Think about it, sir. A man who can stand on a tram platform, gun down another and stroll away as cool as kiss-your-hand isn't going to go shouting his mouth off in the pub about it or come and own up, which is how we usually get on the right track.'

The superintendent pulled a long face. 'Add to that, I presume, because you gentlemen are involved, there's something hush-hush about the whole affair.' He tapped the briefcase. 'I've brought all the evidence with me, as you requested. Do you want to look at it now?'

'I'd rather see the body first,' said Sir Charles.

'Just as you like, Mr Monks.'

The attendant ushered them into the mortuary. They were silent as the sheet was pulled back from the body on the slab, then Anthony gave a gasp of surprise. 'Good Lord, it's the Weasel.'

Sir Charles looked at him sharply. 'Are you sure?'

'Certain.'

The bullet had gone through the back of his head but the face was unharmed. Anthony stared at the dead man. The jaw had fallen open and the upper lip curled away from his teeth in a weaselly snarl. He was unmistakable.

'So you recognize him, Colonel?' asked the superintendent, brightening.

'He broke into my rooms.'

The superintendent nodded. 'That ties in. He was a thief, all right, a real pro. He had a record as long as your arm.' He stared at the figure on the slab. 'I don't know why he was mixed up with the likes of Lieutenant Warren's killer. I wouldn't have thought that was his cup of tea at all. He's been found in possession of a firearm before now, but he's never used one, to the best of our knowledge. Like most professional crooks, he avoided violence if he could.'

'A lovable rogue, Superintendent?' asked Anthony with a lift of his eyebrows.

Superintendent Rothley gave a snort of disagreement. 'There was nothing lovable about Chapman, sir. Not on your life. He avoided violence because he was a sight too fond of his own skin. He'd do down a pal if he thought he'd get something out of it. He's no great loss, that's for sure.'

They went back into the anti room where they pulled up chairs to the table. The superintendent opened his briefcase and handed a cardboard folder to Sir Charles. 'That's a copy of Chapman's record, sir, with a note of his last known address and associates.'

'Did he have anything on him?' Anthony asked. 'Money, papers, that sort of thing?'

'He had a few bits and pieces, including a watch, a box of matches and a packet of Woodbines and nearly five pounds in notes and loose change. That wasn't much to shout about, but this was a bit out of the way.' The superintendent reached in the briefcase once more and took out a cardboard-backed envelope.

Sir Charles opened it, took a photograph from the envelope. He stared at the photograph for a moment, then handed it to Anthony.

Anthony felt the hairs on the back of his neck stand up as he recognized the photo.

It was a studio portrait of a little girl about five years old, the same child whose picture they'd found in Veronica O'Bryan's room. Then she'd been holding a toy cat; now she had a doll. Anthony took the photograph and once again looked into the child's solemn eyes. As before, an adult had written across the bottom of the picture. 'To Mummy'.

'Veronica O'Bryan,' said Sir Charles softly. 'It's a link to Veronica O'Bryan.'

Superintendent Rothley looked at him enquiringly but Sir Charles didn't explain. 'It's a puzzler, isn't it?' he said, putting the photograph back in the envelope. 'I couldn't figure out why Chapman had it on him. It was in that envelope in his breast pocket and it's obviously fairly new. There's no photographer's name on it, worse luck, so we can't trace it that way. Chapman didn't have any family and besides that, I'd say that little girl was a different class altogether from Chapman and his sort.' He looked hopefully at Sir Charles. 'You can't give me a hint, Mr Monks? It obviously means something to you.'

Sir Charles clicked his tongue in irritation. 'You're quite right, Superintendent. It means something but I don't know what.'

'Well, sir, I know better than to ask too many questions, but if it does start making sense, perhaps you could let us know,' said Rothley, standing up.

'I will, Superintendent,' said Sir Charles absently. He shook himself and got to his feet. 'Thank you for your cooperation. It's saved a great deal of unnecessary work. I'm much obliged.'

They all left the mortuary together. As Superintendent Rothley departed down the street, Sir Charles tucked the cardboard folder under his arm and fell into step with Anthony as they rounded the corner of Fennel Street.

'What the devil,' said Anthony, as soon as they were alone, 'was Chapman doing with a photograph of that kid?'

'Blackmail, perhaps?' said Sir Charles. 'Maybe Veronica O'Bryan was blackmailed into cooperating.'

Anthony drew his breath in. 'That's a filthy trick.' He scratched his ear thoughtfully. 'Can it be blackmail, though? Mrs O'Bryan didn't seem an unwilling partner.'

'Maybe it isn't blackmail,' said Sir Charles with a shrug. 'Maybe they, whoever *they* are, are looking after the child and send Mrs O'Bryan photos of her from time to time to keep her sweet. That'd fit the facts. What I'd like to know is why Chapman was killed. We can take it as read that Warren and Chapman were killed by the same man, but why kill Chapman? Was he threatening to blow the gaff, as they say, about Warren's murder? Chapman might have drawn the line there. Most thieves are squeamish about murder.'

'I don't think Chapman was squeamish,' said Anthony, remembering that weaselly face. 'As the superintendent said, as long as he could get away with it, I don't think there's much he'd have blinked at. I think Chapman tried to pinch the diamonds but it didn't come off. It seems as if this organization won't tolerate failure.'

'My God,' breathed Sir Charles. 'We have to get to the bottom of this. I'd give a dickens of a lot to haul Sherston over the coals, but I can't.'

He paused, sunk in thought. 'Miss Holt, the editor of the *Beau Monde*, thinks Frankie's a member of Sherston's household, so, for the time being, I'm going to work on the premise that Veronica O'Bryan is Frankie, with or without Sherston's knowledge. I think there's a good chance she'll get in touch with someone at Starhanger. It might be her daughter or it might be Sherston. If Sherston is involved, he'll want to know what's going on. If he comes back to town, I'll make sure he's kept under observation but I want you at Starhanger.'

'How do I get myself invited back to Starhanger?' asked Anthony.

'You'd better telephone. You can ask to speak to Tara O'Bryan.'

A slightly cynical smile curved Sir Charles's mouth. 'You made quite an impression on her, if I'm not mistaken.'

Anthony was about to deny it, then, with a little jolt, realized that Sir Charles might be right. All sorts of little pointers fell into place, such as the way she had sought him out in the garden and the easy familiarity with which she'd talked to him. Yes, she probably did like him, the poor kid. The idea made him uncomfortable and he tried to pass it off with a dismissive laugh. 'I don't think so, Talbot.'

Sir Charles raised his eyebrows disbelievingly. 'Have it your own way,' he muttered. 'Anyway, you can express your concern and so on, and ask if you can come back and help search for her mother. Unless I'm much mistaken, she'll invite you like a shot.'

Like a shot? That was an unhappy choice of phrase.

Anthony liked Tara O'Bryan. He felt a tender protectiveness towards her, an elder brotherly sort of feeling. He loathed the idea of using her, of pretending to be a friend because – he couldn't pretend otherwise – there was no happy ending for Tara.

Her mother had vanished without trace. Either she would stay lost or be found. If she stayed lost, Tara would never be really at peace again. If she was found, those papers in her room were enough to strap Veronica O'Bryan blindfolded to a wooden Windsor chair in the Tower of London where she would be executed. Shot.

That was the brutal simplicity of war. If Sherston was part of the conspiracy, Tara would lose her home as well. She was innocent and she was going to suffer. He didn't want to be part of it. And then there was Josette . . . The thought of her haunted him and the only cure he could see was to stay away.

Sir Charles looked at him. 'You have to go,' he said with unexpected sympathy. 'We've had too many deaths, Brooke. We have to get to the truth before the fourteenth of June. There's something very nasty planned and we've got to stop it.'

Anthony braced himself. 'If you say so,' he said unhappily.

The next morning, Tara O'Bryan met Anthony on the little platform of Swayling Halt. It was unexpectedly touching to see her there, in her pretty green jacket and green and white hat.

At a guess, she had dressed with especial care to defy the anxiety she so clearly felt. She was putting, thought Anthony as he stepped off the train, a very consciously brave face on it all. The look of relief she gave, as he hefted his bag and stepped down from the train, hurt. After all, he was her mother's enemy and she thought he was a friend.

She stretched out her hand to him. 'I'm so glad you came back, Colonel.' She paused, then added, her voice cracking, 'I'm trying to bear up, but I'm off my head with worry.'

And that, thought Anthony, as he looked at her strained face and the shadows under her eyes, was true. 'Kindred's outside with the pony and trap,' she said, in an attempt at her usual manner.

To see Tara, who was so courageous and – well, so downright *sensible* – so close to tears, moved Anthony more than he could say. He didn't think Veronica O'Bryan had been a very kind or loving mother, but she was the only mother the girl had.

He was about to reply, but the train huffed, sending a whoosh of sooty smoke into the clear air. There was a slamming of doors and shouts of, 'Dover train! Foxley Heath next stop!' which made conversation impossible.

The train gave a deafening whistle and chugged out of the station. The sound of clanking wheels and snorting steam gradually died away.

There was one other passenger who had alighted at Swayling Halt, a stout woman in a pepper-and-salt tweed coat and a hat with berries on it. She was fussing with her bags and looked round impatiently for the porter. Her eyes lit up as she saw Tara and Anthony.

'Good morning, Tara, my dear,' she said cheerfully.

It was Mrs Moulton, who Anthony had sat beside at dinner on Friday night. 'I didn't realize we were fellow-passengers, Colonel,' she added. 'I've been away for a few days, visiting Cynthia,' she went on chattily, looking at Tara. 'My married daughter,' she explained in an aside to Anthony. 'She lives in London. I should have come back last night, but the trains are so bad she persuaded me to stop another night. I'm glad I did, too. Did you see this awful news in the paper this morning about the poor man murdered at the tram station? It's not safe to be out any more. It's the war that's done it. It's *unsettled* everyone so. Cynthia asked after you, Tara. She'd love to have you to stay.' She looked at Tara critically. 'Why don't you consider it, my dear? You're looking a bit peaky. A little holiday might do you good.'

'Haven't you heard the news, Mrs Moulton?' blurted out Tara. 'About my mother, I mean?'

Mrs Moulton stood riveted to the spot as Tara told her about Veronica O'Bryan's disappearance. 'We've searched the entire Slough,' said Tara, despairingly, 'and there's no trace. We've gone over every inch of the ground between here and Carson's Water, but no one's seen her.'

'You poor child,' said Mrs Moulton, deeply moved. She glared at Anthony. 'What are you doing about it?

'I don't . . .' began Anthony.

'You should *do* something,' said Mrs Moulton firmly. 'You're a man! When did she disappear, Tara? Saturday? Saturday evening?' Her face fell with disappointment. 'I saw your mother on Saturday afternoon, but I don't suppose that's much use.'

Anthony felt his pulse quicken. 'You saw her?' he demanded. 'When? Where?'

'Wait a minute, young man. Let me get my thoughts in order.' She looked at Tara and her face softened. 'I'm sure it'll be all right, my dear. Now let me see, when did I see your mother last?' Her face cleared. 'I know. I was on my way to catch the ten past three to London, so it would be about twenty to three. Ralph brought the trap round and we were on our way down the hill, when I saw your mother on the other side of the road. She was on horseback. I didn't have a chance to speak to her.'

'She was on Station Hill?' asked Tara, puzzled. 'But she said she was going to Carson's Water. Whatever was she doing there?'

Mrs Moulton shrugged. 'I don't know, but she was there.'

'Which is Station Hill?' asked Anthony.

For an answer, Mrs Moulton pointed over the platform fence. 'There.'

Station Hill was a long, steep road, dusty white with chalk, leading out of Swayling. The village made a start up the hill then straggled to a halt, leaving the road to run on between fields and woods. There was a substantial wood which cloaked the crown of the slope, and, at the very top, a distant gleam of white from the walls of a house.

'That's my house,' added Mrs Moulton with a wry smile. 'Right on the edge of Ticker's Wood. It's quite a pull up. That's where I saw your mother, Tara. It's one of her favourite rides. I've seen her go into the woods a few times.'

'The horse was found near the Slough,' said Anthony. 'Is it possible to get to the Slough from Ticker's Wood?'

Mrs Moulton pulled a face. 'It's *possible*,' she admitted reluctantly, 'but the path through the woods is very boggy and neglected and there's a couple of fields to cross.'

'It's a way back to Starhanger, though,' said Tara. She clutched at Anthony's arm. 'That must be it. We've been looking in the wrong place. Can we go? Can we go and look now?'

They walked into Ticker's Wood. The path was nothing more than a dirt track, the surface churned up by horses' hooves and thrown into deep ruts by cartwheels. Mrs Moulton's house, a little gem of a Georgian building, stood behind them, just visible through the trees.

Anthony had sent his bag back to Starhanger with Kindred and he and Tara accepted a lift up the hill from Mrs Moulton in the trap driven by her handyman, Ralph.

Anthony was glad Mrs Moulton hadn't come into the woods. Tara was jumping with nerves. She could only, he thought, stand so much of Mrs Moulton's rather clumsy kindness.

It was a walk Anthony would have usually enjoyed, with the sun glancing through the rustling delicate green of the young beech leaves, picking out clumps of purple violets and yellow dandelions, but Tara was so keyed-up she seemed on the point of panic. She was almost, Anthony thought, what the Scots called fey.

'Something awful's happened,' she said, her voice so low Anthony could hardly hear her. He tried to say something comforting but he couldn't find the words.

Tara turned on him suddenly, her eyes studying his face. 'Why are you here?'

'Miss O'Bryan—' he began but she cut him off.

'You're not *real*! You don't really care. You're pretending, aren't you? You're not a friend.'

Profoundly uncomfortable, Anthony glanced away, unable to meet her intense stare, and there, amongst the scrubby undergrowth, he saw a flower – an odd flower – of shining black, nearly covered by harebells. It was rounded and regular. Tara picked it up with a little cry. It was a lady's riding hat.

'Look,' she said in a choked voice. 'It's my mother's.'

With the hat in her hand she stopped, looking round intently. The rustling shade of the woods seemed suddenly sinister, a closed-in green world.

Anthony saw it first, a bundle of brown huddled up beside a moss-covered fallen trunk. The trunk was rotten with decay and loaded with fungus. Anthony had never liked fungus.

'Stay here,' he said, suddenly desperate to save her from seeing the worst, but Tara hardly heard him.

She walked towards the trunk like someone in a trance. The fungus had been broken, leaving clumps of black slime.

Anthony looked acutely at the rough bark of the trunk, the lichen, the moss and the fungus. He knew what the brown bundle was and was putting off facing it.

Tara still hadn't caught on. Anthony gritted his teeth and turned it over. It wasn't nice. It wouldn't have been anyway, but two days in warm, damp woodland hadn't helped.

Tara screamed.

They'd found Veronica O'Bryan all right. She'd been shot.

ELEVEN

Anthony caught hold of Tara and took her to the side of the path where they sat on the grassy verge.

Anthony knew he was speaking a stream of discon-nected, comforting words. He hardly knew what he said and Tara didn't hear him. She sat with her arms gathered round her knees, a tight, defensive ball shutting out the rotting tree trunk and the dreadful bundle beside it. After what seemed like a very long time she raised her head. Her eyes, wide and circled as if they'd been rimmed with soot, stared past him. Her whole body was trembling.

She drew a deep breath and Anthony saw her blink and focus, seeing him once more. Dragging the words out she managed to speak. 'How? *How?*'

'She was shot,' Anthony said, awkwardly.

Tara shuddered once more and bowed her head onto her knees.

Again, time passed. Anthony heard her breathing steady.

'Can you walk?' he asked gently.

She nodded and, like a stiff puppet, let herself be helped to her feet and, with his arm around her, allowed him to guide her down the path to Mrs Moulton's house.

The door was opened by an elderly, neatly-dressed maid. She looked a sensible woman and, thank goodness, knew Tara.

'Why, Miss O'Bryan, whatever is it? Have you had an accident?'

Anthony admired Tara then; she straightened her shoulders and raised her chin. He let her speak, knowing it was important for Tara, the self-possessed Tara, to get back a measure of control.

'I'm all right, Doris, but my mother . . .' Her voice faltered but she forced herself to continue, 'she's dead. We've just found her body.'

Her voice broke on the word 'body' and it galvanized the maid into action. In an incredibly short space of time they were gathered into the sitting room where there was warmth and comfort. Mrs Moulton took charge and Anthony was glad to let her do it.

She insisted on Tara drinking a cup of hot tea laced with sugar and brandy, dispatched the gardener into the woods to watch over the body, instructed Doris to prepare a room for Tara and, summoning her husband, sent him off on his bicycle to the village with a prescription Anthony had written for a sedative.

Anthony knew he should inform the police but he didn't want Tara badgered by the local bobby. The police could wait until he'd seen Tara properly taken care of and upstairs out of harm's way in Mrs Moulton's spare room. Mrs Moulton, who had a healthy disregard for authority, agreed with him completely.

Tara didn't want him to go. Her earlier suspicions of him forgotten, she clung to his hand until Mrs Moulton, with brisk sympathy, dispatched him downstairs. 'Now you just rest a while, Tara, dear, and don't worry about what's to be done. There's plenty of time to sort it all out afterwards.'

All that took time, a great deal of time, and it was over an hour later before Anthony could get back to the railway station and the nearest telephone.

Naturally enough, the first person he rang wasn't a policeman, it was Sir Charles.

He weighed his words carefully while waiting for the trunk call to be put through. He knew the operator in the telephone exchange at the rear of the post office wasn't supposed to listen to calls, but human nature makes short shrift of rules.

Sir Charles's voice came on the line and Anthony braced himself. 'Uncle Albert?' he asked.

There was an infinitesimal pause before Sir Charles replied. 'Good to hear from you, dear boy,' he said jovially. 'Still in the village?'

'I'm still in Swayling, yes.' Sir Charles, he noticed, hadn't used any proper names. The mention of Uncle Albert had warned him to feel his way cautiously. 'That job you asked me to do,' he continued, 'is finished. It's over. In fact you could say we've come to a dead end.' There was a longer pause this time.

'A *dead* end?' repeated Sir Charles.

'I'm afraid so. Normally I'd do it –' he paused – 'like a shot but it's murder down here.'

An even longer pause followed. 'Does Bobby know?' asked Sir Charles.

'I'm going to tell him soon. He'll be able to fill you in in about an hour or so. I'd like Bobby to speak to me, though.'

'All right,' said Sir Charles. 'I'll see he has a word with you. Shall I do that right away?'

'Yes. You'd better make a note of this address.' Anthony gave him the Moultons' address. 'I can be reached here for the time being, but I want to have a look round. Can you ask Bobby if that's OK?'

'I'm sure that'll be fine,' Sir Charles agreed. 'Is there anything more I can do for you? I wish I could get down but it won't be possible, I'm afraid.'

'No, I can see that.' And he could. If Sir Charles wanted to carry on pretending to be nothing more than a government official he could hardly take a visible part in investigating a murder. 'I think that's all at the moment. I'll keep in touch.'

'Good man. And I'll speak to Bobby.'

Anthony rang off, drew a deep breath, picked up the receiver and had a rather less elliptical conversation with the local police sergeant or, as Sir Charles would have said, Bobby. The sergeant was clearly puzzled by his request that he should get in touch with his chief constable before coming out to the Moultons' but he agreed all the same.

Anthony put the phone down and did a rapid calculation. At a guess Sir Charles would even now be talking to the chief constable, who, please God, would be both present and cooperative. That should give him some time to see Veronica O'Bryan's body alone.

It felt odd going up that woodland track again, consciously retracing Veronica O'Bryan's last journey. The weather had been fine recently and the track, churned into ruts by heavy cartwheels, was dry and useless for footprints. He knew from Mrs Moulton that the woods were used for timber. There were some muddy patches to the side, incised with the crescents of horses' hooves, but no footprints. That was much as he'd expected. There was no very good reason why Veronica O'Bryan or her murderer should have sought out the few muddy puddles which remained.

It seemed to be a much shorter walk than he remembered. A little more than five minutes from the Moultons brought him to the rotting tree trunk.

He dispatched the gardener back home and crouched down beside the body. The bullet had passed more or less through the centre of the forehead at a slight upwards angle. There was an exit wound on the upper parietal bone – or, thought Anthony, translating it into the layman's language that Sir Charles would want – the top of the back of her head. That was an entirely natural way to shoot someone who was coming straight towards you and he couldn't read anything significant into the upwards direction of the shot. As he knew, all guns tend to jerk upwards. It took quite a bit of training to hold a pistol steady.

When he'd first found the body all he'd really taken in was that Veronica O'Bryan had been shot and that two days lying face downwards in a damp wood hadn't improved matters.

Now, without Tara, he was able to consider that badly discoloured face more closely. There was a bruise on her cheek and a scratch on her neck, but no other sign of a struggle. Where had she actually been shot?

They'd found her hat in a clump of harebells by the track. He went to investigate. Once again, there were no footprints and the grass had had plenty of time to recover, but on the track itself the dried mud was stained with blood. So this was where Veronica O'Bryan had died. He raised his eyes. A few yards away stood an ash tree, its trunk chipped with a new splinter. That's where the bullet had gone. Now he knew where Veronica O'Bryan had been shot, it was easy to see the telltale marks of broken twigs, disturbed pebbles and crushed plants which marked out where she had been dragged to the trunk.

He stepped back from the trunk to get a full picture of the slope leading to the track and caught his sleeve on a mass of brambles. He shook himself free, leaving a snag of tweed on the thorns and there, slightly lower, were caught some blue-grey tweed threads. The murderer's? Maybe. He put a couple of threads carefully in his pocketbook, leaving the rest for the police.

He glanced at his watch. He didn't have long before the police turned up, but he wanted to see if he could glean anything more from the woods. The track pretty soon petered out into a clearing which, from the ruts on the ground, looked as if it was used for turning the foresters' carts. Beyond the clearing, the path was little used, but the grass, ferns and nettles showed signs of the passage of a heavy animal and, in a damp patch of mud, there was the clear print of a horseshoe. Presumably beyond the wood led the fields and beyond them, the Slough.

Anthony walked back to Veronica O'Bryan's body and sat on the grassy verge. He took out his pipe, tamping down the tobacco thoughtfully.

Veronica O'Bryan had found out about the diamonds on Friday night. She'd want to get that information to someone – call them Mr X – as quickly as possible. She'd be wary of the telephone and a telegram was hardly safe, either.

The robbery of the diamonds and maps and Warren's murder had happened on the Sunday, which didn't leave enough time for a letter, from this rural district, to arrive. What she could do, however, was telephone or telegram Mr X to ask him to meet her at a prearranged spot. This spot. Mrs Moulton had said she'd seen Veronica O'Bryan pass by her house into the woods before.

There was another thing, too. He remembered Tara sitting down on the bench beside him on Saturday morning, just before he'd discovered 'Frankie's Letter'. *The house is like a morgue. I don't know where everyone's got to* . . . At a guess, Veronica O'Bryan had gone to the post office in the village. She wouldn't want to telephone from Starhanger.

He got to his feet as the whistle of a train sounded in the valley. Walking down the hill to where the trees petered out into a scrubby fringe, he looked down into the snuggle of houses that was Swayling.

A gleaming stretch of railway wriggled along the bottom of the valley and he saw a train looking, at this distance, like something from a child's toy box.

He strolled back to the grassy verge. Yes; Veronica O'Bryan had contacted Mr X on Saturday morning and arranged to meet him that afternoon. Granted that Mrs Moulton hadn't seen a car, Mr X had come by train. And that meant that, with even a little bit of luck, someone at the station would have seen him. Anthony smiled grimly to himself. This was hanging together.

By Saturday afternoon, Veronica O'Bryan didn't just have the diamonds to report, she would have wanted help to escape and if the fair-haired robber, Warren's murderer and Chapman's killer was X, then Veronica would have asked in vain.

She had failed. By her own admission 'Frankie's Letter' was a busted flush and she had moved from asset to liability. The fair-haired X, who seemed to have a pretty short way with human obstacles, shot her and moved her body to the fallen tree.

It was a good place, he thought, both for secret meetings and to hide a body. Apart from the occasional forester it seemed little used and Veronica O'Bryan was literally off the beaten track. If it hadn't been for Mrs Moulton, they could have been looking for Veronica O'Bryan for a very long time.

He looked up as he heard voices along the path and the policemen came into view along the tree-girded track. There were a uniformed constable and sergeant and an older man who turned out to be Major Rendall, the chief constable himself. He drew Anthony to one side, out of earshot of the policemen.

Sir Charles had spoken to him and although the chief constable had no choice but to cooperate, Anthony could tell he was unenthusiastic about surrendering his responsibilities to someone who he felt sure categorized him as: 'a jumped-up doctor, one of these Intelligence types, calls himself a colonel, by Gad! I'd like to show him what real soldiering is about!'

The fact Anthony didn't actually want to ride roughshod over him, his men or his procedures and had no desire to give orders to his officers, mollified the major, and when Anthony said they were after a murderer in the pay of the Germans who had killed Peter Warren, Cedric Chapman and had probably killed Veronica O'Bryan as well, Major Rendall was beside himself.

'I've been saying it for years, Colonel,' he snorted, using the title without the audible inverted commas with which he'd adorned it with earlier. 'For years we've let the scum of the earth stroll in to this country without a by-your-leave and look where it's got us! An innocent woman murdered out-of-hand' – Anthony didn't see fit to correct his impression of Veronica O'Bryan's character – 'by some damn foreigner.'

'We're not sure the murderer was a foreigner,' Anthony said mildly.

Anthony thought the chief constable was going to go pop. A German running round killing people was bad enough but to have an Englishman doing it was far, far worse.

By the time they'd finished he was so eager to help that he was disappointed when he found all Anthony wanted was to be kept informed of anything his men should uncover and to lend his weight to Anthony's enquiries at the railway station.

The porter, a Mr Hawley, was sitting on his wooden truck, reading a newspaper. The news had travelled fast. Hawley knew all about the discovery of Veronica O'Bryan's body in Ticker's Wood and, with the official presence of Major Rendall looming behind him, Anthony had no trouble in getting the porter to speak about what he felt would be the main topic of conversation for years to come.

'I reckon we'll be in the paper ourselves when this gets out,' said Hawley, rising stiffly to his feet. 'You're looking for someone off the Lonnon train, you say?' He scratched his chin. 'It's been a couple of days now. The Lonnon train . . . There weren't that many on it, as I recall. Peggy Postling and the Sykeses. Young Wilfred Gordon, he's back on leave, and . . .' Mr Hawley looked up brightly. 'There was another man, sir. He slipped my mind for the moment.'

'Can you describe him?' asked Major Rendall briskly.

Mr Hawley looked puzzled. 'I don't know as I can,' he said slowly. 'I didn't take much notice.'

'What about his clothes?' Anthony asked, trying to pin the porter down to something concrete.

Hawley shrugged. 'Nothing out of the way. He had a dark coat, I think, and a bowler hat. There was nothing special about him.'

'He wasn't fair-haired, was he?'

Again Hawley shrugged. 'I didn't notice as he was. He was just an ordinary sort of bloke.'

Something in Hawley's answer jarred on Anthony. What on earth was it? He looked at Hawley thoughtfully. Like most railway staff he seemed honest and helpful but . . . Bingo! He'd said 'bloke'.

There are few men, as Anthony well knew, as socially aware as railway porters. Their livelihood, like taxi-drivers and hotel commissionaires, depends on them being able to sum up a person's class at a glance, to know that the old lady in the ancient coat is a real lady and good for sixpence, that Flash Harry in his cheap finery will sling a shilling to impress his girlfriend and that a careworn mother or cautious clerk will never part with more than tuppence, however much help they receive. It seemed highly unlikely that Mr Hawley would ever describe a man such as Warren's killer as a bloke.

'He wasn't a gentleman, was he? A toff?' he asked.

Hawley gave a slow smile. 'A toff, sir? Not on your life.' The smile faded. 'There was nothing to him, sir,' he added with a touch of irritation. 'Nothing you could get hold of, I mean.'

The word 'nondescript' formed in Anthony's mind. He gave a jump. Hawley wasn't describing Cedric Chapman's killer but Cedric Chapman himself.

Anthony picked up Mr Hawley's discarded newspaper and there, on the front page, was what he was looking for: 'Kingsway Tram Victim Identified' together with a photograph of Chapman. Sir Charles had authorized its release to the press.

Anthony slewed the paper round so Hawley could see it and immediately knew he was right. His face was a picture.

'Well, I'll be blowed,' he kept muttering. 'Who'd have thought it? Him! On my platform!'

Major Rendall was less impressed. Chapman was dead and therefore the fun of the chase had departed. He stroked his moustache gloomily. 'So that's the chappie, is it? Well, he got what was coming to him all right. What was he doing down here, eh?'

'I don't know,' said Anthony honestly enough, for he didn't. He could guess, but that wasn't knowledge.

The major roused himself from his disappointment. 'It's a case of tying up loose ends now, eh, Colonel? I suppose we'd better call at Starhanger. Mr and Mrs Sherston need to be officially informed.'

'Yes, we'd better call,' agreed Anthony. And after that, he thought, he'd better retrieve his bag and leave. He had come to Starhanger to find Veronica O'Bryan and that was exactly what he'd done.

*   *   *

'So how did Sherston take the news?' asked Sir Charles later that day. They were sitting in Sir Charles's room, the room that always reminded Anthony of a gentleman's club.

'He was thunderstruck,' said Anthony, lighting a cigarette. 'His reaction seemed absolutely genuine, Talbot.' He smiled briefly. 'As a matter of fact he wanted me to investigate.'

'What?'

Anthony nodded. 'That's right. I refused, of course. I told him to wait for the coroner's inquest. I'll have to attend that, of course, as I found the body, but they more or less have to bring in a verdict of murder by Cedric Chapman. Sherston realized that, but couldn't begin to imagine, or so he said, what a crook like Chapman was doing in Ticker's Wood and he certainly couldn't imagine what had taken Veronica O'Bryan there. Now whether he was simply meeting trouble head on, I don't know. After all, he knows exactly who I am, so, if he is involved, he'll know it's an odds-on certainty that I'll investigate Mrs O'Bryan's death.'

'How did Mrs Sherston react?' asked Sir Charles curiously.

Anthony shrugged. 'Very badly, considering we know Veronica O'Bryan wasn't one of her bosom chums. When the chief constable told her the news, I thought she was going to faint. That was quite genuine, by the way,' he added. 'As the doctor on the spot, I can testify to it.'

He paused remembering the scene. Josette had been horrified at the news. 'I knew it,' she had constantly repeated. 'I knew she was dead. I just knew it. I knew something dreadful had happened.'

'Anyway,' he continued, 'we got her up to her room and I prescribed a sedative and waited until her own doctor arrived. That got me upstairs,' he added. 'So I took advantage of the situation and, when the maid thought I was safely downstairs, had another look in Veronica O'Bryan's room.' Sir Charles looked at him alertly. 'I found this,' said Anthony, taking an envelope from his briefcase.

He opened the envelope and carefully shook the contents onto the desk. There were charred scraps of writing paper, browned and burnt, but with the occasional word still visible.

'They were in the grate,' said Anthony. 'They'd fallen into the firebox. I should've checked the firebox when I searched the first time but after I found the papers in the jewellery box, I didn't think to examine the fireplace. It struck me afterwards that although Mrs O'Bryan might have thought her letters in the jewellery box were safe enough, she had very little time on Saturday morning to dispose of anything else and the obvious thing to do was burn any incriminating papers. There's at least one sentence – or part of a sentence anyway – that I recognize.'

Sir Charles turned on the desk light and examined the scraps closely. '"Frankie's Letter",' he said. 'These are notes for "Frankie's Letter".' He carefully put the scraps of paper back in the envelope. 'I'll have these read. There's probably more that can be gleaned, but the central fact of them being "Frankie's Letter" is clear enough.'

He sat down at the desk again. 'So, what now? I'd give a year of my life to grill Sherston, but that's not possible, damnit.' He looked at Anthony squarely. 'What do you think, Brooke? Is he involved or not?'

Anthony hesitated. 'He could be,' he said eventually. 'On the one hand, his reaction to Veronica O'Bryan's death seemed absolutely genuine. On the other hand, if he knew about it, he'd be prepared. When I turned up in company with the chief constable, he'd guess that Veronica O'Bryan's body had been found.'

'Was he upset?'

Anthony shook his head slowly. 'Not excessively so, but he did seem shocked. He told me privately that Veronica had been awkward to live with, particularly since he got married. There's been a lot of tension between her and Mrs Sherston.'

'So why didn't he make her an allowance and suggest she live elsewhere? That's what everyone expected him to do.'

'I asked him that – or, at least, I made it possible for him to volunteer the information. He was concerned for Tara. He thinks the world of her, you know. She's more like a daughter than a niece to him. Veronica had a very uncertain temper and he thought they were better off living with him where, as he put it, he could help take the burden of motherhood off her shoulders.' Anthony sighed. 'That rings true. I simply don't know about Sherston. He might be stringing me along. He's clever enough, that's for sure.'

Sir Charles put his hands behind his head and leaned back in his chair. 'That more or less sums up what I think. Let's say the jury's still out, as far as he's concerned.'

He paused reflectively. '"Frankie's Letter" is finished. That's something, a great big something. However, our killer's out there and we still don't know what atrocity is planned for the fourteenth of June. That's getting horribly close. If we can't find out something soon, we're sunk. We know it's something to do with this Irish-German alliance. Incidentally, I've got confirmation of that from another source. We've got a contact in Camden Town who picks up gossip in the Irish clubs. He's heard a whisper of something big planned.'

He tilted his chair forward. He looked, thought Anthony, so tired he was haggard. 'I don't know what they're planning, but it's evil, Brooke. I hoped Veronica O'Bryan would lead us to the truth, but she's quite literally dead and gone. I wish to God I could work out what to *do*.'

Anthony pushed his chair back and, getting to his feet, walked to the window. 'I've got an idea,' he said at last. 'I couldn't carry it off for long, but it might work for a short time. You've been trying to find out what's planned through the Irish end. What about the German angle? I can be a very convincing German. Let it be known, through your Camden Town man or whoever, that a German agent – me – has landed in Britain and is awaiting further instructions. Even if they guess I'm a phoney, they'll still want to see who I am, but I think we can pull it off. I'd need a lot more information if I was going to pretend to be a German agent for any length of time, but it should be all right for a couple of hours.' He looked at Sir Charles. 'It might give us the break we've been looking for.'

'You're a brave man, Brooke,' muttered Sir Charles. He swallowed. 'A damn brave man.' He drummed his fingers on the desk. 'You do know this is dangerous?'

Anthony nodded. 'Of course I know. You said we were up against something evil. That's not a word you use lightly.'

'No,' said Sir Charles. 'No, it's not.' Relief showed in his eyes. 'It's a chance. My God, it's a real chance. We'll have to think up a credible place for you to stay and a credible character for you to be. It won't take long to put the word out that you've arrived.' He gave a little grunt of annoyance. 'What about the inquest?'

'I'll have to go,' said Anthony after a few moments' thought. 'If I don't, it'll be noted, and we might as well tell the enemy I'm engaged elsewhere.'

'Fair enough,' agreed Sir Charles. 'Now, what name shall we give you?'

TWELVE

Late on Friday evening, John Robinson, a tall, soldierly-looking man with dark hair greying at the temples, disembarked from the *Maid Of Orford.*

The *Maid Of Orford,* a little tub of a boat, regularly plied between the Hook of Holland and Harwich and had, on this trip, been carrying a mixed cargo of lard, chair legs, tallow, stair rods and, as a seeming afterthought, four passengers.

John Robinson had, as the other passengers knew, been in Holland and the Low Countries, buying pigs' bristles for artists' oil brushes. What John Robinson – not so obvious a name as John Smith but still commonplace enough for a German to think of as typically English – knew about artists' oil brushes he owed to an intensive couple of hours with Nathaniel Burgh of Minsmere and Burgh, Artists' Requisites, on Wednesday morning. He had been more than happy to share his knowledge with the other passengers on the *Maid Of Orford.*

The trip to the Hook of Holland for the express purpose of bouncing back across the North Sea in a wallowing tramp cargo boat had been Anthony's idea. Not that he thought of himself as Anthony Brooke anymore. He was Günther Hedtke of Kiel, a German explosives expert pretending to be John Robinson of London. If his vowels were slightly too clipped and his manners rather too formal, that was Hedtke's personality showing through. Anthony had begun to be quite fond of Günther Hedtke in the short time he had known him.

He booked in the Ocean Hotel and waited.

The busy Ocean Hotel was, he thought as he drank a glass of watery wartime beer in the bar that evening, a good choice. Most of the men in the bar were in groups of twos and threes but there were a couple of solitary drinkers.

A thin man in a drab raincoat interested him. There was a pianist in the bar, entertaining the crowd with a selection of sentimental modern songs and ragtime, but the thin man, although he sat near the piano and had the newspaper spread out before him, didn't seem to be reading or listening to the music. Oddly enough, the newspaper was open at today's stirring account of an 'Intrepid Briton's Adventures in the Heart of the Kaiser's Empire'. He, thought Anthony, looked promising.

Waiting until the solitary man had nearly finished his beer, he drained his glass and went to the bar. With a prickle of anticipation he saw the solitary man stand up and, empty glass in hand, come to the bar. The jostle the solitary man gave him seemed reasonably natural in the crowd, but it wasn't.

'I beg your pardon, sir,' said the solitary man.

Anthony politely – perhaps too politely for an Englishman – said it was of no consequence. Contact established.

The solitary man looked over his shoulder at the pianist. 'I wish he'd play some of the old songs,' said the solitary man, and paused expectantly. His voice had the nasal twang of a Liverpool accent.

Anthony swore under his breath. That was a cue if he'd ever heard one. Sir Charles had told him the signs and countersigns that were known to be currently in use, but there were no songs among them. The best he could do was pretend not to have twigged and hope for the best.

The solitary man waited, a slight frown creasing his forehead. 'You know, something with a real tune to it,' he prompted.

Anthony smiled politely.

'An Irish song, perhaps?'

There were hundreds of Irish songs. Anthony continued to smile.

'Like *The Minstrel Boy*?' suggested the solitary man.

It was as well Anthony's mind was running on songs and Irish songs, at that. He supplied the next line quickly. '*To the war has gone, in the ranks of death you'll find him.*'

The Liverpudlian's face cleared. 'I thought you were never going to get it. How about joining me for a drink?'

'My apologies,' Anthony muttered quietly as they sat down at the table by the piano. 'It was very natural, very good, the way you introduced yourself. For the moment I did not realize.'

'You'll have to be a bit quicker off the mark next time,' said the man in a low voice. 'It's lucky I saw you come in on the boat. Otherwise I might just have walked away. You're for London. The big one. If it comes off,' he added unexpectedly.

'Wednesday? The fourteenth?' suggested Anthony.

'That's the one,' agreed the man. 'You'll be contacted next Tuesday.'

'That is a long time,' said Anthony, making his disappointment evident. In one way it suited him very well indeed, as the inquest on Veronica O'Bryan was fixed for Monday, but he was conscious of time slipping away.

The man shrugged. 'It can't be helped. The boss has got something else on. We don't need you till the day itself. We can pull this off alone, but expert help is always welcome, I suppose. Stay in the hotel and make yourself useful. There's a lot of shipping in and out of the docks but don't draw attention to yourself.'

'I am here to make things go with a bang, yes?' said Anthony carefully. 'That is a good way of putting it?'

The man grinned. 'It's a very good way. But listen, Mr Robinson –' Anthony had not introduced himself – 'if you'll be guided by me, you'll not talk to too many strangers. You speak English very well but you've got a way of saying things that might arouse attention.'

'That is good advice,' agreed Anthony, enunciating the words carefully.

The man raised his eyebrows and finished his drink in a few gulps. 'I'm off. Don't stand up as I go. It's not necessary. The chances are you'll bow and click your heels,' he added, more to himself than Anthony.

Anthony looked crestfallen. 'No, this I will not do. It is not the custom here.'

'Just watch who you're speaking to,' the man advised. 'See you, Mr Robinson.' The man stood up, put on his cap, and left.

Anthony sat back. He gave an inward sigh of relief but he was careful not to show too much satisfaction. After all, you never knew who was watching.

The rest of the weekend passed without incident. As Mr Robinson, Anthony stayed quietly at the hotel, ate, slept, walked round the town and noted the shipping in the harbour.

In the very early hours of Monday morning, he departed for London and his club, from where he emerged as Anthony Brooke, complete with uniform, to catch the train to Swayling to give evidence at Veronica O'Bryan's inquest.

The inquest was held at Swayling Assembly Rooms in the middle of the village. To his relief, there were no cameras and precious few reporters. Sherston was in a position to curb the enthusiasm of the gentlemen of Fleet Street.

It was as he was going up the steps into the Assembly Rooms that Anthony felt a definite sense of unease. He stopped and glanced round the crowd, but they were, as far as he could see, only locals.

Nevertheless, as the inquest got under way, his unease grew. Maybe, he thought, as he took the stand and, in answer to the coroner's question, affirmed his identity, it was nothing more than having to declare in public exactly who he was and where he lived. Maybe it was the heart-wrenching sight of Josette, so near and yet so remote, her face strained with nerves. She seemed to be finding the proceedings even more difficult than Tara, whose determined bravery in recounting the discovery of her mother's body won the immediate sympathy of the coroner, courtroom and jury. Maybe – but he didn't quite believe it.

Tara conducted herself with great dignity. *The daughter and only child of the deceased.* That was how she was described.

Only child? There was the little girl in the photograph with 'To Mummy' written across it. Her solemn eyes tugged a chord of memory. Was she really Tara's half-sister? Perhaps, thought Anthony, dissatisfied. She looked an engaging sort of kid, the little girl in the photograph. He'd always liked kids. He'd love to see her smile. Maybe then he would see the resemblance that he frustratingly couldn't sharpen into focus.

The inquest brought in the predictable verdict of wilful murder against Cedric Chapman. Anthony was making his way out of the Assembly Rooms, when his sense of danger flared. He stopped dead. At the back of the crowd was a flurry of movement. At that precise moment Sherston caught up with him and took him by the elbow.

'Can we offer you some refreshment up at the house, my dear fellow?'

'Thank you,' said Anthony abstractedly. 'Yes, thank you very much.'

A little way up the street, walking away very rapidly, Anthony saw the back of a man. As he turned the corner, Anthony could see he was tall and stiff-shouldered, dressed in a dark topcoat and carrying a black stick with a glint of silver at the handle. Under his soft hat Anthony could have sworn he saw a glimpse of fair hair.

Anthony tried to break through the crowd, but the throng on the pavement was too great.

'Is there something wrong?' asked Sherston.

Anthony reluctantly turned back with a shrug of disappointment. 'It's nothing. I thought I saw someone I recognized.'

So he'd been watched. Well, Cedric Chapman had known enough about him to search his rooms, and the fair-haired man was, he had guessed, Chapman's boss. It wasn't remarkable that he should be observed but he still didn't like it.

'You must be mistaken, Colonel,' said Josette. 'Anyone who recognized you would've spoken to you, surely?'

Sherston ushered them both towards the waiting car where they stood, waiting for Tara. Sherston looked dissatisfied. 'I'm glad the inquest's over, but I can't say I'm much wiser. I still can't work out why Veronica was in Ticker's Wood.'

'Do stop, Patrick!' said Josette sharply. She looked at Anthony apologetically. 'I'm sorry, Colonel, but we've gone over this endlessly. I don't know how poor Tara has coped.' She gave them both a warning glance as Tara approached. 'There you are, my dear.'

'What an absolute waste of time!' said Tara. 'I still don't know why my mother was killed.'

'Tara, don't!' pleaded Josette with a shudder. 'You mustn't brood about it. It can't be good for you.'

Tara, pale and heavy-eyed, put her hand on Josette's arm. 'Maybe it isn't, but I find it easier to face things, rather than ignoring them.'

'But you can't *do* anything,' said Josette, sympathetically.

Tara squeezed her arm. 'You are sweet, Josette,' she said seriously. 'Both you and Uncle Patrick couldn't have been more thoughtful. I know you hate anything violent, and I do appreciate your kindness. We won't talk about it if you'd rather not. Perhaps it is better that way.'

Josette looked relived. As they settled into the car, she hunted round for another topic of conversation. 'Colonel, have you seen the articles in the *Sentinel*? The ones about you, I mean?'

'They've caused an absolute sensation,' said Sherston proudly. 'I've rarely known anything like it. By jingo, Colonel, if anyone had the slightest idea that you were the man all the fuss is about, even I couldn't have kept the press away from the inquest. Have you seen the German Town we're building? That's drawing in crowds already and it isn't finished yet.'

Once started, he happily talked about the Town and the *Sentinel* all the way to Starhanger. It was a relief when Anthony, pleading a train to catch, could finally slip away.

It was getting on for dusk when he arrived back at the Ocean Hotel, a golden evening, with the sun catching the clouds in pinks and blues in the big East Anglian sky. As far as he could tell, no one on the journey from Swayling to London had evinced any interest in him or, thank goodness, Günther Hedtke (alias John Robinson) as he went on from Liverpool Street Station to Harwich.

The evening really was lovely, thought Anthony as he walked back from the station, far too pleasant to stay in the bar of the hotel.

He'd picked up a paper at the station and, sitting on the sea wall at Dovercourt, he turned to the latest breathless account of his doings.

Sherston had captured the excitement all right, but what he couldn't describe were the slips which were covered up, the accusations a hairs-breadth away, the sick feeling of over-tightened nerves suddenly relaxed, and the queer bravado which took the place of caution. Yes, it was probably as well he'd left Germany when he did. He had a suspicion he wouldn't have lasted much longer.

He stuffed the paper into his pocket and, with his pipe drawing nicely, walked away from the houses onto a country lane bounded by fields with the sea beyond.

A big black Daimler with its hood closed drove slowly past him. A few hundred yards further on, Anthony rounded a corner and saw the car drawn up to the verge.

A green-liveried chauffeur was standing beside the car, a map spread out on the bonnet. He looked up as Anthony approached, his face brightening with relief.

'Excuse me, sir,' he said touching his cap. 'My master's been taken ill. We've been told the nearest doctor lives on Seaview Road, but I can't find it. Can you direct me?'

'I'm sorry, I don't know the area very well,' said Anthony. 'You should find a doctor easily enough in Harwich, though.'

The chauffeur looked back at the car anxiously. 'I hope so. My master's in a bad way.'

'What's the matter with him?' asked Anthony.

The chauffeur looked puzzled. 'I think it's called mal something. He picked it up in Africa. It comes and goes. He's terribly ill if it's not treated. He sees a special doctor in London.'

The mention of Africa intrigued Anthony. 'Maybe I can help,' he suggested, saying the obvious and decent thing. 'I know something about tropical illness. It sounds as if it might be malaria,' he added, walking round to the passenger door. 'What are his symptoms?'

From behind him the chauffeur gave a funny little gasp. Anthony whirled to see the chauffeur, his face contorted, raising a rubber cosh. Anthony jerked to one side and took the blow on his shoulder.

With tracks of fire lancing down his arm, Anthony lashed out, sending the man sprawling. The chauffeur picked himself up, hefted the cosh and came at him again. This time Anthony wasn't so quick and the chauffeur caught him a glancing blow, knocking him to the ground. Dizzily, Anthony tried to pick himself up but his reactions were slow.

The chauffeur clamped a sweet-smelling pad over his face. Anthony struggled, helplessly trying to get the sickly gauze away from his mouth and nose, then the chloroform sapped his senses and the world turned to black.

He came to gradually. He tried to open his eyes but something was in the way. There was a blindfold over his eyes and a gag round his mouth. His ankles were bound and his wrists tied behind his back.

His face was pressed against the Daimler's seat and he moved fractionally, enjoying the coolness of the leather against his cheek. An engine thrummed and under his ear came the smooth swish of the tyres on the road.

He must have groaned as he woke. He knew that, and stifled any more sounds. Between the gag and the engine, the sound was muffled and he lay quietly. No one spoke and, with infinite caution, Anthony straightened out his cramped limbs, bit by bit, finding huge relief in the tiny movements.

He gradually took in his bearings. He was trussed up like a Christmas turkey in the back of the Daimler, being taken to God knows where. He felt horribly sick, a usual reaction to chloroform. He couldn't believe he'd fallen for the chauffeur's trick.

He'd been off-guard, lulled by the fixed idea that Tuesday (tomorrow? today?) was when it all kicked off.

The hook had been temptingly baited with the mention of Africa and tropical illness, and, for a few fatal seconds, he wasn't Günther Hedtke or John Robinson or even Colonel Brooke, but a doctor about to examine a patient.

Someone had done their homework and he'd come off worse as a result. He knew he should try to escape, but his brain was fogged and his body weak. He drifted back into unconsciousness, lulled by the steady throb of the engine.

The next time he came to the car had stopped. He heard a big, scraping sound that he half recognized, followed by a click. The earlier wakening had helped. This time, although weak, he was able to feign unconsciousness.

With no sight to guide him, he was dependant on his ears and his sense of smell. Wherever he was smelled oily and slightly damp and the sound had a hollow, indoor timbre.

A garage? Of course. The scraping sound was the noise of the double doors being closed. He heard the car door open and sensed someone was very close. A hand briefly lifted the cloth round his eyes.

'He's still out cold, boss.' It was the chauffeur.

'Good.'

It was one word but Anthony caught at the sound. He'd heard that voice before. He wanted the man to say more so he could place the elusive memory, but the cloth was twitched back into place and the car door slammed shut again.

There came the noise of feet walking away over a concrete floor, a door opened and closed and a key turned in the lock. His captors must have worked out their plans while he was unconscious and weren't considerate enough to discuss them now he was awake.

Why had he been left in the car? Presumably because he was to be taken somewhere else. Anthony lay still. After a few moments he became convinced he was alone. How long that would last he didn't know but it seemed likely someone would be back soon. If he was going to escape it had to be now.

He wriggled along the back seat of the car until he reached the door. Set in to the door was a projecting handle and he rubbed his face along it.

The blindfold, probably loosened by the chauffeur's inspection, rucked up. With a few more seconds work it was off altogether and he could see. He set to work on the gag and managed to get it away from his mouth. He drew a deep uninterrupted breath of satisfaction.

He was in a garage. His hands were tied behind him, but he managed to move his back against the car door and grasp the handle. As the door opened he fell out in an ungainly, painful bundle onto the cold concrete floor. He brought his legs round and, pushing his back against the car, hesitantly stood up.

The garage, dimly lit by two windows set into the double doors, was a solid room built of whitewashed brick which had once been a stable. From the light it seemed as if it was very early morning, about four o' clock or so.

He'd hoped to see a tool bench with a file or something to cut the rope round his wrists. There was nothing. He looked vainly round for inspiration. The garage was empty.

A sunbeam, the first rays of dawn, suddenly shot brilliantly though the dusty windows. He was prepared to bet he was right about the time. He *had* to hurry up. They were bound to be back before long.

The sunlight pierced through the gloom like a solid bar of gold. He had a wayward memory of a Salvation Army street meeting, complete with a brass band ompah-ing out hymns and a bonneted lady with a collecting tin. *Jesus wants me for a sunbeam* . . .

Like the pilgrim in the hymn, he followed the beam of light, inching across the floor. He levered himself up to the window, hoping to see a passer-by. There was no one. It looked as if the garage was in an old stable yard.

There was only one thing for it. He drew a deep breath, pulled his head back and smashed his forehead into the window.

It hurt. It hurt even more than he thought it would hurt and, from the blood in his eyes, he knew he'd gashed his forehead, but the window broke and, thank God, some of the glass ended up on the concrete floor.

Anthony sat with his shoulder to the doors, picked up a shard of glass and gingerly began to cut through the rope round his wrists. He couldn't see what he was doing. The glass slipped, cutting his fingers, but he managed to bring the shard between the heels of his hands.

The relief when he finally felt the bonds go was indescribable. He sat for a couple of seconds, feeling life pulse back into his arms before he wiped the blood away from his forehead and got to work on his ankles.

After rubbing life into his cramped feet, he stood up and looked at the window critically. If he cleared away the rest of the broken glass he could possibly fit through the window. He took off his jacket and wrapped it round his hand to protect it from the glass when he had a thought. The car.

Were there papers in the car? He'd better check. He opened the driver's door and slid into the seat. There were maps, a torch and a flask in the pocket of the door. He was about to look in the pocket of the passenger seat, when he heard footsteps outside.

Anthony froze in his seat. There was a gasp as the man saw the smashed window. If Anthony could open the boot, he could probably get a wrench or a jack to use as weapon – the chauffeur must have tools somewhere – but he had no time. The heavy torch could be a weapon but . . .

It was the chance of finding papers which spurred him on. As the key sounded in the lock of the garage, Anthony closed the throttle, checked the ignition and air control, pressed the self-starter and kicked down on the accelerator.

The Daimler, still warm from its journey, roared into life at the first attempt. He knocked the throttle and the air control into the right position, put his foot on the clutch, engaged first gear, released the handbrake and crashed through the doors, busting them open in a splintering explosion.

The chauffeur leapt for dear life. Anthony had a brief glimpse of a shocked white face before he wrestled the steering wheel to bring the heavy car round.

There was a ghastly screech as the side of the car scraped along the stable yard wall and then he was out onto the road.

It might have been sheer foolhardiness, but he nearly crashed the car into the line of trees on the opposite side of the street with sheer exhilaration. He knew he was laughing.

He straightened up the car and in the mirror caught sight of a black-clad figure standing in the middle of the road, silhouetted in the brilliant light. Although he only had fractions of a second to take it in, Anthony could see the sun strike steel light off something in the man's hand.

It was a gun. The silhouette raised the pistol very deliberately, cradling his right hand in his left in a trained marksman's aim, and fired twice. The first bullet smashed through the fabric hood of the

Daimler, creased past Anthony's temple and shattered the windscreen. He didn't see the second bullet but felt a thump in his left shoulder and knew he'd been hit. There wasn't any pain; Anthony knew there often wasn't for the first twenty minutes or so in an injury, but his arm felt like a lead weight.

As he squealed the car round the corner, he saw the marksman drop his arm and walk purposefully back into the yard. Anthony tried to catch the street name but all he saw was an L and a B and a collection of other letters on the road sign as he whipped past.

He came out onto the Embankment. He was in London and the stable yard must have been an old mews. He drove a few hundred yards down the Embankment like a maniac, aware at the back of his mind that it was just as well there was no traffic in this first flush of dawn.

His arm was beginning to bother him. He tried to turn the wheel and yelped with pain. Intense lights danced in front of his eyes and the lamp posts on either side of the road seemed to flicker in and out.

Driving with his good arm, he nursed what had become a brute of a car along. He turned up Horse Guards Avenue and onto Whitehall. By the time he got to the War Office he was surviving by willpower alone.

Two startled soldiers, on guard outside the main entrance, watched him shudder to an unsteady halt. By the time the car stopped, one had run towards him.

Anthony slumped over the driver's door. 'I'm Colonel Brooke,' he managed to say. 'Intelligence.'

Even as he spoke, part of him wondered why the man was gazing at him in such a bewildered way. He only realized afterwards what he looked like, with his shoulder soaked with blood, a deep gash across his temple and his forehead scarred by glass. He felt in his pocket and pulled out his cigarette case with the picture of St Michael inside and thrust it into the man's hand.

'I need Mr Monks. I need an angel.' He pointed at the building. 'Now.'

Anthony didn't really lose consciousness, but he seemed to be only half-aware of what was happening around him. The next thing he clearly knew was an intelligent-looking elderly man shaking him awake.

'You're Colonel Brooke? You need an angel?'

Anthony blinked to try and bring him into focus. Fighting to talk, he gasped out his story.

'Get to the mews. It's off the Embankment. Something like Lamb? Lamb Street? Find who owns the garage in the mews. German agents. Tried to kill me. Arrest them.' Anthony tried to get out of the car but the man restrained him.

'Easy does it.'

'It's urgent,' Anthony said, slurring his words. 'Urgent.'

'We'll take care of it. Don't you worry.'

He heard the sound of running feet as if from a long way off, knew he was going to be horribly sick, then, as all the light seemed to retreat to the end of a deep black tunnel, passed out completely.

Anthony awoke in a white-sheeted institutional bed in a hospital with rain running down the windowpanes. The rain was such a pleasant sound that he lay quietly for a few moments, listening, before the sound made him realize how thirsty he was. He turned his head and saw a nurse smiling at him.

She helped him sit up in bed, poured out a glass of water for him and helped him drink it. At that moment, no woman, not even Josette, had ever seemed as beautiful.

'Good morning, Colonel,' she said, taking his pulse. 'You're doing very well,' she added, after a pause in which she counted out the beats. 'The doctor said you'd wake up about now.'

'I need to see Mr Monks.'

'He's with the doctor.'

Anthony relaxed. 'Where am I? How long have I been out of action?'

'You're in the King Edward the Seventh and you've been unconscious for about three hours.' She walked to the door. 'I'll get Dr Gibbs.'

Dr Gibb's examination was cheerful and professional. 'I guessed you'd been chloroformed, old man,' he said. 'The blisters round your mouth are very distinctive. Don't worry about the head wound. You'll probably need a couple of aspirin for headaches, but it was a nice, clean graze. Your arm will be sore for a few days, I imagine. I understand from Mr Monks that you're a brother medico, so you know the drill.' He stepped back from the bed. 'Mr Monks is outside. I'll show him in.'

Sir Charles looked downright worried when Dr Gibbs ushered him into the room. 'What's the problem?' asked Anthony anxiously.

Sir Charles grinned and pulled a chair up to the bed. 'You, Brooke. Believe it or not, I was concerned about you. I must say you look a damn sight better than you did this morning. Symonds, one of the code people, spoke to you. He was on his way home after spending all night wrestling with a cipher. I don't know how much you remember, but you gave him some very clear instructions, considering the circumstances, then passed out. You gave him your cigarette case and he knew what the picture of St Michael meant. He called his angel, who called me. I got the police and we went in search of your captors.'

'Did you find them?'

Sir Charles hitched himself forward. 'At first I thought we'd missed the bus. By the time we found which house the garage belonged to, the owners had scarpered. The house, or rather flat, in question is 57, Lamb Row. It had been let to a Mr James Smith, who'd lived there with two menservants for the last fortnight. The car came from a commercial garage on Fenton Street.'

Anthony reached out a hand for the water. 'James Smith sounds like an alias. Is he our fair-haired man? The toff?'

Sir Charles pursed his lips. 'I think so. I couldn't find out much about him, worse luck. You clearly put the cat very much among the pigeons, though. From the condition of the flat, he and the servants left in a tearing hurry.'

He leaned forward. 'It was the car which brought the biggest prize. There was a notebook in the glove compartment, giving a description of one Günther Hedtke or John Robinson, comparing him to one Colonel Anthony Brooke.'

Anthony winced. 'I suppose that's predictable. I should've been on my guard. I thought I saw our fair-haired friend at the inquest. Presumably he smelt a rat when Robinson arrived out of the blue.'

Sir Charles nodded agreement. 'It's probably these damned articles in the *Sentinel* that's done it, but James Smith wants you very badly. There were detailed instructions in the notebook for your capture. They know you're a doctor with an interest in tropical medicine, but, what's perhaps more interesting, is what was going to happen to you after you were safely nabbed.'

Anthony looked at Sir Charles suspiciously. 'What was going to happen? You look very smug all of a sudden. You've got an ace up your sleeve. Go on.'

Sir Charles smiled expansively. 'You were going to be picked up by U-boat.'

'I don't see why you're so happy about it.'

Sir Charles held up a finger. 'Listen. Between midnight and two o'clock tonight, a U-boat will be inside the Goodwin Sands, off the coast between Sandwich and Deal. I've got the map reference. The U-boat will flash a signal, Mr Smith will reply and the U-boat lands a boat and takes you off to dear old Germany. Brilliant, eh?'

'I still don't see why you're so thrilled about it.'

'There's more in the notebook. One of the purposes of the U-boat was to deliver a radio transmitter to Mr Smith. The inference is that he hasn't got one, which makes our job all the easier. And, knowing how bulky they are, I'm not surprised. We've captured three since the beginning of the war and they'll be the devil's own job to replace. I think Mr Smith is out of touch with home.'

'Yes, you're probably right.' Anthony looked at Sir Charles suspiciously. 'There's something else, isn't there?'

Sir Charles nodded. 'I saved the best till last. The U-boat is going to give Mr Smith his final instructions for the twenty-ninth.'

'What!' Anthony thrust the bedclothes back in his agitation. 'The twenty-ninth!'

Sir Charles rubbed his hands together and grinned broadly. 'Stay where you are, man,' he added. 'At long last, we've got a chance. And not before time, too,' he added, sobering.

'So what's the plan?'

Sir Charles pushed back his chair and walked round the room. 'We do what James Smith would have done. We flash the signal and, hey presto! We've got a U-boat that'll come meekly in, like a dog to heel. James Smith can't do a thing about it.'

Anthony's eyes widened. 'I see what you mean. He can't get a message to Germany.'

'Exactly,' said Sir Charles with satisfaction. 'Thank God you brought us that car, Brooke. I think our luck's finally turned.'

THIRTEEN

D r Gibb wanted his patient to stay in bed. Eventually he compromised and allowed Anthony to leave hospital on the understanding he'd go quietly back to his club and rest. Anthony agreed to rest during the day – he was quite willing to obey Dr Gibb to that extent – and tactfully said nothing about what he intended to do that evening.

Sir Charles decided that the simplest plan was probably the best. The U-boat expected James Smith and a prisoner, and Sir Charles didn't see any reason to disappoint them. Anthony took the part of James Smith with Sir Charles as his captive, and now the two men, their collars turned up against the cold, waited.

The beach, a long foreshore of sand that stretched darkly for miles in either direction, seemed deserted. The moon was in the first quarter and its fleeting light, hidden behind scudding clouds, showed the black expanse of the North Sea with only the occasional curling tip of white as the quiet waves lapped onto the shore. Out there, Anthony knew, were the Goodwin Sands, a treacherous grave-yard for ships. Out there, Anthony knew, was a German U-boat.

A surge of triumph tingled through him as, from the dark sea, a light pierced the night.

The light flashed three times, a single, brilliant beam. Anthony thought he could just make out the bulk of a conning tower, solid black against the rippling darkness of the sea. Using the torch from James Smith's Daimler, he flashed the signal back.

For a while nothing seemed to happen, then came the distant chink of chains followed by a splash and, from far away, the creak of oars in rowlocks. Before the boat landed, a voice hailed him in German. He replied in the same language.

He waited until the keel of the boat grounded onto the beach before saying, 'Come ashore, all of you. I need some help with the prisoner.'

The boat crew shipped oars and, splashing through the shallows, hauled the boat half out of the water. The captain of the boat, a young lieutenant, waded towards him and saluted. He looked at Sir

Charles, sitting disconsolately on the sand, a little way up the beach, hunched over as if his hands and feet were tied. 'That is the prisoner?'

'Yes,' replied Anthony briskly. 'All trussed up and ready for transport. Tell your crew to carry him into the boat. He's a tricky devil. It's better that his feet remain tied.'

The lieutenant gave a brief order to the crew and they all walked up the beach.

'You have some orders for me, I believe?' asked Anthony as they trudged up the sand.

'Yes, sir,' said the lieutenant. 'And a radio transmitter. The transmitter is in the boat but I have your orders here.' He felt in the pocket of his jacket and drew out an envelope sealed with a double-headed eagle. It was addressed, prosaically enough, to James Smith.

Anthony took the envelope and put it away carefully in his inside coat pocket as they reached Sir Charles.

Anthony looked at the lieutenant apologetically. 'I'm sorry about this,' he said in German, then, in a carrying voice, added in English, 'It's all yours, Captain.'

From the dark sand rose up a party of Royal Navy sailors, guns at the ready.

The boat crew stood frozen in shock but the lieutenant lashed out. Three sailors leapt at him, bearing him to the ground. The lieutenant, scrabbling fiercely in the sand, managed to draw his revolver from its holster. Yelling a warning to the U-boat, he fired the pistol before a sailor kicked it away. He was hauled breathlessly to his feet, his arms securely held.

His eyes blazed at Anthony. 'Traitor!'

'No,' said Anthony quietly. 'No, I'm not. I'm English.'

The lieutenant's shoulders sank, looking at the grinning sailors and their dejected prisoners. 'We are all betrayed.' A gleam of hope came into his eyes. 'The U-boat will escape.'

'Sorry,' said Anthony once more. 'Take a look for yourself.' Behind the U-boat, dark against the moonlight, two British submarines had surfaced. 'It's over, I'm afraid.'

Leaving the German boat crew and the U-boat to the Royal Navy, Sir Charles and Anthony walked back up to the car. The car, with its official driver, was parked by the side of the sea road.

Anthony and Sir Charles climbed into the back and, as Sir Charles held the torch, Anthony ripped open the envelope.

It took him a little time to make sense of the closely-written German text as the writer assumed knowledge Anthony didn't have. He grunted in frustration. 'I'll say this for James Smith. He's fluent in German if he's meant to make sense of this. In fact, I bet he *is* a German. I wonder if the U-boat crew know anything about him?'

'We'll ask them, of course,' said Sir Charles, 'but I doubt it. What do the orders say?'

'Wait a moment.' Anthony waved him quiet and read on. As he reached the end, his face altered and, with a noise in the back of his throat, he put down the document and lit a cigarette.

'Well?' demanded Sir Charles again.

'They're going to kill the King and Queen,' said Anthony quietly.

'*What?*' Sir Charles's voice was incredulous. 'How?'

'There's going to be a bomb at the Marriotvale munitions works.' His voice was very even. 'There's an official visit planned – a secret official visit.' He ran his hands through his hair. 'That's court gossip, isn't it? That's exactly the sort of thing Frankie would know.'

'Never mind about that,' said Sir Charles impatiently. 'What are the details?'

'They plan to blow up the works, taking with it the King and Queen, the factory itself and all the munitions.' Anthony clamped down on his cigarette with trembling fingers. 'And all the people who work there.'

Sir Charles swallowed hard. He tried to speak, failed, and took a cigarette from his case. It took him a couple of attempts to light it. 'Marriotvale,' he muttered. 'Do you know Marriotvale, Brooke?'

Anthony did. It was a densely populated labyrinth, hugging the south side of the Thames, a maze of docks, wharves, workshops, factories and slums between Rotherhithe and Bermondsey.

'There's thousands of people,' said Sir Charles with a catch in his voice. 'Thousands.' He was silent for a few moments then asked wearily. 'When's it going to happen?'

'At ten o'clock this morning.'

'Ten o'clock?' Sir Charles swallowed. 'We'll never evacuate the area in time. We can save the King and Queen, but we'll never save the poor beggars who live there. Dear God, this is worse than I ever imagined.'

Anthony sucked at his cigarette. 'There's a chance, Talbot.' He tapped the document, his mind racing. 'These are James Smith's instructions. Berlin sees the munitions factory as a legitimate military target. They refer to the huge propaganda coup they can make out it, but they're not keen on making hay about the death of the Royal couple. Berlin wants the credit for that to go to the Sons of Hibernia.'

Sir Charles rubbed his chin with his hands. 'The King and the Kaiser are cousins, after all,' he murmured. 'Yes, I can see there'd be some reluctance. I wouldn't be surprised if the Kaiser's been bullied into this.'

Anthony shrugged. 'Perhaps. Anyway, it's been agreed but the bombers don't know that yet. James Smith's instructions are to go to an address in Marriotvale and inspect the arrangements. Then, after a successful outcome, Smith's authorized to pay a credit note for six thousand pounds' worth of German arms to be shipped to Ireland.' He looked up. 'That means it's all right, doesn't it? After all, James Smith hasn't got this letter. We have.'

Sir Charles swallowed once more and drummed his fingers on the car seat. 'I don't like to leave it to chance. It's an Irish plan, is it?'

Anthony nodded. 'I think so, yes.'

'They might decide to go ahead anyway, with or without Smith. I can't gamble on it. Not when the stakes are so high. There's far too many lives at risk. We'll have to evacuate the area, God help us.' His face twisted. 'Even so, if that damn bomb goes off, there's bound to be casualties. I don't see how it can be helped.'

Anthony smoked his cigarette down to the butt and pitched the end out of the car onto the hummocky grass. 'What if I go?' he suggested. 'What if I take James Smith's part?'

Sir Charles stared at him. 'You can't do that. What if they know him?'

'All right, I'll be someone acting on James Smith's behalf. I can say he's had an accident or something but it's a chance, Talbot. I can be a German again.' He jerked his thumb in the direction of the sea. 'I could have arrived on that submarine. We've got the address, after all. I can say that Berlin refused permission to explode the bomb. They can't argue with that.'

'I bet they can,' muttered Sir Charles.

Anthony nearly smiled. 'Even if they do, if I can just get to see this ruddy bomb, maybe I can disarm it. I can even ask them to rendezvous with me somewhere else to plan out another operation, which means you and the police can pick up the swine. In the meantime, you can evacuate the area.'

Sir Charles shook his head. 'Not while you're in the house. They'll smell a rat at once.' He chewed his lip. 'I like the idea of catching the bombers. If you can nip it in the bud, that's their precious propaganda triumph gone west.' His mouth tightened. 'Damnit, they still win, even if we do catch them. If we do manage to evacuate Marriotvale, they've still brought an entire area of London to a standstill.'

He raised his hands and let them fall helplessly. 'We're sunk, Brooke. They've won, whatever happens. If the bomb goes off, they've won. If it doesn't and we evacuate the area, all they have to do in the future is *say* there's going to be a bomb. We can't ignore it. It'll cause endless amounts of disruption and thousands of pounds worth of manufacturing time.'

'Unless I give it a go.'

Sir Charles sucked his cheeks in, then leaned forward and tapped the chauffeur on the shoulder. 'London,' he said, giving an address in Albemarle Row, Westminster. 'We're going to see the Home Secretary,' he said, turning back to Anthony. 'This is too big a decision for me to take alone.'

Anthony knocked softly at the door of 17, Nightingale Street, Marriotvale. A nightingale had never sung here. Nightingale Street was a smoke-blackened terrace among a series of smoke-blackened terraces, hunched against the looming factory wall of the Marriotvale Munitions Company.

Nightingale Street probably referred to the Crimea War, he thought, turning his collar up against the chill of the early morning. The date was about right. He felt nothing but sympathy for people who were forced to live in these jerry-built, two-up and two-down filthy slums.

He had been touched by the sight of a little street shrine, at the corner of the road. A jam jar of wilting flowers stood in front of a handwritten notice listing the names of dead soldiers from the surrounding streets. Marriotvale had very little to give, but it had been given.

He glanced at his watch and knocked once more. This time there was a sound of movement in the house, a few muffled swear-words and, after a short interval, the creak of a window being raised. Anthony looked up as an unshaven jowly face peered down at him.

'What time do you call this?' the man called in a carrying whisper. By his voice, he was from Belfast.

'Five o'clock,' answered Anthony in the precise tones of a German speaker. 'I have a message from James Smith.'

'Christ, I thought you were never coming. Wait there.'

The window was pulled down and, a few moments later, came the noise of feet on the stairs.

Anthony braced himself. He had an hour before the evacuation began. That was the scheme worked out with the Home Secretary and the Chief Commissioner of Scotland Yard. The Home Secretary had wanted to evacuate Marriotvale right away, but the Chief Commissioner was keen to give Anthony a chance. It would take, he argued, at least that amount of time to have enough men in the right place and, while they were being assembled, Anthony might as well try to bluff the bombers.

The door opened a crack. 'Come in.'

Anthony stepped into the front room of the house. It was, predictably, dark, squalid and very dirty. A ragged curtain was pinned across the window and the furniture was a collection of packing cases.

The jowly man, who was barefooted and dressed in a long-sleeved vest tucked into serge trousers, took him into the kitchen, the only other downstairs room, where there was a table and two chairs. Here, with no curtain, there was daylight from the kitchen window which gave onto a tiny yard at the side of the house. The back wall of the yard was the factory wall.

'My name's Joseph,' said the man. 'My God, you're an early bird. Sit down, why don't you?'

Anthony gave a fastidious shudder that wasn't entirely assumed. 'Thank you, no. I will stand.'

Joseph laughed. 'You bloody Germans. You're all the same. You are German, aren't you?'

'Yes, that is so. I arrived on the U-boat last night. My English name is Robert Jones. James Smith had business in Germany.'

There was a clatter of feet on the stairs and another man, dressed in workman's clothes of heavy cloth, came into the kitchen. He looked, thought Anthony, a cut above Joseph. 'This is Kevin,' said Joseph. 'He's in charge here. Kevin, this is Mr Robert Jones, as he wants to be called. He came on the boat last night.'

'So I heard,' said Kevin. He had an educated voice and a thin, ascetic face. 'Well, Mr Jones? Has Berlin agreed at long last?'

'Do we get the money?' asked Joseph.

'You will get a credit note for six thousand pounds to be spent on arms in Germany,' said Anthony. 'I trust you are aware of the generosity of the government in providing such a sum.' Kevin and Joseph looked at each other with a quick nod of approval. 'However, today's scheme will not be carried out.'

Joseph, who had been rolling a cigarette, looked at him in consternation. 'Why the hell not? We can get the King! D'you not realize that? Why, Veronica herself came up with the plan.' With a shock Anthony realized he meant Veronica O'Bryan. 'She worked out how we could do it. We've been planning this for months.'

'It's the Kaiser, isn't it?' said Kevin bitterly. 'He doesn't want to kill his cousin.'

Anthony nodded.

'But his cousin is the *King*,' said Joseph. 'Doesn't he see? The King is the heart of England. We kill him and we'll strike a blow they'll never recover from. By Christ, I'm damned if I'm having some bloody German turn round and tell us we can't do it. We're the men on the ground. We know what should be done.'

'Be quiet, Joseph,' said Kevin. 'These walls are like paper.' Joseph glared at him in frustration. 'However,' continued Kevin, 'I don't think Mr Jones here quite appreciates what's been done. This is a patriotic scheme that will benefit Ireland and Germany.' He drew an automatic pistol from his pocket and put it on the table. 'Once the plan has been carried out, then the Kaiser will see its merits.'

Anthony had been afraid of this. 'You will lose the friendship of Germany,' he said stiffly. Kevin's hand twitched towards the pistol. 'There are matters at stake you cannot grasp. Take the money and forget your ideas. The Kaiser is insistent on this.'

Kevin picked up the pistol. 'And what if we'd never got the message from the Kaiser?' he said softly, pointing the pistol at Anthony. 'I'm an Irishman. I don't care who the Kaiser's relations are. Nobody knows you're here. I can explain the shot.' He gave a jerk of his head towards the factory. 'Living next to that thing, people are used to noise. I think, Mr Jones, it might be better if you'd never come.'

Anthony looked at him. Kevin had the bright, cold eyes of a fanatic. The pistol was rock-solid. The muscles in Kevin's hand tightened and Anthony knew he was a breath away from death.

He allowed himself to look very scared. Oddly enough, it really was all pretence. His mind was working so quickly he didn't have time to be frightened. He wanted to get to the bomb and at least attempt to disarm it.

'Wait! Perhaps if you can show me what you have in mind, how the device will work, I can argue for you in Berlin.' The muscles of Kevin's hand relaxed. 'It is true what you say. After the King is dead, perhaps, it will be different. I agree with you. It will be a mortal blow for England. When the Kaiser sees that, he will change his mind – *if* you let me argue for you,' he added.

Kevin froze, studying Anthony's face. Then he laughed and put the pistol back in his pocket. 'It seems we have an agreement, Mr Jones. Luckily for you.'

Anthony took a deep breath. 'You will show me the arrangements? You will do more than merely throw a bomb, yes?'

'I think,' said Kevin, 'you'd better come with me, Mr Jones.'

He opened the kitchen cupboard, took out a powerful electric torch, then walked across the kitchen and opened a door.

The opening yawned blackly. It was the cellar. 'I think you can go first, Mr Jones,' said Kevin. 'Joe, get a cup of tea brewed, will you? I'm parched.'

The cellar steps, which were very steep and stank of damp, led to a tiny clay-walled room, glistening with slug trails. A small circle of light rimmed the coal-hole on the street above. There was a heap of earth piled up in the cellar. They've dug a tunnel, Anthony thought with sudden understanding.

'Nice, isn't it?' said Kevin ironically, flashing his torch round the cellar. 'This cellar, Mr Jones, is why we chose this house.'

He flashed his torch into the corner, showing a roughly dug hole. It was about six feet deep with a wooden ladder propped against the side. 'Now, I'll go first, but don't try anything. Down we go, Mr Jones.' Anthony could hear the amusement in his voice. 'I'm afraid you're going to get your smart clothes dirty, but it can't be helped.'

The hole opened out onto a narrow tunnel, about three feet wide. Following Kevin and the beam of light, Anthony crawled on his hands and knees through the passage.

'We're under the factory wall,' explained Kevin shortly. 'We'll come to another ladder in a minute. I'll go up first. You'll have to wait a moment while I see it's all right.'

He scrambled up the ladder, leaving Anthony in the tunnel. There was a pause and the creaking sound of wood. A gloomy light shone into the hole. Kevin looked down at him. 'Come on!'

They came out at the back of a warehouse. A wooden pallet that had covered the entrance was pushed to one side.

Anthony stretched, glad to be out of the cramped tunnel. Wooden boxes and piles of shells stood heaped up in a huge, silent room. He looked around with apparent admiration. 'This is clever, yes?' he said quietly.

Kevin put his mouth near Anthony's ear. 'One of the warehouse men is one of ours. The other's an old dodderer and doesn't know anything about it. Altogether, we've got three lads who work here.'

His teeth showed white in a wolfish grin. 'Funnily enough, they're all going to be off sick today. Follow me, Mr Jones.'

He led the way down a corridor formed by piles of crates, waited cautiously at the end and slipped across the gap to the next passage. 'We have to go into the factory yard,' he said in a low whisper. 'Just walk as if you owned the place. There shouldn't be anyone around at this time in the morning.'

Looking round, he waited at the end of the passage. The great double doors of the warehouse were in front of them but, set into the wood, was a smaller wicket door. Kevin took a key from his pocket. 'You see what it is to have friends in the right places, Mr Jones. Me, Joseph, and a couple of the lads made the final preparations last night. There was supposed to be an explosives expert coming from Germany but he never turned up.'

Anthony recognized the description as that of Günther Hedtke and wondered what Kevin would do if he knew he was the missing expert. 'I don't know what happened to him. I don't care, either. Your lot should learn to trust us more, Mr Jones. We don't need anyone to tell us how to do our job.'

He walked across to the wicket door and turned the key in the lock. After a pause to make sure there was no one about, he jerked his head at Anthony to come on.

The cobbled yard of the factory was set between the three-storey high brick walls of the factory, with its rows of long black windows. Dominating everything was the chimney, rising high from the engine shed. Before them were the closed factory gates and beyond, Anthony could hear the early-morning sounds as London stirred into life.

Kevin walked quickly up the yard, away from the gates. 'There's some new buildings beyond the yard.' He grinned again. 'That's what King George and his wife are coming to see. There's going to be a big fuss, with flags waved and a band playing and everything just fit for a king. He's got a beautiful silver trowel, ready inscribed with the date, to lay the foundation stone. That trowel will be the last thing he touches.'

They went up the yard between the main buildings. The land opened out and there, as Kevin had said, was the low brick wall of the foundations of a new factory building, looking very clean and raw. There was a wooden dais beside the wall, evidently prepared for the royal party.

'Now this,' said Kevin, 'is where it happens.' He stopped and pointed. 'Tell them about this in Berlin, Mr Jones.'

He turned and grinned at Anthony. 'Imagination's not any German's strongpoint, but we Irish have imagination. Imagine this. A few hours from now, all the factory hands will be out to see their precious King and Queen. Don't be sorry for them. They're making shells to kill your lads and are as legitimate a target as any soldier in uniform. This common land we're standing on –' he rubbed his foot in the grit – 'will be covered with a red carpet so George won't get his feet dirty. That dais will be covered in fancy cloth with fancy chairs and fancy bunting. The band will play, Mr Noakes, the factory owner will hand George his silver trowel and George will lay the stone for the new building.'

'And then?' asked Anthony. 'What will happen then?'

'Bang,' said Kevin softly. 'That foundation stone has been booby-trapped.' He walked to the wall, resting his hand by the gap left for the stone. Where the stone was to go was a fine layer of cement. 'Under there, under that cement, is a detonator. You can't see the cable because I've covered it up with cement to the ground.' He pointed back towards the warehouse. 'It runs to the warehouse.

It's all buried, out of sight. I tell you, Mr Jones, this is a great device. All we had to do last night was lay the detonators and connect the bomb. It's not a big bomb, but it'll set off a stockpile of high explosive.'

He laced his hands together and cracked his fingers in satisfaction. 'They'll hear it the other side of the Channel. Now tell me the Germans don't need us. This took Irish brains and Irish know-how and because of us, you can strike at the very heart of England.'

Standing in the silent factory yard, Anthony looked at the innocent gap in the wall. Kevin had told him to imagine and he could imagine only too well.

There would be pomp and ceremony and happy faces as the workers looked at the King and Queen. The women – he knew there were many women in the factory – would be admiring the Queen's dress and enjoying the band, glad to have this little holiday, excited to see their Queen and King. Maybe there'd be children in the crowd waving pocket-money penny flags and cheering. Outside the factory, in those mean little houses, the day would seem brighter and life that bit better because of what was happening in those few square yards so near at hand. And then . . .

He *had* to disable the bomb. 'It is impressive,' he said. 'Yes, you are right. You can strike where we cannot. You are sure the bomb is well-hidden? I would like to see it for myself.'

'No problem about that, Mr Jones,' said Kevin. He looked at his watch. 'It's twenty-five to six. I've got time to show you the bomb, then we'd better get going before anyone arrives. And after that, we'll get as far away from Marriotvale as we can.'

He led him back down the yard, through the wicket gate and into the warehouse once more, threading his way confidently through the tall corridors of crates. 'It's at the side of the warehouse,' he explained, coming to a stop before a five-box high stack of crates that ran the length of the wall. 'Now you tell me if you can see anything suspicious.'

Anthony looked. He couldn't.

'And yet it's in there.' He would have said more, but, very faintly from outside, came the thrum of an engine. He looked up sharply. 'What's that? It sounds like a motorbike. Wait here, Mr Jones.'

Kevin ran out of the warehouse. It was the opportunity Anthony had been waiting for. The cable was buried, he knew that, but somewhere, surely, the ground would be disturbed. The crates stood away from the wall on pallets. He squeezed into the narrow dark gap between the crates and the side of the warehouse. Bent double, he ran his hands along the earth, trying to find a space where the ground had been disturbed. Dimly he registered that the motorbike had roared up the yard outside but ignored it in his frantic search.

The minutes ticked away. There! He'd found it! Anthony felt dizzy with relief. He took out his pocket knife and scrabbled in the earth. He heard footsteps behind him but carried on. He was too close to give up now. His hand was on the cable – and a gun barrel dug into the back of his neck.

'Drop the knife, Mr Jones.' It was Kevin.

Anthony froze but didn't obey. Then he was sent sprawling by a kick from Kevin's heavy boots.

'Get up and come outside. Walk backwards towards me. Yes, that's right. We've got a bit of catching up to do, Mr Jones. Hands up!'

Anthony wearily wiped the grit from his face, stood up and raised his hands. His knife gleamed on the dirt in front of him but he daren't go for it. Dead, he was no use to anyone. Alive, he might – just might – have a chance.

Once out of the narrow passageway, Kevin waved him back out of the warehouse into the yard. 'Walk to the dais,' he said grimly. 'Don't try anything.'

By the dais was a motorbike, its rider clad in leather coat, helmet and goggles. 'One of our friends arrived, Mr Jones,' continued Kevin. 'He had something very interesting to say about that U-boat you arrived on last night. Apparently it was captured by the British, which leaves me asking an obvious question. Who the hell are you?'

Anthony didn't answer. There didn't seem much point.

As they approached the motorbike, the rider dismounted and raised his goggles. It was Bertram Farlow.

Anthony stared at him. Bertram Farlow? As he thought of how Sir Charles trusted him, of the information Farlow must have given the enemy, he felt sick.

'Do you know who this is?' demanded Kevin.

Farlow nodded with grim satisfaction. His air of beneficence, like an unworldly vicar or a philosophical cabinet minister, had completely vanished. 'You've caught the big one.' He looked at

Anthony with pure hatred. 'This is Anthony Brooke.' He ground out the name.

Kevin gave a strangled hiss.

'Why are you doing this?' asked Anthony, stunned. 'Why, Farlow?'

Kevin answered for him. 'Money. That's it, isn't it, Farlow?'

'And power,' said Farlow softly. 'You don't know about that, do you, Brooke? You don't know what it's like to be cheated of your rightful place. You've always had it easy. You despised me, didn't you? I didn't go to the right school. I didn't have the right relations. I've been kept down all my life and at long last I've got the chance to get back.'

'You're nothing,' said Anthony. 'You're just an errand boy.'

Farlow's eyes gleamed in fury. 'Nothing? You're wrong, Brooke. I knew exactly where our friends over the water could find Cavanaugh. *And* I found you. You're a bloody spy and you're going to suffer.'

'Never mind that,' interrupted Kevin. 'We'll deal with him later, Farlow. You can see him off, if you like.'

Farlow smiled slowly. 'I'll enjoy that,' he said softly. 'You'll learn what power I've got. You won't die quickly, Brooke.'

'Later, Farlow,' said Kevin impatiently. 'You'll have your chance later. You say they're going to evacuate the area?'

Anthony sprang.

The move was so unexpected, it sent Farlow sprawling off his bike. The heavy machine fell on them as Kevin fired a stream of bullets from the automatic.

Bullets thudded into the petrol tank. Petrol jetted out, then the tank exploded in a deafening whoosh of flame and chunks of flying metal.

Anthony felt Farlow's fist slam into the side of his head, then Farlow's neck jerked back and his body went limp. One of Kevin's bullets had gone home. Anthony rolled to one side as Kevin leapt through the curtain of flames and pointed his gun. Bullets tore into the earth followed by a series of useless clicks. The gun was empty. Kevin flung away the gun and hurled himself forward towards the gap in the bricks.

'Don't be a fool!' yelled Anthony. 'You'll kill us all!' His head still singing with Farlow's blow, Anthony lunged after him, catching his legs.

Kevin kicked out, sending Anthony twisting to one side, but Anthony hung on grimly, desperately trying to stop him reaching the detonator.

Kevin clawed his way across the wooden floor of the dais and kicked out once more. This time, his heavy boot caught Anthony on the chin, sending him reeling away.

With a scream of triumph, Kevin staggered the last couple of feet. There was a fusillade of sharp cracks and he gazed down in absolute shock at the blood on his chest. With his last ounce of strength he reached forward, clutching at the gap in the wall as he fell. Anthony flinched away as Kevin thudded down on the detonators.

Nothing happened.

It suddenly seemed very, very quiet. The motorbike still burned in an acrid, evil-smelling cloud of black smoke. Beside it, lay Farlow's twisted body and, on the dais, sprawled Kevin, his eyes open wide in death, staring at the hand draped across the concrete crust of the detonators.

'Brooke!' He looked up as his name was called. From one of the upstairs open windows of the factory, Sir Charles leaned out and waved. 'I'll be down in a minute.'

Anthony slumped onto the dais and waited. Sir Charles, accompanied by an infantry captain, came out into the yard at the head of a party of soldiers, complete with rifles. 'Brilliant work, Brooke,' he said, enthusiastically shaking Anthony's hand.

Anthony wearily stood up and ran a hand round his tender jaw, sore from the kick he'd received. 'Who killed him?' he asked, looking at Kevin's body.

The captain stepped forward. 'We all shot at him, sir. I suppose we're all responsible.'

Anthony nodded. 'He's probably better off dead. There's another man back at the house. You'd better arrest him.'

'We've done that,' said Sir Charles. 'As soon as we saw you and your pal safely in the factory yard, we collected Master Joseph. He's wanted for a string of murders in Ireland.'

Anthony sat back against the wooden support of the dais. 'I thought we'd had it at the end,' he said, lighting a cigarette. 'I know we had a plan, but I didn't know it had come off.'

Sir Charles nodded. 'You needn't have worried. We were watching the whole time. We saw you point out where the cable and the detonator were hidden and, as soon as you and your Irish friend went back into the warehouse, Captain Black here saw to it, didn't you, Captain?'

'I worked as fast as I could,' said Black. 'You led us to the spot and then gave us enough time to cut the bomb cable.'

'I wish I'd known,' said Anthony, nursing his chin. 'I knew you were somewhere around, but I didn't know where you were or if you'd managed to disable the device. Then when Farlow turned up . . .'

'That was a complete shock,' said Sir Charles. He looked down at the dead man broodingly. 'I wish we'd managed to take him alive.'

'Kevin killed him,' said Anthony.

Sir Charles sighed. 'That's fitting, I suppose.' He looked at Anthony. 'Come on, Brooke. I suppose you'd better go back to hospital to have your jaw looked at.'

'Damn hospital,' said Anthony with a grin. 'I spent long enough there yesterday. I know it's early, but I want a large whisky and soda.'

FOURTEEN

Anthony finished his whisky and soda. 'By jingo, I needed that,' he said in satisfaction. They were in Sir Charles's room in Cockspur Street, and never had whisky tasted so good or the green leather armchair been so welcoming. He stretched out his legs comfortably and took a cigarette from the silver box on the table. 'Well,' he said, cocking an eyebrow at Sir Charles. 'What did the Home Secretary have to say?'

It was nine o'clock in the morning and Sir Charles had returned from an interview with a hugely relieved politician, an eminent soldier and the Chief Commissioner of Scotland Yard.

'He was very complimentary,' said Sir Charles. 'We've been asked to give his sincere thanks to everyone involved, which means, old man, Captain Black and his men, the Scotland Yard people who organized the evacuation which, thank God, never happened, but principally, and richly deserved, you.'

Anthony grinned lazily. 'Just for once, I feel inclined to take the praise. I hope you came in for some as well.'

Sir Charles nodded. 'I did. However, neither of us can afford to sit back on our laurels just yet. We've got a job to do.'

'Blimey, the man's a slave-driver,' said Anthony with a groan. 'What have you got in mind?'

'Finding James Smith.'

Anthony pulled a face. 'Yes, I suppose we've got to.'

Sir Charles sat down in the winged armchair and stuck his feet up on the low table. 'I was thinking,' he said, 'what information Bertram Farlow could have passed on. You're sure, aren't you, that James Smith was at Veronica O'Bryan's inquest?'

'As certain as I can be. I suppose I've got Farlow to thank for that.'

Sir Charles shook his head. 'That's just it. I was the only one in the department who knew you'd be at the inquest, and I certainly didn't tell Farlow.'

'Couldn't he have guessed?' asked Anthony.

Sir Charles swirled the whisky round in his glass. 'That's just it, damnit. He might have, but I don't see how.' He looked at Anthony, his face twisted. 'You see where that gets us?'

Anthony paused. 'Starhanger?'

'Exactly. The Starhanger people knew you found the body and would be called to the inquest. There was virtually no coverage in the press – Sherston saw to that – and of the other people involved, such as the Moultons and the local constabulary, I suppose they could have said something out of turn, but I doubt it. All the attention was on Tara O'Bryan. For Farlow or anyone else to find out from them, they'd have to know enough to ask the right questions, and I don't think they did.' Sir Charles put down his glass and frowned in perplexity. 'I'm not happy about Starhanger and I'm very unhappy about James Smith. Have you considered how he must feel about you, Brooke?'

'I don't suppose I'm on his Christmas card list, if that's what you mean,' said Anthony with a grin.

Sir Charles smiled fleetingly. 'I think it's more profound than that. You've crossed him at every turn. You brought us the notebook and stopped the bomb, turning what should have been one of the biggest blows of the war into a damp squib.' He frowned at his whisky. 'Add to that the loss of a U-boat and crew and I'd say you've made James Smith's life nearly unbearable. I think he must hate you.'

'Hate me?' repeated Anthony startled. 'That's putting it strong.'

'Is it? I think Smith has one chance to re-establish himself. And that's by producing the diamonds and you.' Sir Charles looked up thoughtfully. 'I'm afraid, old friend, as long as James Smith is at large, you're in very real danger.'

Anthony raised his glass ironically. 'Cheers. What do you suggest I do?'

'Remember he's dangerous,' said Sir Charles seriously. 'We *have* to find James Smith, Brooke.'

Anthony stubbed out his cigarette. 'How? The police are looking for him, but there's damn all to go on.'

Sir Charles got up and restlessly walked round the room. He paused by the desk, drumming his fingers on the tabletop. 'That's the problem. I can't see the police are ever going to find him.' He hitched himself onto the desk and looked at Anthony. 'Instead of us trying to find him, I think we have to get him to find us. After all,' he added, 'we've got something he wants.'

Anthony knew the answer but he asked the question anyway. 'And that is?'

Sir Charles grimaced. 'You.'

Anthony looked away, chilled. He'd taken risks, of course, but they were necessary. To trail a broken wing across the path of a cold-blooded killer was a very different matter. He remembered how deliberately Smith had taken aim and fired at him in the Daimler, how he'd brushed Warren out of the way, the icily precise preparations he'd made to kill young Greenwood and how he'd executed Chapman on a crowded tram platform. To say he wasn't scared was ridiculous; of course he was. However, Sir Charles was right. As long as Smith was at large, he would always be looking over his shoulder.

He took a deep breath, looked up and met Sir Charles's eyes squarely. 'All right. I'll be the bait. What do I do?'

'Go back to Starhanger,' suggested Sir Charles. 'After all, I think there's a good chance there's still something to be discovered there.'

'Putting it plainly, you think Sherston is in touch with James Smith? And that if I turn up, James Smith will follow?'

'It's a possibility.' Sir Charles lit a cigarette. 'As far as the public knows, Veronica O'Bryan was murdered by Chapman, but the reason for her murder is as mysterious as ever. As the one who found the body, you've got every reason to be interested in Mrs O'Bryan's murder. What's to stop you getting in touch with Sherston, telling him you're curious, and want to investigate further? If we're right, I bet he'll invite you to Starhanger like a shot.'

Anthony thought for a moment. 'I think you're right. Yes, that would work.' And it probably would work. What he couldn't tell Sir Charles – what he shied from admitting to himself – was how much he both wanted and flinched from being near Josette. While he stayed away from Josette, he could keep his head. Near her, he didn't trust himself and it hurt like hell.

'You won't be alone, Brooke,' urged Sir Charles. He'd seen his hesitation and misinterpreted it. 'I'll have men nearby to keep watch.'

'That's reassuring,' said Anthony matter-of-factly, glad for once of Sir Charles's lack of insight. 'It'll be good to have support, but how do I get in touch with them? Sherston may invite me, but he won't invite your guard dogs.'

'No. They'd better stay in the village inn.' Sir Charles thought for a moment. 'What about the boathouse? You could leave a message under the seats.'

'There's an old canoe lashed to the wall,' suggested Anthony. 'I can leave a message in that and vice versa.'

'That'll do. Well, what d'you think?'

'Have I got any choice?' asked Anthony. 'Either I go to Starhanger and keep my eyes open or I wait for James Smith to nab me when I'm off my guard.' He finished his whisky and stood up. 'I'm going back to the club.' He yawned. 'I know I slept most of yesterday, but I wouldn't mind a bit more rest. Let me know when you've organized your guard dogs and I'll get in touch with Sherston.'

'I'll speak to you soon,' promised Sir Charles, seeing him to the door.

They spoke sooner than Sir Charles had anticipated. Less than half an hour after leaving Cockspur Street, Anthony telephoned. 'Talbot?

There was a letter for me at the club. It arrived this morning. Sherston's invited me to Starhanger.'

Sir Charles was silent for a moment. 'That sounds suspiciously like a trap.'

'I thought so too,' agreed Anthony. 'Make sure I've got good guard dogs, Talbot. I think I'll need them.'

'I must apologize, Colonel,' said Sherston over the apple charlotte at dinner that evening. 'I hoped to be able to take a few days off, but I have to go to London tomorrow.'

'Oh Patrick, you promised,' said Josette reproachfully.

'I'll be back in the evening, my dear,' said Sherston. 'It can't be helped, I'm afraid.' He looked at Anthony. 'In the meantime, my dear chap, I would be very grateful if you could look into poor Veronica's death.'

Anthony cast a quick look at Tara, wondering if she'd care to have her mother's death discussed so openly round the dinner table.

She caught his look. 'I want to know why it happened, Colonel. The police are certain Cedric Chapman killed my mother, but I want to know why.'

'I wish we didn't have to discuss it,' said Josette irritably. 'We've done nothing but ask the same questions endlessly.'

Tara looked surprised. 'But you want to know just as much as we do, Josette. It was you who suggested Colonel Brooke might like to look into the matter.'

'That was to put an end to this ceaseless speculation,' said Josette. She looked at Anthony apologetically. 'I'm sorry, but we've talked about nothing else ever since it happened.' She looked at the butler. 'Vyse, you can clear away now.'

As if to make up for her abruptness, she gave Anthony a consciously friendly smile, adding, with a glance at her husband, 'I'm not going to let you monopolize Colonel Brooke over the port, Patrick. I want to show him the rose garden while there's still light enough to see.' She stood up and put a hand on Sherston's shoulder. 'We'll have our coffee in the drawing room afterwards.'

Anthony stood up and, seeing it was expected, offered Josette his arm. He was keeping a tight grip on his emotions.

With her arm in his, they strolled into the gathering dusk of the rose garden. It was a little way from the house, laid out with grass walks and sheltered by a dark belt of trees, the rich smell of roses filling the evening air. The sun had dipped below the horizon and the bats had started their jerky night-time dance. Josette led him to a seat surrounded by an arch of flowers.

'Please smoke, Colonel, if you want to,' she said, sitting down. She smiled at him hesitantly. 'I want to talk to you and I thought this was the best place.'

It was a wonderful place, but between the smell of the roses and the nearness of Josette, he was finding it difficult to think. There was something else, too. He couldn't quite place it, but he felt as if this had been staged, as if what should have been a private moment was somehow a public performance.

He lit a cigar and took a deep breath of smoke, trying to clear his mind. As he looked at Josette, he didn't see a very lovely woman but a very anxious one.

'You're worried,' he said gently. 'Why?'

Josette took a deep breath. 'Ever since Veronica died we've talked about nothing else. I'm very sorry for Tara but it's hard to be sorry in the right way. Tara's so strong-minded and so clear-headed she seems ruthless at times. I . . . I don't know if she really loved Veronica. That's wrong, isn't it?'

'Did Veronica love Tara?'

'Of course she did! She was her mother. I wish Veronica had been nicer. It would be easier to be sorry then, but she wasn't nice at all. She hated me. Patrick doesn't understand how much Veronica hated me. She stored up resentment and would never forgive or forget. God help anyone she ever took against.'

She clearly meant herself. Anthony thought he could guess why Veronica O'Bryan resented Josette so much. After all, Veronica had ruled the roost for years and to have Sherston's beautiful new wife thrown into the mix must have upset the apple cart good and proper. That could be more or less taken as read. However, there was someone else Veronica had her knife into and he wondered exactly what Josette knew.

'She disliked Terence Cavanaugh, didn't she?' he asked. 'Why?'

Anthony thought she was going to faint. She started forward and he caught her from falling. 'No,' she whispered. 'I won't talk about him.' She shook herself free.

Anthony reached out. 'Cavanaugh was my friend.'

She looked up at him. 'Then . . .' She hesitated, then spoke in a rush. 'You don't understand. Veronica didn't hate Terry. She loved him and he didn't love her. All her love turned to hate. She told Patrick it was all Terry's fault, that he had led her to believe he cared for her. Patrick was furious. I knew the truth and she hated me for knowing. I tried to tell Patrick but he wouldn't listen. He got angry. You don't know what a temper he has, but it's frightening sometimes. He didn't like me taking Terry's part.' She hesitated once more. 'I've been scared. It's stupid, but I've been scared.'

It was dusk; she was beautiful; the smell of the roses and the scent of her perfume mingled in intoxicating closeness. She was a frightened woman and she turned to him. Anthony reached out his arms and she lent forward. Almost unconsciously he leaned forward to kiss her . . . and she screamed.

'Look!' she yelped, pointing.

Anthony whirled in time to see a man disappear into the trees. He hurtled after him, thudding across the lawn. The man looked back, his face a white blur in the gloom.

It was James Smith's chauffeur. Anthony made a desperate leap, managed to get within a hand's breadth, grabbed out and caught his leg, sprawling into the leaves on the ground. The chauffeur kicked out, shaking off Anthony's grasping hand, and vanished into the wood. Three men burst out of the bushes across the lawn and plunged into the wood after him. Anthony got to his knees, staring after them, as the roar of a motorbike bit through the air.

He glanced at Josette. She was standing framed in the arch of roses, her hand to her mouth. 'Who were those men?' she demanded. 'Who were they?'

Anthony knew very well who they were. Their names were Bedford, Cooke and Parkinson, Sir Charles's watchdogs, but he could hardly tell her that. 'Burglars?' he suggested.

Unbelievably and much to Anthony's relief, she bought it. 'I must tell Patrick,' she said. She ignored the hand he held out to her. 'Patrick will know what to do.'

She walked back into the house alone, leaving him in the darkening garden.

Anthony waited, looking after her, then turned back to the woods and gave a low whistle.

Bedford, Cooke and Parkinson emerged from the trees. 'He got away, sir,' said Bedford in disgust. 'He's been creeping about the place for around half an hour. When you and the lady came out he settled down to watch.'

'Why didn't you arrest him?' snapped Anthony, his temper at fraying point.

Bedford shook his head. 'We wanted to see what he'd do. We hoped he'd take us to Smith. He's the one we want.'

They were right; even though he was boiling with frustration, Anthony knew they were right. Smith *was* the one they wanted. With the chauffeur so close at hand the danger had been very real and he couldn't fault the men for keeping such an excellent watch. They should be congratulated but all he could really think of was that he'd been about to kiss Josette with the chauffeur, Bedford, Cooke and Parkinson as his audience. So much for romance. He felt an absolute fool.

Sherston insisted on calling out the menservants, arming them with shotguns and searching the grounds. Predictably, they found nothing and Anthony was hailed as a hero for dispatching four burglars single-handed.

He took the unmerited praise with as good a grace as he could muster. Although uncomfortable in his new role as strongman, he chose discretion as the better part of valour. Sherston might not like the idea of burglars, but Anthony thought he'd like the idea of his gardens as the rendezvous for secret service men and enemy agents even less. It was a relief when Sherston finally finished chasing imaginary crooks and, ensuring that all the doors were firmly barred, suggested the household retire to bed.

Once in his own room, Anthony's first thought was to open his window, lean out and take a few deep breaths. He stopped. Out there, despite the burglar hunt, and perhaps very close, was Smith and at least one of his men. Anthony didn't want to tell them which room he was in. Careful not to show himself against the light, he closed the curtains and retreated to the chair by the fireplace.

This couldn't go on. Smith had to be caught and he had to find out, once and for all, if Sherston was a friend or an enemy.

He stayed awake, listening and half-heartedly reading, as the house settled down for the night. Eventually the stairs stopped creaking and the noises in the corridor were stilled. From somewhere down below a grandfather clock softly marked the passage of time in mellow chimes.

It seemed a long time before the clock chimed twice. Silence wrapped the house like a blanket. He put on his pyjamas and dressing gown. If he was found creeping round in someone else's house in the dead of night, it would be a great deal easier to pretend he couldn't get off to sleep and needed a book to read if he wasn't fully clothed.

Torch in pocket, he stood behind his bedroom door, listening, before slipping out into the corridor. Keeping to the side of the stairs – he didn't want them to creak – he walked down into the moonlit hall and along to Sherston's study.

The door was locked but, to his surprise, the key was in the lock. He wouldn't need the bunch of picklocks in his dressing-gown pocket.

The moonlight shining through the study window was very bright, making deep pools of sharp-edged blackness. He didn't know exactly what he was looking for but hoped that somewhere in this room would be a note, a message, some record of contact between Sherston and the enemy.

Sherston was, Anthony knew, a methodical man and, at a guess, would keep his notes at home rather than his office in Sherston House. It was probably safer here than in his London office. As far as he knew, Sherston and his secretary were the only people who came in the study.

The walls of the study were lined with box files. A whole section concerned the house and estate but the ones which interested him were the press files, each labelled with a name of a newspaper or magazine.

The *Sentinel*, Sherston's flagship paper, had four boxes, which were, according to the notes on the spine of the files, split between a record of contributors and their specialities, a note of special features the paper had run, circulation figures arranged by region and an account of money paid and received. Anthony guessed these papers would be duplicated at Sherston House together with more extensive records. He was looking at information Sherston needed at his fingertips. It was a digest of his entire business.

Anthony flicked his torch along the shelves, looking for the *Beau Monde*. There it was. He pulled it down and opened it on the desk.

Here, separated into Manila folders, was information classified as it had been on the *Sentinel*. In the record of contributors was Frankie.

Frustratingly, that was the only name she appeared under. Anthony spread the papers out, looking for a note of payment, but there wasn't any. He wanted some evidence that Patrick Sherston knew who Frankie was and how she was using the 'Letters'.

He put the papers back in the file and returned it to the shelf, and, sitting on the chair at Sherston's desk, forced himself to look methodically round the room. He needed something out of place, something that didn't seem right. He used the picklocks to open the desk drawer. The right-hand side contained a cash box and chequebooks. The left-hand side drawer was unlocked and contained stationery.

He really needed to examine every piece of paper in the place but he couldn't see Sherston letting him do— Bloody *hell*!

It was there. Anthony put the torch down on the desk beside the typewriter and a wedge of light shone on the papers beside the machine. The top sheet had a neatly typed title. 'Frankie's Letter'.

He picked up the typed sheet and read it through. 'Frankie's Letter'. Frivolous, inconsequential and apparently trivial. And *new*.

He stared at the piece of paper. Veronica O'Bryan had written 'Frankie's Letter'. Veronica O'Bryan was dead. This was a new 'Letter' so Veronica *couldn't* be Frankie. They'd been wrong.

His name was in the 'Letter'. Anthony couldn't read the code, but there was a reference to 'babbling brooks'. He'd eat the damn thing if that didn't mean him. Sir Charles had to see this right away. He picked up a pencil and turned to find a piece of blank paper so he could copy it out.

Anthony froze. The window was outlined in moonlight on the floor and, cast in clear silhouette, was the shape of a man's head and shoulders.

He kept very still, leaving the torch on the desk. Although the man could see there was a light. Anthony didn't think the man could see him. He slid off the chair and crept into the shadows, working his way round the walls, out of the study and into the hallway. The garden door, he knew, would bring him out onto the terrace. As quietly as he could, Anthony unlocked the door and stole round the corner of the house.

The man was crouched by the window. Anthony had no weapon

apart from his fist, but he knew that one sharp blow in the right place was as effective as a cosh.

He was at arms' length before the man realized he was there. Anthony's fist was raised when he turned – and he very nearly hit Bedford.

Bedford gave a little yelp of surprise. Anthony let out his breath in a gasp and jerked his thumb behind him to indicate they should move away from the house.

'What the devil,' he demanded in a whisper when they were far enough away from the house and the shadow of some bushes, 'are you doing here?'

Bedford was still recovering from Anthony's near-miss. 'I had no idea you were there, sir,' he said admiringly. 'I thought I was pretty good, but that takes the biscuit.'

'Never mind that,' Anthony broke in impatiently. 'Answer the question.'

'Mr Monk's orders are to keep watch, sir. I saw torchlight in that room and was trying to make out what was going on.'

'That was me. How about earlier? Did you follow the chauffeur?'

Bedford shook his head. 'No, sir. We tried to follow the bike-tracks but the main road was too hard to take a print. The bike had a sidecar, so I don't know if he was alone or not.'

'He could have been,' said Anthony. 'It depends if he was planning to kill me or abduct me.' He sucked in his cheeks thoughtfully. 'Never mind that now. We know they're here and they know I'm guarded. Quits. Are you in touch with Mr Monks?'

'Yes, sir.'

'Good.' Anthony pointed to where the boathouse stood dark against the moonlit lake. 'You see the boathouse?'

'Yes, sir. I know that's our letter box.'

'Good. I'll have a message for Mr Monks inside it within an hour. There's another thing. Sherston is planning to go to London tomorrow. Have him followed.'

'Will do, sir.'

They parted, Bedford to God knows where, Anthony back to Sherston's study. He took 'Frankie's Letter' up to his room to copy out and, rather to his surprise, was able to return the original and deliver the copy to the boathouse without further ado.

*   *   *

The next day, Sherston, with apologies to his guest, left for London.

Anthony picked up a heap of magazines from the hall table and took them into the garden. The other magazines were camouflage. The first time he'd seen 'Frankie's Letter', he'd been too stunned to take in anything more than the fact that he'd found it and last night his emotions had been much the same.

Frankie's literary style was a matter he hadn't considered but now he wanted to read the 'Letters' themselves. He didn't expect to find anything that the code breakers hadn't seen, but hoped for an insight into Frankie by reading the words around the messages.

Veronica O'Bryan certainly hadn't written the 'Letter' he'd found last night, but that wasn't to say she hadn't written the others. Somebody else – Sherston, at a guess – could easily have written the latest one. And really, with such an excellent method of communication to hand, it made sense to keep 'Frankie's Letter' going.

He didn't have the last 'Letter' but, having copied it out only hours earlier, knew exactly what was in it. Was there any difference in style between it and the earlier 'Letters'?

If there was, he couldn't see it. Frankie's gossipy, trivial style seemed consistent throughout. It wouldn't, he thought, be a difficult style to mimic but if the last 'Letter' was written by another person they'd done it very well.

Annoyed, he lit his pipe and looked yet again at the light-hearted sentences.

'Good heavens! What on earth are you reading, Colonel?'

Anthony started. It was Tara O'Bryan. Her feet had made no noise on the grass as she crossed the lawn behind him. She was looking at the magazine over his shoulder. She came round the bench, picked up the magazines, put them on the lawn and sat down beside him.

'I found you reading Uncle Patrick's magazines once before,' she said chattily, 'but I never expected to find you with your nose in the *Beau Monde*. I wouldn't have thought it was your sort of thing.'

Anthony summoned up a smile. 'I'm just passing the time, really. Seeing how the other half lives and all that.'

'The other half being the mysterious female sex?' For some reason that seemed to amuse her. 'You won't find many clues by reading magazines, you know. Especially,' she added, looking at the magazine on his knee, '"Frankie's Letter".'

'Why not?' Tara didn't answer and Anthony carried on. 'After all, it's about things girls do talk about, isn't it? Fashion and gossip and so on.'

'Not all the time,' she said in a pained voice.

He pulled at his pipe and plunged in. 'As a matter of fact, I wondered who actually did write it. I know it's a secret . . .'

'A very closely guarded secret.'

'But I wondered if Frankie was your mother. Sorry to mention it, but I did.'

The humour vanished from her face. 'Whatever gave you that idea? You're wrong.'

'Are you certain?'

'Absolutely.'

Anthony sat back. 'Why?' he asked pleasantly. 'After all, if you don't know who wrote "Frankie's Letter", why shouldn't it have been your mother?'

'Because . . .' She stopped, biting her lip. Anthony felt a sudden conviction. She knew! 'She couldn't,' she finished, avoiding his eyes.

'You know who Frankie is,' he stated. It wasn't a question.

Again, she avoided his eyes. 'So what if I do? After all, it's just a newspaper stunt. It doesn't matter.'

'If your mother wrote it, it does. And, as Mr Sherston has asked me to investigate what happened to your mother, if she did write "Frankie's Letter", I need to know. There has to be some link between her and Cedric Chapman. This could be it.'

A line creased her forehead. 'Don't be ridiculous. Chapman was a criminal.'

'A blackmailer, perhaps? If your mother was Frankie, she'd have to do some digging around. She could easily have found out something disreputable about someone. Maybe Chapman was acting on their behalf.'

She threw her hands up impatiently. 'For heaven's sake! Colonel, this is idiotic. You're barking up the wrong tree.' She looked round, saw they were alone and drew closer. 'I'm only telling you because I can't let you waste your time.' She lowered her voice. 'Frankie isn't a woman at all. It's Uncle Patrick.'

Time seemed to stand still. Anthony looked at Tara. She had recovered her poise and her eyes met his in an amused challenge. He forced himself to laugh. 'What? Patrick Sherston writes "Frankie's Letter"?'

'Shush!' She raised a hand. 'Uncle Patrick would have a fit if he knew I'd told you. But you can see why I said you won't find out much about women from "Frankie's Letter".'

'But . . .' Anthony pretended to be bewildered. Perhaps he wasn't pretending. He'd suspected Sherston right enough, but to have it confirmed was stunning. 'How do you know?'

Tara became confidential. 'It was ages ago. I wanted to see Uncle Patrick and went into the study. He wasn't there, but on the type-writer was "Frankie's Letter". He was halfway though it. When he came back I said, It's you! You're Frankie! He swore me to secrecy. He said that "Frankie's Letter" was shaping up to being one of his best stunts. It had pushed the circulation of the *Beau Monde* past *Vogue* for the first time ever.' She laid a hand on his arm. 'Don't say anything, will you? It's only a joke but it'd be ruined if the truth got out. Promise?'

Anthony looked at her bright eyes. 'Promise,' he said, lying with a heavy heart. Yes, the joke would be ruined.

Not only that, he thought, half an hour later as he left his message inside the canoe, Patrick Sherston would be ruined. He knew 'Frankie's Letter' – that joke – had killed Terence Cavanaugh, but he hated the part he had to play.

FIFTEEN

Josette expected Sherston at seven. When eight o'clock arrived and he still hadn't returned, Josette ordered dinner to be served in his absence. 'I do apologize, Colonel,' she said, taking her seat at the table. 'It's too bad of Patrick.'

'He'll bustle in soon saying he was unavoidably detained,' said Tara, cheerfully. She cocked her head as the telephone rang in the hall. 'Hello, this is probably him now.'

Anthony, who knew only too well who was detaining Sherston and how unavoidable it was, found it difficult to play his allotted part of easy unconcern as Vyse, the butler, went to answer the call. Josette looked up as Vyse came into the dining room.

'Mr Elswick, the solicitor, would be obliged if you would speak to him on the telephone, madam.' Vyse coughed. 'He says it's important.'

Josette was on the telephone for a matter of minutes, some of the longest minutes Anthony had ever spent.

She came back into the dining room like someone in a trance. 'Patrick's been arrested,' she said without preamble, then collapsed into tears.

Early next day, Anthony walked to the boathouse. He hadn't seen either Josette or Tara that morning and, after the previous evening, he didn't want to. Tara had reacted with fury, Josette with silent horror.

There was, as he had hoped, a letter in the canoe.

Dear Brooke,

Congratulations. We've got him. It took some doing to get the authorities to act but, after your information, I had no choice. He doesn't suspect we had any part in it.

He was arrested at Sherston House. He was taken to Carey Street Police Station and charged. His solicitor, Elswick of Harwood, Elswick and Kendal, was in attendance. We don't want him wriggling out on a technicality. He stormed and blustered and indignantly rejected the charge, especially when the police spelled out, and Elswick confirmed, that the only penalty for High Treason is death.

It was the sight of all the 'Frankie's Letters' that got him, laid out neatly with their transcribed messages beside them. It was like pricking a balloon. All the fight went out of him. Elswick asked him to deny he was the author. Sherston admitted he'd written them. He wouldn't say much else, despite Elswick's promptings. So there we are. If we can nail Smith as well, we could rest easy, so stay put until you receive further instructions.

With best wishes,

W. Gabriel Monks

Anthony read the letter through again then stuck a match and set fire to it, making sure the pieces of charred ash went into the lake. They'd won. Half-won, anyway.

Smith was still out there and he was still in danger. He sat against the boathouse wall, sightlessly watching the water lapping round the piles of the wooden jetty.

It was so damn difficult to *feel* anything. He remembered how determined he'd been to get whoever was responsible for Terence Cavanaugh's death but now, with Sherston safely behind bars, he couldn't summon up any emotion but pity.

He couldn't face the house and slipped away without fuss. He didn't know if he was followed. He didn't really care.

It was late that afternoon when he returned to Starhanger. He had lunched at the village pub and then sat by the river, trying to put his thoughts in order. He must leave Starhanger.

Despite Sir Charles's instructions, he couldn't, in all decency, continue to inflict his presence on the stricken household and, now Sherston was taken care of and the link between Starhanger and Smith broken, he had no reason to stay.

Despite the apparent solitude of the riverbank, he knew that one of his guard dogs, at least, was near at hand.

Anthony longed for an encounter with Smith. He was in the mood to relish a fight. He'd half-expected Smith to make a move, now he was alone and apparently unprotected, but Smith, frustratingly, left him unmolested.

The door to Starhanger was open. He squared his shoulders and walked up the steps and into the hall. Vyse was crossing from the morning room into the library. He stopped as Anthony walked in, evidently surprised to see him.

Anthony paused enquiringly. 'Was there something you wanted, Vyse?'

Vyse picked up a silver salver from the hall table. 'There's a letter for you, sir. It was delivered by hand this morning.'

Anthony took the letter. Vyse cleared his throat, looking at Anthony awkwardly. 'I beg your pardon, sir, but could I enquire—'

'Colonel!' Tara stood at the end of the hall. 'I've been waiting for you.' She came a few steps into the hall. 'That will be all, Vyse.'

'Very good, Miss.'

Vyse gave a small bow and withdrew.

Anthony stuffed the letter into his pocket and followed Tara into the conservatory. 'I had the idea Vyse wanted to say something to me.'

Tara shut the door behind them. 'I'm sure he did,' she said grimly.

'But although Vyse is one of the best, I'm not having the servants discuss family affairs with a guest.'

She looked at him appraisingly, her face white with tension. She started to speak, swallowed hard, and tried again. 'Colonel Brooke, where is Josette?'

Anthony stared at her. At the back of his mind, a little shoot of fear took root and started to grow. 'What d'you mean?'

'Josette. She's with you, isn't she?'

'No. I haven't seen her today.'

Tara's eyes widened. 'Then where is she? She's gone.'

Anthony looked at her, unable, for the moment, to make sense of her words. Then he grabbed hold of her arms, his face very close to hers. 'Gone? What do you mean, gone?'

Tara's startled eyes met his. 'We don't know. Her maid said she was in her room last night, but her bed's not been slept in.' Her voice broke. 'I thought she'd gone with you.'

'*What!*' His grip tightened.

Tara's lip trembled. 'You're hurting me.'

He let her go, then, realizing what strain she was under, helped her to a seat. 'Tell me what this is all about.'

Tara slumped helplessly. 'I thought you and Josette had gone off together.' She moved her head to one side, avoiding looking at him directly. 'I know how you feel about her. It's obvious. It's the way you look at her, the way your face lights up when she comes in the room. I know.'

Anthony looked at her silently.

'It's a nightmare,' she added desperately. 'First Uncle Patrick was arrested, then Josette disappeared and you couldn't be found. I can't understand what's happening but it's you, isn't it? You're responsible for everything.'

He met her eyes, schooling his face into blankness. She reacted with sudden fury. 'For heaven's sake, Colonel, don't pretend!' Her voice was savage. 'You know, don't you?'

Anthony couldn't hold out any longer. Silently he inclined his head.

Tara gave a little choking gasp.

'I know some of it,' said Anthony quietly. 'I don't know what's happened to Mrs Sherston. Haven't you any idea? Could she have gone up to London, say?'

'She wouldn't go off by herself to London in the middle of the night. I rang Mr Elswick and he hasn't seen her. He said he'd telephone if she turned up, but there's been no word.'

'What about the police?'

Tara shook her head. 'I didn't want to tell them.' She paused, looking at him reluctantly. 'Not in the circumstances. What I thought were the circumstances, anyway. Shall I ring them now?'

Anthony hesitated. If the police were called that meant interviews, an investigation, and delays. He suddenly remembered the letter Vyse had given him. 'Wait a moment,' he said. 'This could tell us something.'

He pulled out the letter, Tara watching him. 'That's not Josette's writing,' she said.

As Anthony read the letter, his stomach turned over. He'd wanted Smith to make his move. He'd got his wish.

Dear Colonel Brooke,

By this time you will be aware that a certain lady of your acquaintance has disappeared. If you want to see her again, be on the main road outside Starhanger at six o'clock this evening. You will, of course, be unarmed and alone.

James Smith

He met Tara's watchful, apprehensive gaze and decided to trust her. It was, perhaps, weakness on his part but, in a world of shadows, misunderstandings and half-truths, there was something deeply appealing about her honesty. She hadn't beaten about the bush but asked him an awkward question straight out. He wanted Tara to understand why he acted as he had done. He wanted that very much. He held out the letter to her. 'Read that.'

Tara frowned and took the letter. She read it through and looked up, puzzled. 'What's this about? Who's James Smith?'

Anthony sat down on the sofa and lit a cigarette. 'James Smith wants to kill me.' Tara made an incredulous noise but he waved her quiet. 'He's an enemy agent. We've crossed swords before now and I've escaped by the skin of my teeth.'

'Are you serious, Colonel?'

'Perfectly serious. He's killed at least two others.'

Tara put her hand to her mouth. 'I don't believe it,' she whispered.

'I don't believe any of it. Josette can't have been kidnapped. This is England, for heaven's sake. You're up to something. I know you're a spy. You came here to spy on my mother, didn't you? She's dead and Uncle Patrick's in prison, and it's all down to you. I knew you weren't real. I don't believe in James Smith. I don't believe that's a real letter. You wrote it.' She stopped and her voice wavered. 'Didn't you?'

Anthony didn't answer her directly. Instead he got up and went to the conservatory door leading into the garden and opened it.

With Tara following him, he walked out onto the terrace, into the garden and down to the copse of trees flanking the wall that separated Starhanger from the road. He stood beside the trees and whistled. Tara gave a yelp of surprise as Cooke emerged from the wood. 'Meet Lieutenant Cooke.'

'At your service, Miss,' Cooke said with a smile.

Anthony could see Cooke's appearance like a rabbit from a hat dealt the final blow to Tara's scepticism. 'It's all right,' he said reassuringly. 'This is one of my men.' He smiled fleetingly. 'He was one of the burglars the other night.' He gave Cooke the letter. 'It's from Smith. He's got Mrs Sherston.'

Cooke read the letter quickly with a growing smile of satisfaction. 'And I'd say we'd got him, Colonel. If he turns up at six, we'll have him on ice. What's your idea, sir? Parkinson's back at the inn but Bedford and I are ready and waiting. If he shows up, we've got him.'

'As a plan, that's simple enough to work,' said Anthony. 'I presume Smith's going to abduct me, not gun me down in the road.'

Cooke sucked his cheeks in. 'He might try, sir, but I doubt it. He'll want to find out exactly what happened at Marriotvale, to say nothing of the U-boat. I think you're right. I don't think he'll kill you out of hand. My guess is Smith or one of his confederates will show up in either his car or that motorbike and expect you to step aboard nice and quietly.'

'Which I will do, of course,' said Anthony. 'He's got Mrs Sherston. We can't risk anything happening to her.'

'We can't guarantee anything with a man like Smith,' said Cooke. 'I wish we'd nailed him last night. He must have enticed Mrs Sherston outside somehow.'

'Can we *do* something,' Tara broke in impatiently. 'Other than just wait for this Smith, I mean? Can't we look for Josette?'

'Where do you suggest looking?'

Tara brushed her hair back from her face. 'I don't know but I want to try. Someone might have seen something.'

'They might,' Anthony admitted. 'And you'd know who to ask.' He hesitated. 'The only thing is, you could be running into danger.'

Cooke shook his head. 'If you'll excuse me, sir, I can't see it. Smith won't want another hostage. He'll be strained as it is, keeping Mrs Sherston under wraps. He'd expect Miss O'Bryan to look for Mrs Sherston. It's the natural thing to do. He won't realize she knows the truth and, with Miss O'Bryan knowing the area, she might find something out.'

Anthony put a restraining hand on Tara's arm. 'Be careful. We're dealing with a very ruthless man. No heroics.'

'No heroics,' she repeated. 'All right. I'll take one of the horses out. I'll cover more ground that way.'

'If you must,' said Anthony reluctantly. 'Cooke, can you keep an eye on Miss O'Bryan?'

Cooke shook his head. 'I'm sorry, sir, but our instructions are to keep tabs on you.' He smiled at Tara. 'After all, the young lady's only taking a look around, aren't you, Miss?' He touched his hat to her and disappeared into the bushes once more.

Anthony turned to Tara and led the way back across the garden into the conservatory. 'Do you believe me now?'

'Of course,' she said abstractedly.

'In that case,' said Anthony settling down on the conservatory sofa, 'I've got a question. You said I'd come here to spy on your mother. Why did you think that?'

She drew a deep breath. 'Uncle Patrick was excited about you. He said you were this marvellous man who'd done all sorts of incredible things in Germany, and he'd invited you down here to interview you. My mother smelt a rat at once. She . . . Well, she'd got involved with some very odd people.'

Tara's brow furrowed. 'I didn't like them.' She hunched forward earnestly. 'You must understand. She was passionate about Ireland. When the war started she was convinced Germany would win and this was Ireland's opportunity at last.' She looked at him in perplexity. 'I don't know what she did. Can you tell me?'

'She sent information to the Germans,' Anthony said quietly.

Tara drew her breath in sharply, studying his face with wide, frightened eyes. 'I don't believe you,' she said uncertainly.

Anthony remained silent.

'It can't be true!' Tara broke out. 'What about Terry? Did Terry know? Terry Cavanaugh?'

Anthony nodded.

'So she was right about him, too. She said he was a spy. Worse than that, a traitor. After all, he was as Irish as she was.'

'He was American,' corrected Anthony.

She waved his objection aside. 'That's just where he was born, not who he was.' Her voice wavered. 'Did you . . . Did you have her killed?'

'Good God, no!' The exclamation was startled out of him. 'Miss O'Bryan, we don't do things like that.' He saw the doubt in her face. 'No, really we don't. Cedric Chapman killed your mother and he was on her side.'

She bowed her head and sat for a long moment. When she spoke, Anthony could tell she was trying hard not to let her voice betray her emotions. 'Are you sure it was Chapman?'

'As sure as we can be. I came here to find a spy. I'm not proud of my profession, but it's necessary. I found positive proof your mother had been dealing with dangerous men. The most dangerous man of all is James Smith. I think Chapman worked for him.'

She looked at him, meeting his gaze square on. 'Colonel Brooke, swear to me you are telling the truth.'

'I am,' said Anthony quietly.

He saw the belief in her eyes. She put her hand to her mouth and sat without speaking.

'I never suspected a thing,' she said at last. 'Now that you've told me – well, I'm not surprised. It was all for my father, you know? It was all for him.' Once again she was silent for a while, then she shook her head impatiently. 'It still doesn't make sense! Why should Chapman turn on my mother?'

Anthony shrugged. 'I don't know what went wrong that afternoon your mother met Chapman.'

'Haven't you any idea? Wasn't there any clue?'

Anthony was about to deny it, but was struck by a sudden thought. He took a small cardboard envelope out of his pocket and handed it to her. 'There's this.'

She opened the envelope and took out the photograph of the little girl, the child with the solemn eyes.

As she looked at the picture, a grim suspicion grew in Anthony's mind, a suspicion he fought hard to deny.

It was obvious the picture meant something to her. He could see her body grow rigid as she stared at the little square of cardboard. He could see her pull herself together, see the effort she made to relax. He could see the muscles in her throat contract.

'I don't know anything about it.' She put the photograph back in the envelope and handed it back to him. 'Where did you get it?'

Anthony felt a frozen chill of disappointment. Tara, honest Tara, had just told a deliberate lie.

'Never mind,' he said, taking back the envelope and returning it to his pocket. 'I don't suppose it's important.'

'No,' she agreed, her eyes very thoughtful. 'No, I don't suppose it is.' She didn't speak for a few moments. 'What about Uncle Patrick?' she asked eventually. 'Why was he arrested?'

Anthony looked away. 'He was passing information to the Germans.'

'That's nonsense,' she said, her voice shaky. 'Absolute nonsense. Look, you came here to find a spy. You found my mother. Isn't that enough?'

'I'm sorry,' was all he could say.

She sat for a few more moments then abruptly rose to her feet. 'Colonel Brooke, I apologize for the suspicions I harboured about you and Josette. I was wrong. I see that now.' She walked to the door leading back into the house and then stopped, her hand on the handle and turned back to him. 'Are you really going to wait for Smith?'

'It might be as well, don't you think?'

She shuddered. 'Good luck.'

Anthony went onto the terrace and, taking his pipe from his pocket, walked slowly round the garden at the back of the house. He should, he knew, be thinking of James Smith but just for the moment he was more interested in Tara.

He was worried about Tara's reactions. That child in the photo-graph meant something to her, but what? Could it possibly be *her* child? Almost as soon as he'd asked himself the question, he'd dismissed it. Not only was the little girl in the photograph too old to be Tara's child, but Tara had been puzzled by the photograph, not frightened, as she would be if it were a guilty secret of her own she was concealing.

So was it Veronica O'Bryan's child? Tara could know all about it. Naturally enough, she wouldn't want to tell him. Her mother had precious little reputation left, but Tara could want to salvage whatever remnants she could.

His walk took him round to the stables and he stood for a moment by the whitewashed walls. The inside of the stable-block was quiet. All the horses were out to grass at this time of year. He slipped into the stable block and stood for a few minutes in the dusty light.

There was a collection of straps, hats and tackle on a shelf at the far end of the stable and, underneath the shelf, hanging from hooks, a couple of old hacking jackets. Something about the jackets bothered him. There was the clip-clopping of hooves on the cobbles in the yard outside and Kindred, the groom, called, close at hand.

It took that moment of distraction for a memory to click into place and his suspicions to flare. From his wallet he took the blue-grey thread he had picked from the brambles in Ticker's Wood, the day he had found Veronica O'Bryan's body, and placed it against one of the jackets.

It was a perfect match.

Biting down hard on his pipe-stem, he put the thread back in his wallet. The jacket, although old, was a fine quality tweed, a lady's coat. He could see the rough patch on the sleeve where the threads had been pulled.

There was the sound of hobnailed boots and Kindred came into the stables. 'Afternoon, sir,' he said placidly. 'Were you wanting a horse?'

'No thanks,' said Anthony. 'Kindred, who does this jacket belong to?'

Kindred peered at the jacket. 'That's an old one of Miss Tara's, sir. She keeps it here to be handy, so to speak. She often takes one of the horses out first thing and she dresses very workmanlike, knowing that she's going to be all alone, as you might say. It wouldn't do for some ladies but Miss Tara's got a fine, independent spirit. She'd rather ride by herself than in company. She knows the country for miles around like the back of her hand. You've only just missed her, sir. She's going out this afternoon. I've just been getting Moondancer in from the paddock for her.'

Anthony put the jacket back on the peg. Tara had been in Ticker's

Wood. It was Tara who had left the thread on the brambles, Tara who had so convincingly been near to fainting when they had found the body, Tara who had so cleverly carried the war into the enemy's camp by accusing him of murdering her mother. His stomach twisted.

Tara had got him to tell her about James Smith.

A blistering anger filled him. Tara had lied about the photograph and she had lied about her mother. He should have remembered Veronica was Tara's mother. Now she was off to hunt Josette. He had a suspicion that she'd know exactly where to find her. And he'd told Tara O'Bryan exactly who he was and what he was doing. He nodded to Kindred, not wanting to trust his voice and walked swiftly round to the trees edging the garden.

His first thought had been to wait for Tara, but what then? He couldn't restrain her by force and one word from her would bring the servants to her aid. What he wanted to do was get to Smith. Tara, he decided, could wait. However, what he could do was warn Cooke.

He stood by the line of trees and called softly. This time there was no answer. Anthony tried again, but the only sounds were those of the wind in the trees. He skirted round the trees, whistling. There was no response. With a little knot of anxiety in his stomach, Anthony walked round the bulk of the house towards the gates. Sticking out from the bushes was a shoe. Anthony walked forward softly, fearing a trap.

In a few minutes he pulled Bedford's body out from under the bushes. Thank God, he was still alive, but he had a huge lump on the side of his head and he'd obviously been in a fight. Anthony tried to get him to wake up but he was out cold. He'd been coshed.

Anthony's lips set in a grim line. There was only one man he'd come across recently who used a cosh and that was the chauffeur. He crouched beside Bedford and looked among the trees. There was another grey bundle in the wood about a hundred yards away. It was Cooke. He, too, had been coshed.

Anthony knelt by Cooke's body. It was one thing to calmly wait for Smith, knowing that Cooke and Bedford were watching his every move. It was quite another to put himself at the mercy of a ruthless killer when he was alone. The chauffeur must be close by.

As quietly as he could, he made his way through the trees to the high brick wall of Starhanger. Choosing a likely-looking tree, he swung himself up into the branches and stealthily climbed high enough to look over the wall.

He pulled back into the shelter of the branches. Not more than ten yards away stood a big green car, a tourer with its hood raised. The chauffeur and a second man were leaning against the car, smoking cigarettes. The second man wasn't Smith but a dark-haired man in a brown suit, someone he had never seen before.

Their voices were low and Anthony inched himself along the branch, trying to get close enough to overhear. He caught the word 'woman', and the chauffeur laughed. The branch had grown out over the wall, part of it resting on the brick coping stones. Again Anthony pulled himself forward. From his vantage point above their heads, he saw the man in the brown suit look at his watch and throw away his cigarette. 'It's about time . . .' he said, when the branch creaked ominously.

The two men looked round. Anthony tried to pull back before they looked up, slipped, put his weight on a rotten branch and, with a rending crack from the tree, fell heavily into the muddy ditch, in a welter of leaves, twigs and rotten wood.

'Bloody *hell*!' yelled the chauffeur.

In an explosion of movement, the chauffeur hurtled himself towards Anthony.

Winded from the fall, Anthony, his ribs in agony from his returning breath, managed to pull himself away. The chauffeur's hands reached out for him, but Anthony moved once more and the chauffeur grasped air and twigs. Half in and out of the ditch, Anthony reached out and held onto the polished leather of the chauffeur's boot and brought him crashing down into the ditch beside him.

Still on his knees, Anthony made a wild grab. The chauffeur rolled to one side, struggling like a maniac. Some of those blows from his flailing fists and kicking feet went home, but Anthony shook them off, desperately trying to land one piledriving punch. He seized the chauffeur by the front of his uniform, raised him up, his right hand clenched into a fist.

Anthony saw his eyes widen, waiting for the punch, then a searing pain blasted his left shoulder as a shot rang out. He fell away, rolling back into the ditch.

The other man was by the car, gun in hand. 'Get him!' he yelled.

The chauffeur picked himself up, straightened his tunic and lunged at Anthony with murder in his eyes.

From somewhere in the distance came a shout, the crack of a whip and the sound of wheels and horse's hooves. Sprawled on the edge of the ditch, Anthony could see a horse and cart, the driver whipping the horse into a canter, rattling down the road towards them. The driver shouted, his words lost over the racket of the cart.

The man by the car looked round wildly. 'Leave it!' he shouted. 'Come on!'

The chauffeur stopped, drew back his foot and landed a kick in Anthony's ribs. For a second or so everything went black. Lights scratched jagged lines of pain in his head, then there was the sound of swearing, a revving engine and Anthony felt a hand on his collar.

He opened his eyes and saw the carter bending over him, hauling him out of the ditch. Anthony made a vague gesture with his hand – he was halfway to being strangled – and, raising himself on his elbow, managed to get unsteadily to his feet.

The car was already some distance away, a cloud of dust marking its passage.

The carter, a big man, stood back. 'Was that a gun?' he said incredulously. Anthony nodded, unable, for the moment, to speak. 'A real gun? A pistol, I mean?' Anthony still couldn't speak.

'You need a doctor,' said the carter. 'The police will have to know too, I reckon. Who were they?'

Anthony didn't want a doctor and he certainly didn't want the police. And, although the carter had been useful, he didn't want him, either. All he wanted was to get his hands first of all on the chauffeur and then on James Smith. He straightened up and took a deep, gasping breath.

'It's all right,' he said to the carter's obvious incredulity. 'The gun wasn't real. I'm an actor. We were trying out a scene for a film.'

'A film?' echoed the carter. 'Moving pictures, like?'

'Yes,' said Anthony, brushing twigs and leaves off his clothes with his right hand. His left arm, the same arm that had been injured before, felt like a block of wood. 'It's a spy story about the war,' he said. 'Mr Sherston's making it.'

At the mention of Sherston's name, the carter's face cleared. 'It should be a good film,' he said. 'It looked real, so it did.'

Anthony laughed dismissively. 'No, but if the fight was real, I'd have been very grateful to you. I think I'll put the bit where you save me into the film.' He felt in his pocket and drew out two half-crowns. 'Here you are. Thanks very much.'

The carter shrugged and took the money. 'Thank you, sir. And you say it's a film?'

'That's right,' said Anthony, removing leaves from his hair and forcing a smile. He cast a look downwards. 'We're thinking of calling it *Ditched*!'

The carter looked at him uncomprehendingly, then at the ditch by the side of the road, and suddenly threw back his head and roared with laughter. '*Ditched*! That's a good one, that. Wait till I tell everyone about that. *Ditched*!'

Still laughing he went back to the horse, climbed back up to his seat, jiggled the reins and slowly clopped away.

Anthony watched him go, the sound of the horse's hooves gradually fading into silence. He moved his left arm tentatively and winced. The bone hadn't been touched, thank God, but the muscle was damaged. His ribs were incredibly sore. He was desperate to follow the car but his arm was screaming for attention.

He managed to pull off his jacket. The bullet had creased his biceps and his sleeve was wet with blood. He thought of going back to the house for help but all he wanted to do was follow that bloody chauffeur and his car.

His shirtsleeve was ripped already and he tore the fabric off. Using his teeth and his good hand he managed to make a passable bandage with his handkerchief. He draped his jacket round his shoulders to cover his arm – he didn't want to have to explain myself to any kindly passer-by – and set out to follow the car.

He was alone. Cooke and Bedford would take a long time to recover and he didn't have a clue where Parkinson was. In the meantime he had a fresh trail to follow.

SIXTEEN

For about a mile there was no turning in the road. He should, Anthony realized, after walking for ten minutes or so, have left some sort of note for Cooke and Bedford, but he couldn't face the thought of going back. He trudged along, gradually recovering his strength. There was a horse-trough on the road fed by a spring and Anthony had a rudimentary wash.

He plunged his head into the clear water, taking off the worst of the dirt and the mud. It would take more than a wash to make him feel better but it did him a lot of good. He could feel his arm stiffening and, gritting his teeth, forced himself to move the damaged muscles.

Then came a choice. The road proper continued on, but a cart track stretched off to the right. It wound off between the trees, dark underneath the overhanging branches. It looked little used. Anthony followed it for a few yards, looking intently at the ground. After a few minutes' walk he was rewarded with a fresh tyre-track in the red clay soil.

A little further and he saw where the bank had been scraped by something large. Crushed grass-stems and cow parsley hung forlornly, but the flowers on the cow parsley were still fresh. They had been broken very recently. Less than ten minutes later the track widened out into a clearing.

He crouched down behind some shrubby undergrowth. Before him stood a cottage with its door open and, to the side of the cottage, was the big green tourer.

The clearing was deserted but, from the open door of the cottage, he could hear the murmur of voices. The place looked as if it'd been abandoned for years.

Tiles hung off the roof, the glass in three of the windows was smashed and the lean-to privy at the side stood with its door hanging drunkenly from broken hinges. What had been a kitchen garden was overgrown with nettles, loosestrife, brambles and scrubby trees, surrounded by a low, broken wall.

The only people he could imagine finding shelter here were passing tramps, glad of any sort of protection from the elements.

He shrank back into the bushes as the chauffeur and the man in the brown suit came out of the cottage door. They had mugs in their hands and they were both smoking cigarettes.

'Please God we don't have to spend the night here,' said the brown-suited man, taking a drink from his mug. From his accent, he was from Belfast. He pulled a face. 'Why didn't you bring sugar? I can't abide tea without sugar.'

'I put it in the box,' said the chauffeur, drinking his tea. 'You're blind, Keegan.'

'Blind yourself,' said Keegan morosely. 'I've had enough of this job. For two pins I'd be on the next boat. To listen to the boss, you'd think all we had to do was whistle for that bastard Brooke and he'd come running. I'd like to see the boss get his hands dirty.'

'The boss is tough enough,' said the chauffeur. 'And he is the boss. Don't get any fancy ideas about leaving. You wouldn't get far.'

'D'you think I'm scared?'

'You should be,' said the chauffeur grimly.

Keegan looked back at the cottage and shifted uncomfortably. 'Maybe. But no one's ever spoken to me like that.' He spat in disgust. 'It's going to be dark soon, all under these trees as we are. What's the boss going to do? We can't stop here. It's not fit for a pig. And what will we do with the girl?'

'Don't you worry,' said the chauffeur with a laugh. 'The boss'll see to her.' He inclined his head and lowered his voice. Anthony had to strain to hear. 'She's not going anywhere.' To Anthony's horror he mimed taking a gun from his pocket. 'Bang. End of problem.'

Keegan started away and swore. 'Jesus, what about the cops? Count me out.'

'You're in if the boss says so,' said the chauffeur. 'You don't say no to him.' He laughed at Keegan's expression. 'Relax. He'll see to it. He enjoys it. He wants to find out what she knows first, though.' He laughed once more. 'He'll enjoy that too.'

Keegan shuddered and threw away his cigarette end. 'I'm going back in. These bloody midges are biting me to death and I can't see a thing out here. Fancy a game of cards?'

'We might as well.'

The two men went back into the cottage. Anthony saw a glow from the room as they lit the lamp.

He sat back on his heels. His original idea had been to find Smith, then get help. Well, he'd found Smith all right but he couldn't afford to waste a minute. Somehow he had to get into that cottage. The thought of Josette in Smith's hands made his blood run cold.

He dropped back into the woods and made a wide circle round the cottage, coming round to the back. A tumbledown wall with a broken gate enclosed what had been the yard. The windows were unlit and the back door stood half-open. Judging from the heap of leaves that had blown against it, it had been that way for years. Anthony looked up. There was a light from an upper window. He crept forward cautiously.

Through the back door he could see into the deserted room. He stepped over the leaves and into the cottage.

This had been the kitchen. The door to the front room was ajar, framed in the light from the chauffeur and Keegan's lamp. He heard their voices and the chink of coins from their game of cards.

An old sink was against the wall and, on the draining board, were two new wooden boxes. A spirit stove and a kettle stood on one and the other contained a few groceries from, incongruously enough, Fortnum and Masons.

Anthony's heart sank. He'd hoped at the very best to find some sort of weapon but all he had was one good hand. It would have to be enough.

The stairs led upstairs from the kitchen, a black, enclosed pit of darkness. Anthony paused, listening intently. He could hear voices upstairs. Frustratingly, he couldn't distinguish either the words or the speakers. As quietly as he could he slipped up the stairs. Despite his caution they creaked horribly.

At the top of the stairs was a tiny landing with three doors. He heard someone in one of the rooms stand up and their footsteps crossing the floor. Anthony flattened himself against the wall beside the door, hoping to avoid being seen.

The door opened and Josette, holding an oil-lamp high, looked out. She called back to someone in the room. 'There's no one here.' She took a couple of steps forward to look down the stairs, turned back and gasped as she saw Anthony.

Anthony, spread against the wall, put a finger to his lips, begging her to keep quiet.

Without saying a word, she opened the bedroom door again and stood in the entrance. 'He's here,' she said to the person in the room. 'Colonel Brooke's here.' She turned to Anthony with a delighted smile. 'Come in, Colonel. We've been waiting for you.'

Anthony had no choice. With a stomach like lead he followed her into the room, blinking in the lamplight.

Josette shut the door behind him and stood in front of it, barring his way.

There was a man in the room, a fair-haired man whose eyes burned with triumph.

'Well, well,' said the man. 'Colonel Brooke. At last.'

Anthony gaped at him.

This was Warren's murderer and Chapman's killer. The gent, the toff, the boss. James Smith.

And James Smith was the same man who Anthony had cheated and humiliated in Kiel: Oberstleutnant von Hagen. And he had a gun pointed at Anthony's chest.

Von Hagen waved the gun towards a chair. There was furniture in the room, cheap wicker picnic chairs and a tray with a coffee pot and cups beside the empty fireplace.

'Please sit down, Colonel,' he said in German. 'I have been to some trouble to prepare this cottage for you.'

Anthony didn't have any choice but to obey. 'For me?' he repeated stupidly.

'Oh yes. Haven't you realized?' Von Hagen laughed. 'Yes, I moved from my comfortable hotel to prepare this cottage expressly for your benefit.'

He picked up a cup. 'I would offer you a drink, but I remember what you did once before when you had coffee.'

His eyes gleamed and in that split second Anthony realized just how deep von Hagen's hatred for him was. 'I have been looking forward to this,' he said. 'I requested to be sent to England solely to hunt you down.' He gestured towards Josette. 'Once I had the missing lady, I knew you would follow.'

Josette, her head on one side, could obviously follow something of what was being said.

'I wanted to write to you,' Josette said. 'I wanted to tell you where I was, but Mr Smith said you'd find us. What's happened to your arm?'

Von Hagen smiled icily. 'His arm, my dear,' he said in

heavily-accented English, 'is the least of his worries. You took a great deal longer than I expected, Colonel Brooke.'

Anthony wasn't going to be drawn. Not by him. Instead he looked at Josette. 'What are you doing here?' Anthony could hardly credit her manner.

She seemed so completely at home and in control of herself that it beggared belief. She smiled as happily as if she had been in the drawing room at Starhanger.

'Please, Colonel, don't be angry with me.' She clasped her hands together in a childish gesture of apology. 'After Patrick was arrested I had to do something. I knew Mr Smith could help poor Patrick.'

Stupefied, Anthony went to draw his cigarette case from his pocket. Von Hagen stopped him with a gesture of his gun.

'I'm sorry,' said Anthony. He knew he was being absurdly polite but he couldn't help himself. Josette seemed so bewilderingly at home that it was easier to take his tone from her, rather than the brutal fact that a cold-blooded killer was pointing a gun at him. 'Do you mind if I smoke?' He instinctively looked towards Josette for permission as if she was his hostess and he was her guest.

'Please do,' said Josette.

Von Hagen nodded warily. 'No tricks, Colonel Brooke. I understand English very well.'

Anthony lit a cigarette, glad of the few seconds respite while his mind readjusted itself. He looked from von Hagen to Josette. 'Mrs Sherston, does your husband know anything about your association with this man?'

She clasped her hands eagerly once more. 'Not a thing. You've got to believe me.'

'Oh, I do,' said Anthony slowly. 'I'm coming to believe quite a few things, as a matter of fact. There's a lot Mr Sherston doesn't know, isn't there? I'm surprised I haven't tumbled to a good many of them before. "Frankie's Letter", for instance. It's bright and lively and contains all sorts of gossip about fashion and fashionable people. You wrote it, didn't you?'

Josette's smile faded. 'I don't understand, Colonel. Why are you talking to me like this? You've always been so nice before and you're not being at all nice now. Why? I haven't done anything wrong. Not really wrong.'

Anthony looked at her steadily. Incredible as it seemed, she believed what she said. 'Writing "Frankie's Letter" was wrong. Letting Patrick Sherston take the blame for writing "Frankie's Letter" was wrong.'

Her eyes widened. 'But it was Patrick's idea. He asked me to write "Frankie's Letter".'

'Did he ask you to use it to send information to the enemy?'

She wriggled uncomfortably. 'Of course he didn't. He'd have been horrified, so I never told him. I didn't want to upset him. Patrick doesn't like being upset. I had to do it, you know. I didn't have any choice. If you're looking for someone to blame, blame Veronica. She told me what to put in the "Letters". She'd have written it herself if she had any talent for writing but she didn't. You don't understand.'

Her lip trembled. 'Veronica threatened . . . Well, I had to do what Veronica said. Besides that, it wasn't wrong. It was only trivial gossip. It wasn't really wrong. It was all a joke.'

She meant it. 'A joke?' he repeated. 'It might have started as a joke.'

'But that's all it was,' she said eagerly. 'Patrick said it was a joke. He suggested the title and it seemed so funny. He called it "Frankie's Letter" because that was his middle name. But that's all it was. A joke.'

Anthony stared at her. 'For God's sake, Mrs Sherston, it's no joke. After all,' he said acutely, 'you knew enough to burn the drafts of "Frankie's Letter" in Veronica O'Bryan's grate, didn't you?'

She swallowed. 'So what if I did? If she'd been capable of writing it, she would have. It doesn't matter, I tell you. It was only a joke.'

Anthony's voice was very quiet. 'That joke, as you called it, killed Terence Cavanaugh.'

Her head jerked up. 'That wasn't my fault!' Anthony said nothing. 'Don't look at me like that,' she added desperately. 'I wouldn't have harmed Terry.'

'You told the Germans where he was.'

'I didn't know it was Terry.' She looked at Anthony with an expression that caught his heart. 'Terry told me he was a journalist. Veronica asked me to write about a spy. I didn't know it was Terry. When Patrick told us Terry had died, Veronica laughed and said it was my fault, but it *wasn't*.' She swallowed. 'I would never have harmed Terry.'

Anthony looked at her wonderingly. She was utterly convinced of what she said. 'You loved him, didn't you?' he asked, wondering once again how he could have been so slow.

Her sudden intake of breath told him he was correct. 'You told me it was Veronica who was in love with Cavanaugh but it was you, wasn't it? Terry Cavanaugh was in love with you and your husband found out. That's why Patrick Sherston disliked him. That's why Cavanaugh was forbidden in the house.'

'I didn't do anything wrong!' she said desperately. 'I couldn't help Terry falling in love with me.'

For his own sake Anthony had to know the answer to the next question. 'Did you love him?' he asked quietly.

Josette dropped her eyes. 'Yes.' Her voice was a whisper. She looked up, her eyes bright with defiance. 'How can you blame me?' she said savagely. 'After all, you . . .' She left the sentence unfinished but her eyes seemed to lance through him.

Anthony writhed inside. Yes, she was right. He had loved her. Her face had filled his dreams and, given any encouragement, God alone knew what he would have been capable of.

She saw his expression and gave a slow nod of recognition. 'We can't always choose, can we?' she said softly. 'And then . . .' she shrugged. 'Veronica found out. She told Patrick and he was furious. He threw Terry out of the house. I told Patrick that I didn't love Terry. Perhaps that was wrong, but I wouldn't leave Patrick, even though Terry begged me to. I didn't want to hurt Patrick and I didn't want to hurt Terry.' Her face grew puzzled. 'Even now I can't see how what I wrote could have harmed Terry. I only asked for him to be taken care of. There's nothing wrong in that, is there?'

Anthony swallowed. Yes, maybe the irony of the phrase had been lost on her. 'He was taken care of, sure enough.'

She looked at him, bewildered. 'So how can I be responsible? I don't understand. "Frankie's Letter" was just a joke. Patrick was the one who wanted it kept secret.'

Anthony sighed heavily. 'Patrick Sherston wanted it kept secret because he thought it really was a joke. A newspaper joke. He kept Frankie's identity secret because it was one of his best stunts. He even went to the lengths of telling Tara O'Bryan he'd written it to put her off the scent.'

'I know,' she said vigorously. 'Patrick told me. Tara came into his study when he was typing it out. Tara was so pleased with herself that Patrick played along.' Josette's eyes narrowed. 'She promised she'd keep it a secret. She lied. She told you and poor Patrick was arrested. It's all Tara's fault. She shouldn't have told you.'

This was staggering. 'Excuse me, Mrs Sherston, but compared to High Treason, breaking an unimportant promise isn't serious.'

She wrinkled her nose and shuddered. 'Don't say things like High Treason. I don't want to think of it like that.'

'No matter how you want to think of it, your husband has confessed rather than incriminate you and he'll be executed.'

She gave a little shriek. 'He won't! Mr Smith's going to help. They can't hang Patrick for doing something he didn't do.' She sunk her head in her hands for a few moments. 'I suppose you think I'm horrible,' she said eventually, 'but you don't know why I did it.'

Anthony dropped his cigarette end to the bare boards of the floor and ground it out. Ideas and half-guessed truths were chasing round in his mind. Josette had been forced to write 'Frankie's Letter' by Veronica O'Bryan. How had Veronica forced her? If Cavanaugh had had an affair with Josette, that would explain it, but Sherston knew about Cavanaugh. No, there was something else, something far more important than a passing love affair.

He looked at von Hagen. 'Excuse me, Oberstleutnant. Can I show Mrs Sherston a photograph?'

Von Hagen glanced at his watch. 'Be my guest,' he said, again speaking in German. 'I can understand you wanting to satisfy your curiosity, Colonel.' He grinned wolfishly. 'Even though your pleasure is likely to be short-lived.' He brought the gun up to the ready. 'Once again, I warn you. No tricks.'

Anthony gave a little bow of thanks. 'No tricks,' he agreed. Moving slowly, he took a little cardboard envelope from his jacket pocket and handed it to Josette. 'That's the reason, isn't it?'

She opened the envelope and took out the photograph, the picture of the child with solemn eyes. The colour drained out of her face and she stood holding it for a few moments. Then, with a little dry sob, she clutched the photograph to her bosom in a useless, instinctive, gesture of protection.

'She's your daughter,' said Anthony. 'She's your child.'

Josette didn't answer but nodded agreement, her eyes wide.

'Your husband doesn't know you had a child, does he?'

Again, Josette nodded. 'It's Milly,' she broke out desperately. 'Her name's Milly. Her father and I should have married, but he died.' She looked imploringly at Anthony. 'Please understand, Colonel. It was when I was in France. I put Milly in the charge of some good people – some nuns – and paid for her to be looked after. I loved Milly. Then Patrick came to Paris.'

Her face changed, softening as she remembered the past. 'I knew who he was, of course. He was a rich man, the owner of the magazine and the owner of the Sherston Press. He was lonely, Colonel, and I felt sorry for him. I liked him. He was kind and he was good but he was very, very respectable.'

She made a frustrated gesture with her hands. 'I knew he wanted to marry me. What could I do? I wanted to marry him. I wanted to leave France, to have a home in England once more, to stop writing about pretty clothes and actually have the money to buy them. Patrick offered me all that. If I'd told him about Milly I'd have been ruined.'

'So you married Patrick for what he could provide?'

'How dare you?' she snapped. 'Have you ever scraped and struggled? I was surrounded by rich women with beautiful things. I wanted those things. I wanted to be happy and secure and not worry about stupid things like food and paying the rent. I was fond of Patrick. I've been a good wife. I could never have told Patrick I had a child.'

'But didn't he guess? After you were married, I mean?'

'No.' Josette looked at him wonderingly. 'Why should he have done?'

Anthony left it. As a doctor he could have easily guessed if a woman was a mother, but what even the closest married couples didn't know about each other had long since ceased to surprise him. 'Go on,' he said heavily. 'Tell me what happened to Milly.'

She gave a ragged sigh. 'The war started and the convent Milly lived in was in an area occupied by the Germans. I was desperate for news and wrote to the convent, asking what had become of her.' She put her hand to her mouth. 'Veronica gave me the answer. She'd found out. She knew everything. She could ruin me and . . . and I was worried about Milly.'

Anthony flicked a glance of deep contempt towards von Hagen.

'So you're part of a scheme which uses a desperate woman and a helpless child, eh? You can be proud of a country which fights with such weapons.'

Von Hagen shrugged. 'We will fight with any weapon we have. Germany's survival is threatened. We didn't harm the child,' he added in English.

'No, they didn't,' said Josette eagerly. 'She was safe as long as I cooperated and what harm did I do? I had to protect Milly, so I wrote what Veronica told me to and she gave me news and photographs of Milly. I had to earn them. She had a picture in her room, a picture of Milly, but she wouldn't give it to me. That was wrong. Milly's *my* child. You see why I had to do it, don't you? And it was all right. Everything was all right until you came. You showed us those diamonds. Veronica was excited about them. I don't know why. She never cared for pretty things, but she was excited about those diamonds. When she went out I thought she was going to meet someone to tell them about the diamonds.'

'You're right,' said Anthony. 'She went to meet Chapman.'

Josette shuddered. 'He was a horrid little man. Veronica met him in Ticker's Wood. I followed her—'

'You took Tara's jacket from the stables,' said Anthony, illumination dawning.

'What does it matter?' said Josette impatiently. 'I had to follow Veronica quickly, otherwise I'd lose her. I saw Veronica talking to a man and I wanted to hear what he said. I thought he was telling her about Milly. Veronica had to get her news from somewhere and it wasn't right. He should have told me, not Veronica. Milly's my daughter.'

She swallowed convulsively. 'I crept as close as I could.' She glanced at the photograph in her hand and looked at Anthony indignantly. 'They talked about the diamonds but he *did* have a photograph of Milly. He showed Veronica the envelope and she said – her voice was horrible – "We'll keep that for later". I wanted it then. I must have made a noise because Veronica saw me.'

She blinked rapidly. 'She dragged me out of the bushes and I fought back. She was vicious. She gave me a real bruise. I had to cover it up with make-up for days. I was so angry I didn't know she'd hurt me. How dare they talk about my daughter? That little man, Chapman, tried to stop us. He had a gun. Veronica grabbed it from him and Chapman tried to get it back. He dropped it and I picked it up and it went off. I didn't mean it to. Veronica's face went all stiff and twisted and she crumpled up. She was dead. I asked Chapman what I should do and he told me to say nothing and it'd be all right. If I said nothing Milly would be all right. He dragged the body into the bushes and told me to go home.'

Josette looked at him appealingly. 'Please understand. He told me it'd be all right if I did what he said. So . . . so I went home and it *was* all right. He wouldn't take the gun. He didn't want to touch it. I didn't want to keep it, so I threw it into the lake. Veronica was dead and I was glad.'

'I imagine you were,' said Anthony wearily. 'What happened then?' he asked. He looked towards von Hagen. 'Where does our friend here fit in?'

'Mr Smith?' asked Josette, brightening. 'Mr Smith met me in London and said he'd look after me. All I had to do was write the "Letter".'

'I think he was interested in me as well, wasn't he?' asked Anthony.

Josette looked uncomfortable. 'What if he was? I told him you'd be at the inquest. Mr Smith wanted to see you. He didn't mean you any harm. Then, after he'd seen you, he wanted to ask you a few questions, but it was difficult. I knew Patrick was puzzled about Veronica. He thought you were clever enough to work out what had happened. I couldn't see how you'd guess the truth, but I suggested Patrick ask you to stay and then Mr Smith could talk to you, and it would all be all right. And then . . . it wasn't all right at all. Patrick was arrested. I thought Mr Smith would know what to do, so I telephoned him and he sent the car for me and then we came here and waited for you. That's all.'

Anthony sank back in his chair, his head in his hands. Terence Cavanaugh had been wrong. Sir Charles had been wrong. He had been wrong.

They thought they were on the trail of a ruthless mastermind of a spy and all the time what they had to deal with was a woman; a beautiful woman, admittedly, but not a femme fatale, not a mysterious temptress, not even a woman who was particularly clever, but simply a mother protecting her child.

Josette looked at von Hagen. 'It's all going to be all right, isn't it?

After all, Colonel Brooke's here now so you can say whatever it is
you want to say and you can help Patrick, as you promised, and we
can all go home.'

Von Hagen drained his coffee and rose to his feet. 'Yes, Mrs
Sherston. It is going to be all right.' He gestured with the gun
towards Anthony. 'I think, Colonel Brooke, it is about time we left.'
He gave a thin smile. 'You can think of it as home if you prefer.'

Anthony looked bleakly at Josette. 'Did you really believe the
Oberstleutnant – Mr Smith, I mean – when he said all he wanted
was to talk to me?'

She nodded. Anthony could see her fighting down her anxiety.

'Let me tell you what's going to happen, Mrs Sherston.' Anthony
cocked an eyebrow at von Hagen. 'I imagine I'll be drugged. When
I'm helpless, I'll be smuggled to Germany or the occupied territories
and I'll be questioned. I don't know if I'll say anything of any use,
but I'll be questioned. And, after that, I'll be killed.'

She drew her breath in sharply. 'Don't say that!'

'I do say that, Mrs Sherston. We're at war. Do you know what
that means? It's not brass bands and patriotic songs and saving
waste paper and planting extra vegetables, it's war. You want to
save your daughter. There's other people's children fighting and
dying as we speak. This man, Mr Smith, the Oberstleutnant von
Hagen, isn't concerned about Patrick Sherston or you or your child.
He's fighting with any weapon he can get to help his country. I
stood in his way, so he's going to have me killed. Chapman might
have been a horrid little man, as you say, but he stood in von Hagen's
way too. Von Hagen murdered him in broad daylight, as he'd murder
anyone else who inconvenienced him.'

'Enough!' said von Hagen sharply.

Anthony looked at him steadily, ignoring the gun. 'Tell Mrs
Sherston the truth. Tell her that you're going to let her husband die.
With me gone, who will be left to speak for him? Tell her how you
killed Warren at the hotel when you stole the diamonds and how
you gunned down Chapman on the tram platform.'

Von Hagen smiled contemptuously. 'You think she cares about
Chapman? He attempted to double-cross me. What did he expect? As
for the rest, as you so eloquently said, Colonel Brooke, we are at war.'

Josette gulped, her fingers playing nervously with the lace trim-
ming at her neck. 'You are going to help Patrick?' Von Hagen's

smile grew. 'And Colonel Brooke? I . . . I won't let you harm Colonel Brooke.'

Without taking his eyes from Anthony, von Hagen strode to the door and flung it open. 'Wait downstairs.'

Josette didn't move. 'It's true, what Colonel Brooke said, isn't it? You aren't going to help. You did shoot Chapman, didn't you? I read about it. You were the mysterious man on the platform. Even if he was a horrid little man, you shouldn't have done that.'

'Enough, I say,' repeated von Hagen. 'Go downstairs.'

Josette shook her head. 'I trusted you. You said that you wanted to talk to Colonel Brooke. You said you'd protect Milly if I brought the colonel to you. You said you'd help Patrick if I brought the colonel to you.'

She went to stand beside Anthony, putting her hand protectively on his shoulder. Anthony covered her hand with his, feeling her emotions trembling through her. 'You're going to kill him,' she said wonderingly. 'I can't let you do that.'

Very deliberately, she dropped her hands, squared her shoulders and walked towards von Hagen. 'I can't let you do it.'

The gun came up. Von Hagen's eyes were like chips of ice.

Anthony saw his finger twitch on the trigger. 'Josette!' he shouted. 'Get back!'

Her hand reached out and took hold of the muzzle of the gun. She turned her head. 'Anthony,' she said, very quietly. 'Go downstairs.'

Anthony saw von Hagen's finger tighten and, as if time had slowed to a crawl, the hammer on the gun go back. He flung himself across the room to pull her away.

In a deafening blast the gun went off.

Anthony crunched into von Hagen, the weight of his charge knocking von Hagen off his feet. They rolled over on the filthy floorboards together, the gun flying out of von Hagen's hand. Anthony scrambled for it desperately as von Hagen's hands closed round his throat. He found the muzzle, grasped it, and cracked it down hard on the side of von Hagen's head. Von Hagen's eyes rolled back and his body went limp. Anthony lay still for a moment, then painfully shook off the other man's dead weight.

He could hear shouts and footsteps on the stairs, but they seemed to be in another world. All he could think of was Josette sprawled on the floor, her dress stained with blood. 'Josette?' Anthony knelt beside her and reached for her hand. 'Josette?'

Her eyes flickered open. They were glazed and sightless. Her lips moved as she tried to speak, then her head fell back and she died.

The door opened and he knew someone had come into the room. He tore his gaze away from Josette and, still kneeling beside her and holding her lifeless hand, looked at the chauffeur and Keegan.

'Jesus,' said Keegan softly.

'Watch him!' warned the chauffeur as Keegan walked across the room, but Anthony didn't have the strength to resist. Keegan hauled him to his feet and Anthony slumped into one of the flimsy chairs.

Keegan picked up the gun and covered Anthony with it.

'Tie him up,' said the chauffeur. 'Use your belt if you have to. I want the swine safe and sound.'

Anthony made no resistance. He couldn't have moved to save his life, but Keegan pulled his hands behind his back and tied them at the wrists. His injured arm screamed a protest. Dimly, Anthony knew it was hurting like hell, but even the pain seemed far away.

The chauffeur stooped over von Hagen, shaking him awake. Von Hagen stirred and groaned.

Von Hagen lifted himself up and, with the chauffeur's help, got to his feet. He steadied himself for a moment, looking first at Josette and then at Anthony. He flexed his muscles, walked across to the chair, drew back his hand and walloped Anthony across the face.

Anthony's head crashed back and the chair went over. Again, it hurt, but he was so numb he hardly felt it. Anthony knew von Hagen was barking instructions, but he couldn't make out what he said. His whole world centred on Josette and that ghastly stain on the front of her dress.

Anthony was made to stand up and the gun was thrust in his back. His legs trembled with the effort of walking and he nearly fell down the stairs. He was led outside and, with the gun in his back, he stumbled across to a tree and sank onto the ground.

It was dark now and the chauffeur brought the paraffin lamp from the sitting room, resting it on the old wall.

'Keep watch,' said von Hagen to Keegan. 'I'll go and take care of things inside.' He turned to the chauffeur. 'Start the car.'

Anthony slowly started to put coherent thoughts together. Why had they left his ankles free? Of course. He was going to get in the car.

Von Hagen paused before he went into the house, looking at Anthony in the dim light. 'You will pay for what you have done,' he said quietly.

Anthony didn't answer.

Leaving Keegan to keep watch, the chauffeur went to the car. Even though Anthony felt utterly beaten and wearily detached, he couldn't help notice what was going on.

The first was that the chauffeur started the car.

The second was that he felt a hand touch the back of his wrist.

It was utterly unexpected. The hand squeezed his tightly and it was as if strength flowed into him from that touch. With the touch came back sensation. First, pain from his arm and his face and then a slow, steadily growing anger.

He felt the cold metal of a knife work through the leather belt and, feeling the warning pat of the unknown hand, stayed exactly as he was, as if his hands were still tied. He felt the knife being put into his hands and, as he grasped the handle, another pat of approval came from the hand behind him.

Anthony tensed himself to creep away but he was brought up short by a commotion from the cottage.

There was the sound of running feet and von Hagen stormed out of the house in a towering fury. 'She's gone!' he shouted. 'The woman's gone!'

Keegan snapped his head round and the chauffeur got out of the car. 'She can't have gone, boss,' he stammered.

'She has,' ground out von Hagen. He marched up to Anthony and stood, hands on hips, glaring at him. 'Where is she?'

A deep fear gripped Anthony. *She* could only be one person. 'I don't know,' he said with as much conviction as he could muster.

Von Hagen started forward. Anthony readied himself, bunching the muscles in his legs. Then once again, von Hagen raised his hand and struck out in a stunning blow.

He'd made a mistake. This time Anthony wasn't tied up.

Anthony launched himself away from the blow and flung himself at von Hagen, knife at the ready. Keegan, taken by surprise, fumbled the gun, dropped it and tried to knock the knife out of Anthony's hand. Von Hagen jumped back but Anthony felt the knife dig into something solid.

Keegan kicked out, Anthony staggered back, crashed into von

Hagen and they all went down together. Anthony felt a knee on his chest and hit out wildly. Someone crunched into his wounded arm and Anthony, mad with pain, hit blindly at the body in front of him.

He heard a gasp. Not a big gasp, but a sound as if a heavy man had sat on a cushion. Von Hagen stared at him with wide open eyes that showed nothing but absolute astonishment. He put a hand to his white shirt-front and brought it away black with something. It seemed to take Anthony ages to work out it was blood. Still with his eyes wide open, von Hagen tried to speak, gave another gasp, and fell, the knife buried in his chest.

'Where's the bloody gun?' shouted the chauffeur.

'I dropped it,' yelled Keegan. 'The boss is a gonner.'

The chauffeur took one look at von Hagen's staring eyes. 'Bloody hell!' he muttered, backing away. 'Bloody hell, Keegan, let's get out of here.' He groped his way into the car.

'Wait!' shouted Keegan, over the revving of the engine. He vaulted into the car beside the chauffeur. 'Go! Go!'

The headlights snapped on and the car lurched out of the clearing, missing the trees by inches.

Anthony slumped down against the old garden wall.

'Tara,' he called, raising his head. 'You can come out now.'

She came out of the darkness to sit beside him. Anthony realized she was crying. He reached out and comforted her with his good arm, holding her close to his chest, her head on his shoulder.

With a lifting of his heart he realized what he'd always known. Tara, clever, resourceful, passionate, loyal Tara was his; had to be his. As he realized the dangers she had faced and the trials she had surmounted to be safe with him at last, he was too happy to speak. He mourned Josette, mourned her deeply, but as he sat, holding Tara close, he felt a wave of deep contentment wash over him.

'I'm sorry,' she said eventually, drying her eyes with her sleeve. 'I'm sorry to cry, but I've been so scared. Josette was with them. Where is she?'

Anthony didn't say anything. She looked at his face and understood. 'She's dead?'

'Von Hagen killed her,' said Anthony.

She shuddered. 'Poor Josette.'

It seemed as good an epitaph as any.

'What were you doing here?' asked Anthony. 'It seemed like a miracle when you patted my hand.'

'They captured me,' she said simply. 'I'd got into the kitchen and seen them in the sitting room. I was outside when they caught me. It was the chauffeur and that other man. They argued what to do with me, then said they'd leave it up to the boss to decide.' Anthony pulled her closer to him with a convulsive shudder. 'They tied me up and locked me in the shed but they didn't know I'd put the bread knife down my riding boot. I managed to get the knife out and cut myself free, then I broke the window and escaped.'

'But why were you here in the first place?' asked Anthony.

'I met Matthew Stoker, the carter, on the road. He was talking to Ben Travis, which I thought was odd. Ben's done odd-jobs for us lots of times but he's a tramp, really. He's usually beneath Stoker's notice, but Stoker wanted to share a joke with him about a ditch and I imagine he thought Ben would do as well as anyone. Ben asked me if they needed any men for this film being made at Starhanger. I guessed what had happened from what Stoker told me. Then Ben said he wondered if this film was to blame for his usual sleeping-place, the old gamekeeper's cottage, being taken over by a bunch of toffs in a car. Well, that sounded unusual, so I went to have a look. I left my horse tethered, walked to the edge of the clearing and saw Josette by the car. I knew Josette was involved, after you'd showed me that photograph of the little girl. I'd seen a similar photo in her room and I knew there was a secret about her. I didn't say anything because it wasn't my secret to give away.'

'She's Josette's daughter,' Anthony said.

Tara nodded. 'I thought so. Anyway, Josette went inside and, as I listened to the men, I realized they were waiting for you. They said you were bound to turn up.'

Anthony said nothing but held her close.

It seemed like a long time before she spoke again. 'I'm sorry the men in the car got away. They shouldn't have done.'

'What d'you mean?'

'I stole their sugar from the kitchen and put it in the petrol. It was something I learned when I wrote the motoring pieces. I thought it would stop the car.'

Anthony threw back his head and laughed. 'You wonderful, wonderful girl. Of course it'll stop the car. It'll run for a couple of miles at the most before the sugared petrol feeds through and then it'll stop, sure enough.' He tried to stand up. 'Give me a hand, will you? We need to tell my people. They'll round them up all right.'

Tara gently restrained him. 'Stay there, Anthony.' It was the first time she had ever called him by his name, not his title, and the sound of it thrilled him. 'I'll go. My horse is nearby. Who do I tell?'

Anthony reached awkwardly into his jacket pocket and handed her his notebook. Even that small movement hurt and he relapsed gratefully against the tree. 'Look in there. There's a list of telephone numbers. Ring Sir Charles Talbot and tell him Keegan and the chauffeur need picking up. Say we need an angel.'

She took the book. 'Sir Charles Talbot? I thought he was more than he seemed.' She paused for a brief moment and smiled, her eyes lighting up. 'That sounds like top-secret information. Should you have told me?'

'It doesn't matter. Go on, Tara. It's urgent.'

She walked away quickly, then, just before she plunged into the trees, turned round. 'Why doesn't it matter?'

Anthony raised his head. 'Because I'm going to marry you. If you'll have me.'

She grinned. 'I hoped that was it.'

'I seem,' said Sir Charles, 'to spend far too much of my time visiting you in hospital.'

It was the next day. Anthony had been taken to a private ward in a hospital in Canterbury. Sir Charles had called last night and Anthony had wearily told him the truth about Josette Sherston. With his mind buzzing, Anthony thought he would never sleep, but nature had taken its eventual toll on his exhausted body. This morning he'd been allowed to get up and, now that his arm and an array of cuts and bruises had been attended to, he'd been told he could leave that day.

'However,' continued Sir Charles, 'you can be very pleased with yourself. With Keegan and Gallagher safe in custody . . .'

'Gallagher?' Anthony questioned.

'The chauffeur. His name's Gallagher. He's a key member of the Sons of Hibernia and a very dangerous man. He's wanted both here and in New York for a string of crimes.' He coughed and cleared his throat. 'It's a pity about Mrs Sherston.'

Yes, thought Anthony with a twist of compassion. He thought it was a pity about Mrs Sherston.

'We released Patrick Sherston this morning. I don't know how the poor devil will put his life back together after something like this. He knew his wife was guilty, of course, after we'd arrested him. I admire him for what he did, even though it confused matters. It was a noble thing to carry the can like that. He was devastated to hear she was dead.'

Sir Charles sighed. 'I can't help feeling it's for the best, though. I know it was Veronica O'Bryan's doing, but there's no doubt Josette Sherston was up to her neck in it, no matter how compelling the motive was. The main thing is Tara O'Bryan's all right. I spoke to her earlier. She's someone I admire, Brooke. She's a very tough-minded girl.'

'That's just as well,' said Anthony with the beginnings of a smile. 'She's going to marry me.'

Sir Charles raised his eyebrows. 'Is she, by jingo? I always thought she was fond of you. Congratulations. She didn't mention that. Well, that's one good thing to come out of it all, to say nothing of "Frankie's Letter" being finally dead. I told Miss O'Bryan about "Frankie's Letter", by the way, and the truth about her mother's involvement.'

'Did you?' said Anthony, startled. 'Blimey, Talbot, how did she take it?'

'She wasn't happy but she wanted the truth. If you're going to marry her, I'd recommend the truth. She's incredibly sharp.'

'She's simply incredible,' murmured Anthony. 'Talbot, I know I've mentioned this before, but this time I mean it. If I'm going to be a sober married man, I can't carry on working for you. I'm going to join the Medical Corps.'

Sir Charles looked at him ruefully. 'I thought you might.' He saw the determination in Anthony's face and shrugged. 'I'll be sorry to see you go. You might be safer staying in the Service. Being an army doctor is no picnic.'

'I'll take my chances,' said Anthony firmly. 'Having said that, there's one more mission I want to do off my own bat.'

'Which is?' asked Sir Charles sharply.

'I want to go France. That kid Milly – I want to bring her home. Ever since I saw her picture her face has got to me.'

'Take it up with your future wife,' said Sir Charles after a few moments thought. 'France, eh? D'you know, I might have a job for you in France.'

Anthony put down the letter from Patrick Sherston and looked through the open French windows into the garden. The war had been over for three years. Life – his life, Tara's life, everyone's life – had been altered out of all recognition by the war. For a moment, a deep longing for that happy, settled time before the war engulfed him, then he heard Tara laugh as she played with the children on the lawn. He sat back, lit his pipe, and let contentment wash over him.

Patrick Sherston had gone to Australia, leaving Britain for good. The letter said he was marrying again. Poor beggar, he deserved some happiness at last. Anthony thought of taking Sherston's letter into the garden, but treated himself to a few more minutes of quiet reflection, looking through the windows.

Tara was engrossed in the children's game. She had worked all morning, busy on her new novel. Her last book was a success. She was a far better writer than her father had ever been.

Milly, very much in charge, was laying out toys on the grass for a game of shop. Milly; exactly how he'd got into France and brought her home would make a book in itself. Perhaps Tara would write it one of these days, but that, added Anthony to himself, as he picked up the letter and walked outside, was quite another story.